The Eternal Geets of Bhagavad Gita

"Haiku" Gita
With more than 2600 interpretative Haiku

My joy in his
And his tears in my crisis
Is above earth, a bliss.

akhilesh gumashta

PRABHAT
PAPERBACKS

Published by
PRABHAT PAPERBACKS
An imprint of Prabhat Prakashan Pvt. Ltd.
4/19 Asaf Ali Road,
New Delhi-110002 (INDIA)
e-mail: prabhatbooks@gmail.com

ISBN 978-93-5521-183-5

The Eternal Geets of BHAGAVAD GITA
by Dr. Akhilesh Gumashta

Edition
2022

Price
₹ 750.00 (Rupees Seven Hundred Fifty only)

Printed at
R-Tech Offset Printers, Delhi

Dedicated to

Two Reformers of Bhaarat

Swami Vivekanand
(12 Jan 1863 - 4 July 1902)

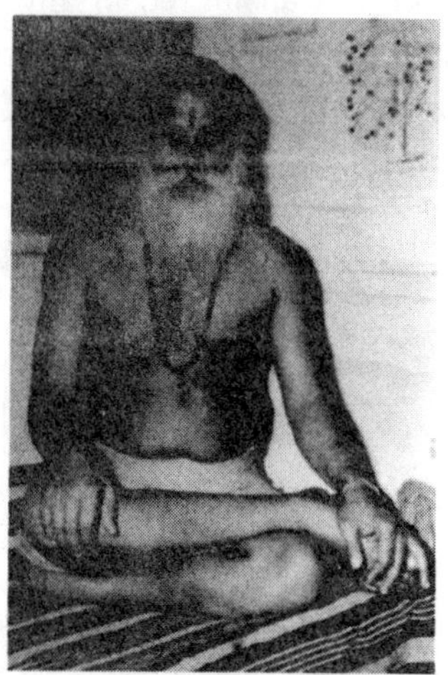

Brahmrishi Vishwatma Bawra
(11 Jan 1934 - 8 Feb 2002)

Reformers know this
Their worships tell through human service
God is as man is.

In Memory

Sarkis Ohanjanyan

He was an Armenian, who left his body for krishna's Abode on December 26, 1988 at an early age of 23. He was found guilty for printing and distributing Bhagavad Gita which was banned in his country. He was punished and sentenced for two years of rigorous imprisonment in Siberian Labour comps. He used to chant Krishna's Mantra everyday 16 rounds. Because he adopted Vaishnav cult and ate vegetarian only, which was rare finding in diet of that Prison, thus he could survive for few months and died ultimately earlier to full term of imprisonment. This cruelty shocked the world. His Life is motivating and encouraging.

In Eternity's recent past
The Lord talked to Arjun to impart
His heart in every heart.

FOREWORD

Dr Akhilesh Gumashta sent his book **'The Eternal Geets of Bhagavad Gita'** to me to write foreword. As Mananeeya Parameshwarnji, the President of Vivekananda Kendra is not keeping good health, the responsibility of writing the foreword came on me. And it is a tough job as the time is very short to go through the book carefully enjoying the philosophy embedded in Haikus.

Bhagavad Gita is a book for contemplation and practice. It is the only book perhaps which fascinates men and women, scholars and common-men, literates and illiterates, young and old alike. Many people who contemplate on the eternal message of Bhagavad Gita, get inspired to internalize that message by expressing it in their own words. Thus there are innumerable books, commentaries on Gita by scholars, critics, philosophers, seekers, Acharyas and others.

After going through the Haiku-poems one sees Dr Gumashta as a seeker, a devotee and a philosopher rolled into one. Clearly his work is written for 'Swantah Sukhaya' i.e. for one's own bliss. The bliss that comes by dwelling upon the words of Divine. Thus he writes—

"After every Shloka being versified in English, metaphysical interpretations are composed in the form of Haiku to make my own mind understand and if it creates happiness in all readers then it's only Lord's grace. Fortunately these haikus are composed in such a way to create a difference by having 'end-rhyming', of course without changing the very soul in these short poems."

It is said in our tradition that one must regularly take to study of scriptures and the study should be expressed in suitable words for others. 'Swadhyayat pravachanat ma pramditavyam'— One should not miss out on self study and intense expression of the study. Author seems to be following this Vedic injunction in spite of his busy schedule as a surgeon. After the creative work on Ramayana (Ramayana; The Hymns of Himalaya) he has taken up the study of Bhagavad Gita. The Gita-Sholkas are written in English verses by him and then he expresses his contemplations on the verses in Haiku—a form of poetry in which brevity and intensity of thought compete with each other. For example see these few

The culprit
Is punished by sin Spirit
And not for it.

All my steps
Should go ahead unstrayed
To the Ultimate.

In the mansized world
Lord compresses Himself from Infinite
To the individual limits.

There are total 2000 Haikus as powerful capsules for contemplation in the book. This book is another valuable addition to the texts on Gita for the English readers throughout world. I am sure while writing this book the Author must have enjoyed thoroughly. To express in brief words, needs the intensity of feelings and understanding. This work would propel him to dive deep into other scriptures, as well benefitting interested readers in the process.

01.10.2018

—**Nivedita Raghunath bhide** (Padmashri)
All-India Vice president,
Vivekanand Kendra, Kanyakumari

PREFACE

'What's next?'— after the work on Ramayan; The Hymns of Himalaya took the form of a book, my close friends and well wishers asked me. I replied that I would now read the Ramayan again and again till it becomes Soul of my soul.

I realized soon that the Lord's Plan was slightly different; He was to prepare me as an instrument for a greater task and further bestow His blessings

Vital grey's His tool,
Through which Divine planner reveals His plan,
Lest mortal coil is fool. (Ch VII)

I understood soon that the Ramayana was guiding and motivating me towards Krishna; more precisely Krshna of Bhagavad Gita.

Innumerable volumes on Eternal hymns of Bhagavad Gita, have come to us as interpretative and elaborative texts by seers and sagacious writers since it was discovered and picked by Adi Shankaracharya from the Mahabharat. I submit this work to His Lotus feet saying

Whatever inked the page.,
As evolution of Man's Sulciigyrii,
Is all Lord's Brain-child. (Ch XV)

After every Shloka being versified in English, metaphysical interpretations are composed in the form of Haiku to make my own mind comprehend the ruiances of the philosophical text. It creates happiness in all its readers then I shall deem it only Lord's grace. Fortunately these haikus are composed in a style with, a difference, by having end-rhymes. This is done without changing the very essence of these short poems. For eg—

Great Archer, his prow,
Bows to the Lord, for he knows,
Lord's strength in his bow.

Before Lord Krshna's advent, the tradition of 'shruti'— the listening and learning was in vogue. Then breaking away from this tradition, the Ancient bard-sage Vedavyas, wrote texts and Shlokas in Sanskrit. The Bhagavad Gita has 700/701* Shlokasas part of the epic Mahabharat.

Wordless scattered words,
Vedavyas picked, collected and took,
Lord turned into blessed book.

Such interpretative short poems along with the English version of the shlokas explore the practical approach to various realms of our lives. In a world where materialistic comfort is set as the ultimate goal; every chapter, every Shloka, every word of the Bhagavad Gita turns into a 'Mantra' (Holy Guide), to explain how every Being is a part and parcel of the Lord, the same Lord who is omnipresent in the Universe and thus it is every human's sacred duty to render his services to Him, and also to fathom His divine Plan in sending humans on this earth. Unfortunately however caught in the maze of unending mundane desires, bound in the shackles of Maya, we humans are increasingly turning self-centered materialistic and worldly.

People with tubular visions view their holy scriptures from a narrow perspective. They build walls of distinction between ideologies which isolates them from imbibing the best from other schools of metaphysical understanding. These Shlokas are sharp-edged blade to excise this delusion of parting man—

Left to sink or swim,
In man's such whim, Vedavyas limned
With The Gita's hymns

I started this particular work in September, 2011, and it reached the final comment (Ch 18/ verse 78) of Commentator Sanjay in September, 2018. My work proceeded at snail's pace, due to my first commitment to medical profession.

The guidance of Pujya Sadhvi Gyaneshwari Didi remains unparalleled. As she helped me with Ramayana; the Hymns of Himalaya with enthusiasm; this time also she did this huge work with commitment and brought the words and verses from diary to manifest as a book. Smt. Sadhna, my wife and Varsha and Kartikey, my children were keen and supportive during these years, while I kept engaged for hours on my desk flooded with many reference books and metaphysical and critical texts. It is again a matter of immense pleasure that world renowned Prabhat Prakashan, New Delhi has taken great interest in publishing this book. Mr Sharad Tiwari, Jabalpur put in all his efforts with promptness day and night, in the making of this text.

Literature exists in abundance to be holy guide to man. In this egoistic world, as a preliminary step we all need to realize—

Thews, throne, thorn, thought, text
Everything is His Theme, thus is concluded
Nothing is man-made.

Whatever has been prayed by me every day in the last seven years during composing these pages is condensed in the following lines:

Into mine, O Soul Supreme ,
May fill everyday, to the brim,
Should overflow as Hymn.

Jai Shri Ram... Jai Shri Krshna

Deepawali, 2021
4th November, 2021

—Akhilesh Gumashta

BLESSINGS

Dr Akhilesh Gumashta is embodiment of multifold possibilities. We could know him through his phenomenal marvel, when his inner conscience streamed as divine flow in Ramayan; The Hymns of Himalaya.

After accomplishing own pen and ink with Ramayana author has poetically exalted Shrimad Bhagavad Gita and this work is unparallel and unique.

I bless author for bringing to the world neonate sapling of Bhagavad Gita as an innovative creation in English.

—Swami Shyam Devacharya ji Maharaj

The societies outside India who are leading a materialistic way of life are now attracted towards Indian philosophy as they have now keen desire to understand real purpose and meaning of human life.

I am sure this seven years arduous work of the author on Gita would benefit the spiritual quest of the English knowing readers in India and abroad and would help them to enrich their lives to attain real joy and contentment .

I also hope that Dr. Gumashta would continue to snatch time from his busy medical profession to take up many such endeavours in the field of scriptures and philosophy for the upliftment of the human society.

May Lord Krishna bestow on the author necessary wisdom and sound mental and physical health to carry on similar works for the ultimate good of the human family.

—Justice D M Dharmadhikari
Rtd. Judge Supreme Court

The rendering of the timeless teachings of the Bhagavad Gita into the rhythms of Haiku is an impossible task. Such a task is possible only with divine inspiration and dedication. He added rhyming endings to the lines which adds to the sweetness of his work, without sacrificing the original intent of either the haiku or the Bhagavad Gita

—William and Margot Milcetich
Gita and Yog Scholar, USA

Arjuna was standing in the midst of the battlefield. Still. Overwhelmed with emotions. Unable to fight against his own clan. Krishna made him understand the law of karma. The law of dharma. The law of life. And also helped him get a glimpse of life after death.

Gita contains the complete truth about life.

His statements are no less than gospel truth, so meaningful and so deep.

I have read his previous volume of Ramayana, versified in English. I was aware that he was working on Gita for the last seven years. And from time to time, I used to request him to read out parts from his interpretations. The rhyming Haikus is yet again a novel experiment, and has come out magnificently.

— Sanjay Sinha
Author and journalist
New Delhi

From the sublime *Ramayana— Hymns of the Himalayas* to its sequel, the Haiku verses on the *BhagavadGita*, the same creative muse continues its adventurous journey of aesthetically exploring eternal truths. For us the readers, it is a step from delight to wisdom. The charm of these "moment's monuments" unfolds in its multiple shades as we glide over from one poem to the other. The true lover of poetry is left in awe at the precision, profundity and power of these incantatory verses. A steep decline in values in the present times, demands serious rethinking and a return to our roots for imbibing values crystallized in ancient texts.

Drawing on a lifetime of rewarding human experiences supplemented with profound prolific reading of ancient treasures, Dr. Gumastha displaying the power of a bard, has succeeded in crafting an inspirational piece of art that advises, consoles, heals, radiates hope and gives reasons to celebrate the joy of living.

—Dr Neelanjana Pathak
Prof. of English Lit.

Verses and short poetic interpretations make this work scholarly and metaphysical purport in the form of haikus has authenticated the book making the meanings of Shlokas self-evident. One who is aware of author's previous work on Ramayana will definitely be keen to read this book and imbibe it.

Hope, the readers will be benefitted, as Spiritualists in deriving path, as Scientists in deriving theories of Science, as scholars in perfecting themselves, as Judges in judicial decisions, as writers and teachers in preaching through references and quotable messages in haikus .

—Justice Deepak Verma
Rtd. Judge Supreme Court

INDEX

INVOCATION

"The Invocation"

Ganesh

The Nature doth, what it must,
Through the genesis of Genius,
Tinctured wi the seraphic thrust.
Wherever, that Genius is unfurlt,
I worship that, as Ganesh, first (1)

Hanuman

As the frontlet on the pennant,
As the boast of the battle-front,
As crown over Archer on wheel of Truth,*
To unfurl gnosis of glorious gallant,
For the bays; its way of Hanumant, (2)

Krshna

In the per diem, inner melee,
Bring me Triumph, which the soul agree,
Between power of love and love of power,
O Charioteer! reveal Thy vast and Thy wee,
Me, afficted be freed,
O Lord Krshna! I prithee!! (3)

Not just the ritualistic worship,
But for perdiem, duty and practice,
The Great Charioteer didth guide,
In the field holding rein and whip. (4)

Prithee = I pray thee, Bays = wreathe of victory
*Pennant = small triangular flag, Rein = Bridle, *Arjun*

O Krshna ! to my defeating doubts
O Hope !! Ope divine lips, speak now,
May Thy voice echo in me, O Wisest voice !
May Thy holiness elixir my ink, wise. *(5)*

With my humble gaze, drooping lids, dropt eyes,
Barren vision, blunt weapons, and blurred sight,
And benumbed hilt and succumbing hold,
Keen on Thy face, I dost behold. *(6)*

BHAGAVAD GITA

1

Thoughtful whispers asked...
The voiceless questions in mind-rivercrossed...
Dipped entranced Vedavyas.

2

The maker's 'own make'
Theory of theories the Lord spake..
Practically all to Awake..

3

'I know is but none'-
Is only vastest knowledge big wisdom..
Need be known, to know.

4

Only worth..
In this and next world...
Is HIS word.

5

The brimming old urn..
To elixir the conscious of modern
I mean to learn.

6

His exhaustive details..
Are as if my Soul 's cradled..
In repose Eternal.

7

Left to sink or swim..
In man's such whim, Heart sage limned..
The Geeta's Hymns..

8 THE SUPREME PREACHER
Where both have ideal keenness..
The Teacher fullest and Taught emptiest..
Completely poured and completely grasped..

9

Wandering with text..
Pondering on it is further blessed..
Living in it is Best.

10

Themed the Supreme...
Reinstalled lost hymns...
Effaced corrupt whims.

11

Future is blest..
When today's Wisdom accepts..
The past quest.

CHAPTER ONE

Battlefield and despondency of Arjun

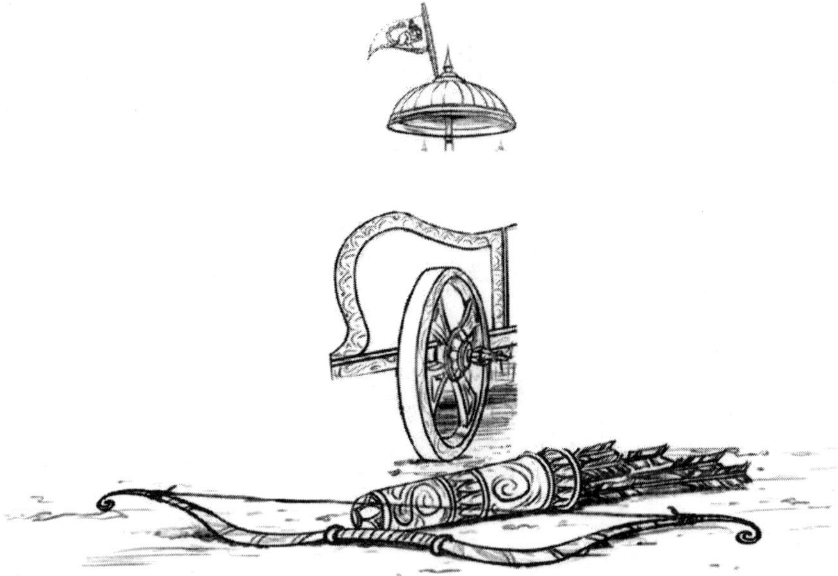

If I ignore conflict
For the sake of the peace
From peace I drift.

Breaking point of war

Should be making point

For no further war.

Chapter One

BATTLEFIELD OF KURUKSHETRA

Verse 1

Dhratrashtra asked-

On the sacral field, on the battle field
For the glorious sway, for victorious yield,
My and Pandav's combative sons arrayed,
What do they do in thick of the fray,
O Far-sighted Sanjay! Say!

1
Doped in the wine
Of brewing thoughts of me and mine,
Inner Dhratrashtra anoints.

2
Virtues and sins
Born of same clan are cousins
Mind! Where stays Krshna.

3
When the Soul reclaims
The fallen reign of holy plain
Faces mayhem.

4
Where blind Ego is King
Soul is exiled from inner plains
And cruel sceptre reigns.

5
Before my truth and his
When the thoughts find a breach
How could wrought peace.

6
Closest of your inside
You would not see with naked eye
Need a far-sight.

Verse 2

Sanjay commented-

Pandav's array having observed; The rush
Of Duryodhan repaired to Drona spake thus-*

**Drona-Dronacharya, Preceptor, Guru of Kauravas and Pandavas*

धृतराष्ट्र उवाच
धर्मक्षेत्रे कुरुक्षेत्रे समवेता युयुत्सवः।
मामकाः पाण्डवाश्चैव किमकुर्वत सञ्जय।। *1.1*।।

सञ्जय उवाच
दृष्ट्वा तु पाण्डवानीकं व्यूढं दुर्योधनस्तदा।
आचार्यमुपसङ्गम्य राजा वचनमब्रवीत्।। *1.2*।।

1
Among hundred sins born
Of the blind darkness as sire,
First born is the 'Desire'.

2
Once wisdom prevailed
By the Egoism of desires' spell
Strength drains in pell mell.

3 FOOLISH SILENCE
Introspection, the Preceptor
Why is silent ? and Not interferes
O me fool ! be aware!!

4
In anxiety, the lust
Even while seeing virtues' hush
Restlessly ever rush.

5
The Tyrants
Are ants
Before innocents

6 INTROSPECTION
Before battle
Inner battle ever fought in inner field
Between the self and guilt

Verse 3

O *Guru! Behold !! the bold array*
Of Pandav's sons in field of affray,
Arranged by thy wise disciple, Dhristadyumn,*
Lo ! the massive formation and stratagem.

1 GURU'S INDIFFERENCE
Ploy of desire play
Overpowering Guru to dictate own sway
In daily battle array

2
Habits and sensory passion
As Duryodhan fight with soul-perception
are conned with false conation.

3
Guru, the intuitive habit
Watches exile of the Truth, in tacit
Ensures defeat.

4
Soldier of inner calm
Against evils of Mind, when throng
Should win the palm.

** Chief commandant of Pandav's army,   Pell-mell = Desparation*

पश्यैतां पाण्डुपुत्राणामाचार्य महतीं चमूम्।
व्यूढां द्रुपदपुत्रेण तव शिष्येण धीमता।। *1.3*।।

Verse 4-6

Lo! glow of heroes of bow, Arjun n Bheem,
Skilled in battle, trained to fight in extremes.
Not just youngster archers, but veteran as well thronged,
Yuyudhan, Virat, Drupad many more strong.

Namely Dhrishtaketu, Chekitan, Kashiraaj.
Manly Purujit, Kuntibhoj, Shaibya-All bellicose.

Though tender but tend to run riot
Yudhamanyu, Uttamanjas All great Chariots.*
The son of Subhadra, and Draupadi's Sons
Art the boast of battle, commandants.

1
Spirit on both sides
Never names or numbers won fight
But the Pennant right.

2
On the soul canvas
Some gaudy some pastel colours emboss
The reflections of the mass.

3
Confronts the passionate team
With devotion and chastity Incarnate Arjun, Bheem
One inner field, two extremes.

4
In man to man fight
Both have right to fight
Wins the right.

5
The Self-Kingdom
With compelling Urge of evil in bellum
Fall in grip of thralldom.

Thraldom = slavery   ** Great Chariot warriors*

अत्र शूरा महेष्वासा भीमार्जुनसमा युधि।
युयुधानो विराटश्च द्रुपदश्च महारथः।। *1.4*।।

धृष्टकेतुश्चेकितानः काशिराजश्च वीर्यवान्।
पुरुजित्कुन्तिभोजश्च शैब्यश्च नरपुङ्गवः।। *1.5*।।

युधामन्युश्च विक्रान्त उत्तमौजाश्च वीर्यवान्।
सौभद्रो द्रौपदेयाश्च सर्व एव महारथाः।। *1.6*।।

Verse 7

To counter, the Encounter, for thy account*
My tough generals, now I do count.

1
Where Dark blacklists the Good
The Evil blackballs in ostracizing mood
The very Truth.

2
The Desires impure
Count materialistic allies that rear
To escape fear of Pure.

3 EVIL BOASTING
Bubbles of Ignorance swell
Looking to swell of rivals' prow
In fear babble and crow

Verse 8

Thy self, Bhishma, Kripa, Karn, Vikarn,
Ashvatthama, Jayadrath and Somdatt's son
Ever in the field laurels earned.

1
Past bad Karma
In battalions of evil make stratagem,
To fight Soul-Kingdom.

2
Sense-focused mind
Through distorted lens of delusion
Blurs inner Divine.

3 EVIL ARRAY
Bhishma, the Chief Urge
I, me, mine as pseudo weapons treasured
Backs Desire-born desires.

4 EGO
Little ' i ' is humble
That wins in the field laurels
Big I is own rival.

Blackball = ban **Guru Dronacharya*

अस्माकं तु विशिष्टा ये तान्निबोध द्विजोत्तम।
नायका मम सैन्यस्य संज्ञार्थं तान्ब्रवीमि ते।।*1.7*।

भवान्भीष्मश्च कर्णश्च कृपश्च समितिञ्जयः।
अश्वत्थामा विकर्णश्च सौमदत्तिस्तथैव च।।*1.8*।।

Verse 9

Many more countless with arms and armours, trained;
Who are ready to give life for my sake.

1 LIFE BATTLE
Desires are well armed
All about the Soul-field swarm
With power of luring charm.

2
Exile of the soul
Stiffens body wings and delusive grip hauls,
Into mental scheol.

3 TENTACLE-EGO
Little worm with tentacles great
Fetters, feuds, fights and arrays
For its blind faith.

4
Ego-kingdom ever does clinch
The mind through sensory weapons; for Soul
Would not share an inch.

5
Forgotten, know must
Weapon of Soul victorious
Is not the lust.

Verse 10

Army of Bhishma, that rearth, hath endless ends
That of Bhima merely has counted traineds.

1
Before virtues extent
The wrong doers look endless
But to end.

2
With cataleptic forces couched
The consciousness in anarchic delusive drowse
Be as Bhima be aroused.

अन्ये च बहवः शूरा मदर्थे त्यक्तजीविताः।
नानाशस्त्रप्रहरणाः सर्वे युद्धविशारदाः।। *1.9*।।

अपर्याप्तं तदस्माकं बलं भीष्माभिरक्षितम्।
पर्याप्तं त्विदमेतेषां बलं भीमाभिरक्षितम्।। *1.10*।।

Verse 11

Ye all art well marshalled in the field
Now need alone, Bhishma to shield.

1 PSEUDO-EGO
Where consciousness offend
The Aged ego, the chief of sense
find die hard delusive phalanx.

2
Matter-desires though fetter
Its big army has no innate mettle
To fight spiritual battle.

THE CONCH-SHELLS BLOWN

Verse 12

Grey aged yet grave caged veteran,
Bhisma blewth conch like roar of lion,
To spur rearing legion and Duryodhan,
To stir the forces in the front.

1
Alas ! war is called on
Provoked by false identity of existence
But for its consequence.

2
Innate interiorized calm
Is strayed by restless ego to prompt
And call on arms.

3
My name my frame claim
My fame; my game blow and bellow
With pride untamed.

4
If I ignore conflict
For the sake of the peace
From peace I drift.

अयनेषु च सर्वेषु यथाभागमवस्थिताः।
भीष्ममेवाभिरक्षन्तु भवन्तः सर्व एव हि। *1.11*।।

तस्य संजनयन्हर्षं कुरुवृद्धः पितामहः।
सिंहनादं विनद्योच्चैः शङ्खं दध्मौ प्रतापवान्।। *1.12*।।

Verse 13

Even as all waited the chieftain's call,
Following first note, thus instigated all
Sounded conch shells, tabors, cymbals
And war-drum making clamors to appal.

1
With whim of head high
Where soul kept dissolved in biased I
Falsehood instigates fight.

2
Breaking point of war
Should be making point
For no further war.

3
In Ego's noise blast
Own fine astral melody
Alas ! is lost.

Verse 14

Krshna and Arjuna by such yond call, provoked
Seated in great chariot with white horses yoked,
In the battle scene, then as well
Superbly blew their divine conch-shells.

1
At demonic challenge
The Calm with its divine image
Should never escape.

2
For my clear endeavor
May the senses be horsed to bring
Krshna as actions' charioteer

3 ACCEPTING WAR
For challenges it behoved
A warrior, ever yoked with doves
Him, wheels of war drove.

Appal = terrify   Yond = mad

ततः शङ्खाश्च भेर्यश्च पणवानकगोमुखाः।
सहसैवाभ्यहन्यन्त स शब्दस्तुमुलोऽभवत्।।1.13।।

ततः श्वेतैर्हयैर्युक्ते महति स्यन्दने स्थितौ।
माधवः पाण्डवश्चैव दिव्यौ शङ्खौ प्रदध्मतुः।।1.14।।

Verse 15-18

Krshna blew His Panchajanya,
Arjun his Devadatt,
Bhima of terrific act
Blew Paundra, his conch great

King Yudhisthir, unstirred as speakth the name,
Blew his Anantvijaya, at the same
Nakul and Sahdev, now blew,
Sughosh and Manipushpak, anew.

Sanjay further continued-

The King of Kashi, the toxophilite,
And Shikhandi, the boast of war exploits

Dhristadyumna, Virat, Satyaki, the champion,
And Drupad, all Draupadi's sons,
And son of Subhadra of great might,
*All blew their conches, O King of all wides ! **

1
Life never ends
When it accepting the challenge
Keeps not silence.

2
Its not the conch
But blower's fight within
Should be staunch.

Toxophilite = lover of archery   ** Sanjay says to Dhratrashtra.*

पाञ्चजन्यं हृषीकेशो देवदत्तं धनंजयः।
पौण्ड्रं दध्मौ महाशङ्खं भीमकर्मा वृकोदरः।। *1.15*।।

अनन्तविजयं राजा कुन्तीपुत्रो युधिष्ठिरः।
नकुलः सहदेवश्च सुघोषमणिपुष्पकौ।। *1.16*।।

काश्यश्च परमेष्वासः शिखण्डी च महारथः।
धृष्टद्युम्नो विराटश्च सात्यकिश्चापराजितः।। *1.17*।।

द्रुपदो द्रौपदेयाश्च सर्वशः पृथिवीपते।
सौभद्रश्च महाबाहुः शङ्खान्दध्मुः पृथक्पृथक्।। *1.18*।।

3 HALLOW VOICE
In the selfish realm
Stunned by hubbub of own cerebrum
Blow! conch of Divine dictum.

Verse 19

Keen shrill pinked through welkin and the field,
And filled Kaurav forces with rills of chill.

1
Mundane senses uncontrolled
In casus belli be dumb-struck
Before echo of soul.

Verse 20-23

Yes ! the restless fronts, had come to blows
To meet the challenge, Arjun lifted his bow.
And held his flag with Kapi emblem
Addressed Krshna in the field of bellum.

O Rishikesh ! O Changeless !! thus Arjun spake-
My chariot between facing arrays be placed.

Whom must I fight, let me conceive,
At this very mo, on this war eve.

Casus belli= Provocation of war

स घोषो धार्तराष्ट्राणां हृदयानि व्यदारयत्।
नभश्च पृथिवीं चैव तुमुलो व्यनुनादयन्।।*1.19*।।

अथ व्यवस्थितान् दृष्ट्वा धार्तराष्ट्रान्कपिध्वजः।
प्रवृत्ते शस्त्रसंपाते धनुरुद्यम्य पाण्डवः।।*1.20*।।

हृषीकेशं तदा वाक्यमिदमाह महीपते।
सेनयोरुभयोर्मध्ये रथं स्थापय मेऽच्युत।।*1.21*।।

यावदेतान्निरीक्षेऽहं योद्धुकामानवस्थितान्।
कैर्मया सह योद्धव्यमस्मिन्रणसमुद्यमे।।*1.22*।।

Restless desires of the bellicose'
I wish to spot, all those.
And the Kings and friends of Duryodhan, crooked
Gathered who dare, I wish to look at.

1
In war with the crooked
The Divine charioteer on wheels of Truth
Lends a hand of boost.

2 OBSESSED WARRIOR
On the intuitive chariot
Tendencies of irrational uncertain rut
Bring to indecisive alerts

3
Flag is essence
Not just through armies n weapons transcend
Fills with patriotism, the land.

4
In middle of array
A vantage point in thick of fray
Warrior first wins dismay

IN MIDDLE OF FIELD

Verse 24-25

Sanjay narrated-

O King ! thus on Arjun's request
Krshna drove that among chariots, very best,
At the point between two forces,
Affronting Bhishma, Drona, many known faces.
Krsna, the great charioteer asked now-
" Behold ! O Arjun the Kuru's crowd"

1
From do or die
Fearing the ruins of the fight
The Escape, I rationalize.

2
Lord messaged a warrior
Worth living for, what's to the fore
What backs is worth dying for.

Rut = grooves made by wheels on track.

योत्स्यमानानवेक्षेऽहं य एतेऽत्र समागताः।
धार्तराष्ट्रस्य दुर्बुद्धेर्युद्धे प्रियचिकीर्षवः।। *1.23*।।

एवमुक्तो हृषीकेशो गुडाकेशेन भारत।
सेनयोरुभयोर्मध्ये स्थापयित्वा रथोत्तमम्।। *1.24*।।

भीष्मद्रोणप्रमुखतः सर्वेषां च महीक्षिताम्।
उवाच पार्थ पश्यैतान्समवेतान्कुरूनिति।। *1.25*।।

3
Against enemy swarms
Lord forewarns and also Lord forearms
In varied forms.

ARJUN'S REFUSAL TO FIGHT

Verse 26-31

Came into Arjun's view,
Positioned there, armies of Kurus,
Grand paters, kindreds, preachers, cousins,
Comrades, confrere kith and kins .

Very next perplexed with deep set back,
Filled with chill, he thus spake-
O Krshna ! finding kins, keen at battle,
My mouth shrivelth and my limbs fail.

This very sight creeps in me with bumps' goose,
Grip of the Gandiv glideth, and skin agued.
My stance trembles, my mind rambles,
O Keshav ! I forebode omens' bale

O Krshna ! none the worth I dost weigh,
To slay my own, in thick of the fray.

Agued=fevered

तत्रापश्यत्स्थितान्पार्थः पितॄनथ पितामहान्।
आचार्यान्मातुलान्भ्रातॄन्पुत्रान्पौत्रान्सखींस्तथा।। *1.26*।।

श्वशुरान्सुहृदश्चैव सेनयोरुभयोरपि।
तान्समीक्ष्य स कौन्तेयः
सर्वान्बन्धूनवस्थितान्।। *1.27*।।

कृपया परयाऽऽविष्टो विषीदन्निदमब्रवीत्।
दृष्ट्वेमं स्वजनं कृष्ण युयुत्सुं समुपस्थितम्।। *1.28*।।

सीदन्ति मम गात्राणि मुखं च परिशुष्यति।
वेपथुश्च शरीरे मे रोमहर्षश्च जायते।। *1.29*।।

गाण्डीवं स्रंसते हस्तात्त्वक्चैव परिदह्यते।
न च शक्नोम्यवस्थातुं भ्रमतीव च मे मनः।। *1.30*।।

निमित्तानि च पश्यामि विपरीतानि केशव।
न च श्रेयोऽनुपश्यामि हत्वा स्वजनमाहवे।। *1.31*।।

1
Dilemma cursed
where faces look our own
and hearts are worse.

2
Where mind keep
kinship with carnal wrongs
soul keeps aplomb.

3 ESCAPISM
Escaping mind just exerts
to turn workable soil of the soul
in barren peace of deserts.

4
Between the reason
and agitation which has won
decided the evolution .

5
With loose grip
of owned arms of self control
thoughts turn arid.

Verse 32-35

Arjun continues-

Of what avail is the State and Throne,
Even continuation of life, all alone.

For whose sake, we desire Empire,
Enjoyment, elation entity entire,
Preceptors, paters and other kins close,
Array here for war and came to blows.

Kins tho' should try me to wreck,
Keen to give up their lives and wealth,
Yet O Krshna ! I wish not to perish them,
Even if lordship of all worlds I attain.

न काङ्क्षे विजयं कृष्ण न च राज्यं सुखानि च।
किं नो राज्येन गोविन्द किं भोगैर्जीवितेन वा।। *1.32*।।

येषामर्थे काङ्क्षितं नो राज्यं भोगाः सुखानि च।
त इमेऽवस्थिता युद्धे प्राणांस्त्यक्त्वा धनानि च।। *1.33*।।

आचार्याः पितरः पुत्रास्तथैव च पितामहाः।
मातुलाः श्चशुराः पौत्राः श्यालाः म्ब्रन्धिनस्तथा।। *1.34*।।

एतान्न हन्तुमिच्छामि घ्नतोऽपि मधुसूदन।
अपि त्रैलोक्यराज्यस्य हेतोः किं नु महीकृते।। *1.35*।।

1

On welkin of ego
My imaginary pencil draws shallow
Desire's rainbow.

2

I give up and fend
With my false plea in hand
Remain empty hands.

3 *ESCAPE*

Senses' seine very close
Since ages I lived with those foes
As kin fail to oppose

4

Where emptiness prevails
Many heartful excuses it avails
Never wins laurels.

5

In kinship with sense matrix
To escape from challenges I trick
Give up the bliss.

Verse 36-37

O Krshna ! what the Gain we could gain,
If Dhratrashtya's clan is slain
More so, if these fallen felons are zapped
Would bring to us a fall from grace.

O Madho ! doth it vindicate
And could ever it maketh us elate
laying low our own kindred
How indeed could we be glad.

1

I do not brave
Trumpeting sensual haves
Being natural slave.

2

A potential Brave
with inherited habits entangling haves
imprisons soul as slave.

Seine = net

निहत्य धार्तराष्ट्रान्नः का प्रीतिः स्याज्जनार्दन।
पापमेवाश्रयेदस्मान्हत्वैतानाततायिनः।।*1.36*।।

तस्मान्नार्हा वयं हन्तुं धार्तराष्ट्रान्स्वबान्धवान्।
स्वजनं हि कथं हत्वा सुखिनः स्याम माधव।।*1.37*।।

3
In my comfort mood
With false reasoning I confront the Truth
In ease of habitual route.

4 ACCEPT CHALLENGE
Come out of comfort zone
Before challenges, with the riddance n moan
Dharma can't be enthroned.

Verse 38-39

Their wisdom ; the greed had pruned
They behold not rack and ruins.
Should we not think of sin against friend,
And also destruction of Dynasty O Janardan !

1 ACCEPT CHALLENGE
Where wisdom declines
the challenges of sense blinds
Wise have foresight eyes.

2 REASONING
Wrongs in me are seasoned
Those erupt, challenge me with evil weapons
To corrupt my reason

3 EVIL FORCES
Bad habits are bad
Unscarred of consequences ever bade
Arrogantly unafraid.

4 EXTINGUISH EVIL
Where Evil sets afire
For own sack should the Good retire
Watering pseudo peace to Altar.

यद्यप्येते न पश्यन्ति लोभोपहतचेतसः।
कुलक्षयकृतं दोषं मित्रद्रोहे च पातकम्।।1.38।।

कथं न ज्ञेयमस्माभिः पापादस्मान्निवर्तितुम्।
कुलक्षयकृतं दोषं प्रपश्यद्भिर्जनार्दन।।1.39।।

Verse 40-41

Where Family thus, decimates
Good rites rituals as well fade
Up keeping thoughts annihilate
Unwomanhood in women pervadeth,

And scattered split sect
Woos not the customs of lineage,
Filth corrupts filial bonds
Cross off-springs bringeth crass traits.

1
Keeping first, the sequels
The fighter in mid of battle
How could prevail?

2 DESPONDENT ARJUN
Ethics commit sin
In its hide when a warrior thinks
Of unfought win.

3
Seeing too far
In spite of closing foes in war
Is self-mar.

4 HYBRIDIZED CULTURE
Inheritance admixtured
Diffusing discrete lineage denatures
And create confused culture.

Verse 42-43

The adulterated blood, thus gush
Adulateth the wreckers of race,
Disennobled paters, then, blush
Getting no oblations, degrade.

Adulate= flatter(make friends with)

कुलक्षये प्रणश्यन्ति कुलधर्माः सनातनाः।
धर्मे नष्टे कुलं कृत्स्नमधर्मोऽभिभवत्युत।। *1.40*।।

अधर्माभिभवात्कृष्ण प्रदुष्यन्ति कुलस्त्रियः।
स्त्रीषु दुष्टासु वार्ष्णेय जायते वर्णसङ्करः।। *1.41*।।

सङ्करो नरकायैव कुलघ्नानां कुलस्य च।
पतन्ति पितरो ह्येषां लुप्तपिण्डोदकक्रियाः।। *1.42*।।

Cross blood thus admixed,
Fadeth good customs' practice,
With its misdeeds and lapse
Race and clan collapse.

1
My arguments synthesize
From falsehood, the truth of my size
As reason to compromise.

2 RITUALS TO PATERS
I offer inward quest
An inherited flame of ancient heritage
As paters' appetite I oblate.

3
Escaping from the Present
Caught into jaws of future obsessions
I justify my indifference.

4 INHERITANCE
One more me in me
Is offspring of past pedigree
My Present trait should carry.

Verse 44-46

O Krshna ! O Janardana !! It's learnt
Family rites and customs, who miss
Most certainly its meant
The doom of everlasting abyss.

Alas ! for possession of the Throne
We, wise are ready to kill our own
Actuated by greed, this deed
Is a great misdeed, indeed.

Me, unarmed
and wholly resigned,
If the sons of Dhritrashtra lay me low,
This, as better option I do find.

दोषैरेतैः कुलघ्नानां वर्णसङ्करकारकैः।
उत्साद्यन्ते जातिधर्माः कुलधर्माश्च शाश्वताः।। *1.43*।।

उत्सन्नकुलधर्माणां मनुष्याणां जनार्दन।
नरकेऽनियतं वासो भवतीत्यनुशुश्रुम।। *1.44*।।

अहो बत महत्पापं कर्तुं व्यवसिता वयम्।
यद्राज्यसुखलोभेन हन्तुं स्वजनमुद्यताः।। *1.45*।।

यदि मामप्रतीकारमशस्त्रं शस्त्रपाणयः।
धार्तराष्ट्रा रणे हन्युस्तन्मे क्षेमतरं भवेत्।। *1.46*।।

1
Rites and customs
Has mechanized my family wisdom
Devolved from what I'm

2
Circumstances may be vehicle
To the war, but can't be
Weapon of the defence.

3
Surrender to dismay
Before and during thick of the fray
Is bravery astrayed.

4
Warm skill
Of warrior in despondent chill
Is vain skill.

Verse 47

Spake Sanjay-

In midst of field spoken thus
Arjun sat on rear seat of chariot
Casting away his arrow and bow
His mind distressed with sorrow.

1
In middle of inner row
Indecisive self behold
An alter-ego in foe.

2 PUZZLED HOPES
With brows knitted to qualm,
Thoughts unbridled on intuitive wheels
Get astrayed and jammed.

3
Dipt in shallow kinship
My discriminative weapons in depth slip
To keen, longings I kneel.

4
The Present of despondent
Is transient, but even momentary quittance
Sticks to future till end.

एवमुक्त्वाऽर्जुनः संख्ये रथोपस्थ उपाविशत्।
विसृज्य सशरं चापं शोकसंविग्नमानसः।। *1.47*।।

CHAPTER TWO

Sankhya and Yoga: The cosmic wisdom

*I'm Pritha's son**
In every coming to listen
To inner Krshna.

* Arjun

Our dilemma is

that we hate the challenge

At the same want change.

Chapter Two

LORD'S EXHORTATION

Verse 1

Sanjay commented—

Dipt in pain, with unnerved brain,
Through his eyes, brimming melancholy drained,
Madhusudan spake, then -

1
For the lost past
I fill my efforts and lament
Emptiness I attain.

2 GEETA IN LIFE
On one dejected sun
My concious attuned to Krishna
A vision, all of a sudden.

Verse 2

The Blessed Lord said—

O Arjun ! At such untimely mo,
This dejection for Aryas doth not behove
It bringeth infamy here and
Here after earns no heavenly abode.

1 REAL ATTUNEMENT
Till I knew
' I' am just body' I never have heard
The voice of rescue

2
Between polar thoughts
A vantage point ever been brought
By Himself, the God.

3 GOD'S WORDS
In fray of matter
After momentary lapse in battling barter
The spirit, I should hear.

4 PRAYER
To my aged quest
O Krshna ! as intuitive charioteer of vision
In wisest Geets manifest.

तं तथा कृपयाऽविष्टमश्रुपूर्णाकुलेक्षणम्।
विषीदन्तमिदं वाक्यमुवाच मधुसूदनः।।2.1।।

श्री भगवानुवाच
कुतस्त्वा कश्मलमिदं विषमे समुपस्थितम्।
अनार्यजुष्टमस्वर्ग्यमकीर्तिकरमर्जुन।।2.2।।

Verse 3

O Parth ! no worth; it's not fit
To unmanliness, if thou doth submit.
This frailty is so petite
Arise ! Arise !! and not quit.

1 MOTIVATOR LORD
The Unseen sees me
Through hope, through hold, through heart
Me never to flunk.

2 WARRIOR OF MOTHERLAND
I should esteem my birth
Borne of womanhood, indebted to Mother
For manly worth.

3
O Seed ! Arise !!
Ope thy tender potential coil
Bring life above soil.

4
O Bhaarat ! don't recant
Up with Gandiva in hand
War ! the war to end.

5 I AM ARJUN
I'm Pritha's son
In every coming to listen
To inner Krshna.

6 RISING CALL
From mucky mud
Arise ! O Soul of Lotus !!
Feel fathom's thud.

7
O Pellucid soul ! Arise !!
On the horizon of life's blues
But as rainbow's hues.

Verse 4

Arjun said-
O Madhusudan ! O Destroyer of foes !!
How can I come to blows,
Against Bhishma, Drona; with arrows,
Before whom should I bow.

Bhishm-Grandfather of family; Drona-Guru   flunk = fail   mucky = dirty

---

क्लैब्यं मा स्म गमः पार्थ नैतत्त्वय्युपपद्यते।
क्षुद्रं हृदयदौर्बल्यं त्यक्त्वोत्तिष्ठ परन्तप।।2.3।।

अर्जुन उवाच
कथं भीष्ममहं संख्ये द्रोणं च मधुसूदन।
इषुभिः प्रतियोत्स्यामि पूजार्हावरिसूदन।।2.4।।

1
Instincts and Ego
Are enemies though seem my own
as Bhishm and Drona.

2
The individualized person
Should be institutionalized into arrayed legion
Above egoist misconception.

3
What's unnatural to soul
Deluded, to me seem so innate
I make them intimate.

Verse 5

Better to live in dearth,
Then to batter lives of dears,
For me, the life will be marred
By slaying Guru, highly honoured.

If I dost slay these mentors
For mere pottage and power,
Then my worldly lavishes sure,
Would be daubed in dreadful gore.

1 LIFE ON SAIL
With Ego on helms
My past ride on thought boat
Take no soul's wind note.

2 GREAT GUIDE
With my Narrow watch
Driftless I float on life-Yacht
Looking to His Beacon torch.

3 ASTRAYED THOUGHTS
Habits past
Rust needle of the Just compass
Boat finds itself lost.

4 BHAKTI
In my daily muse*
The moment I surrendered I discovered
His presence, His refuge.

** Inspiration*

गुरूनहत्वा हि महानुभावान्, श्रेयो भोक्तुं भैक्ष्यमपीह लोके।
हत्वार्थकामांस्तु गुरूनिहैव, भुञ्जीय भोगान् रुधिरप्रदिग्धान्।।2.5।।

Verse 6

Its hard ! I can hardly decide,
Which would be better, the winning side !
Should they win us or we should
What's good and better I Canst not brood.
Sons of Dhratrashtra stand vis a vis
Whose death would again, for us be amiss

1
In the dilemma of core
Knowing this is the knowable lore
What's to be ignored.

2
Our dilemma is
that we hate the challenge
At the same want change.

3
East or west horizon
Both have same spread of crimson
But one have more sun.

4 DILEMMA
Light and shadow join
Bring dilemma when we stand
At their meeting point.

5
Dilemma blocks the mind
Where staunch thought of fullness
Are incomplete.

Verse 7

Infirmity overshadows my innate glow,
For onus my mind lays low,
Me, Thy Disciple! For the best path beseech !
I'm in Thy refuge, Teach me ! Teach !!

1 UNFIRM AMBITION
The mare nectaris
I would drink, but on quick sand
My feet sink.

2
With loads of infirm feet
I dig my own chilly pit
I gravitate into it.

न चैतद्विद्मः कतरन्नो गरीयो
यद्वा जयेम यदि वा नो जयेयुः।
यानेव हत्वा न जिजीविषाम
स्तेऽवस्थिताः प्रमुखे धार्तराष्ट्राः।।2.6।।

कार्पण्यदोषोपहतस्वभावः
पृच्छामि त्वां धर्मसंमूढचेताः।
यच्छ्रेयः स्यान्निश्चितं ब्रूहि तन्मे
शिष्यस्तेऽहं शाधि मां त्वां प्रपन्नम्।।2.7।।

3 ONLY HELP
My lost canoe
On the vast of the Blue
And only Thy refuge.

4 BHAKT
Mired upto groin
With my palsied limbs
and still hands sublime.

Verse 8

None ! Nothing I discern,
For miseries in me that stung,
And my senses get stunned,
Find none to cure affliction
Nor unrivalled reign, nor even
Lordship over the Heaven.

1 INTROSPECTION
Filled with soiled thoughts
A hollow pot shaped by fraud
Am I just this odd?

2
My puffs' dance
On beats of sense to become
My entity's nuance.

3 BODY
A clay not the soul
Sensual hammering framed the mould
Under misery's control.

4 SUBLIMITY
On carnal plane accessed
Those petty joys, diffuse into eternal bliss
Once beyond I assessed.

Canoe = Little Boat Nuance = Synonym with little difference

न हि प्रपश्यामि ममापनुद्या
द्यच्छोकमुच्छोषणमिन्द्रियाणाम्।
अवाप्य भूमावसपत्नमृद्धम्
राज्यं सुराणामपि चाधिपत्यम्।।2.8।।

Verse 9

Sanjay commented (to Dhritrashtra)-

To Krshna, having thus spake
Arjun worded to roll back-
" I will not combat"
And then he remained quiet.

1 CARNAL WORLD
Shrunk to mortal extents
Dictated by, of and for the sense
Ruled by its unruly reign.

2 NEED TO FIGHT
Be subdued or subdue
If you are in foe's range
So is the foe too.

3
In the need acute
At peace with weapons' pessimist mute
Alas ! inner soldier is subdued.

Verse 10

O Dhristrashtra !, to Arjun, while
He was lamenting between two arrays
Lord Krshna, as if with smile
Spake in the following ways-

1
During my trial
I look or not look at Lord
Need His merciful smile.

2 O LORD ! BLESS WITH GEETA
Drizzle quenches thirsts
Its nectar blankets with bliss, the Earth
Likewise, shower ! Thy word.

3 FROM HOPELESSNESS TO HOPE
A bloom, butterfly puffs
On the tendril of pip it hops
With hopes through toughs.

4 PRAYER
Eastern halo ! on bedewed meadows
Crayons empty dew with rich rainbow
Much like O Lord ! bestow!!.

एवमुक्त्वा हृषीकेशं गुडाकेशः परन्तप।
न योत्स्य इति गोविन्दमुक्त्वा तूष्णीं बभूव ह।।2.9।।

तमुवाच हृषीकेशः प्रहसन्निव भारत।
सेनयोरुभयोर्मध्ये विषीदन्तमिदं वचः।।2.10।।

5
Unto my spirit
May Thy voice echo the melody
Of the Divine Geet.

THE ETERNAL NATURE OF SOUL

Verse 11

Lord Krshna said-

Thou dost utter words of Lore
Yet hast been heaving sighs
Its no worth, thou dost deplore;
Because, mourn not the truly wise
For the living, nor for no-more.

1 TRUE WISDOM
Truly not mine
Seeming mine is though Lord's world
In ignorance I whirled.

2 PESSIMIST UTTERANCE
My inflated wisdom
Limited me to shallows of tongue
But the spirit choked

3 KRSHNA'S WORD
In the gloomy silence
Unto grip of hilt, gyrii of brain
Let His oracles bang.

4
Each time man claimed*
On Master's world, my brick, my bread
My brain and my brand.

5 NO SADNESS
Its Wisdom's prerequisite
The Deep, from shallows they perceive
Thus Never grieve.

Verse 12

I havest never been befo' -its not true
Nor these royal ones, nor for you
And never in coming times too,
Nor any one's existence, shall not continue.

** Every Birth*

अशोच्यानन्वशोचस्त्वं प्रज्ञावादांश्च भाषसे।
गतासूनगतासूंश्च नानुशोचन्ति पण्डिताः।।2.11।।

न त्वेवाहं जातु नासं न त्वं नेमे जनाधिपाः।
न चैव न भविष्यामः सर्वे वयमतः परम्।।2.12।।

1
I am same plume
From infant world to grown up cosm*
Evolving into innocent.

2 **PERMANENCE**
'I' am elixired-being'
"what's this word –death"
Write on cenotaph.

3 'PILGRIMAGE'
In Every framed being
Whether finned, winged and skinned
I was a pilgrim.

4 BIRTH BY BIRTH
Many short sojourns
From ages from cages, in every turn
By degrees became Human.

5 LORD
O Ancient Hand !
I continued my travel holding Thou
Even as now.

Verse 13

As the embodied self, passes through,
The childhood to the youth
Then to the old-age too,
So is its way to body next;
The wise are not stirred there at.

1
Life has permanence
I limit my 'now' to one span
Of the Time Unchanged.

2
From Time-peaks engrossed
The 'Now' expands into future and past
Broad and vast.

3 UNDERSTAND TIME
Should my concept sublime
Rise up and up a endless 'Now'
On mount of the time.

4
But through Ego perceived
In 'eternal Now' truly I live,
Time's chronicled to piece'.

* *Macrocosm. Plume = feather*

देहिनोऽस्मिन्यथा देहे कौमारं यौवनं जरा।
तथा देहान्तरप्राप्तिर्धीरस्तत्र न मुह्यति।।2.13।।

Verse 14

Cold or warmth, Sore or Charms
Are in context of the contacts,
Are short-lived, begin to culminate,
So, with patience O Arjun ! react.

1 ENDURANCE
Every feeling is touch
n touch is ache, the Endured feeler undisturbed
Keep unruffled as such.

2
Pinked by the tides
Of matter having no inherent size
Judge ! pacific benthos.

Verse 15

O Prime among men !, who possess-
A Poise in pleasure and pain,
In these, who is firm and serene,
Befits 'Moksha' and be Amarantin .

1 SELF-CONTROL
Existence has intrinsic odds
Everything apparently in duality records,
Keep ! hold on cords.

2 BE PACIFIC
Should sirens
And its earthly din may not ruin
The immortal serene.

3
A Firm oars-man
Can row a boat in gyrri of brain
Through roaring main.

Main = Ocean

4 BLISS IS ETERNAL
An eternal infant in mind
To flickers of out riders keeping blind
Lie in cradle of content.

5
Roots of evergreen orchard
In fall or winter or in Spring
Never wither.

मात्रास्पर्शास्तु कौन्तेय शीतोष्णसुखदुःखदाः।
आगमापायिनोऽनित्यास्तांस्तितिक्षस्व भारत।।2.14।।

यं हि न व्यथयन्त्येते पुरुषं पुरुषर्षभ।
समदुःखसुखं धीरं सोऽमृतत्वाय कल्पते।।2.15।।

Verse 16

The unreal subsists never more,
The real exists ever more,
This final Truth cometh to the fore
And is known to the men of lore.

1 NON EXISTENCE
Quick sand tickles sole,
My foot prints remain under foamy control
Changeable foam changes Changeable.

2
Lord created what exists
The spirit and domain of spirit
Rest all are non-existent.

Verse 17

Know ! Him as Immoral
Who in everything does dwell
And in everything doth imbue,
This unchangeable Spirit
None the power can subdue.

1
His pervasion,
Is vision for His Creation
Keep from perversion.

2
My all learning thoughts
Come to one consensual mind
'All is All God'.

नासतो विद्यते भावो नाभावो विद्यते सतः।
उभयोरपि दृष्टोऽन्तस्त्वनयोस्तत्त्वदर्शिभिः।।2.16।।

अविनाशि तु तद्विद्धि येन सर्वमिदं ततम्।
विनाशमव्ययस्यास्य न कश्चित् कर्तुमर्हति।।2.17।।

Verse 18

'Ts presumed the existence is flesh
Consumed by the death,
But sans bounds, sans transumes
Dwellth the Self wrapped in dying costumes
O Bhaarat ! so with this fact
Up ! take up the combat."

1 SPIRIT
I'm unchanging spirit,
These changeable changes are changes
Of the outfit.

2 WORLD STAGE
Its Director's wish,
From Ant to lion, to Eagle to fish
Costumed, same eternal spirit.

3
Fear not for sinew
What dwells within you
Is perpetual you.

Verse 19

The self can be slain, he who doth think
Or who feels the self as assassin
The Truth; neither of them knows,
The Self slayth not, nor is layed low.

1 THE AMRIT SELF
Beyond straps and traps
Unstructured immortal synapse,
never does collapse.

2
The Beauty of Spirit
Is that it lacks all merits-demerits
Only eternally exists.

3 THE SELF
Within worldly mattered webs
'Non matter', seeming nothing, never saps
This 'Nothing' is 'Everything'.

अन्तवन्त इमे देहा नित्यस्योक्ताः शरीरिणः।
अनाशिनोऽप्रमेयस्य तस्माद्युध्यस्व भारत।।2.18।।

य एनं वेत्ति हन्तारं यश्चैनं मन्यते हतम्।
उभौ तौ न विजानीतो नायं हन्ति न
हन्यते।।2.19।।

Verse 20

Never born, Never ruined; the Self.
Once came to the being, never endth again,
It's constant, eternal, ever the same,
When the flesh is killed, it's not slain.

1
The unborn Immortal
with time-bound-womb articled
beyond womb, Eternal.

2
Nothing is so certain
Within me exists, never be slain
As it is my Self.

3
What flows in vein
Is not my gore but the current
Of Eternal existence.

4 ONLY BODY CARED
Creases are Time-made
For would be corpse, for graying head
Man hath much paid.

Verse 21-22

How can he who weighs,
'The Self' as unborn, ever to stay,
O Parth ! how can that man
Slay or cause others be slain?

Dilapidated and worn
Cloths, casts off he; and donth
New one in the same note
Spirit casts off worn out bodily abode
Another new one to own.

न जायते म्रियते वा कदाचि न्नायं भूत्वा भविता वा न भूयः।
अजो नित्यः शाश्वतोऽयं पुराणो, न हन्यते हन्यमाने शरीरे।।2.20।।

वेदाविनाशिनं नित्यं य एनमजमव्ययम्।
कथं स पुरुषः पार्थ कं घातयति हन्ति कम्।।2.21।।

वासांसि जीर्णानि यथा विहाय, नवानि गृह्णाति नरोऽपराणि।
तथा शरीराणि विहाय जीर्णा, न्यन्यानि संयाति नवानि देही।।2.22।।

1 AT DEATH
My pupils while
At Thy beauty arrest, uncoiled
'ts long awaited- 'While'.

2
*Seeming Gloomy, The Cyanose**
Reflects on my lips, nails, nose
That swarthy Krshna is close.

3
Is it gloom of death?
Thy ope hands doffs worn out wraps
For a-newed finery layette.

Verse 23-25

No fire can ablaze the spirit
No weapon can pierce through
Nor wind can wither it
Nor water can bedew.

Can not be charred, nor be charred,
Can not be drenched, nor be parched.
All present changeth never, never doth constrain,
Eternally the same, unstirred, contained.

It's declared that this,
Soul is unthinkable, can't be conceived,
And Immutable, Clearly knowing this,
For body thou shouldst not grieve.

** Turning Bluish at death (Medical Term) layette = new clothing of newborn*

नैनं छिन्दन्ति शस्त्राणि नैनं दहति पावकः।
न चैनं क्लेदयन्त्यापो न शोषयति मारुतः।।2.23।।

अच्छेद्योऽयमदाह्योऽयमक्लेद्योऽशोष्य एव च।
नित्यः सर्वगतः स्थाणुरचलोऽयं सनातनः।।2.24।।

अव्यक्तोऽयमचिन्त्योऽयमविकार्योऽयमुच्यते।
तस्मादेवं विदित्वैनं नानुशोचितुमर्हसि।।2.25।।

1 SPIRIT
Nor chopped nor be charred
Nor it be drenched nor be parched
This thing is 'Non-Thing'

2 WATER (JAL)
On winged vapours flew
And, to dive into roaring blue.
I'm Ocean with in dew.

3 ALL- PERVADING FIRE
On Altar hallowing purpose
Shrivels jungle shrubs, for pyre ashe's hush
It hides in flint's rub.

4 ETHER
Rising from mortal swoon
I'm permeating puff out of stuffy cocoon
with Virat commune.*

5 SKY (AKASH)
Not just framed skin
But a compressed welkin under welkin
All of it within.

6 FIRE (AGNI)
Beyond senses and sinew
My Infinite glow with Eternal fuel
Is a kindled flambeau.

7 EARTH
From atom to Alps
Clayed existence is nothing else
But projection of the Self.

8 FIVE ELEMENTS
Five life ingredients
From the Vast in symmetry condense
Bringing a unit of existence.

Verse 26-27

O Mighty Arjun ! if thou dost conceive
This soul is ever to be born and to leave
Even then, thou shouldst not grieve.
For, being born, the death is due,
For, the dead must be born anew,
Then thou shouldst why
For the certain inevitable, cry?

**Enormous form*

अथ चैनं नित्यजातं नित्यं वा मन्यसे मृतम्।
तथापि त्वं महाबाहो नैवं शोचितुमर्हसि।।2.26।।

जातस्य हि ध्रुवो मृत्युर्ध्रुवं जन्म मृतस्य च।
तस्मादपरिहार्येऽर्थे न त्वं शोचितुमर्हसि।।2.27।।

1 THE INEVITABLE DEATH
Never did fade
My bold signature till it is shaped
Thick on epitaph.

2 MORTAL FACE OF LIFE
This faceless mask,
With outward colours of grief and grin
Alas ! engaged me to preen.

3 SHORT LIVED FRAME
Mirror what had approved
Short lived non-entity as identity stood,
Soon into Shapeless diffuse.

4
On the ocean of Almanac
Tides wiped surf of my named Name
Merging into nameless Sand.

5 BIRTH BY BIRTH
In Time-roll
Signed mark, designed mask died n thrived
For new unknown mould.

Verse 28-30

Genesis of All beings, is in mist
Only are known manifested in the midst,
O Arjun ! again the End is latent,
For this state why then lament?

The soul in amazement some glimpsed-
As the marvel, others limned
Still others heard of the Soul, in wonder
For some, it remained un-illumined.

This soul in every mould dwells
and its eternally inviolable
O Bhaarat ! thou dost lament!
Why for such beings in vain?

Preen = Spend time in make up

अव्यक्तादीनि भूतानि व्यक्तमध्यानि भारत।
अव्यक्तनिधनान्येव तत्र का परिदेवना।।2.28।।

आश्चर्यवत्पश्यति कश्िचदेन, माश्चर्यवद्वदति तथैव चान्यः।
आश्चर्यवच्चैनमन्यः श्रृणोति, श्रुत्वाप्येनं वेद न चैव
कश्िचत्।।2.29।।

देही नित्यमवध्योऽयं देहे सर्वस्य भारत।
तस्मात्सर्वाणि भूतानि न त्वं शोचितुमर्हसि।।2.30।।

1 BODY
Jobbed to fiery puffs
Sob not for extinguishing empty stuff
In Invisible hands, the stub
2
Berceuse to threnode
All harsher dins of life mode
Dissolve in Eternal hush.
3 A FIGHT FOR PEACE
Strange soldier's untold epic
Dawns through days on his debris,
Dovish flag, such war breeds.

4
'Name', claimed as own
On the Engraved epitaph stone
The Unnamed fate disown.
5
Where Non-violence brings defeat
To bring about the lasting peace
Need a warrior's feat.
6 THOUGHT-JOURNEY
My thought journey rolled
From I'm body with a Soul
To Soul with a mould.

RIGHTE OUS BATTLE IS MAN'S DUTY

Verse 31-32

Even from this point of view,
It's thine own Dharma's due
Tremble not ! for Kshatriya nothing else behooves,*
Than battle for the righteous move.

For the born warriors are blest,
When such righteous battle are provoked
To their fortune chanceth,
Find; ope doors to High abode.

1 EVOCATION
Trumpeting win needs gore
The trummed up kins ignore !
A Warrior, within explore !

2 A KSHTRIYA'S SACRIFICE
Gory rush in the sinew
Through wound when gushes ever woo
Warrior to pay his due.

Stub=tail end of cigarette or pencil empty stuff=physical body Berceuse = cradle song
Threnode= funeral song * Warrior class

स्वधर्ममपि चावेक्ष्य न विकम्पितुमर्हसि।
धर्म्याद्धि युद्धाछ्रेयोऽन्यत्क्षत्रियस्य न विद्यते।।2.31।।

यदृच्छया चोपपन्नं स्वर्गद्वारमपावृतम्।
सुखिनः क्षत्रियाः पार्थ लभन्ते युद्धमीदृशम्।।2.32।।

3
Over forecasted stars
Right fight of un-scared scar
Ope sure the heaven's bar.

4 WINNING HEAVEN
Born- warriors never wilt
These Brave brandish upto the hilt
Sure ! Paradise up they build.

Verse 33

But, if thou declinest
This very righteous combat,
Then abandoning duteous onus,
The Sin, thou shalt incur.

1
Me, my, mine, narrow
In timeless journey to and fro
Learn ! universal love.

2 SIN
If laden strides kneel, drop,
Sunk feet get palsied and stop
Further laden by blot.

Verse 34

Men will ever narrate,
About thy ignominy and shame,
Sure ! dishonour is worse than death,
To the man of name.

1 TO ESCAPE IS TAINTED
Where my shanks sink,
To glazing flanks, fazed I wink
Face I daub with ink.

2 BRAVE WARRIOR
With buried bruised knees
Into fought sands of enemies
The badged breast buries.

3 DEFAMING ACT
Escaping soldierly part,
Failing his country's heart
From the society, depart.

Hilt handle of sword Upto the hilt=as much as possible wilt=become less confident
Shanks = legs Faze = Unnerve

अथ चैत्त्वमिमं धर्म्यं संग्रामं न करिष्यसि।
ततः स्वधर्मं कीर्तिं च हित्वा पापमवाप्स्यसि।।2.33।।

अकीर्तिं चापि भूतानि कथयिष्यन्ति तेऽव्ययाम्।
संभावितस्य चाकीर्तिर्मरणादतिरिच्यते।।2.34।।

Verse 35-37

Great commanders will opine
Out of fear, thou dost decline.
Who held in esteem; now
They will belittle thou.

Contemptuous words of foe
Shall malign thy prowess
What could be above
Such an aching woe?

In the battle field thine demise
Is the gain of paradise,
Or Else thy triumph is the gain,
Of all the cheers of mundane.
So, O Arjun !, thou shouldst stand,
To fight, be ascertained.

1 DOVISH/HAWKISH
My instinct is dove
But a hawk I cherished and loved
In a havoc, it behoves.

2 SINNING
Shrivels me on war path
I call peace, its but a sloth
Contempt I plot.

3
The Escape crownth a blot
Who die by the sword, die not
The uncrowned patriot.

4
Funk of wound's hot spill
Who lives on cold sweat's will,
Is no warmer than death's chill.

5 GIFTED FORTUNE
The fortune, warring efforts declare,
The Heaven, martyrs share,
Or ope relishes to Victor.

भयाद्रणादुपरतं मंस्यन्ते त्वां महारथाः।
येषां च त्वं बहुमतो भूत्वा यास्यसि
लाघवम्।।2.35।।

अवाच्यवादांश्च बहून् वदिष्यन्ति तवाहिताः।
निन्दन्तस्तव सामर्थ्यं ततो दुःखतरं नु
किम्।।2.36।।

हतो वा प्राप्स्यसि स्वर्गं जित्वा वा भोक्ष्यसे महीम्।
तस्मादुत्तिष्ठ कौन्तेय युद्धाय कृतनिश्चयः।।2.37।।

YOGA - THE REMEDY

Verse 38

Be even to gaiety and grief,
Profit -loss, triumph and defeat.
To the battle, thou shouldst turn
The Sin, thou, thus wilt not earn.

1 EVEN MIND
The aroma of stoicism,
Fill contrasted stinks
and suffuse triumph.

2 EVEN-TEMPER
Gandiv, gladius, grenade, gun*
Blitz with countless odd weapons
The Wreath, even-mind won.

3 STOICISM
Over the ebby conscious
Ever surfs empty frothy sandy gush,
Pearls breed in even-hush.

4
In jungle infernal dance
On stoic fireline pilgrim's stance
Fail extinguishing plans.

Verse 39-40

Sankhya's ultimate knowledge
To thee I havest explained
Now, facts of Yoga, thou must attend,
Equipped with which O Arjun!
Thou shalt shatter Karma's chain.

In the path of Yoga's act
Even if not reached the ultimate,
A bit of this Dharma protectth
From mundane's great threat.

**Name of Bow of Arjun.*

सुखदुःखे समे कृत्वा लाभालाभौ जयाजयौ।
ततो युद्धाय युज्यस्व नैवं पापमवाप्स्यसि।।2.38।।

एषा तेऽभिहिता सांख्ये बुद्धिर्योगे त्विमां श्रृणु।
बुद्ध्यायुक्तो यया पार्थ कर्मबन्धं प्रहास्यसि।।2.39।।

नेहाभिक्रमनाशोऽस्ति प्रत्यवायो न विद्यते।
स्वल्पमप्यस्य धर्मस्य त्रायते महतो भयात्।।2.40।।

1 YOGIC ACT
Iron curtain of matter-sense
Is melted by Yogic penance,
Reveals real-substance.

2 NO EFFORT IS WASTED
Traps to God contact
Mo in some life man steps
No holy crawl is wasted.

3 YOGA
Blind renunciation is none,
It blunts senses to breathing automaton,
Senses be sublimed to Nirvana.

4 FEARLESSNESS OF YOGI
Yogic-Self doth realize
Same Eternity transmuteth to man size
Threat of being-'mortal', dies.

Verse 41

In Yoga, O Kuru's Scion !
Soul's goal is one pointed
While undecided mind's reason
Ramifies with endless ambitions.

1 INDECISIVE WANDERER
Hopping on undecided toes
Chronic wanderer in Labyrinth roves,
Till on Yoga zeroes.

2 TAKE UP ONE IDEA
In misty gyrii many grown,
From that course single out one alone,
Make that idea your own.

3 YOGIC ABSORPTION
Flavoured trial of sips
Tooth into Endless desires, parches lips
Quenched by aimed dip.

Mo = Moment

व्यवसायात्मिका बुद्धिरेकेह कुरुनन्दन।
बहुशाखा ह्यनन्ताश्च बुद्धयोऽव्यवसायिनाम्।।2.41।।

Verse 42 – 44

Mislead by flowery words of Ignorants
To power and eros adamant
To the Karma's reward who are bent,
In Laudary aphorism of Veds, who pretend,

Heaven is their highest gain,
Through many rites they claim,
Pomp and pleasure to obtain
But Desire-instigated acts have on chance
To reach holy communion of trance.

1 BARGAIN
Pseudo Yogna I immerse
Lesser prayers aim at lucrative perks
It's but commerce.

2 RITUALS
Vespers, flowers offers in clutch
Of desired heaven go waste as such
Till aimed at Holy touch.

3 WRONG PATHS
Misled map-lines
In lust-lustre, the heaven I design
Highest Goal need be redefined.

Verse 45

Vedas validatest three-fold traits
For triadic qualities of the Created
O Arjun ! free thyself from contrast vibes,
Above seizing and securing thrives,
In the 'self' compose thy drive.

यामिमां पुष्पितां वाचं प्रवदन्त्यविपश्चितः।
वेदवादरताः पार्थ नान्यदस्तीति वादिनः।।2.42।।

कामात्मानः स्वर्गपरा जन्मकर्मफलप्रदाम्।
क्रियाविशेषबहुलां भोगैश्वर्यगतिं प्रति।।2.43।।

भोगैश्वर्यप्रसक्तानां तयापहृतचेतसाम्।
व्यवसायात्मिका बुद्धिः समाधौ न विधीयते।।2.44।।

त्रैगुण्यविषया वेदा निस्त्रैगुण्यो भवार्जुन।
निर्द्वन्द्वो नित्यसत्त्वस्थो निर्योगक्षेम
आत्मवान्।।2.45।।

1

In pro tem contrasts waves
Once handful quicksand drains thro' webs
This empty hand grasps 'the Self'.

2

Rebirths' dizzy gyrii tied
Encircling in greedy goods, godules cheap-buy.
Need centrifugal escape from me-my.

3 WORDS OF VED

Rote left my treatise to rot
Beyond vibes veds belaud-
'thou art full of God'.

4 ABOVE YOGKSHEM

Possessions tempts to procure
Preservations tempts further to secure
Getting rid is the cure.

Verse 46

Veds are of little avail,
To the knower of the Supreme Self.
Having got the oceanous swell,
Man needth no little well.

1 BRIMMING POT MOKSHA

A filled vault urn
Floats not, sinks and turns,
Into ocean dissolve all learnt.

2

Epistle, message, sermons, buzz
Dins, chants, discourse vespers or hush
Ousted by fullness of touch.

3 ACCOMPLISHED

From ponds, lakes, stews
From rites, rotes, recitations; withdrew
Once dipt in nectarine deluge.

Verse 47

Thy right, is alone to execute
The Action; is never for the fruit.
Nor to fruits of Action be attached
Nor to Inaction be annexed.

Vibes=emotions Stew=waterbody deluge=flood. pro tem = for now

---

यावानर्थ उदपाने सर्वतः संप्लुतोदके।
तावान्सर्वेषु वेदेषु ब्राह्मणस्य विजानतः।।2.46।।

कर्मण्येवाधिकारस्ते मा फलेषु कदाचन।
मा कर्मफलहेतुर्भूर्मा ते सङ्गोऽस्त्वकर्मणि।।2.47।।

1 LARK

The Spirit of melody, hark !
For no Claim, no gain, no mark
For the Infinite, sings a lark.

2 ATTEMPS-NOTEMPTS

Works, worships, wails, wants
Fruitless to spiritual advance,
In vain, idle stance.

3 RIGHT

Toiling Right blisters
Pearls on my soles my hands appear
Claim no gems in barter.

Verse 48

To success or defeat unconcern,
Being established in Yoga, Performs !
O Arjun ! all the Karma,
Unattached to the outcome,
In poise of equilibrium,
As 'Yoga' its term.

1 YOGA -SERENITY

On steady wings 'Soul' flies
High in native repose of hushed skies
Ever dipt in perfect poise.

2 GOD – UNION-ADVAIT

Mind with soul be tuned
Lesser 'me' with Lost Greater Me to commune,
From duality first be immuned.

3 YOGA OF GENESIS

Essence and colour's lush
All the pomp rot into dust
Seeds ope again in hush.

Verse 49

Action with desire is lesser
Than one which, the Even-wisdom steer.
O Arjun ! go to wisdom's shelter
Its pity for who actth for desires.

योगस्थः कुरु कर्माणि सङ्गं त्यक्त्वा धनञ्जय।
सिद्ध्यसिद्ध्योः समो भूत्वा समत्वं योग उच्यते।।2.48।।

दूरेण ह्यवरं कर्म बुद्धियोगाद्धनञ्जय।
बुद्धौ शरणमन्विच्छ कृपणाः फलहेतवः।।2.49।।

1 DESIRES

Action be wisdom's tool
Lest burdened deeds drown in greed pool
Gold profits not laden mule.

2

Calculative toils count hope
But in wine of desires doped
Astrayed 'Karma' in misery grope.

Verse 50

Even here in this life,
Whose wisdom with 'even-ness' comprise
Sublime above virtues and vice,
So devote ! to yoga, which's Karma's expertise.

1

A prisoner suffers full term
Once wisdom-diary enrolls right 'Karma'
Parole, the Warden affirms.

2 ALAS !

Up high above earthlings
A falcon in gyrii evenly should swing
But in gold cage frustrates wings.

Verse 51

Rapt in wisdom, who mastered their mind,
To the fruits of Action they never incline,
Thus freed from bounds to and fro
Get an state beyond sorrow.

1

Every sun brings Lord's theme.
Man ignored His, over own dream
Desires corrupt God's scheme

2 'SOUL AND MIND'

Reigning beaut of Soul resignth
Before as ugly as sin, the mind
Brought misery, is no God's design.

Grope=to try to find something in dark.

बुद्धियुक्तो जहातीह उभे सुकृतदुष्कृते।
तस्माद्योगाय युज्यस्व योगः कर्मसु
कौशलम्।।2.50।।

कर्मजं बुद्धियुक्ता हि फलं त्यक्त्वा मनीषिणः।
जन्मबन्धविनिर्मुक्ताः पदं गच्छन्त्यनामयम्।।2.51।।

Verse 52

Whenever thou, dost well cross
Dark delusive morass,
Wilt be detached from 'trite'
What mundane, voiced and would be voiced.

1 ACROSS TIME
God conscious soul rout,
Future birth's wow, and past woe
To dissolve into Infinite Now.

2
Deaf to din, clamour
This orchestrated soul, only hear
Tuned up melodic whisper.

Verse 53

Thine baffled core
By very many revealed lore'
Once settle in ecstatic Samadhi,
'Divine-union' chance upon thee.

1 MEDITATION
Many surfing waves toss
The Anchor bindth to grave benthos
To serene marge ships close.

2 YOGIC MONSOON
The noisy vapours pace
To hush of steady Mounts, to embrace
Rain all around the grace.

Trite matter=expressed so many times to become boring and dull. Benthos=bed of ocean

---

यदा ते मोहकलिलं बुद्धिर्व्यतितरिष्यति।
तदा गन्तासि निर्वेदं श्रोतव्यस्य श्रुतस्य च।।2.52।।

श्रुतिविप्रतिपन्ना ते यदा स्थास्यति निश्चला।
समाधावचला बुद्धिस्तदा योगमवाप्स्यसि।।2.53।।

ATTRIBUTES OF REALIZED PERSON

Verse 54

Arjun asked -

"What are features O Keshav !
Of stable wisdom, who have ?
In Samadhi who are steeped
How do they sit, step and speak?

1 CURIOUS ARJUN
Bee askth bud in hope
Seed probeth through envelope.
The path, those queries ope.

2 DAILY TOIL
Wisdom serene
Needth no unearthly advanced mean
But sublime through routine.

3
Curiosity is child
Evolves from infancy to man-sized
Through queries mild.

Verse 55

The Blessed Lord said-

O Parth ! when a man waiveth
All desires, what the mind hast,
Within the self, by the self fulfilled
'settled in wisdom'- he is entitled.

1
Toxic desires as chalk -cheese
Or elixired with nectar the wisdom chalice
Wise chose this brimming bliss.

2
Stony - Self buried in desires,
Unearthed rinsed with nectar
Statued out 'True-Self' clear.

Chalice= big wine cup

अर्जुन उवाच
स्थितप्रज्ञस्य का भाषा समाधिस्थस्य केशव।
स्थितधीः किं प्रभाषेत किमासीत व्रजेत
किम्।।2.54।।

श्री भगवानुवाच
प्रजहाति यदा कामान् सर्वान् पार्थ मनोगतान्।
आत्मन्येवात्मना तुष्टः स्थितप्रज्ञस्तदोच्यते।।2.55।।

3
Peel pulp sap lured me,
Through time's lens now I see
In stable stone, a tree.

4 SELFLESS SELF
With I-ness lost in I
Yet search of I lasted till I eyed
And discovered I-less I.

Verse 56-57

Whose consciousness ist never alarmed
Nor glad by charms, nor ached by harms
Who is free from worldly lust, qualm, rage
Is termed a steady minded sage.

Dispassionate all over
Who is not excited by pleasure,
Nor perplexed by the dolour
Has wisdom, all honoured.

1 SUBLIMITY
Vivid Kites under welkin
Though threaded whirl and swing,
Rise in unseen calm wind.

2 NATURE OF SOUL
While the beam pierces through
Spectrum appears in colourless dew,
Possesses none of own hue.

3 POMPS OF COLOURS
Through rays of wisdom, come
The delusive arc of cosmic spectrum
Again dissolved in conscious sun.

4
An stranger puffed into flesh
Mind-stuff making it closest friend
Though (That)stranger is bosom-flame.

दुःखेष्वनुद्विग्नमनाः सुखेषु विगतस्पृहः।
वीतरागभयक्रोधः स्थितधीर्मुनिरुच्यते।।2.56।।

यः सर्वत्रानभिस्नेहस्तत्तत्प्राप्य शुभाशुभम्।
नाभिनन्दति न द्वेष्टि तस्य प्रज्ञा
प्रतिष्ठिता।।2.57।।

Verse 58

When a Yogi; like a tortoise
Own limbs as it coils,
Fully retireth from senses likewise
His wisdom manifestth poised.

1
Unsatiable big palate
Aimed at lie-around mirage
Interiorize ! the target

2 SOUL'S FOOD
Hunger bringth more hungerly attack
Of five relishes*, never to sate
Soul eats senses and satiates.

Verse 59

The senses, man who quitth
Senses fall aside little bit
Only to have longings avidly persists
But the Supreme who perceiveth
Even from such longings is freed.

1 TAPA THE CHURNING
Water added milk dilutes
Its lacteal nature gets reproved
Once churned, creams off aloof.

2 SENSES PREDOMINATE
Mind's dragged by senses
Toiling to control senses is in vain
Established by Intellect, truly gains.

3 ENLIGHTENMENT
In glittering dusk I seized
Little glowworms into craving fist
Till knocked crimson of East.

**olfactory, optical, auditory, gustatory and tactual*

यदा संहरते चायं कूर्मोऽङ्गानीव सर्वशः।
इन्द्रियाणीन्द्रियार्थेभ्यस्तस्य प्रज्ञा प्रतिष्ठिता।।2.58।।

विषया विनिवर्तन्ते निराहारस्य देहिनः।
रसवर्जं रसोऽप्यस्य परं दृष्ट्वा निवर्तते।।2.59।।

Verse 60-61

Who is enlightened to high degrees,
O Arjun ! who is striving to be freed,
Even them athirst senses forcibly seize,
But who with me communeth
Remainth to me attuned
Thus whose Conscious subdueth 'Sense'
His wisdom turnth 'Balanced.'

1 DEFECT (LOOPHOLE)
Wishing to brim with divine
This thirsty bowl of foible design
May spill old carnal wine.

2 BEWARE !
Where predatory sense
Had slain inner Supreme Consciousness
Every move is 'tempt-providence'.

3 BALANCED WISDOM
The ship on the voyage
With its balanced mast has
Touched the destined edge.

4 BE VIGILANT
Wisdom with no tocsin
Only fueled the flambeau with toxins
Extinguishes torch of win.

Verse 62-63

Once thoughts in 'senses' doth indulge
Those lead to longing urge
With longings, the Anger eruptth
The Mind, this anger disruptth
With such mind the Ingenious interruptth
The Genius, which further corruptth
Thus the Corrupt fallth and fallth abrupt.

Foible = weak aspect of character. *Tempt -Providence = Confidently move to Bad luck.*
Tocsin = warning bell.

यततो ह्यपि कौन्तेय पुरुषस्य विपश्चितः।
इन्द्रियाणि प्रमाथीनि हरन्ति प्रसभं मनः।।2.60।।

तानि सर्वाणि संयम्य युक्त आसीत मत्परः।
वशे हि यस्येन्द्रियाणि तस्य प्रज्ञा
प्रतिष्ठिता।।2.61।।

ध्यायतो विषयान्पुंसः सङ्गस्तेषूपजायते।
सङ्गात् संजायते कामः
कामात्क्रोधोऽभिजायते।।2.62।।

क्रोधाद्भवति संमोहः संमोहात्स्मृतिविभ्रमः।
स्मृतिभ्रंशाद् बुद्धिनाशो बुद्धिनाशात्प्रणश्यति।।2.63।।

1 SUBLIMITY
Forgotten I'm; know must
What would not raise and upthrust
The soul; is heightening lust.

3 FRACTURED IDOL
Carved chip by chip
Statue, deshaped in a chisel slip*
Is not worshipped.

2 ANGER
Shortlived thunderbolt
Its' own story told
In ashes and coal.

4 SOUL, THE KING
Desires conquered the Empire
Should the conquered conquer the
Conqueror
Let hidden King-Soul take over.

Verse 64

The man of Self curb,
Mastered Cupidity, roaming in world's charms
To hates and baits undisturbed,
Attain unstirred calm.

1
On Board of ladder and trap,
With dice of hate and bait
None gets passes straight.

3 GOOD AND RIGHT DOINGS
Given enough rope
Grazed not ropy charms - dopes
Further serene glebe ope.

2 SELF CONTROL
On high pole rope of cupid
He crosseth with balancing stick
Meditating acrobatics.

** committed sin Self curb = Self control. Baits = attraction*
Give enough rope = freedom ropy = sickly glebe = land

रागद्वेषवियुक्तैस्तु विषयानिन्द्रियैश्चरन्।
आत्मवश्यैर्विधेयात्मा प्रसादमधिगच्छति।।2.64।।

Verse 65

With this unstirred calm state
All grief annihilates,
In fact ! the Insight of the Elated
Soon establisheth in the Self.

1 AIMED
On wrinkled sailing quest
On 'One twinkle mini magnet fixeth*
Guideth boat through tempest.

2
In comparison
Between grief and elation
Its only the perception.

3 INSIGHT
Weathering the storm
Is hard but on helms little arms
Can shore to calm.

Verse 66

While the inner self is un-established
It lacks in the wisdom-gnosis
Nor hath a genial fix
Unmeditative fix bringth no peace,
Then, to the Peaceless how cometh bliss ?

1 BOOKISH KNOWLEDGE
Even unlettered insight intuits
But with astrayed discursive books,
The reasoning is overlooked.

2 SOUL-FORCE
Aroma never halts
With in man-made barbed walls
Fix ! on this innate call.

3 UNGENIAL HEIGHT
'Disunion' cultured winged notion
In vulture-gyrii** high like felcon
From high eyeth carrion.

**polar star **punning for Vulture whirls and brain gyrii. Carrion = flesh of dead animals.*

प्रसादे सर्वदुःखानां हानिरस्योपजायते।
प्रसन्नचेतसो ह्याशु बुद्धिः पर्यवतिष्ठते।।2.65।।

नास्ति बुद्धिरयुक्तस्य न चायुक्तस्य भावना।
न चाभावयतः शान्तिरशान्तस्य कुतः सुखम्।।2.66।।

Verse 67

As, a boat is tossed
Astrayed by the wind blows
So, is driven off from its course
The wisdom, by the senses' force
To such senses while the Mind bows.

1 *TRAPS*
Boat made to cross
O Carpenter ! O Creator !! Alas
In the shallow lost.

2 *DISCRIMINATION*
The Crew is trained
To avail the forcing hurricane,
Thus mileage gained.

3 *SENSES ON HELM*
Unlearnt full rigged sail,
Even in the favouring gale
With untrained trimming, trail.

Verse 68

O Arjun ! O Mighty armed !!
His Wisdom is set perfect
In regard to sensual charms
Whose sense faculties art wholly subjugated.

1 *RIGHT WISDOM*
Fearing wild off-beat,
I bridle and whip ; instead
Should train steeds.

2 *CONTROL – IMPULSE IN MIND*
To lavishes abstinent blind,
Peepth into charms through palpable mind,
Must evil-impulse resign.

Trim=to adjust sail to catch wind.
Full rigged sail = ship with all masts and ropes cables.

इन्द्रियाणां हि चरतां यन्मनोऽनुविधीयते।
तदस्य हरति प्रज्ञां वायुर्नावमिवाम्भसि।।2.67।।

तस्माद्यस्य महाबाहो निगृहीतानि सर्वशः।
इन्द्रियाणीन्द्रियार्थेभ्यस्तस्य प्रज्ञा प्रतिष्ठिता।।2.68।।

Verse 69

'What is Night' to all creatures
Is wakefulness to the self-mastered.
What is wakefulness to the masses,
That is night to the divine sage.

1 DELUDED MAN
Wakeful who ever dreamt
Deluded that he's not in delusion
Ope eyed mesmerized he is.

2
Night or Days
Cannot discriminate the ecstatic state
Of the sage.

3 WAKEFUL TO VIRTUES
Weeds immersed in dazzling wake,
From elixired orb lilies nightly partake*
Yet, keeping above lake.

4
The inner Sun
of sages is beyond the horizon
And so never sets.

Verse 70

Like the ocean, full to the banks
By adding in water, it remainth unchanged,
Who absorbth all desires within,
He is content full to the brim,
Not he, who after desires keen.

1 THE LOSS
Handful of infant bliss,
For Handsome spoils, spills
Through aging creases.

2 HUNGER
Desires arise from lacking
Desireless but accepts desire's stream
Unaffected like an ocean.

3 CALM WITHIN
In vast space of core
Brimming oceanous peace, explore !
Unchanged by ripples poured.

** Moon*

या निशा सर्वभूतानां तस्यां जागर्ति संयमी।
यस्यां जाग्रति भूतानि सा निशा पश्यतो मुनेः।।2.69।।

आपूर्यमाणमचलप्रतिष्ठं, समुद्रमापः प्रविशन्ति यद्वत्।
तद्वत्कामा यं प्रविशन्ति सर्वे, स शान्तिमाप्नोति न कामकामी।।2.70।।

Verse 71

All desires who relinquish,
With no craving who existth
That person realizeth peace,
Who's nor with 'mortal-I' known,
Nor sense of I-ness who doth own
That person realizeth 'Peace'.

1 FALSE EGO IN LIFE
I-ness in tight grasp
Like sweaty camphor faster escapes
Empties in barren epitaphs.

2 **PEACE**
Owning even not the Own,
This 'emptied- I' come into its own,
is Blessed with serene throne.

3 **SELFLESSNESS**
Studded marrow of bamboo,
Once hollowed through and through
Hallowed flute's peace blew.

Verse 72

In this state of final gain
One is never deluded again
Even touched such state, just at end
O Arjun ! 'Brahmn-Nirvan' he attainth.

1 NIRVANA
Once Honeyed; its waste
To add more lesser tastes
On the tongue, thus blest.

2 GOD UNION
The nearing ship with undertows
At swells of flows may toss
Till anchored to benthos.

विहाय कामान्यः सर्वान्पुमांश्चरति निःस्पृहः।
निर्ममो निरहंकारः स शांतिमधिगच्छति।।2.71।।

एषा ब्राह्मी स्थितिः पार्थ नैनां प्राप्य विमुह्यति।
स्थित्वाऽस्यामन्तकालेऽपि ह्मनिर्वाणमृच्छति।।2.72।।

CHAPTER THREE

Karma Yog: Path of Action

Mould is fool's gold
Battered, bartered and sold
At cost of the soul.

KARMA

Lord worked pearls in benthos

Yet He avowed and chose,

Man's toiling pearls on brows.

Chapter Three

KARMA LEADS TO LIBERATION- 'MOKSHA'

Verse 1

Arjun asked-

If Thou O Janardhan !
Dost judge the Gyan
To be Superior to the Action
Why then O Krshna!
Dost Thou direct
Me to this Terrible act ?

1 COMPROMISE
Grey – labyrinths vibes
Bring 'peace' as unjust bribe,
But Just-war is sacrificed.

2 INACTION/ ACTION
Sublime woolpack snooze*
The treasured sky not ooze
Only Active clouds droop.

Verse 2

Arjun continues-

My mind is dazed
In Thy cryptic speech,
Let me know certain ways
The highest good I reach.

1
Adult mind is adulterated,
Though the path is torched straight
Let infant faith tread.

2 COUNTER POINT
Action to attain inaction
Weaponise for era of no weapon
Seems a paradox compulsion.

**Wooly inactive cloud.*

ज्यायसी चेत्कर्मणस्ते मता बुद्धिर्जनार्दन।
तत्किं कर्मणि घोरे मां नियोजयसि केशव।।3.1।।

व्यामिश्रेणेव वाक्येन बुद्धिं मोहयसीव मे।
तदेकं वद निश्चित्य येन श्रेयोऽहमाप्नुयाम्।।3.2।।

Verse 3

The Blessed Lord said-

O Sinless one !
Two ways of devotion
Was given by Me to the creation,
For wise through wisdom
For the Yogis, through Karma-Yog
Way to the Divine-Union.

1
One Droplet quenched the wheat,
Else shelled to pearl the seed
Two ways to nature's meet.

2 FIRST STEP- KARMA
After the season of 'Karma'
Followth vernal blossomming bliss
Fructifieth gnosis.

3 GYAN / KARMA
One knowth- 'He Knowth nought'
'He doth know', the other knowth not,
Two folds, one path.

Verse 4

To undercut mundane Action-ties
The Action, do not avoid.
Once the 'Karma' is forsaken
No one reacheth Perfection.

1 ACTION/INACTION
Buds work hard to blossom
Petals fall back to inaction,
At shaping fruition.

2 KARMA
The final action-less peace
This leisure soul hath achieved
Only through sole's trodden crease.

लोकेऽस्मिन्द्विविधा निष्ठा पुरा प्रोक्ता मयानघ।
ज्ञानयोगेन सांख्यानां कर्मयोगेन योगिनाम्।।3.3।।

न कर्मणामनारम्भान्नैष्कर्म्यं पुरुषोऽश्नुते।
न च संन्यसनादेव सिद्धिं समधिगच्छति।।3.4।।

3 NON ACTIVITY

Workless hush of the Idol
Is the enshrined divine symbol
Of prior din of working chisel.

Verse 5

Verily work deprived,
One canst not survive
Even for a trice.
All are compelled indeed,
To perform some deeds
Prodded by the drive
Which from Nature, is derived.

1 NATURAL EVOLUTION

Actively Inactive to actively active
Unto calmly active The Nature gifts
To Actively calm, at length, achieved*

2 DYNAMISM

In motionless framed landscape
Mute mounts have lively said-
Stillness is stilted.

Verse 6

Own organs of action, who subdueth,
But mind broodth carnal views
Is said to be hypocrite
Himself, he deludeth.

1 NURTURE THOUGHT

The visible morning dew,
Is bound to vapourize can't be rescued
Rosy-soil be imbued.

2 IMPOSTER

Through lenses I read,
And costumed n' adorned holy text; instead
Into senses, seed ! good read.

**final non-action of Samadhi (God Union)*

stilted=Unnatural.

न हि कश्चित्क्षणमपि जातु तिष्ठत्यकर्मकृत्।
कार्यते ह्यवशः कर्म सर्वः प्रकृतिजैर्गुणैः।।3.5।।

कर्मेन्द्रियाणि संयम्य य आस्ते मनसा स्मरन्।
इन्द्रियार्थान्विमूढात्मा मिथ्याचारः स उच्यते।।3.6।।

3
Lord doth watch,
Words, text, thoughts, with very acts
Must match.

Verse 7

Achieves supremacy that man,
Who disciplineth his sense
Keepth his action-organs unattached
Keeping Divine path intact.

1 WORTHLESS TOIL
Would be ash, I groomed
Wick of aged toils lit no commune
Well-chanced flame, thus consumed.

3 WORK ! AT AIM
On flotsam little ant's chore,
Over foam, flood with working Oar,
Reaches the honeyed shore.

2 KARMA-YOG
Discipline be disciplined
Bit by bit, so that its spirit
Turn into habit.

Verse 8

Thou perform !, essential bounden duty
For 'Action' is superior to passivity
Even the routine vital needs
Are impossible without obligatory deeds.

1 ACTION IN INACTION
The balanced rock on hill top
In saintly hushed non-motion, yet jobbed
To neutralize imbalance.

2 SEEMING IDLE GALAXIES
On vault passive twinkling spread
'on hault', through lenses read
Act on tugged unseen threads.

Flotsam = piece of wood floating on sea.

यस्त्विन्द्रियाणि मनसा नियम्यारभतेऽर्जुन।
कर्मेन्द्रियैः कर्मयोगमसक्तः स विशिष्यते।।3.7।।

नियतं कुरु कर्म त्वं कर्म ज्यायो ह्यकर्मणः।
शरीरयात्रापि च ते न प्रसिद्ध्येदकर्मणः।।3.8।।

3 DYNAMIC INACTION

Acrobats, on rope-shows
Unmoved, as an idle, pose
Workst on unseen toes

4 WORTHLESS-WORK

Any mundane sized pastimes
Of active toils may be spiritual crime,
Work shouldth make soul sublime.

ALL ACTIONS AS YAGNA

Verse 9

All the actions of mundane,
Ever chain the man,
But 'Karma' sacrificed for spiritual gain
Those are different.
So, in spirit of Yagna, non-attached
O Arjun ! thou shouldst act
As oblations, all actions are consecrate.

1 THE SACRIFICE

On call of quenched altar,
Match stick with own inner fire,
Oblates to be consumed entire.

2 KARMA YOG

Any self sacrificing act
In spirit of self dedication is blest
ever liberates.

3 WASTEFUL CHORE

Glitters* and Cheese
go waste in treasuries,
Even breath is His.

4 LIBERATING ACT IS YAGNA

Krshna's words resolve
Karma which from Relativity evolve
Is sacrifice to the Absolute.

*Worldly earnings.

यज्ञार्थात्कर्मणोऽन्यत्र लोकोऽयं कर्मबन्धनः।
तदर्थं कर्म कौन्तेय मुक्तसंगः समाचर।।3.9।।

Verse 10-12

At the Genesis of Cosmos,
The Creator, Brahma hadth caused
Mankind also The Yagna, to prosper thou
For thy wishes its milch-cow.

Through this act of Yagna
Thou mayst sustain Devas
And they mayst in turn sustain thou
And this commune of mutual care,
Wilt lead thou all to Supreme welfare.

Devas, through Yagna, communed thus
Unasked fruition, they will entrust.
But then, who enjoyth such bestowed gifts,
Repaying no due offerings, is a thief.

1 FIRE OF KARMA
Man's hands since Genesis
At the same hath igneous crease
Torched just by the deeds.

2 KARMA'S POWER
Orphaned zodiac signs
Brought up in Karmic science
Works out fate's designs.

3 SELF HELP
Birth by birth this snail,
With own angelic hands' help
Evolved sudden out of shell.

4 WORK WORKS
On forelot a laden wish
If perspires out of Knuckles; squeezed
Through creases all accomplished.

5 'A DRIVE' ABOVE LUCK
My free choice within
Hath inherent will to win
Over mute stars' din.

6 NOT GIVING
With ope blessings dropt
Whose closed fist giving nought
Such thrift is theft fraud.

Igneous = fiery thrift = miserly

सहयज्ञाः प्रजाः सृष्ट्वा पुरोवाच प्रजापतिः।
अनेन प्रसविष्यध्वमेष वोऽस्त्विष्टकामधुक्।।3.10।।

देवान्भावयतानेन ते देवा भावयन्तु वः।
परस्परं भावयन्तः श्रेयः परमवाप्स्यथ।।3.11।।

इष्टान्भोगान्हि वो देवा दास्यन्ते यज्ञभाविताः।
तैर्दत्तानप्रदायैभ्यो यो भुङ्क्ते स्तेन एव सः।।3.12।।

7

In sacrifices* employed
Its not just a good Karma to deities
But is a mutual joy.

Verse 13

Sharing due offerings, the Sages
The remnants, who dost partake
Are freed from all lapses;
But the sinners, those who make
Food just for the self
They feast on sacrilege.

1 OBLATIONS

Mortal offerings of mortals
Morsels, florals, candles
Make a bit, Immortal.

2 SELF CENTERED MAN

In own cocoon, man flaws
Has to repay to the natural laws,
Even moths give floss.

3 SCIENCE OF LIVING

*Cells** feast mortal way, die*
Better fed in astral way, survive
Souls way, wilt immortalize.

4 UNSHARING SINNER

The mortgaged cage blufft
Added debts, every breath pufft.
Debtor declared bankrupt.

**Good acts **Unit of Body Floss= Silk*

देवान्भाव यज्ञशिष्टाशिनः सन्तो मुच्यन्ते सर्वकिल्बिषैः।
भुञ्जते ते त्वघं पापा ये पचन्त्यात्मकारणात्।।3.13।।

Verse 14-15

The Creature springth from food grains,
Food begetth from the rain,
Rain from fire of the Yagna
And Yagna from performed Action..

This divine Karma's squad
Know ! be begotten from the Veds.
Veds, Ancient texts in its turn
Art derived from imperishable 'Brahmn'.

Therefore, in Karma-Yagna, its established
All inseparably,
Omnipresent Brahmn existth.

1 ACTIVE YAGNA-WITH IN
Lush or lesser earths
Trash, ashen all inerts hath
Very same afired hearth.

2 ONE NESS
In Man, grain, sand
Hidden blaze seemth alien,
The fire is same Ancient.

3
Blessings rain
Upon man of righteousness performance
Thus cosmic nature sustains.

4 FIRE-WITHIN
Sparkled sweet or sore
On the inner altar poured
Igniteth enlightened chore.

5
With Inner fire, that dwells
To meet ocean, the Karma's debacles melt,
Lest chilly tough Glacier swells.

6 TWO ASPECTS OF KARMA
Gross yagnic Acts are meant
For the gross gain, But the subtlest
Unto the Absolute transcend.

Debacles = Breaking up of ice over river surface Trash = Rubbish

---

अन्नाद्भवन्ति भूतानि पर्जन्यादन्नसम्भवः।
यज्ञाद्भवति पर्जन्यो यज्ञः कर्मसमुद्भवः।।3.14।।

कर्म ब्रह्मोद्भवं विद्धि ब्रह्माक्षरसमुद्भवम्।
तस्मात्सर्वगतं ब्रह्म नित्यं यज्ञे तिष्ठितम्।।3.15।।

Verse 16

O Arjun ! that man
Who followth not this nature's wheel
Living in all ill,
In senses get content,
That sinner liveth in vain.

1 LIABILITY

On giant wheel evolving shift
Had to repay through descending drift
For the diagonal uplift.

2 CLOSING ACCOUNT

A mammonist grasp
Alas ! at last gasp
Tightens fist holding lapse.

3 REPAY

Wicked sowed no seeds
Can't harvest grace or deeds,
'll reap barren weeds.

Mammonist = Greedy

एवं प्रवर्तितं चक्रं नानुवर्तयतीह यः।
अघायुरिन्द्रियारामो मोघं पार्थ स जीवति।।3.16।।

Verse 17 -18

But the one, who truly,
Loveth the Self, satiated fully,
Finds content in the Soul only
For him there ist no duty.

Such a self realized man,
Hath no purpose to treasure in mundane,
For his inaction or performance
Hath nothing to lose or gain,
Also, on none he dependth.

1 HURDLE OF EGO
I – ness blurth eyes
Lest no wail lies
' Most-Intimate' to visualize.
2 REALIZATION BEYOND KARMA
Lamps burnt midnight oil
Then dawning embrace of rays coiled
Freed it from duty n toil.

3 VAIN GLORY OF GLOWWORM
Glow of mammonist
That of worm size egoist
Fade at knocking East.*

* Sunrise

यस्त्वात्मरतिरेव स्यादात्मतृप्तश्च मानवः।
आत्मन्येव च सन्तुष्टस्तस्य कार्यं न द्यते।।*3.17*।।

नैव तस्य कृतेनार्थो नाकृतेनेह कश्चन।
न चास्य सर्वभूतेषु कश्चिदर्थव्यपाश्रयः।।*3.18*।।

NON ATTACHED DUTY IS GODLY

Verse 19

So, deeds telluric or seraphic*
To senses need not stick,
Sans-attachment to sense, these deeds
Meet the Supreme summit.

1 NON-ATTACHMENT
Unattached to frothy swell,
In benthos, aloof Drop dwells
Evolves to pearl in shell.

2 MUNDANE LIFE
Tagged name, decked tavern
Alas ! Lagged behind, lacked Aim
The Aimless aimed at sojourn.

3 FIRE – NON ATTACHED
To the finery from nuggets
The fire toils, carve crown, crest,
all aloof yet.

4
Mould is fool's gold
Battered, bartered and sold
At cost of the soul.

Verse 20

Janak and others are known to attain perfection
Through righteous actions alone,
Further thou shouldst perform deeds
Simply, in masses weal.

1 BENEVOLENCE OF ACHIEVER
He paved reached the summit
Then descended through steeps
For down-trodden to uplift.

2 WELFARE
Surpassing cliffs and slopes
He climbed peaks, yet belayed ropes
As low dwellers' hope.

3 RIGHT DUTY OF RAIN
Ocean's vaporizing rush,
Descends as dutiful gush,
In pond uplifts lotus.

**Telluric = earthly Sans=without Nugget=a Lump of gold Tavern=Inn. Benthos=bed of sea.*

तस्मादसक्तः सततं कार्यं कर्म समाचर।
असक्तो ह्याचरन्कर्म परमाप्नोति पूरुषः।।*3.19*।।

कर्मणैव हि संसिद्धिमास्थिता जनकादयः।
लोकसंग्रहमेवापि संपश्यन्कर्तुमर्हसि।।*3.20*।।

Verse 21

The path Virtuous beings lead,
Exactly, the others repeat,
Thus the Action what they perform
For the masses set a norm.

1 THE PATH MAKER
Shouts in hush would sink
Text would fade in own ink
Last untrodden imprints.

2 THE HIGH SOUL
Having mastered the fragrance
Jasmine with elixired essence,
Fills bushes in the dense.

3 THE WORK WORKS
Quotes, slogans lectures,
All din is futile whisper
Mute example speaks louder.

4 STANDARD MOULD
A cast layed
Unnumbered shapes
In mouldless clay.

Verse 22

Arjun ! for no duty I'm compelled
In the world at any level
None I havest which I havest not gained,
For Me none to acquire remainth.
I'm consciously engaged, yet
In performance of act.

1 GOD-WILLING
For desireless desires I do,
Through individualized dreams anew,
For dreamless bliss to pursue.

2 CONSCIOUSNESS –MORE INTENSE
Nor mind, heart nor eyes
But Lord hath chosen to reside
Intensely in hands at work.

यद्यदाचरति श्रेष्ठस्तत्तदेवेतरो जनः।
स यत्प्रमाणं कुरुते लोकस्तदनुवर्तते।।3.21।।

न मे पार्थास्ति कर्तव्यं त्रिषु लोकेषु किञ्चन।
नानवाप्तमवाप्तव्यं वर्त एव च कर्मणि।।3.22।।

3 KARMA

Lord worked pearls in benthos
Yet He avowed and chose,
Man's toiling pearls on brows.

Verse 23

For If certainly I,
With care, dost not comply
With performance of 'Karma'
Then in all respect O Parth !
Men would follow My Path.

1 GOD'S POLICY

His unchanging plan, is one,
Through ever changing divine phenomenon
Evolve man, unto Him.

2 BE ALERT LEADERS(INFLUENTIALS)

Ignored, miles of ants' toil
While An inch of model step's slip
Ist enough ages to spoil.

3 MENTOR

Consciously He guides strayed lot
Ceaselessly He works on untrodden path
Oh ! foot prints I ignored.

Verse 24

So, If Myself I dost not employ
Humankind would be destroyed.
Then, the Hybrid inequity's qualm
Would cause admixing of Karma
Thus, whole mankind, I wouldst harm.

1 ONE FATHER

Jungle is hued motley
Siblings lie on same soil bed
All elixired with one sap.

2 DISCRETE TASK, NO ADMIXTURE

Clay quenched as urn
Same clay's dudeen burnth
Tasked to potter's scerne.

Dudeen = Short tobacco pipe of clay Scerne = Wit, Discretion

यदि ह्यहं न वर्तेयं जातु कर्मण्यतन्द्रितः।
मम वर्त्मानुवर्तन्ते मनुष्याः पार्थ सर्वशः।।3.23।।

उत्सीदेयुरिमे लोका न कुर्यां कर्म चेदहम्।
सङ्करस्य च कर्ता स्यामुपहन्यामिमाः प्रजाः।।3.24।।

3 EVOLUTION KEY
The Maker, in every bit chanced
With ceaseless duty to evolving advance
For Karma is Lord's stance.

Verse 25-26

As the Benighted pursue
Act, attached to it's fruits;
O Bhaarat ! as much as must do

With the Enlightened attitude
Being Non-attached to its fruit,
As a guide to the multitudes.

Let the learned not confuse
The Naives, for their work for fruits,
By not refraining but with own Karma, the wise
Should encourage them to abide.

1 THE NON ATTACHED GUIDE
Longing act that won
Through brandishing hilt at bellum
Is inspired by non attached pennon.

2 DETACHED KARMA
Non chalant to lustre or murk
The mirror, reflects not figures
But, own selfless work.

3
A boat with no oar
Be not barred its active flow
Some eve finds shore.

4 ILLUMINED ACT
Over, Act attached to motives,
The Act detached to achieve
Gets bliss as incentive.

5 KARMA AS HOBBY
Lord's hobby, I take
I bless, with work, myself
Lest work to eke, aches.

6 PERFORMER IN SACK OF ATTACHMENT
On sack-race
No stake to my pace
Yet I progress.

Pennon = Triangular flag at war Bellum = war Non chalant = dispassionate Buff = Expert, Guru,

---

सक्ताः कर्मण्यविद्वांसो यथा कुर्वन्ति भारत।
कुर्याद्विद्वांस्तथासक्तश्चिकीर्षुर्लोकसंग्रहम्।।3.25।।

न बुद्धिभेदं जनयेदज्ञानां कर्मसङ्गिनाम्।
जोषयेत्सर्वकर्माणि विद्वान् युक्तः समाचरन्।।3.26।।

I-LESSNESS AND BONDAGE OF KARMA

Verse 27

All activities, in actuality
Are carried out by Promordial Prikrti.
Who thinkth of him as doer
Ist his owned foolish egoity.

1 THE REAL DOER
The invisible Absolute
Visible in vibrating attribute
Is it blower's flute?

2 BEHIND ALL SCIENCE
Manifested God head,
As apple, fell on Man's head;
All mankind rocketed.

3 NO ONE IS PIONEER
Long past words those babbled
Evolved to this great level
Today my text got laurels.

4 NATURE, THE DOER
Begets in Nature's womb
He forgets that acts of his loom
Naturally with nature commune.

Verse 28

O Arjun ! the Knower of the Truth,
Knowth the dissimilitude
Among Works in devotion and for fruits,*
Keepth his 'self' nonattached
To Nature's and sense's attributes.

1 ILLUMINED ONE-NON ATTACHED
Bosom of the dew
Treasures none of attributes
In play of rainbow's hue.

2
His work alone workth
Worked not for passionate perks
Nothing bargains from work.

3 RIGHT THOUGHT
I, Being compressed Absolute,
Beyond worldly attributes,
Should brood.

4 THE KNOWER
The Illumined one, knows
The torch in and out glows
To the Supreme source, owes.

**Karma/Action*

प्रकृतेः क्रियमाणानि गुणैः कर्माणि सर्वशः।
अहङ्कारविमूढात्मा कर्ताऽहमिति मन्यते।।3.27।।

तत्त्ववित्तु महाबाहो गुणकर्मविभागयोः।
गुणा गुणेषु वर्तन्त इति मत्वा न सज्जते।।3.28।।

Verse 29

Having imperfect knowledge,
Those, befooled and attached,
Into material attributes engaged,
But the Perfect wise may not, yet
Distract them from their acts.

1 HELP
Gushing with flooding pour,
Boat mayst slowly evolve to shore
Keels over by helping oar.

2 DISCRIMINATION OF WAYS
May not seem wise
But the path of own choice
Be there for tortoise.

3 SELF HELP
Through waves taking up helm
The avail from within prevails,
Only you are your help.

Verse 30

In Omniscient Me, mayst thou rapt
All Karma's unto Me, waive
Nor Desire nor fond thou shouldst have,
Be free from worked up sloth,
The Battle, O Arjun ! be braved,

1 NO RIGHT TO DESIRE
Acts The Lord consigned
For Karma very Hands He designed
But desires, be declined.

2 HE, THE DOER
Our True duteous acts
Threaded through unseen fantoccini
We, the Krshna's conscious puppet.

3 DESIST DESIRE
His paint, canvas, His brush,
In frame and beyond frame His opus
My claim now blush.

4 NOTICE ! DIVINITY
Renounce all unlettered absurd
Be conscious of the Divine words,
Intuitive epistle be heard.

fantoccini = puppet show

प्रकृतेर्गुणसम्मूढाः सज्जन्ते गुणकर्मसु।
तानकृत्स्नविदो मन्दान्कृत्स्नविन्न विचालयेत्।।3.29।।

मयि सर्वाणि कर्माणि संन्यस्याध्यात्मचेतसा।
निराशीर्निर्ममो भूत्वा युध्यस्व विगतज्वरः।।3.30।।

RIGHT ATTITUDE

Verse 31

To My injunction who execute
The duties regularly, those;
What I tutor this Truth
Sans fault finding who follows
Ist freed from Karma and fruits.

1 EVER NEW GEETA
In Cradle of Holy pages
Ancient verse hadst incarnate
Cherish ! this Neonate.

2 RIGHT PATH OPENS
Guru's precept goad
With none of desires' loads
And intuitive Truth decodeth.

3 OBEDIENCE
Automaton of skilled Guru
Through threads to summit drew,
like, Kites never argue

Verse 32

This teaching of Mine
Who critically declines,
Consequently doth not live,
To this, but to his misbelief
With own foolish conceit
Wilt be doomed ; Perceive !

1 FALSE INTELLIGENCE
Wisdom with ego
Like fireworks glow
Fade quickly though.

2 IGNORANCE
Where Skill exhausts
For own haphazard malign cause
Gets delusive applause.

ये मे मतमिदं नित्यमनुतिष्ठन्ति मानवाः।
श्रद्धावन्तोऽनसूयन्तो मुच्यन्ते तेऽपि कर्मभिः।।3.31।।

ये त्वेतदभ्यसूयन्तो नानुतिष्ठन्ति मे मतम्।
सर्वज्ञानविमूढांस्तान्विद्धि नष्टानचेतसः।।3.32।।

3 ASTRAYED REASONING
Mighty nous grey,
While justifying dazzling way
Spiritual riches pay

Verse 33-34

Enacts, even the wise
To his own nature's drive,
His own instinctive nature pursue
So what can restraint do?

The aversions and attachments
To the senses are nature - ordained
Influence of this duality, know !
The two, are stumbling foes.

1 INNER CHANGE, NOT JUST SUPRESSION
My bias behaves
Compelled to the instinct haves
Change ! O Born slave !!

2 DOUBLENESS COMBINED
In cinders the warmth lies,
Hath a chill in its Ash
This duality doth disguise.

3 VAIN KNOWLEDGE
Learning maps
Within tendencies frame
guide to unworkable treks.

4 SHALLOW REPRESSION
No crude force
Could really endorse
Change to prejudiced course.

5 INCLINATION-SOUL IS UNBIAS
Inclination-born Nature
Of man, is naturally unnatural
For the forgotten soul.

Nous= Intellect

सदृशं चेष्टते स्वस्याः प्रकृतेर्ज्ञानवानपि।
प्रकृतिं यान्ति भूतानि निग्रहः किं करिष्यति।।3.33।।

इन्द्रियस्येन्द्रियस्यार्थे रागद्वेषौ व्यवस्थितौ।
तयोर्न वशमागच्छेत्तौ ह्यस्य परिपन्थिनौ।।3.34।।

CONQUERING CONTRASTS

Verse 35

Own duty, may in merits dearth
Over perfectly done duties of others,
Yet, own duty's path is worth.
In own duty even the death,
Benevolence it doth bequeath
While, the Awe, other's path bringeth.

1 DUTY, AT ODD(IN BATTLE FIELD)
At the front, his brows
Knitted against violent provoking shows
Thus more, peace grows.

2
Spectacular worldly zeal
Making duty to glitter's deal
Rides dangerous ferris wheel.

3 WORTHLESS SENSES
Real 'Own' to survive
Long before so called death
What dies not , should die.

4 SOUL'S SILENT PATH
In the tuneless din
Muting mutating desires within
Dutiful hush blissfully wins.

Verse 36

Arjun said-

O Krshna! By what
A man is impelled
Even against his own thought,
To perform the sin compelled,
As if engaged by force.

1 THE SIN WITHIN
Outshining coal cellar
Self's gleaming white never perverts
Instinctive smoke hurts.

2 MORALIST STRUGGLE
On steeps I cope
Yet resisting my demand and hope
Which's worldly slope.

श्रेयान्स्वधर्मो विगुणः परधर्मात्स्वनुष्ठितात्।
स्वधर्मे निधनं श्रेयः परधर्मो यावहः।।*3.35*।।

अथ केन प्रयुक्तोऽयं पापं चरति पूरुषः।
अनिच्छन्नपि वार्ष्णेय बलादिव नियोजितः।।*3.36*।।

3 GROWING SIN
With a Lie I deceive
Then, repeat it with ease
Now this ease deceives me.

4 CARELESS FARMER
A thought, bad seed
Was mood, then tendency, then habit
Became crop of weeds

Verse 37

Shri Krshna said-

Born of passionate trait of Nature
Which is sire of ire and desire
Are Capital sins all to devour,
So, here in the world know !
These, to be the foulest foe.

1 REFORMER
In cocoon the moth,
Lost in toil of making floss
Which reforms to fine cloth.

2 DIVERGENCE
Expanding circle by circle,
Ever-whirling desires, centrifugal
With central poise, struggle.

3 TRAP
Knocked one of desires,
Flocked many more desires
Locked me, in desires.

4 DESERT OF DELUSION
Chasing the mirage
Endless road of thirsty rage
Here the Self, scorches.

5 DELUSION
Conditioned to unnumbered sins
Exteriorized foes multiplied umpteen
Zeroed not at pal within.

Umpteen=Infinite/ very many

काम एष क्रोध एष रजोगुणसमुद्भवः।
महाशनो महापाप्मा विद्ध्येनमिह वैरिणम्।।3.37।।

Verse 38-39

As, by smoke The Fire is gloomed
As a mirror by the dust
An embryo is covered by womb
So, is Wisdom by the lust.

This Lust ist endless foe
Which satiateth never
Burning as if inferno
Man's Gyan it coverth.

1 NO DESIRE
His Grace is graced
When our consciousness
Needs less.

2 HIDDEN BLISS
Covered in feverish shore
Deep in Sandy tortuous cores
Rippling course explore !

3
Wisdom combusts
Into ashes at its worst
If fueled by the lust.

4
Darkness is less shine,
Evil is less divine.
Potential to refine.

5 WISDOM WITHIN
The theatrical mask
Is unveiled at curtain fall
Real face gets applause.

धूमेनाव्रियते वह्निर्यथाऽऽदर्शो मलेन च।
यथोल्बेनावृतो गर्भस्तथा तेनेदमावृतम्।।*3.38*।।

आवृतं ज्ञानमेतेन ज्ञानिनो नित्यवैरिणा।
कामरूपेण कौन्तेय दुष्पूरेणानलेन च।।*3.39*।।

Verse 40

Own abode, the lust maketh
Over senses, the mind and intellect,
Veilth knowledge of the Living,
And bewilderth him.

1 CONDITIONED SOUL
Pellucid canvas
Daubed in colours gross,
Looses its gloss.

2 EMBODIED IGNORANCE
In damp and dark
Befogged match stick figures
Fail to spark.

3 BODILY KINGDOM
King soul doth dwell
On anthill in wooden citadel,
Put to daily struggle.

Verse 41

O Arjun ! in the beginning
So, bring senses in the discipline
Then lust, the symbol of sins
Which ist wisdom's sure assassin.

1 GOOD THOUGHTS
The Crop-seed,
Lest would recede
If grown with weeds.

2
Small grin, small win
If tempts indiscipline
Slay ! this assassin.

3 CAUTION
Step even a bit
Ope to matter or spirit
Both lie opposite.

इन्द्रियाणि मनो बुद्धिरस्याधिष्ठानमुच्यते।
एतैर्विमोहयत्येष ज्ञानमावृत्य देहिनम्।।3.40।।

तस्मात्त्वमिन्द्रियाण्यादौ नियम्य भरतर्षभ।
पाप्मानं प्रजहि ह्येनं ज्ञानविज्ञाननाशनम्।।3.41।।

Verse 42-43

The senses are defined
To be strong and very fine,
Yet superior to senses, ist mind
Above mind though the Genius excelth
Yet superior to the Genius is 'The Self'.

O Arjun ! learning thus-
'The Self' as above genius,
Commanding the mind with wisdom
Further, very foe, the Lust
Hard to conquer, though be crushed.

1 INERT BODY
With Stallion ten
The Owner over Chariot reign
Never the wheels dominant.

2 AM I BODY?
The Ancient flame
Embodied into Lamp
Is this smoky, 'the same'?

3 CONSTITUTIONAL POSITION OF SOUL
As a rule
The Overlord Superior doth rule,
Lest lesser might overrule.

4
Hates and baits
Are short lived batty mates
Only Poise of soul stays.

Batty = foolish

5 BODY –CHARIOT
On slopes, hurdles,
Discriminative disciplined bridles
Destined the vehicle.

6 SOUL CONTROLS SENSE
Poisonous serpents
Play on charmers' pipe
With broken fangs.

7 TRANSCENDENTAL JUSTICE
Nature's laws
Workst for Super-Natural cause
And equated cosmos.

इन्द्रियाणि पराण्याहुरिन्द्रियेभ्यः परं मनः।
मनसस्तु परा बुद्धिर्यो बुद्धेः परतस्तु सः।।3.42।।

एवं बुद्धेः परं बुद्ध्वा संस्तभ्यात्मानमात्मना।
जहि शत्रुं महाबाहो कामरूपं दुरासदम्।।3.43।।

CHAPTER FOUR

Gnostic Talk: Gyan-Yog

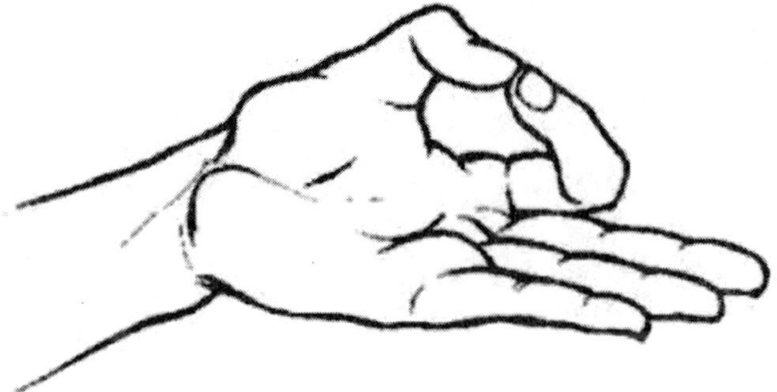

O Flesh-identified pleb !
O Ash –identified on epitaph
Be blest ! identified as His.

Many suns crawled,

One ray then dawned

Never to set.

CHAPTER FOUR

SECRETS OF YOGA

VERSE 1-2

Thus said the Blessed Lord-

This imperishable knowledge of Yog
I imparted to the Sun-God,
In turn the Sun-God, who
Passed it on to Manu
Manu told it to Ikshvaku.

Thus Supreme Science through
Disciplic order all, Rajarshis knew*
O Arjun ! As the long time passed
This Yog from sight was lost.

1 THE LORD, THE SUN
With the cosmic grace
My nest next to palace
Both were equally blessed

2 DISCIPLIC SUCCESSION OF YOG
Most Ancient Eye
In unbroken succession of ties
Limned new born's sight.

3 BIG-BANG
Supreme Echo stretched,
And conscious energy hatched
The life in time-space.

4 ENLIGHTENED BY YOG
My Yogic stride
Deep in sundial ride
Never faced eve tide.

5 UNENDING GAME
Witnessed He, I played
Changing sides, flags, flanks and arrays
On this eternal Holiday.

Limned = illumined ** Royal rishis*

इमं विवस्वते योगं प्रोक्तवानहमव्ययम्।
विवस्वान् मनवे प्राह मनुरिक्ष्वाकवेऽब्रवीत्।।4.1।।

एवं परम्पराप्राप्तमिमं राजर्षयो विदुः।
स कालेनेह महता योगो नष्टः परन्तप।।4.2।।

Verse 3

Today, unto thee,
This ancient Yog, I spake
For thou art my pal, my devotee
Sure ! this is transcendental secret.

1 GEETA
Themed, the Supreme,
Reinstalled lost hymns
Effaced corrupt whims.

2 APPEAL TO DEVOTEE
O Flesh-identified pleb !
O Ash –identified on epitaph
Be blest ! identified as His.

3 SALVATION
Ego-centric Names
Off loading those; the self same
Sublimeth to final aim.

4 MEDIATION
With oldest Pal
The Ancient threads reinstall
Into Him to dissolve.

5 COMMUNION-TODAY
Since births, many aeons
To Limn Souls' eveless horizon
The Divine perceptively dawns.

स एवायं मया तेऽद्य योगः प्रोक्तः पुरातनः।
भक्तोऽसि मे सखा चेति रहस्यं ह्येतदुत्तमम्।।4.3।।

INCARNATION – THE AVTAAR

Verse 4-5

Arjun asked –

The Sun, existed first
Afterward, occurred Thy birth.
Thy words, How then
Can I do comprehend-
This 'Yoga' Thou didst
Pass on at the Genesis.

The Blessed Lord said –

O Arjun ! Very many birth havest been
Experienced by Me and by thee,
I'm acquainted with them all
Tho' thou canst not recall.

1 KNOWLEDGE / IGNORANCE
The Sun, Lord's gift
Slipped from my fist
Ope in mist.

2 GEETA
A vigilante asked
Into timeless span brought
A distant virtuous past.

3 YOG – GOD UNION
The Immortal Togetherness
Above mortal consciousness
Witnesses unbroken existence.

4 INQUEST
Unquestioning wrongs
If quizzes throng
Weaken the Faith-strong.

5 TIME
Mine is in fragments
Lord's past and future drains
Into Prolonged Present.

6 LORD'S TIME PIECE
Expands the past on tonneau,
But at timeless centric screw
The Present is eternally anew.

Tonneau = wrist watch.

अपरं भवतो जन्म परं जन्म विवस्वतः।
कथमेतद्विजानीयां त्वमादौ प्रोक्तवानिति।।4.4।।

बहूनि मे व्यतीतानि जन्मानि तव चार्जुन।
तान्यहं वेद सर्वाणि न त्वं वेत्थ परन्तप।।4.5।।

Verse 6

Though unborn and changeless,
Yet being Lord of Universe
By own vital verve
I embody Myself,
In My transcendental visage.

1 HIS AVATARS

The Unmanifest transcendth
Also as leaves, rays, drops descendth
Not just Human mien.

2 CAUSE OF CAUSES

The Causeless caused
Abiding by Own Natural laws
Personified the cause.

3 SHAPED THE SHAPELESS

From Infinite came,
Before mirror, the very same,
Visage in finite frame.

4 INCARNATED BEING

All garbs my own
Upon entering Nature, I don
As Avatar 'm known.

5 HIS COMING – AVATARA

That invisible Essence,
No man can perceive; hence
This Visible Advent.

6 GOD IS NATURE'S YIELD

No Bets, debates, threats
But in innate untext text
Godliness incarnates.

अजोऽपि सन्नव्ययात्मा भूतानामीश्वरोऽपि सन्।
प्रकृतिं स्वामधिष्ठाय संभवाम्यात्ममायया।।4.6।।

Verse 7-8

Whenever shouldst virtue fail
And unvirtuous prevails
O Bhaarat ! At that spell,
As Avatar I manifest Myself.

Age after the age,
To save the sage
And ravage the savage
In the visible visage
I dost firmly come
To re establish the Dharma.

1 ANSWER TO ADHARM
A seed seedth
In even corrupt extremes
An evolved yield.

2 GOD'S DECLARATION
O Hell ! Hear
The Paradise that existed ever
Is now and here.

3 AVATAAR
Employing into limits
The Vast, compressing into relative finite
Descends the Infinite.

4 SAVIOUR – ONLY HOPE
When the destined curse
Accepts this Anarchy ist worst
Then savior doth putsch.

Putsch = Remove (Anarchy) by force.

5 RESTORATION OF DHARMA
In chaos
Of Anarchy, grows
The Taos.

6 PURPOSE OF INCARNATION
That very shapeless
To reshape the Deshaped
He, Himself shapes.

7 EVOLUTION CYCLE
Day of Creation
Evolve to Night of dissolution,
Evolve to day of Creation.

8 MANIFEST
Never changing Spirit,
Cometh to Ever changing pit
Revealing the Infinite.

यदा यदा हि धर्मस्य ग्लानिर्भवति भारत।
अभ्युत्थानमधर्मस्य तदाऽऽत्मानं सृजाम्यहम्।।4.7।।

परित्राणाय साधूनां विनाशाय च दुष्कृताम्।
धर्मसंस्थापनार्थाय संभवामि युगे युगे।।4.8।।

Verse 9

Arjun ! My coming , My deeds are Divine,
In own essence, who findth,
After leaving, is not reborn again,
My eternal abode he obtainth.

1 MY SMALL PRAYERS
Worshiping thoughts
Expressed compressed and brought
The embodied Virat.*

2 EVOLUTION OF EMBODIED HUMAN
Disguised as Non Divine,
Inner divinity is regained refined
But through that Divine.

3 THE LEELA
His pastime
Above causative space
Is timed timeless.

4 SALVATION
Melts that alone,
Into Thy unknowable own
Whom Thou makest known.

5 MY FOLLY
Otherwise wise,
I didn't realize
The Divine comes man-sized.

Verse 10

Chastised by Tapa of wisdom
From passion, piques, panics freed
Absorbed in Me, My refugees,
Many havest, to Me, reached.

1 ACHIEVABLE GOD
Unlocked to very many traits
With innate key of wisdom of the chaste
Opened door to the Ultimate.

2 SIMPLY DETERMINED
Standing to my stand,
Not a bit I moved
Journeyed to the Goal.

3 DEVOTEES PATH
Ascetic sibs,
Simply shading fibs,
Reformed into Libs.

4 PUREST
Laid at feet, the Lotus
Flowers freshest unsmelt, untouched
Lord receives such.

**The Vast, The Supreme.* *Libs = Liberated*

जन्म कर्म च मे दिव्यमेवं यो वेत्ति तत्त्वतः।
त्यक्त्वा देहं पुनर्जन्म नैति मामेति सोऽर्जुन।।4.9।।

वीतरागभयक्रोधा मन्मया मामुपाश्रिताः।
बहवो ज्ञानतपसा पूता मद्भावमागताः।।4.10।।

5 PENANCE OF WISDOM

Achievers are very rare
The penance, others not dare
In theories ensnare.

Verse 11

O Arjun ! As men do,
Approach Me, in that view,
I reciprocate to them too.
And All men in all respect
A path to Me, pursue.

1 DEVOTION

A tiny tear
Ever adhered
Each other.

2 DIVINE OCEAN

Mounts' ope door
Through ripples surrender to shore
Thus returnth the pour

3 ALL SEEKERS/ ALL GODWARD

An atheist ! who said?
Seems astrayed; even his tread
Leads to God head.

4 MUTUAL

A little but keen thought
In rebounce - response brought
Equally keen Virat Lord.

5 ALL PATHS LEAD TO GOD.

Man's any stride
Whether firm or tried
Hath cosmic Guide.

6 ALL PATHS ARE HIS

All walks all stance
Reach to God in the end,
Because Lord is omnipresent.

ये यथा मां प्रपद्यन्ते तांस्तथैव भजाम्यहम्।
मम वर्त्मानुवर्तन्ते मनुष्याः पार्थ सर्वशः।।4.11।।

Verse 12

In fruitive work, The Men
Do crave a fulfillment
For which, demigods they worship,
Of course, they get success quick
In the men's mundane.

1 SHORTLIVED GOALS
Worked to desire
It worked quick, but fruit vapoured
Was a camphor.

2
Mans unquenching thirst
Pray God, godules and their worships
Are thus made worst.

3 MUNDANE WISH
My Nutshell, my will
Against His will
Is barley's weevil.

4 BUILDING DESIRES
I Desired brick on brick
Got quick edifice
On the Self debris.

5 A SLAVE WITHIN
My inner fool
Looked at lesser godules
Making me, my tool.

TRAITS OF ACTION (KARMA)

Verse 13

As per virtues and acts
I havest created
The four fold sects
Though I'm its author,
Yet, being Immutable,
Know Me to be Non-doer.

काङ्क्षन्तः कर्मणां सिद्धिं यजन्त इह देवताः।
क्षिप्रं हि मानुषे लोके सिद्धिर्भवति कर्मजा।।4.12।।

चातुर्वर्ण्यं मया सृष्टं गुणकर्मविभागशः।
तस्य कर्तारमपि मां विद्ध्यकर्तारमव्ययम्।।4.13।।

1 HUMAN
The Doer
Uninvolved in evolution
Hence non-doer.

2
Water, Ice, vapours
Very states same element has authored
But as Non-doer.

3 MAKER'S PLAN
Its the Doer's wish
Let the Gunas* and deeds
Be doer instead.

4 NON-PERFORMER
Involved in creation,
But the Creator, ist non-involved
In attributes and actions.

5 GOOD DEEDS
Attributes, the Lord admixed
My very Being I fixed
Conditioned to deeds.

Verse 14

Involves Me none the actions
Nor I havest any longing for fruition
One, who truly knowth Me thus,
Also is free from fetters of works.

1 NON ATTACHMENT
A Divine skill-
Potter workth on making wheel
Never stickth the argil.

2 MOTIVE OF DESIRE
The better work
In fetters of perk
Battered the work.

3 THE MASTER VIEWER
Maker of grains, rains, field
Now, interruptth not to keep weevil
From the yield.

4 DIVINE HARMONY
Any Action non-attached
Is Divine; because
Lord's work it matched.

Argil = clay used for pottery *Attributes/Traits

न मां कर्माणि लिम्पन्ति न मे कर्मफले स्पृहा।
इति मां योऽभिजानाति कर्मभिर्न स बध्यते।।4.14।।

5 WISH-FREE KARMA

While the work pursued
None the fruits due or undue
Worked God in you.

Verse 15

With this very knowledge,
Since pristine age
Wise-seekers of liberation
Have performed their Action;
So take up thy deeds
As the Ancients did.

1 OLD SEEKER I'M

Fresh mirror image
Should recover the ancient visage
On my unaltered face.

2 UNWISE TRAPS

Impulsed sense haunt
The thoughts, with desires' lance
Trapping into 'wants'.

3 STRETCHED 'NOW'

Many pasts condensed
Into futuristic today in me
As eternal present tense.

4 ANCIENT TEXTS

The brimming old urn
To elixir the conscious of moderns
I lean to learn.

5 OLD TEXTS

Evolved from the Crude
Time tested words withstood
To pursuit of Truth.

6 TIME TESTED

What the Time accrued,
Learnings brought to you is true
Or else becometh true.

Accrue-Accumulate.

एवं ज्ञात्वा कृतं कर्म पूर्वैरपि मुमुक्षुभिः।
कुरु कर्मैव तस्मात्त्वं पूर्वैः पूर्वतरं कृतम्।।4.15।।

FREEDOM FROM KARMA

Verse 16

Even the wise,
Here are mystified,
To make out
What is Action and Inaction?
What's action about,
I shalt clear doubts
A knowledge which will free
From the Evils thee.

1 TRUE ACTION
When gray zone rise
Need a single stride
God sized.

2 GYAN
Not the doing of Deed
Even knowing the Deed
Would have freed.

3 DEVOTEE
What, why and how,
Me, with the breathing doubts
I surrender to Thou.

4 HIS GRACE
One touch, One glance
Ist the enough chance
For Lord's grants.

Verse 17

One shouldst, indeed, perceive,
What Action, what forbidden is
As well what Inaction is
'Cos unfathomable are Actions' intricacies.

1 RIGHT PATH
Not simply intellect,
But what discriminateth
Liberateth.

2 REALIZATION THROUGH KARMA
The knowledge exists,
In the laboratory of the Action
Man discovered it.

किं कर्म किमकर्मेति कवयोऽप्यत्र मोहिताः।
तत्ते कर्म प्रवक्ष्यामि यज्ज्ञात्वा
मोक्ष्यसेऽशुभात्।।4.16।।

कर्मणो ह्यपि बोद्धव्यं बोद्धव्यं च विकर्मणः।
अकर्मणश्च बोद्धव्यं गहना कर्मणो गतिः।।4.17।।

3 RELATIVITY
Same Action diversely endorsed
In Relative World, on Conscious scores
The right or wrong course.

4
Krshna's Geets
Are not just for learnings
But effect on deeds.

5 JUDGE ! THE ACTION
That cures
That work is sure
The pure.

6 MEDITATION
Changing idle mute
Into awakening mute,
Transmutes.

7 ART OF GOOD ACTION
Gardener waters Rose,
Need not know, how vivid it glows?
Root-sap He knows.

8 JUDGE ! THE ACTION
Enslaves or salves-
Path of Action so Solved
Confusion dissolved.

9 ACTION AND CONSEQUENCE
All deeds,
Like sweet and poisoned sweet
Look same though discrete.

10 INACTION/ AKARMA
Sated Action
Has shed Action
Headed to Liberation.

Verse 18

In the Action, the inaction
And in Inaction the Action,
A wise he is, who beholdth
United to his Karma
He attainth the goal.

1 INACTION IN ACTION
The voice of flute
To the inner mute
Introduce.

2 WISE-INACTION
Colourless drone,
Of a drop; within own
A spectrum shown.

3 ACTION IN INACTION
The passive Earth
In its wordless arms
Seeds new birth

4 RELATIVE MULTIPLICITY
This that and that
Into all contrasts permeate
Thus relative world is made.

कर्मण्यकर्म यः पश्येदकर्मणि च कर्म यः।
स बुद्धिमान् मनुष्येषु स युक्तः कृत्स्नकर्मकृत्।।4.18।।

5 CONSCIOUS INACTION
Say –the Absolute laws
Pause is relative pause
All have Active cause.

6 LIBERATION FROM KARMA
The Creator decreed
Assigned divine deeds
I finished and am freed.

7 NO WANDERING INACTION
Seekers' wish
From searching to No searching
Is at finish.

8 KRSNA CONSCIOUSNESS
Activity is relatively passive
Passivity is relatively active
The Divine to achieve.

Verse 19

Purified in fire of gnosis
Whose every pursuit is freed
Of selfish motive and greed
The sages distinguish
That performer as Pandit.

1
The only desire
Which burnth all desires
Lit ! that inner fire.

2 INACTION ACHIEVED AFTER ACTION
Working waves designed
In the deepest of the Brine,
Inaction's pearly shine.

3 NON ATTACHED ACTION
The fireline, the wise finds
Amid Activity and fire of desire
Thus His Action not binds.

4
From desire freed
In such Action meet
Inaction's serene seed.

5 WISE ACTION
Involved yet not involved
From God Actions unto good Inaction
Thus evolved.

6 PURIFICATION
The pinchbeck * scorches
The Gold in the fire separates
Transmutes to the purest.

*Immitation gold.

यस्य सर्वे समारम्भाः कामसङ्कल्पवर्जिताः।
ज्ञानाग्निदग्धकर्माणं तमाहुः पण्डितं बुधाः।।4.19।।

Verse 20

Who Never is attached,
To the fruits of Act
Dependth on none
Ever is satiated
Although fully engaged
He doth not, at all act.

1 SATIATED IN GOD-CONSCIOUSNESS
Other sweetening tastes
On the tongue fade
At honey –droplet.

2 GOD ACTS
Working on Lord's plot
One acts, yet acts not,
Only acts the Lord.

3 BONDAGE FREE WORK
Butterfly hopped
Unattached to pollen, jobbed.
Seeded the blossom.

4 NON ATTACHED-SILENT WORK
Harmony in violin
In the wolf of orchestral din
Has bow's silence within.*

5 NON-ATTACHED KARMA
To the fruits resigned
All such acts Lord designed
To be Divine.

Verse 21

Desiring nothing;
Without and within
Who is disciplined,
None the possessions who own,
Workth by body alone,
Also incurth no sin.

*violin bow, wolf = harsh sound of faulty Vibrations

त्यक्त्वा कर्मफलासङ्गं नित्यतृप्तो निराश्रयः।
कर्मण्यभिप्रवृत्तोऽपि नैव किञ्चित्करोति सः।।4.20।।

निराशीर्यतचित्तात्मा त्यक्तसर्वपरिग्रहः।
शारीरं केवलं कर्म कुर्वन्नाप्नोति किल्बिषम् ।।4.21।।

1
Non attached work
To any of the perks
The sin, never incurs.

2 DESIRE FREE
Hands, engaged,
In the non-engaged wake;
Liberate.

3
Every work is sacred
Work never sins, till is engaged
In fruitive Bondage.

4 POSSESSED WORK
Non possessive opus
Never trieth incentive bonus,
Which is sin in disguise.

5
Actions desired
To be desireless,
Ever are blessed.

Verse 22

Satiated, unasked
In dualities of contrasts
Equal on gain and loss
Free of all envy
Such man of Karma is free.

1 POISE
Unified with fire Divine
Consumed all me and mine
Here dualities decline.

2 WORLD OF DUALITIES
Phenomenon toys
Most cunningly ploy,
Even-mind to destroy.

3 AS INSTRUMENT OF THE DIVINE
The Deed
To His need
Has never worried.

4 YOGIC BLISS
Imposed body crude,
But reach how could,
The deep final Good.

5 UNDOUBTED GOOD KARMA
Who's Divinely tasked;
To welcome all unasked,
Is never asked.

6 COMMERCE OF POISE MIND
Above phenomenal crises
Above fluctuating market indices
Unaffected is rich business.

यदृच्छालाभसन्तुष्टो द्वन्द्वातीतो विमत्सरः।
समः सिद्धावसिद्धौ च कृत्वापि न निबध्यते।।4.22।।

7 NO ENVY
Envy targets
The close person very Next,
Till the closest Lord Manifests.

8 SIBLINGS ENVY
Jealous in me, means,
On Lord's ope hands of equal means
I do not ween.

SPIRITUAL FIRE – THE YAGNA

Verse 23

Freed from material urge
Whose mind in wisdom, is immersed
For the sake of Yagna who work
His action is entirely merged.

1
Only Wisdom seedth
Enough for satiating needs
Not for the greed.

2 ACTION IS YAGNA
Action with its urge
In the fire of working altar
Should dissolve and merge.

3 YAGNA
Inaction to fruition
Of Action in the altar of perfection
Workth as sacred oblation.

4 SELF CENTRED ACTION (No Yagna)
Owned in tight fist
The work becomes unworkably stiff
Opened by grasping wit.

5 FREE ACTION
Wisely if realized
*Any of the works is sacrifice**
Naturally it satisfies.

Ween = Believe, Opine **Yagna*

गतसङ्गस्य मुक्तस्य ज्ञानावस्थितचेतसः।
यज्ञायाचरतः कर्म समग्रं प्रविलीयते।।4.23।।

Verse 24

Brahm is sacrificial work
*Brahm is oblation and also incensory poured**
Into fire of Brahm as altar
In all works who fixes
In Brahm, his lore.
To Brahm alone he goes sure.

1
All the Actions' diversity
Focusing on Oneness of existence
Convergeth on Divinity

2 THE KARMA
Fixed in Divine
Perfectth all the Action; thus refined
At the same time.

3 DELUSIVE RELATIVITY
Outer Showy rituals
Bring rewards, hazards, reversals
All dual world's visuals.

4 ENLIGHTENMENT
Absent to individuality
Enterth, not there in Duality
But in Omnipresent Reality.

5 SURRENDER
Infused with Being
Is confused with shallow feelings,
Need own Beings offering.

6
Once in Him established
Work, wakening, worship is His
Bliss too is 'His Bliss'

7 DIVINITY SPECTRUM
Frame filled with contrasts
Thus shades coloured the entire canvas
Derived of one colourless Vast.

8 YAGYA
Established in conscious plane,
Irrespective of engaged sense,
Work, on transcendence , intents.

Verse 25

In the Yagna perfected a few
Mere worshiping demigods godules,
Yet others offer their 'own'
In the fire that is Supreme, alone.

*incensory = Combustible thing offered (Havi)

ब्रह्मार्पणं ब्रह्महविर्ब्रह्माग्नौ ब्रह्मणा हुतम्।
ब्रह्मैव तेन गन्तव्यं ब्रह्मकर्मसमाधिना।।4.24।।

दैवमेवापरे यज्ञं योगिनः पर्युपासते।
ब्रह्माग्नावपरे यज्ञं यज्ञेनैवोपजुह्वति।।4.25।।

1 PURE WORK
Conscious beyond flesh,
All Actions assume state
Of Yagna, Sacred.

2 MANY FORMS/ MANY WORSHIPS
O Thou ! indeed
As Manifest of my need
In wide spectrum* revealed.

3 GYAN/ BHAKTI
In mind's eye He freezes
Else, through some eyes He melts
In each perception Lord dwells.

4 MANY PATHS
The streaming flotsams
All along the river have won,
And reached the ocean.

5 MULTIFACED DIVINITY
As seeker doth perfect
The Supreme also Transmuteth to manifest
In to feelable aspects.

6 CONSECRATION
Must I offer my entire
As subtlest incensory in Virat fire
Of Eternal Altar.

Verse 26

Certain devouts as offering
Oblate their power of hearing
And other senses on the whole
In the fire of inner control;
And few others offer their sacrifices
In the fire of senses and objects.

1 SELF CONTROL
Senses dissolved in stable urn
Thus conflated perceptions turn
Into one wine of bliss.

2 NATIVE SOUL
Smelting ore of senses
In furnace of Control, extractth
The gold purest.

3 SENSIBLE SACRIFICE
Object of senses
Once becomes incense burner in senses' altar
Fuels to enlighten

4 MUTATION OF SENSES
All the harsh rush
Converged into inner hush
Sanctify even worst.

5 ACTION'S MISSION
Any trivial good
Costing final good
Bringth little good.

6 PURE CONSCIOUSNESS
Once closed the eyes
To the sensual tides
Openth the eyes.

*Lowest to the Supremest

श्रोत्रादीनीन्द्रियाण्यन्ये संयमाग्निषु जुह्वति।
शब्दादीन्विषयानन्य इन्द्रियाग्निषु जुह्वति।।4.26।।

Verse 27

Again, devouts some
Kindled by the pure wisdom,
In that flame of self control
As oblation in their yogic course,
Offer all their senses activities
And all their actions of life force.

1 MUNDANE INFERNO
Stray fire scorches,
The very Inner fire itself -
Till inner fire torches.

2 A YOGIC WALK
A chariot with unbridled horses
Runs riot as anarchic forces
Wise, slowly on foot courses.

3 BODY AND MIND OFFERED
Clay's vis, grey's bliss
Offered to fuel gnosis
Further bringth bliss.

4 YOGI'S OFFERING
All me, mine is His
Realizing His energy puffed in my effigy
I oblate all this.

Verse 28

Some, likewise oblate,
As offerings, the material assets
And penance and Yogic practices; yet
Dost offer some, as sacrifices
Taken to vows strict,
Some offer their Natural Gyan and Studies.

1 WAYS OF RITUALS
Through serving grain
Or through deserving brain
A Wise reciprocally gains.

2 KNOWLEDGE SYNERGISM
The inherent genius helped
Acquired gnosis penance, Yagna
The Wise to explore Self.

Vis = Power Clay (Bodily) Grey (Wisdom)

सर्वाणीन्द्रियकर्माणि प्राणकर्माणि चापरे।
आत्मसंयमयोगाग्नौ जुह्वति ज्ञानदीपिते।।4.27।।

द्रव्ययज्ञास्तपोयज्ञा योगयज्ञास्तथापरे।
स्वाध्यायज्ञानयज्ञाश्च यतयः संशितव्रताः।।4.28।।

3 MANYFOLD PATHS
Through don'ts of monks' austere
Or through do's the plebs mastered
The Great Master.

4
The learner to become Learned,
All scriptures conclusively said,
Its All one touch Ahead.

Verse 29-30

Devoted yogis to breathing practices
Offer they as sacrifices,
Pour the inward breath
Into the outward breath
And outward breath into inward,
Keeping course of breath under sway
Thus in Life control trance, some stay.

And some controlling the palate,
As sacrifice offer their outward breath,
Into vital air itself.
Through these sacrifices seekers; are cleansed
Of reactions of performing sins,
Thus they are knowers of Yagna and its meanings.

1 PRANAAYAAM – Yogic Breathing
Trapped soul in cage
Restrained breath vitally distills the flesh
Winged soul gets liberated.

2 BREATHING EQUILIBRIUM OF LIFE
Indrawing to the Infinite
Forcing out to the matter's pit
A tug of war that breathes.

3 BREATH
Not the puffs of fancy,
Breath is friction of immanent energy
To lit the Reality.

4 TOWARDS IMMORTALITY
A yogi transmuted
A breathing death
Into undying breath.

अपाने जुह्वति प्राण प्राणेऽपानं तथाऽपरे।
प्राणापानगती रुद्ध्वा प्राणायामपरायणाः।।4.29।।

अपरे नियताहाराः प्राणान्प्राणेषु जुह्वति।
सर्वेऽप्येते यज्ञविदो यज्ञक्षपितकल्मषाः।।4.30।।

5 INTUITIVE PERCEPTION
Lord, puffed in me
The controlled breath; vitalized to see-
Beyond breath I can see

6 THE CREATION
The formless Infinite
Into unnumbered vitalities did split
Own dreams to meet.

7 FASTING- A Yogic way
On gross; least they depend
For greater is their gain
Yogis, thus sustain.

8 PRANAAYAAM
In the breathing mould
The breath free soul offers
Breaths in to breath altar.

9 FASTING
Fast is the feast,
The spiritual palate surfeits
Demon in me it eats

10 DEATH-UNTYING OF BREATH
The heap of lifetrons
Tied through breathing axons
Dematerialized and withdrawn.

11 PRANAAYAAM-The Yogic breathing
The breathing could decode
In its finest astral mode
The mystery of grosser abode.*

12 SENSUAL APPETITE
Choked by bread,
Craving further, ladens the palate
And Soul suffocateth.

13 MEDITATION- a purifier
Turbid, in a calm urn,
In gravity of retroactive discern,
Effort free clarity returns.

14 PALATE CONTROL
Poor in cuisines
Is a rich salver
To salve from sins.

Verse 31

Nectar the Yagna's residue
Having thus tasted,
Eternal Brahm they winningly pursue.
But here in world O Best of Kurus !
No Yagna who offer
This world is never
For them a happy planet
What's then of the next?

**Soul in the body. Salver = plate, surfeit = overfeed.*

यज्ञशिष्टामृतभुजो यान्ति ब्रह्म सनातनम्।
नायं लोकोऽस्त्ययज्ञस्य कुतोऽन्यः कुरुसत्तम।।4.31।।

1 YAGNA-THE WORSHIP
Bliss of my soul
All I offer to the Supreme soul,
What remained is blest Goal.

2 YAGNA AT EACH STEP
In His Omnipresent's altar
Fuel worship and worshipped work,
Ignited the nectar.

3 GOD CONSCIOUS KARMA
Oblations spirited or mechanized;
Paeans, penance, even breath, arite
The ultimate Union, decide.

4 PURER RESIDUE
Digged the quick sand,
Within pit now drained
Purer, than the flow main.

5 PIOUS PERFORMANCE
Hands oblate bliss
In Yagna, that in lush bringth
Again Bliss to the brim.

6 VIRTUES CARRIED TO NEXT WORLD
Here below performing virtues
Fire of the existence consumeth
And Kindleth here after too.

Verse 32

These Yagna Sacrifices are different,
Set forth by the Veds chants
All of them are offsprings
Of different performances
Knowing them all as such,
Thou shallst find salvation thus.

1 MANY TYPES OF YAGNA
All odds beliefs, odd modes
Texts, breaths, mantras, quotes
All, but, to Oneness trode.

2 SUITABLE WAY
Many paths not confused
All intuitions into 'one' Suit
Into that One to diffuse.

3 CHOOSING PATH
Gleaned all intuitions
Then, means of suiting action
Cleansed to liberation.

4 SACRED WORK- All Yagna
All holy ceremonies
Are born of spiritual activities
Freed, who knows this.

Gleaned = to collect. Arite = Alright

एवं बहुविधा यज्ञा वितता ब्रह्मणो मुखे।
कर्मजान्विद्धि तान्सर्वानेवं ज्ञात्वा विमोक्ष्यसे।।4.32।।

5 INNER FIGHT- A YAGNA
The Wisdom is known
During carnal rules, to rebel alone
Astral prince to enthrone.

6
Any rite is right
Thy truthful insight
Owns its height.

Verse 33

O Arjun ! O foes chastiser !!
Yagna of gnosis is greater
Over Yagna of rituals of matter.
O Parth !! All and all the Actions
End in enlightenment, no exceptions.

1 REFINED ACTIONS
Over the ritual fire
The spiritual fire
Is eternally brighter.

2
Any Yagna action achieved-
Purification by certain degrees,
And in the end freed.

3 RITUAL FIELD
Outward Yagna more and more
Is drilling, warming up of the core
For inner fire to score.

4 DESTINATION ACHIEVED
As means of evolution
Action once embrace Union
Evolveth to non-Action.

5 KNOWLEDGE
All rites, worships, vigils
Themselves, all these fulfilled
By merging into Gyan-field.

6
All Actions
end in the end
into enlightenment.

Verse 34

Must thou know this !
Through Homage to men of Gnosis,
By repeated modest queries
And by submissive service,
To those, the Truth who have fathomed
They wilt teach thou that wisdom.

श्रेयान्द्रव्यमयाद्यज्ञाज्ज्ञानयज्ञः परन्तप।
सर्वं कर्माखिलं पार्थ ज्ञाने परिसमाप्यते।।4.33।।

तद्विद्धि प्रणिपातेन परिप्रश्नेन सेवया।
उपदेक्ष्यन्ति ते ज्ञानं ज्ञानिनस्तत्त्वदर्शिनः।।4.34।।

1 TEACHER-TAUGHT
In fully humble
Towards the Knowledgeable
Manifests the Unknowable.

2 TO SERVE GURU
My wit in cocoon closed
Submits to know, the shell thus opposed
Through service metamorphosed.

3 HUMBLED SUBMISSION
Dependable learning,
Let be dependent on yearning
With depended leaning.

4 MENTORSHIP
I asked my Mentor
He asked me further
To be mentor better.

5 TO SURRENDER TO GURU
Limited individuality
Humbled before Reality
Boosts receptivity

6 POTENTIAL
Modest queries
Like a flint sparks in Guru,
Torches latent in you.

7 EVOLVED KNOWLEDGE
A kindled coach
With further evolved torch,
Lighted my approach.

8 REAL SUBMISSION
Once learner submits his own
Then, not just the knowledge known
But Guru reveals his own.

Verse 35

Thus comprehending from Guru
The wisdom, O Arjun ! you
Shall behold the Truth,
Without falling again in fancy.
Through this you will see
All beings in you and further see
All as Mine and in Me.

1 GURU'S INSIGHT
The Knower's perception owns
Which transcends to the Unknown
The Unknowable trans-shaped to the Known.

2 GURU'S GUIDANCE
A tiny dew
Along river's guidance, drew
To ocean, became Vast Blue

यज्ज्ञात्वा न पुनर्मोहमेवं यास्यसि पाण्डव।
येन भूतान्यशेषेण द्रक्ष्यस्यात्मन्यथो मयि।।4.35।।

3 PRAYERS FAILED
My fancy, among Mankind
Found none as brother of mine
How the Father be enshrined?

4 KNOW BEYOND DUALITY
In wall of Dual ego,
God installed high a unity-window
Guru help me tiptoe.

5 INSEPARABLE UNION
Into Supreme Self melts
All diversities of tiny self
Grows to Supreme Self itself

6 ONE WISDOM OF ONENESS
In peopled dense
Chilly fence of separating ignorance
Melts in warmth of co-existence.

7 TRANSFORMATION
Man, the unlimited
High to the Life of God relate,
Then up to God elevate.

Verse 36

Thou art; even if
Among sinners, the sinner chief,
Yet by alone the Wisdom's skiff
Sure shalt cross ocean of miseries.

1 WISDOM, THE SAVIOR
Evil or bad earnt
All sinful actions are burnt,
In the wisdom Yagn.

2 DELUSION OVERCOME
In grey zone,
Sublime grey matter alone
Rights all wrong.

3 SINNERS SALVATION
However dense
However murk hadst bluffed
One ray ist enough

4 LIGHT BOAT OF KNOWLEDGE
A word of the Divine,
Shedth texts and texts behind
And crosseth the Brine.

5 TRANSCENDENTAL KNOWLEDGE
Own halo
Alone couldst glow
All shadow.

6 WISDOM
Alone, the knowledge
In itself couldst pledge
To be and to make purest.

अपि चेदसि पापेभ्यः सर्वेभ्यः पापकृत्तमः।
सर्वं ज्ञानप्लवेनैव वृजिनं सन्तरिष्यसि।।4.36।।

7 NO MORE SINNING
Man doth sin,
The sinless same man brings
From within.

8 INNATE WISDOM
Thorns, the sins of a shrub
Through knowledge of blooming bud
Naturally purged.

Verse 37

As the fire setth ablaze
Fuel wood into ash,
So doth fire of knowledge
Burnth all Karmas to ash.

1 GLOW OF KNOWLEDGE
Appeared millions Suns,
In midnight oil that burnt
Into timeless day it turned.

2 ENLIGHTENED
In God conscious Inferno
All show, shadow, all ego
Fueled into 'One Glow'

3 DELUSIVE ACTION (KARMA)
The Wisdom alone saw,
In the barren mirror of Karma's Law
Brazen mirage of Maya.

4 ETERNAL WISODM
Priori-posteriori mocked
Making face of the relative clock
Till the Timeless broke it.

5 NON ACTION OF GYAN
During wisdom's voyage
Once reached destined knowledge
Endth the trek.

6 SELFLESS REALIZATION
Gross melts into fine
Matter into non matter resigns
In knowledge combusts me, mine.

Brazen = shameless

यथैधांसि समिद्धोऽग्निर्भस्मसात्कुरुतेऽर्जुन।
ज्ञानाग्निः सर्वकर्माणि भस्मसात्कुरुते तथा।।4.37।।

Verse 38

In this world, existth
Truly, nothing else,
As purifying as the Gnosis.
The Yoga, who hath perfected
In a time stretch
Will realize this Gnostic Knowledge.
Within himself.

1 REALIZATION
State of perfect knowing
Explores in the state of Being
A Transformed purest within.

2 ENLIGHTENED IN DUE COURSE OF TIME.
Many suns crawled,
One ray then dawned
Never to set.

3 SAMADHI- THE SATURATION
In course, rayon fadeth
Dyeing on and on repeated,
Full infusion of Yarn, needed.

4
The time itself somehow,
Shoulst purify into the Timeless
the Eternal Now.

5 IN GOOD TIME
To Unlock The Perfect
In the bosom of treasured self
The Time-key never trails.

6 PURE CONSCIOUSNESS
The knowledge is all about
From phases of relativity, single out
Phase of the Absolute.

7 SPONTANEOUS ENGLIGHTENMENT
The Gnostic waves fill
In Relativity room by degrees, till
Transcend over the Absolute sill.

8 YOGIC UNION
Into Dyes hue
For union of separate two
The fabric be imbued.

9 GNOTIC SAMADHI
Waking and beyond waking
These Dual Consciousness when cling
Main streams to the Supreme.

न हि ज्ञानेन सदृशं पवित्रमिह विद्यते।
तत्स्वयं योगसंसिद्धः कालेनात्मनि विन्दति।।4.38।।

Verse 39

Being absorbed in Him, who
The senses, has subdued
Being blessed with faith,
Is blessed with Knowledge,
With The Supreme Knowledge achieved,
He, quickly, cometh to Supreme peace.

1 *QUICK BLESSINGS*
Of faith Possessed,
Lord needth nothing else
In Time bound Promises.

2 *INTELLECTUAL FAITH*
Faith is, lest
No faith
Till illuminateth.

3 *NATURAL FAITH*
My inclination
Is an evolution
Into upright transcendence.

4 *INCLINATION (THE FAITH)*
The more steep
More I achieve
Dip into deep.

5 *BLESSED WITH TRUST*
My only faith
Is, that even this faith
Is His grace.

6 *KNOWLEDGE BRINGS PEACE*
*From Roars to stridulations**
All Dark forest's darkening noise
At dawn come to poise.

Verse 40

The doubting man, but
Is ignorant lacking the Trust.
Finally destructs(self),
Such sceptic is never blest
Nor here nor in the next.

*Noise of crickets

श्रद्धावाँल्लभते ज्ञानं तत्परः संयतेन्द्रियः।
ज्ञानं लब्ध्वा परां शान्तिमचिरेणाधिगच्छति।।4.39।।

अज्ञश्चाश्रद्दधानश्च संशयात्मा विनश्यति।
नायं लोकोऽस्ति न परो न सुखं संशयात्मनः।।4.40।।

1 DIVINITY CARVED
All doubts in man,
When died then ascertained,
God alone remained.

2
Nay-Sayer is that wise
Whose mind as a rule compromise
With a 'Nay' to realize.

3 A RAY OF COGNITION IS ENOUGH.
Pharos beams encircle
Hath more of dark intervals
Yet beached the vessels

4 WAVERING IGNORANCE
The Darkness hath none,
While light hath its conception
To the perception.

5 SCEPTIC FAITH
Aye and Nay war
Permeates naturally far
Beyond the life-bar.

6
Knowledge fed the faith
And Doubts made starved
To the Death.

7 READING / KNOWING
Doubts prevailed
In the studded book-shelf
Then Learned, looked at self

8 DOUBTFUL MIND
Air surfed in pace,
Wrinkled the lakes surface
Corrupted the moon's image.

9 FAITHLESS WISDOM
Complexity of knowing, argued
With simple knowing of simple Truth
Of certainty that intuites.

Verse 41

O Arjun ! O winner of riches !!
He who, his actions, relinquishes
Whose doubts rent asunder by Gnostic knowledge,
Becometh poised in the Self
Him, The Karma never entangle.

Pharos = Light house at Shore

योगसंन्यस्तकर्माणं ज्ञानसंछिन्नसंशयम्।
आत्मवन्तं न कर्माणि निबध्नन्ति धनञ्जय।।4.41।।

1 BONDAGE
For the Karma's fruits;
The Doubts argued
Turned to noose

2 YOGIC ACTION
Doing the work
Who think to be non-doer
Dwell in them Divine Doer.

3 A TOOL OF SUPREME
A being of doing
Turned to Being of doing for Doer
Knowth himself as non-Doer.

4 EGOSTIC ACTION
The phenomenal activity
On ego trip of Identity
Hath lost the Reality.

5 SELFLESS ACTION
"Non-Identity",
Is my Identity, alone
That I own.

6 KNOWLEDGE WITHIN
Bound to Gnostic self
Bound to the holy text
Found poise, very next.

7 YOGIC NON ACTION
Action as Non-Action
With ego's renunciation
Is Yogic Non Action.

8 NOT BINDING TO FRUITS
Piece of work, I pick
As Jack fruit, with rubbed grease
Hands never to stick.

9 WORLD OF MARIONETTES
Actions bind not,
For strings that knot
Puppet to his Lord.

10 PERFECT KARMA
An action
With surrendered fruition
Is ripeness of Action.

Verse 42

Which, in thy heart dwell on,
Out of mere oblivion,
Shouldst be slashed that qualm
By the Gnostic brand ;*
Bhaarat ! Resort to Yoga and stand !!

O Lotus eater = O deluded one.   ** Sword*

तस्मादज्ञानसंभूतं हृत्स्थं ज्ञानासिनाऽऽत्मनः।
छित्त्वैनं संशयं योगमातिष्ठोत्तिष्ठ भारत।।4.42।।

1
Knowledge pleaded
And doubted the doubts
Thus the wise succeeded.

2 SCEPTISM
A chronic sore
Slough and Debris not ignored
Excised; got cured.

3 ARISE ! FROM APATHY.
Like treasured Lotus bud !
Fighting the encircled mud
O Lotus eater ! stand up.

4 AWARENESS OF BEING
Brandished the Gnosis
Severed the sceptical hypnosis
Vivified awakening bliss.

5 DOUBTLESS MERCY
How hard for Man
O Lord ! to believe
Thy relief !!

CHAPTER FIVE

Inner Renunciation

Workfree wishes of brain-sap
Working fishes of Biceps
All equally blessed.

The Sun is viewed
Alone in the Sun,
Thus, the Knowledge too.

Chapter Five

WHICH, THE BETTER PATH?

Verse 1

Arjun Said –

O Krshna ! Thou dost praise
The renunciation of the Acts,
At the Same yet
Praise performance of Acts,
Tell me O Krshna exact
Which is better of
These two.

1 QUESTIONING BY DEVOTEE
The True –heart's love,
In the initial throbs of love
Keepth the Mind above.
2 GEETA
Ancient queries
Of mindful Progenitor brought
The soulful thought.
3 SPEAKING OUT
Only wisdom speakth
Higher wisdom to seek
Which meetth not the meek.

4 GRATEFUL TO ARJUN
To fathom the maximum
Indebted are many future intellects
To that asking wisdom.
5 WISDOM BEGS MORE WISDOM
At unuttered door
Seeking wisdom knocked to explore
The Supreme Discourse.
6 ADMISSIBLE GEETA
The future is blest
When today's wisdom accepts
The past quests.

अर्जुन उवाच
संन्यासं कर्मणां कृष्ण पुनर्योगं च शंससि।
यच्छ्रेय एतयोरेकं तन्मे ब्रूहि सुनिश्चितम्।।5.1।।

Verse 2

The Blessed Lord said –

The renunciation of deeds
And performance of deeds
Both, to 'Supreme Good' lead.
But in two of these
Performance of deeds for its ease
Over renunciation of deeds exceedth.

1 CLEAR PATH
No labryrinth-
For me, Once I think
Of me, what He thinkth.

2 TYAG AND KARMA
Renunciation may go forced
But Karma in its pious course
The perfect renunciation endorse.

3 KARMA YOGA
Self manifestation thru deeds
Over self-discovery thru beads
The Creator and Creation esteem.

4 KARMA'S SUPERIORITY
Secluded raw stone
Worked unto workable form
Preciously performs.

5 GOD UNION
The String in itself lags
But then attached to violin pegs
For God, God's world plays.

Verse 3

Beyond hates and desires
Liberated from duality pairs,
Easily gets bondage-free.
O Arjun! Know him to be a renunciant, steady.*

*Sanyasi.

संन्यासः कर्मयोगश्च निःश्रेयसकरावुभौ।
तयोस्तु कर्मसंन्यासात्कर्मयोगो विशिष्यते।।5.2।।

ज्ञेयः स नित्यसंन्यासी यो न द्वेष्टि न काङ्क्षति।
निर्द्वन्द्वो हि महाबाहो सुखं बन्धात्प्रमुच्यते।।5.3।।

1
All that is,
I renounced; was His
My Renunciation where is?

2 SANYAS
Unconditioned to nerve
Should spirit, in high spirit conserve,
Its Ancient savour.

3 CLARITY IN LIFE
Where the duality dilutes,
Relatively Relative field could
Transcendent into absolutely Absolute.

4 LIKES AND DISLIKES ARE BONDAGES
The forehead crease,
And the palmer crease,
All hurdled, to release.

5 DUALITY / OPPOSITES OF PAIRS
Through worldly portal of joy
Trespasses evil-weevil, destroys
The shelled inner poise.

6 EQUALIZING CONTRASTS OF LIFE
Distracting duals that oppose,
Where contrasts consciously come close
Condense into 'Composed'.

Verse 4-5

Only childish ignorance,
Observeth the very difference
Between the Gnostic path
And path of Karma's performance
Into any one path who well devotes
Gainth the results of both.

The state, Gnostic Yogis succeed
Same ist attained by doers of good deeds,
He, who seeth path of gnosis
And that of deeds as one,
He seeth as they art indeed.

Savour = pleasurableness

सांख्ययोगौ पृथग्बालाः प्रवदन्ति न पण्डिताः।
एकमप्यास्थितः सम्यगुभयोर्विन्दते फलम्।।5.4।।

यत्सांख्यैः प्राप्यते स्थानं तद्योगैरपि गम्यते।
एकं सांख्यं च योगं च यः पश्यति स पश्यति।।5.5।।

1

Workfree wishes of brain-sap
Working fishes of Biceps
All equally blessed.

2

Gnosis at summit,
Saw 'Karma' to meet
Very same benefit.

3 ACUMEN OF NON PERFORMER.

Non Action is inner Action
To work out, through renunciation
The Karma's ecstatic union.

4

Wisdom perceives One
Action feels One
Two ways to achieve One.

5 BASICALLY THE SAME PATH

Divine path has shown
And established seeker, is made known
A common milestone.

6

Established Yogis urged
At ultimate goal it emerged
All paths merged.

7

Dutiful to meditation
Meditating on duty
Are divine equally.

8 YOGIC ACTION/ WISDOM OF YOG

Unlettered Hands of plebs
Reached the same Acumen's same depth
In this divine lab.

9 GYAN YOG/ KARMA YOG

Wisdom rooting the root
Karma watering the root
All for same fruit.

10 PATH OF RECLUSE AND WORLDY PATHS

A path lost from world,
Other path lost in world
Both resolve at goal.

11 EASY PATH-EASY GOAL

Act purified the intellect.
Intellect purified the Act
In two steps found the Purest.

PATH TO MOKSHA

Verse 6-7

Mere Renunciation is indeed hard,
*O Arjun ! unless the deeds are absorbed**
Sages intentst in Yogic practice
And achieve 'The Brahm' quick.

On 'Karma Yoga' who intent
Who mastered mind and sense
Whose self doth comprehend
As the Self in all beings extend
His deeds are not chained to taints.

1 UNION YOGA
Kinetics of Action
Naturally over static Non-action
Transcendent fast into Union.

2 RENUNCIATION IS HARD
On mossy steeps
Contentment naturally grow,
Better on cosy steps though.

3 YOGIC – PRACTICES
Nor the hollow reed,
Nor the blowing air's deed
Its flutist's skill.

4 SELF TURNS TO THE SELF-UNION
One drop is though 'none'
But So great is fullness of Union
Called 'compressed ocean'.

5 UNION WITH SUPREME
Utter doer from his doings
Once separates his own being
His doings attain the Doer.

6 ACTION PLAN OF SANJAY
With renunciation, established in Absolute
Though action in relative field continued
Daily in me the Supreme grew.

7 LIMITED SELF
Eternal freedom is caged
In the transitory bondage
Of relativity of lower self.

**devotional services (Bhakti)*

संन्यासस्तु महाबाहो दुःखमाप्तुमयोगतः।
योगयुक्तो मुनिर्ब्रह्म नचिरेणाधिगच्छति।।5.6।।

योगयुक्तो विशुद्धात्मा विजितात्मा जितेन्द्रियः।
सर्वभूतात्मभूतात्मा कुर्वन्नपि न लिप्यते।।5.7।।

Verse 8-9

In God's union, the knower of the fact
Thinks in very certain consciousness
I dost not at all act
Though he lookth at, heedth, contactth
Olfactth, tasteth, speakth and breatheth
Speakth and graspth and rejects
Even openth and closeth eyes
All Aloof, he doth realize
Simply the senses act
Among the sensory objects.

1 GOD UNION
Its so ecstatic
Dissolveth all discriminating abyss
Remains absolute Bliss.

2 ETERNAL UNION/ DIVINE AFFINITY
Unexplored thing in me
Beyond this 'me' though is free
Ever bound to Thee

3
See ! beyond cage
In fascinating vastness yogis engage
Belittling their ' Little-self '.

4 DARKS OF WORLDLY SENSES
Murky, senses discriminate
While enlightenment ever integrates
All shadows into shadowless.

5 THE REAL PERFORMER
The doer, I'm not
Even this very thought
Only the Doer could impart.

6 ENLIGHTENING YOGIC PRACTICE
Ever changing sense,
In stable-consciousness transcend
Into Never changing content.

7
Floating senses never meet
Conscious depth , hence mind is not freed
Yoga grounds ' the Being ' deep.

नैव किंचित्करोमीति युक्तो मन्येत तत्त्ववित्।
पश्यन्‌ शृणवन्स्पृशञ्जिघ्रन्नश्नन्गच्छन्स्वपन्‌
श्वसन्।।5.8।।

प्रलपन्विसृजन्गृह्णन्नुन्मिषन्निमिषन्नपि।
इन्द्रियाणीन्द्रियार्थेषु वर्तन्त इति धारयन्।।5.9।।

Verse 10

*Who giveth over all Karma**
Surrendering fruits to the Brahm,
All attachments abandoned
Ist not tainted by sin,
Just as lotus leaf
By water is unsullied.

1 CALMNESS OF YOGI
Soil can't soil
Till this permeable mortal coil
Let it spoil.

2
Ego-realized souls
Attuned to perfect the goal
Turn to soul-realized ego.

3 ACTION AND OBJECTS – NON ATTACHMENT.
While Jack Fruit is sliced
I apply nonsticky oil
Acting hands on knife.

4 NON – ATTACHED REALIZATION
Ridding waves he crossed
Unattached could assess from marge
Vast oceanic mass.

5 REAL NATURE IS PERFECTION
Distortion of my reflection,
Cannot be my imperfection
*Rather mirror's aberration***

6 NON ATTACHED LIKE A LOTUS LEAF
All sap it drew
Lived and died in water-dew
Yet all aloof.

Verse 11

Giving up Attachments
Yogis dost act
With mind, body, intellect
And even with the senses
Directed to purify ' the Self'.

*work / action **Defect in mirror.

ब्रह्मण्याधाय कर्माणि सङ्गं त्यक्त्वा करोति यः।
लिप्यते न स पापेन पद्मपत्रमिवाम्भसा।।5.10।।

कायेन मनसा बुद्ध्या केवलैरिन्द्रियैरपि।
योगिनः कर्म कुर्वन्ति सङ्गं
त्यक्त्वाऽऽत्मशुद्धये।।5.11।।

1 ATTACHMENTS

The Attachment, as offspring
In the womb of ego, brings
Desire and its sibling sins.

2 PURIFIED EGO

Even this flesh and beat
May be sanctified beyond limit
As yogic receptacle of the Infinite.

3 SELF PURIFICATION

In the way Yogic
The Self distills out the self
Remains Non - self in alembic.*

4 OBSERVERS UNBIAS

Detached yet stood
On platform of witness-attitude,
Pure footings observed Truth.

5 MEDITATION

In the closing externals
Intensify ! the Internal
To meet the Eternal.

6 PURE PERFORMANCE

Flowers at Lord's feet
Alone unsmelt, unsullied.
Dost meet.

Verse 12

He, the God united, who
Abandoned the Karma's fruit,
Sure attain to the perfect peace,
Yet not united who is
By action's fruit spurred
To bondage remain anchored.

1 GOD-UNION

Bound to the Bindings
Till this binding transcends to the Finding
Of the Divine binding.

2 NON ATTACHED ACTION

Hands drawn
Where work rises to the Soul's calm
Is Non attached working plan.

3 LORD'S PLAN

The Master's voice
Is to master louder poise
Over demanding noise.

4 GOD'S PLAN

Working pace maker,
Making it as peace maker
Is expression of the Great Maker.

*Distillation flask(Here used for Body)

युक्तः कर्मफलं त्यक्त्वा शान्तिमाप्नोति नैष्ठिकीम्।
अयुक्तः कामकारेण फले सक्तो निबध्यते।।5.12।।

5 NON ATTACHED YET CONCERNED
All free linchpin, hold
Wheeling activities, that roll,
Both Reach the lasting goal.

6
On the free axle
Unbound activity is unentangled
Lest the wheel trundles.

ENSCONCED IN BLISS

Verse 13

The embodied soul,
With senses being in control
Mentally renounceth all the acts
Dwellth happily in the hamlet,
Of nine gates
Nor performing himself,
Nor making the senses enact.

1 FORTIFICATION
Nine gates of citadel
With glacis for King Soul
Secured strong hold.

2 CONDITIONED SOUL
In this stuffy frame,
Till, is as free as the Lord; same
Remains crammed.

3 HAPPY DWELLING CONTROLLING SENSES
A jail bird-soul
Custodian life with good control,
Enjoys parole.

4 YES, TO ACTIVITY
No the escapism could
But withdrawal from fruit
The bliss in me root.

5 TRANSCENDENTAL CONSCIOUSNESS
Although, The Soul
To the frame hath conditioned bond,
Aloof, must go beyond.

6 THE BEING
Subtle protoplasm in me,
In this Grosser gross
Is the doer and cause.

7 BE ONE WITH LORD'S PLAN
A Mortal impedes Immortal's dream
The Yogi owns no own dream
Learns to dream with Him.

Trundles=Noisy rolling of wheel Glacis=protection making attackers vulnerable to defenders.

सर्वकर्माणि मनसा संन्यस्यास्ते सुखं वशी।
नवद्वारे पुरे देही नैव कुर्वन्न कारयन्।।5.13।।

Verse 14

Lord, the Creator doth not create,
In men, the thought of doer of act,
Through men, nor doth He cause act
With fruits, nor doth He make men thrive
Its his delusive Nature that derives.

1
The Lord-made Being thinks,
He Becometh own Lord and prinks
With action, the fruits he links.

2
In Divine puppetry-show
With Non doers' weightless ego,
Succumbs not, thread in load.

3 NON DOER THOUGHT
The sublime pollen
Authored none the Earth of own
Is carried by wind blown.

4 *DELUSIVE LIFE*
His words, His text
His Hands His Action blest
But denaturalized delusion dictated.

5 *UNBOUND EVOLUTION*
Being Lord – made Being
From Lord made web, this inner thing
Is free to take wings.

CONDITIONING OF SOUL BY VIRTUES AND EVIL

Verse 15

The Supreme doth admit,
Nor any of the sins nor virtuous deeds
'Cos, the folly covers the intellect
So the men art deluded.

1
Satiated Supreme
With everything to the Brim
Accepts none acts for Him.

2 *PSUEDO ACHIEVEMENTS*
In the circumstantial shell,
In false fulfillment, man dwells
Delusion surrounds and prevails.

न कर्तृत्वं न कर्माणि लोकस्य सृजति प्रभुः।
न कर्मफलसंयोगं स्वभावस्तु प्रवर्तते।।5.14।।

नादत्ते कस्यचित्पापं न चैव सुकृतं विभुः।
अज्ञानेनावृतं ज्ञानं तेन मुह्यन्ति जन्तवः।।5.15।।

3 ACTIVITY AND DESIRES

Action proposed Gold,
Reaction disposed God
Lord stood Aloof with the soul.

4

Any Bias,
Though The Lord never knew,
Though it appears to us.

5 GOD WILL

Lord's lordly 'Hope'
Put same hope in delusive envelope
With man's free-will to ope.

6 GOD-WILL

At the Son's free will
Though Father neutrally fulfills,
His plan is to lift.

7 WIN-WIN

A discipline beyond frame,
Rules of game He framed
Joy, the soul claim.

8 FREE CHOICE TO EVOLVE

Even unending perdition
Endless delusive immersion
May end in Perfection

Verse 16

But in whom by the Gnosis
The Ignorance is banished,
Their wisdom like sun illumineth
The Supreme-Self within.

1 A SEARCH OF KNOWLEDGE

In this very Mortal
Power of knowing exploreth
The Inner Immortal.

2

This Omnipresent
Seems transcendent actually is at hand
But for Ignorance.

3 KNOWLEDGE IS FACULTY OF KNOWING

The Self to sight;
As sun needs no other light,
You needs no other's Insight.

4 KNOWLEDGE

Long smoky Altar
Impossibly remains unaltered
Without a lit fire.

5 IGNORANCE, I OWN

Gyan hideth Knowledge none
But the mist before my eyes
Till realized the sun.

6 PSUEDO KNOWLEDGE OF IGNORANT

In dream, a dreamer
Until really wakes to rediscover
Dreams like a waker.

ज्ञानेन तु तदज्ञानं येषां नाशितमात्मनः।
तेषामादित्यवज्ज्ञानं प्रकाशयति तत्परम्।।5.16।।

THE KNOWER OF SELF

Verse 17

Whose intellect, mind and faith
And refuge are one with 'That'
Cleansed of sins through pure knowledge
*Reach Non-return state**

1 ETERNAL PEACE
Rebirths Pendulum
Intent to gravitate to the pure wisdom
To end in static equilibrium.

2
Unison with pure
Seeth impurities
No more.

3
Knowable alone is the Knowledge
That brings Him in closer embrace
Where sins die crashed.

4
That Ego dissolved
Then from that Egoless evolved
This 'closest Self'.

5
The Sun is viewed
Alone in the Sun,
Thus, the Knowledge too.

6 EVOLUTION OF SELF
Broody of self-made Shell
Brooding over evolutionary struggle
Brooded into the Infinite.

Verse 18

The enlightened Sage,
With an equal eye weighs
A Brahmin learned and benign
And cow, elephant, a canine
And a low pleb even.

1 GOLD STANDARD
Alchemist weighed
Equally the coronet
And crude nugget.

2 ONE NESS
The wise eye Casts
Not on Caste or outcast
But the same Vast.

**liberated (Moksha) Broody= unhappily thinking, Brooded=hatched.*

तद्बुद्धयस्तदात्मानस्तन्निष्ठास्तत्परायणाः।
गच्छन्त्यपुनरावृत्तिं ज्ञाननिर्धूतकल्मषाः।।5.17।।

विद्याविनयसंपन्ने ब्राह्मणे गवि हस्तिनि।
शुनि चैव श्वपाके च पण्डिताः समदर्शिनः।।5.18।।

3 ONE NESS
In His show-case,
Potter's thrown-vases
Used clay, the same.

4 ENLIGHTENED VISION
Realized state include
In the existence of fine or crude
The very same Absolute.

5 EVENNESS OF EYE
Sagacious Eyes
All distinct price tags, denied
Valued all Priceless.

6 ONENESS IN RELATIVE COSMOS
Ocean, stars, atoms,
Part of the same Wholesome
All linked to one continuum.

7 EVEN – EYE
To this world, the Blind
Who perceives this phenomenon kind
Is not really Blind.

Verse 19

In this very life, even,
By the Even minds is won,
This world of differentiation;
Getting established in Oneness,
Like Omnipresent Brahm flawless
Verily those very ones
Perfect the same Brahm.

1
*All differentiations arrest**
On Evenness once mind perfects
In real Heaven rests.

2 THE CONQUEROR
A Slave to the universe
With engraved evenness
Enslaved the Universe.

3 INTENT OF MIND
The uneven Brainy flesh
Hath in Gyrii impulse of evenness
With divinity to synapse.

4 KING SOUL
Sufferings of flesh and bone,
Once Mortal's mind disown
On Immortal bliss enthroned.

**Bondage. continuum = continuity*

इहैव तैर्जितः सर्गो येषां साम्ये स्थितं मनः।
निर्दोषं हि समं ब्रह्म तस्माद्ब्रह्मणि ते स्थिताः।।5.19।।

5 REFLECTION OF THE LORD IN ME
Inner mirror, is mirror image,
Of taintless Lord's visage
Non possessed, Changeless.

6 GOAL
Suffering struggle
Of Mortals efforts to equal
The Non suffering of Immortals.

Verse 20

One deserveth
Resting in Supreme being
Who with steady Nerve,
Free from delusion, unswerved
Nor rejoice in Pleasant
Nor in Unpleasant disturbed.

1 STEADY NERVE
In Hush or Noise
The attuned melody of equipoise
Is the Master's Voice.

2 FINAL PATH
Turns to Supreme
One, Learns the Supreme
Earns the Supreme.

3 ENLIGHTENED MIND
Being awaken in Truth,
Relative dreaming one never overtook
Getting established in the Absolute.

4 LIFE'S CURRENT
Both banks' flood
Carries flotsams and mud
Mid-Stream is lucid but.

5 ELEVATED MIND
Likings' and dislikings' tides
The mind nor likes nor dislikes
With constant bliss on steady height.

REALIZATION

Verse 21

By external touches untouched
With inner bliss well-versed
His self, with Supreme alliance
Enjoys the Eternal trance.

न प्रहृष्येत्प्रियं प्राप्य नोद्विजेत्प्राप्य चाप्रियम्।
स्थिरबुद्धिरसम्मूढो ब्रह्मविद्ब्रह्मणि स्थितः।।5.20।।

बाह्यस्पर्शेष्वसक्तात्मा विन्दत्यात्मनि यत्सुखम्।
स ब्रह्मयोगयुक्तात्मा सुखमक्षयमश्नुते।।5.21।।

1 NATURAL SEED
The Nutshell
Detached from the shell
Discovered 'real-Self'.

2
Drowns, this floating urge
But once self in ' the Self ' immersed
Crossed, as the bliss emerged.

3 BEYOND FANTASY
In dream I dreamt
I was untouched by dreaming wake
Transformed to Waking Self.

4 BLISS CONSCIOUSNESS
Statue of inner joy
Once idolized in timeless shrine,
Worships not short lived toys.

Verse 22

O Arjun ! that sense-feelings
From outward contacts spring
And have the end and beginning,
Sure, are begetter of sufferings.
In such pleasures, the sage
Never doth engage.

1 SHORT LIVED JOY OF WORLD
Fiery touch is picked
By the chandelier's wick
Into chill to extinguish.

2
Anything that leads
To the outward needs,
Inner bliss defeatth.

3
With joy-hunting
For finite objects
Getth no Infinite Joy.

4 EVOLUTION TO FULFILL
Worm grew to manhood,
Not be wasted, should
Obtain serenest good.

5 WORLDLY BINDINGS
Moored to worldly anchor,
Can't sail to bliss of the Self
Here mind seems not yare.

6 SEASONAL JOY
Vernal carpet vivid
Its blossom ends to wilt
Unchanged Azure hath bliss.

7
Finite pleasures
Have Infinite desires,
As the torture's sire

Yare=dexterous, eager

ये हि संस्पर्शजा भोगा दुःखयोनय एव ते।
आद्यन्तवन्तः कौन्तेय न तेषु रमते बुधः।।5.22।।

Verse 23

Even here before his Last,
Who masterth every lust and wrath,
Is a blessed man,
He is truly on Yogic path.

1 'BALANCED' YOGIC LIFE
Every step discreet
On rope with balanced ease
Acrobat crosses through trapeze.

2 LORD'S ASSURANCE
Refine ! further Refine !!
Even this very process will design,
To be finally Divine.

3 SUBDUE DESIRES
Life flows through Desires
May not be overpowered
Yet, by its flood.

4
Only Desire that frees
From desires and its miseries
Is 'May desires be ceased'.

5 FIRM MIND
In tides of bore
Flotsam though stray in river course
But succumb not in parados shore.

6 REALIZATION FACT
Alive ire and lust
Lively expressed in Action's gush
All die in 'Realized Hush'.

7 DESIRES ABANDONED
Where exists,
With Divine that Union-bliss,
Enables us to resist.

Verse 24

Inner Bliss who possessth,
In inner joy who restth
Whose Inner fire illuminateth,
Is certainly a Yogi Perfect.
He perfectth to Eternal freedom,
The Absolute Divine he becometh.

Trapeze = bar supporting the hanging acrobatic rope. Parados = earth's protection of banks
Bore = strong wave that rushes along river from sea.

शक्नोतीहैव यः सोढुं प्राक्शरीरविमोक्षणात्।
कामक्रोधोद्भवं वेगं स युक्तः स सुखी नरः।।5.23।।

योऽन्तःसुखोऽन्तरारामस्तथान्तर्ज्योतिरेव यः।
स योगी ब्रह्मनिर्वाणं ब्रह्मभूतोऽधिगच्छति।।5.24।।

1 ENLIGHTENING WITH INNER FIRE
Asked failing lantern,
The glowing-Gems-filled urn,
Take up in its turn.

2 LONELY YET WITH HAPPINESS
But seems alone
What he treasured and ever owned
Is his eternal bliss.

3 INNER HAPPINESS
Set and Suns to come
Never changed in changing bosom,
That inner joyous chum.

4 AN EXCURSION WITHIN
As convoy with the Self
I journeyed entered into the Self
Enjoyed the 'Eternal Self '.

5
Worldly blazes scorch,
While the inner fire doth torch,
The Moksha-march.

Verse 25

With sins all ceased,
Who got rid of dualities
Who are self controlled
Intent on welfare of all souls
Those seers, Rishis
To the Ultimate Perfection reach.

1 A SEER IN THE WORLD
Picked from the sludge,
Is serenest untouched
' Worth-offering ' a Lotus.

2 WELFARE – HOLY MESSAGE
Seers subsist
Alone, on Welfare as gist
Of all Divine scripts.

3 HUMAN SERVICE
The Supreme, they discovered,
In the shaped creation of the Shapeless,
Thus, 'Him' they served.

4 SEERS
Evolved self orientates
Once dawns in perfected nexts.*
Never sets.

5 SEERS WELFARE WORK
An Evolved mortal coil,
For walking corpses' glum-turmoil
Immortally, toils.

Orientate = face to east (to enlightenment)

**Next days and Next births.*

लभन्ते ब्रह्मनिर्वाणमृषयः क्षीणकल्मषाः।
छिन्नद्वैधा यतात्मानः सर्वभूतहिते रताः।।5.25।।

Verse 26

Free from lust and piques
Who have won their wits,
For such self-disciplined ascetics
The Very Absolute Bliss
Everywhere doth exist.

1 THE RENUNCIANT -TYAGII
The uninvolved
Is in reality involved
To evolve.

2 SELF-DISCIPLINED NATURE
The self discerned
Here and here after earn
Naturally to govern.

3 FREE BLISS
The Discipline-bound
Is never found
-Bound

4 BLISS EVERYWHERE
The tortoise
Underwater broods in poise
And on land eggs broods.

Verse 27-28

Outer world having left
Between eyebrows bringing gaze
With in and out going breaths
Flow through nostrils, equated,
And whose senses, mind intellect
Are controlled, to aim freed state,
From whom desires, dread, rage
Have departed; that sage
Is forever free, in fact.

1 MEDITATION
Through mind's gaze,
The Mind finds the Ultimate
Turning blind to the rest.

2 HOLY INSTINCT
Nor teachings, nor assistance
But every 'self' naturally intend
To be self-restrained.

कामक्रोधवियुक्तानां यतीनां यतचेतसाम्।
अभितो ब्रह्मनिर्वाणं वर्तते विदितात्मनाम्।।5.26।।

स्पर्शान्कृत्वा बहिर्बाह्यांश्चक्षुश्चैवान्तरे भ्रुवोः।
प्राणापानौ समौ कृत्वा नासाभ्यन्तरचारिणौ।।5.27।।

यतेन्द्रियमनोबुद्धिर्मुनिर्मोक्षपरायणः।
विगतेच्छाभयक्रोधो यः सदा मुक्त एव सः।।5.28।।

3 PRANAYAAM-CONTROLLING BREATH
Sacred life-force in Breath,
Sages felt and read
Beyond sustaining bread.

4 ASTRAL ANATOMY
Body, Breath and Mind,
As encasement, the soul finds
Are vitals of Divine.

5
I gazed into breath
All breath's universality equated
With inner 'Astral-self '.

6 ONE VISION
Dark world mingled
The Dark change to astral
Thine eye be 'single'.

7 PRANAYAAM-DIVINE BREATH
O Breath ! dissolve
All mortal signs in me,
Immortality to solve.

8 COLLECTING MY SELF
My Scattered attitude
In diligent pursuit
Gained perfect integration.

Verse 29

One who realize
Me, as enjoyer of offerings and sacrifice
And Me, as Great Lord of All
And Me, as everyone's Pal;
He attainth equipoise.

1
Daily joy within
When discovered the Lord as enjoyer
'Peace ' I win.

2 FRIENDLY CREATOR
Of two Creating Hands,
He creates with one hand
With other holds a friend.

3 LORD BLESSED THUS
Perceived my paeans
Received my pains
Weaved in me a friend.

4
The Deeds employed
To evolve and purify
The Nature enjoys.

5 THE REAL JOY
My austerities,
Once merge into Lord's bliss
Is boon companion of peace.

6 PATH OF RENUNCIATION
In 'Giving –up' he found,
Active non-Action that paved-
Have-not's path to have.

भोक्तारं यज्ञतपसां सर्वलोकमहेश्वरम्।
सुहृदं सर्वभूतानां ज्ञात्वा मां शान्तिमृच्छति।।5.29।।

CHAPTER SIX

Conscious Meditation: Self Discipline

While calmness pervades
Into all Actions, desires transform
Into tranquil of God-head.

Hurdling stone

Set aside will be known

As Mile stone.

Chapter Six

MEDITATION

Verse 1

Who performth Actions 'due',
Depending not on fruits
Is Renunciant and Yogi true;
And nor the one who
Is sans working Action
Nor the one, who
Is sans firing ignition.

1 ACTIVELY NON-ACTIVE
Inert to the world
Not idle to the world
Thus yogic way works.

2 NOT FOR FRUITS
Divine work's attempted
To make sublime Template
That never is tempted

3 DUTIFUL IGNITION
The Ageless sacred Altar
Consumes not fireless matter
Being lit by duteous fire.

4
Journeyed non-attached
In reality integrate
With the Ultimate.

5 NON ATTACHED WORKING
Renunciant never shirks
Works as warm as world works
Only, lures not his work.

6 UNIGNITED WORK
Many handsome hands
Work in handicapped worldly trend,
In ashes, end.

7 PATH OF PEACE
Who rightly acts
He loves God best, lest
No rest for the rest.

8 UNIGNITED SOUL
Fireless ness
Consumes the Kindled consciousness
Into ash.

Shirk= lazy to work

अनाश्रितः कर्मफलं कार्यं कर्म करोति यः।
स संन्यासी च योगी च न निरग्निर्न चाक्रियः।।6.1।।

Verse 2

'Sanyasa' what's said – so
Arjun ! it to be 'Yoga', know !
For without renouncing personal volitions,
'the Yogi', none verily becometh.

1 PERSONAL DESIRES
Volition seeds
Sown in self – need
Reaped only weeds.

2 SANYAAS AND YOG ARE SAME
Non-Action of renunciant
And Action leading to renunciation,
Both lead to God-Union.

3
The very self renounced
Into Non-self; found
Self redemption.

4 ONLY PERSONAL MOTIVES
Weedy motives,
Of thoughtless thought volitive,
Do desire corrupt incentives.

5 DESIRES OF INCENTIVES
Wishing mere pottage
With astrayed steps and goals faded
Begins no pilgrimage.

Verse 3

For the Muni's wise life
Who wisheth yogic rise,
Fruitless Action is spoken of as his means;
And thus attuned to Yoga, for him,
'The Desireless ness', in such serene
Is said to be his means.

Personal volitions=self satisfying desires.

यं संन्यासमिति प्राहुर्योगं तं विद्धि पाण्डव।
न ह्यसंन्यस्तसङ्कल्पो योगी भवति कश्चन।।6.2।।

आरुरुक्षोर्मुनेर्योगं कर्म कारणमुच्यते।
योगारूढस्य तस्यैव शमः कारणमुच्यते।।6.3।।

1 Divine Uprise
Whose Action
Rise to calmness through Action
Is yogic ascension.

2 MEDITATION IN ACTION
The waking Act
Harmonizing with serenest depth
In eternal consciousness rest.

3 THE SAGE
He meditates,
His calmness separates
Duality of Activity and Self.

4 SAMADHI
Restfulness advanced,
And quietly Quietness chanced
Unto the conscious trance.

5 ASCENDING TO YOGA
Refined Activity,
Which designed serenity
Finds Divinity.

6 DIVINE ASCENT
From his active rush,
Who is activated to Non - action's hush
Is God – Conscious.

7 DESIRES' DIN DIFFUSED
While calmness pervades
Into all Actions, desires transform
Into tranquil of God-head.

8 SPIRITUAL CLIMBER
The Selfless work
Is the workable means
To work on – 'Self' afterward.

Verse 4

When a man is non-indulgent
To the Lures of acts and Lust of sense
Man, to have attained
To Yoga; thus is claimed.

1 YOGIC WAY
The seeking gait,
Passing through selfless gates
Self-perfection gets.

2 MEDITATIVE CONSCIOUSNESS
'All – withdrawn' state
Finds the Vast – spread
Of inner God-head.

Ascension = spiritual rise

यदा हि नेन्द्रियार्थेषु न कर्मस्वनुषज्जते।
सर्वसङ्कल्पसंन्यासी योगारूढस्तदोच्यते।।6.4।।

3 DESIRES DISFIGURE
The fruition - greed rots,
Grotesquely distorts
Real face of task.

4 PERFECT UNION
Clung to the Supremest,
None the one, engages
To any of the rests.

EGO AND SOUL

Verse 5

By Alone, man's self
Must he improve
And must not devalue;
For, this self ist pal of conditioned soul
And this self is enemy too.

1 SUBJECTED TO DEVALUE
The laden Desires,
Conditioned and laden my Entire
Further pull in mire.

2 UNCORRUPT EYE
Transparent view
Could alone perceive the hue-
Which's True.?

3 SELF DISCOVERY
To make known
What I should own
tread All Alone.

4 CONDITIONING TO TRUTH
No means, methods, moulds
But the conditioned Self unfolds
By itself to the Self.

5 SELF MANIFESTATION
This very Self
Is conditioned by the self
And none else.

6 PERFECT MIND
Thought Stuff,
Amid 'Actual- Me 'and' Ideal – Me'
Should fill the gulf.

7 CONDITIONED SOUL
Any aid conditions mind
But it's not any odd outside
Only inner Self decides.

उद्धरेदात्मनाऽऽत्मानं नात्मानमवसादयेत्।
आत्मैव ह्यात्मनो बन्धुरात्मैव रिपुरात्मनः ||6.5||

Verse 6

'The Self' is a pal to the one,
Whose self who hath won;*
But who hath not done so,
His self workth as a foe.

1
In his forlorn attempt,
Lonesome companion, one owns
'The Self' alone.

2
Not the senses slave
But who surrenders to Lord
Masters the Lord.

3
The lesser self acts
Though from action innately separate
Is higher Self's intimate.

4 *DISCIPLINED MIND*
The Stone teased
On the stony street,
Paved and eased.

5 *SENSES CONQUERED*
Hurdling stone
Set aside will be known
As Mile stone.

6 *NOT ATTUNED TO HIGHER*
Relative-self if dumb
To the Self in transcendental bosom
All his existence succumbs.

Verse 7

The tranquil sage
Victorious over the self
Ever establisheth
In transcendental state;
Is above grace or disgrace
Is above heat or floes
Is above pleasure or throes.

**Body with Mind and Senses.*

बन्धुरात्माऽऽत्मनस्तस्य येनात्मैवात्मना जितः।
अनात्मनस्तु शत्रुत्वे वर्तेतात्मैव शत्रुवत्।।6.6।।

जितात्मनः प्रशान्तस्य परमात्मा समाहितः।
शीतोष्णसुखदुःखेषु तथा मानापमानयोः।।6.7।।

1 ABOVE DIVERSE MIND
Absolute peace
Above relativities
Is thus achieved.

2 CONQUERING DUALITIES
Transforming mind asked
For unification of extremes on face
Taking off the Janus Mask.

3 SAMADHI, ABSORBED IN SUPREME
The mind journeyed
Beyond Nerves transcended in realm
Of unnerved nerves reached.

SAGACIOUS VIEW

Verse 8

The Yogi thus is,
Said to be established;
Who is filled with acquired gnosis
And with self-realized bliss,
Mastering senses, poised
Who look with equal eyes
The gold, stone and soil.

1 KNOWLEDGE
The academic ink,
On the intuitive pages imprint
The Lord's Plan map.

2
Knowledge that thought
That the knowledge is God,
Is wisdom of the Self.

3
The knowledge exists
Man creates no Gnosis
Only discovers it.

4 YOGI'S DENIAL OF RELATIVITY
Transfused with single beam
Amused not in relative glittering of dream
Felt same one light of Supreme.

Janus Mask = two faces which are opposite.

ज्ञानविज्ञानतृप्तात्मा कूटस्थो विजितेन्द्रियः।
युक्त इत्युच्यते योगी समलोष्टाश्मकाञ्चनः।।6.8।।

5 STEADY YOGI
In vibrating dimly ray
Of phenomenal gold or clay
Can't the Sun be betrayed.

Verse 9

A Yogi further surpass
Whose equal mind is unbiased,
Among polite, pals and foes
Among strangers, kinsman and jealous
Among Virtuous and even impious.

1 UNBIAS SELF
On Blacksmith's will,
All got changed but for the tranquil
Of the Anvil.

2 EVEN MINDED
The Man reads
One word of Oneness
Is 'Learned' indeed.

3 EVIL IS LESS GOOD
Through unbiased door
Darkness as less light is endorsed
Only the light understands.

4 YOGIC SILENCE
Reaching repose
Fainted and died all echoes
Of being pal or foes.

5 EVIL SEES EVIL
Mind's eye read
And distinguished good-bad
My sight was bad.

6 SIN, THE JUDGE IN ITSELF.
The culprit
Is punished by the sin
And not for it.

KRSHNA'S ADVICE FOR YOGA

Verse 10

A Yogi should ever
Be rid of desire and aver
Remaining lonely in solitude
Constantly try to unite with Lord
With mind – body- senses subdued.

Aver = possessions/ claims

सुहृन्मित्रार्युदासीनमध्यस्थद्वेष्यबन्धुषु।
साधुष्वपि च पापेषु समबुद्धिर्विशिष्यते।।6.9।।

योगी युञ्जीत सततमात्मानं रहसि स्थितः।
एकाकी यतचित्तात्मा निराशीरपरिग्रहः।।6.10।।

1 YOGIC CONQUEST
Outer solitude
Brings inward quietude
Further fulfills pursuit.

2 BLISS IN LONELINESS
Super-conscious solitude
Subconsciously has learnt
Here interrupts none.

3 MEDITATIVE SEARCH
Searched in shallow multitude
Till Ancient depth of bosom introduced
To friend, the solitude.

4
The Yogic state
Perfected in itself validitate
None the senses to invade.

5 YET NOT ALONE
I found myself lost
In me no crowd could trespass
All Alone with 'the Vast'.

6 YOGIC VISION
A Yogi sees
How unlonely companion is
The loner's bliss.

Verse 11-12

On the place neat
Having established a firm seat,
Nor very high nor very low
Having placed Kush grass hallow,
Upon it or the cervine fell,
Then further a cloth as well;
Having seated on such mat
Having made the mind one-pointed
With controlled mind and sense
Shouldst thou practice yoga
For purification of the self.

1 REAL LEARNING
Study and study
Theoretically studded me
Let practice make steady.

2 SACRED SEAT
To attune with me
Surroundings and seat may
Not strangulate me.

Cervine fell=deer skin

शुचौ देशे प्रतिष्ठाप्य स्थिरमासनमात्मनः।
नात्युच्छ्रितं नातिनीचं चैलाजिनकुशोत्तरम्।।6.11।।

तत्रैकाग्रं मनः कृत्वा यतचित्तेन्द्रियक्रियः।
उपविश्यासने युञ्ज्याद्योगमात्मविशुद्धये।।6.12।।

3 LORD'S WORDS IN GEETA
His exhaustive details
Are as if my soul's cradled
In repose Eternal.

4
Mind intends to corrupt
One thinking 'you are only soul'
This soul purifies mind.

5 YOGIC BODY
In the purest mind,
The body becomes shrine
To enshrine the Divine.

6 UNREAL APPROACH TO NATURAL MIND
Wandering dissipation dictates
The mind's innate state
Of single pointedness.

7
Nor high Head
Nor low spirit
Make Yogic seat.

8 SENSES AND THOUGHT SUBDUED.
Felt fulfilled,
Once full to the brim
-The emptiest mind.

9 NATURAL INCLINATION OF MIND
Blocking venues of fuss,-
Inward fantasy and outward lust
Singled mind thus focused.

Verse 13-14

Holding body, neck head
Motionless and erect
Having gaze nor right nor left
Focusing eyes on tip of nose,
Subduing the mind in repose
In restrained vow of Brahmcharya
Sit alert and unfeared;
Within him; man should hold
-Me ; meditating on Me as final goal.

समं कायशिरोग्रीवं धारयन्नचलं स्थिरः।
संप्रेक्ष्य नासिकाग्रं स्वं दिशश्चानवलोकयन्।।6.13।।

प्रशान्तात्मा विगतभीर्ब्रह्मचारिव्रते स्थितः।
मनः संयम्य मच्चित्तो युक्त आसीत मत्परः।।6.14।।

1
All my steps
Should go ahead, unstrayed
To the Ultimate.

2 SCIENCE OF PRAANAYAM
In palpable breath
Visualizing mind's eye gaze
Dissolves mundane maze.

3 YOGASANAS
Lord ope the strictures
Of filthy body to soul's worthy nature
Through gestures and postures.

4 MEDITATION FOR REAL PERCEPTION
Between these blind eyes
An Astral eye lies
To cognize 'I'.

5 UNSTABLE VISUALS
Nomadic gaze
blurs the vision's image
Of mind's eye target.

6 CONSCIOUS CALMNESS
The static body wins
The still world beyond this world
Dynamically serene.

7 SELF ILLUMINATION
Objects and long-shadows
Long fancied me under relative lamp
Now I'm luminous source.

8 PRACTISING YOGI
Surface dual vision
Turned to inner singular intuition
Ope All-wise perception.

Verse 15-16

Thus, the constant Yogic practice
Of collecting himself; The Mystic
Transcendth to Me
Attainth to the Peace,
The final Release.*

Yoga, is not indeed
For the one, with eating greed
Nor for who doth not eat
Nor for who sleepth too much
Nor for who doth not sleep enough.

**Redemption.*

युञ्जन्नेवं सदाऽऽत्मानं योगी नियतमानसः।
शान्तिं निर्वाणपरमां मत्संस्थामधिगच्छति।।6.15।।

नात्यश्नतस्तु योगोऽस्ति न चैकान्तमनश्नतः।
न चातिस्वप्नशीलस्य जाग्रतो नैव चार्जुन।।6.16।।

1

Should I reside
In the very peace
That resides in me.

2 FIELD

*Collecting mind's impures**
On the soil of peace manured
Sprouts the Pure.

3 REDEMPTION KEY – BE CONSTANTIVE

Ever the 'Always'
Brings the accomplishing ways
That opens the cage.

4

Any act,
Over sized or minimized
Victimized.

5 WITHIN BOUNDS

No more, 'The More'
Excepting the more; but in core
More of moderation.

6

*In the lid-spasm***
Palate too chill too warm
Bring a brittle charm.

7 TAPA

Unaffected state
Of 'Karma', in abundance or lack
Is penance.

8 MEDITATING MOUNTAINEER

Alone that Yogi achieves
Who merely not touches the Peak
But halts there in peace.

9 CONSTANCY

In constant discipline
The seed, bud, pollen bring
Fragrant spring.

10 REDEMPTION SIGN

Like fragrance at door sil,
*Of Temple of the Release **
Comes 'The Peace'.

11 *Extremists fail*

Excessive, abundance
And obsessive, the abstinence
Are empty hands.

12 EXTREMES

Over stepping the crease,
Infringes that doth cease
The winning step which frees.

13 TEMPERANCE

Too much or too trifling
Beyond Active moderation ring
All passivity brings.

Impurities.* * too much sleep or too much awake*

Verse 17

The Yoga, only those achieve,
As destroyer of all grief,
The feeds, deeds, recreation and sleeps
In moderation who keep.

1 YOGIC MATURITY
From infantile greed
To the mature moderation of need,
In Yogic flow, is achieved.

2 NON – TEMPERANCE (MAKE HABITS)
With too much shift
Even Redeeming efforts, instead
Enslaves to exhaustive drifts.

3 MODERATION SCALE
How much
is too less or too much,
Judged by grief's touch.

4
No extreme tempts
But, To temperate, the attempts
The Yoga, aims.

5 YOGI – 'BEING UNITED WITH IN'
Yogi enjoys luxuries
But never employs as necessities
Thus destroys miseries.

SELF-CONTROL

Verse 18

Where mind perfects
In the Self alone rests
All free, never desiderates
Is spoken of as the God-united.

1 PERFECT – SURRENDER
All rhythm
All* attuned to Him
Hum ever Master's hymn.

2
None who abnegates
But who never desiderates;
Perfects.

*Desiderate=craves Hum=sing *Deeds, feeds, recreation, sleep.*

युक्ताहारविहारस्य युक्तचेष्टस्य कर्मसु।
युक्तस्वप्नावबोधस्य योगो भवति दुःखहा।।6.17।।

यदा विनियतं चित्तमात्मन्येवावतिष्ठते।
निःस्पृहः सर्वकामेभ्यो युक्त इत्युच्यते तदा।।6.18।।

3 DESIRE-FREE ZONE

In Converged Limits
Solidity spreads illimitably
The spirit.

4 CRAVING HEART

Non-availability of Bliss
Or Non perception of available bliss
Is bound to miss.

Verse 19

As lamp wavers not,
In the windless spot
For Yogi, such simile is brought
Who hath conquered his thought
Practising union with the Lord.

1 STILLNESS OF MIND

In the Sheltering calm
The luminous path is formed
Against the storm.

2 CALMNESS

Thought and flame
Only in the unflickerings, acclaimed
The Light.

3 WAVY THOUGHTS WIN

Torched weather within
Fights and wins dark draught
Of the weather without.

4 BE FIXED

Be steady ! steady !!
Is the message to study
The sturdy Divine.

Verse 20

In the restrained Yogic quiets
Mind's self getth pacified
And through this little self eyes
And perceiveth 'The Self'
And in the Self getth satisfied.

यथा दीपो निवातस्थो नेङ्गते सोपमा स्मृता।
योगिनो यतचित्तस्य युञ्जतो योगमात्मनः।।6.19।।

यत्रोपरमते चित्तं निरुद्धं योगसेवया।
यत्र चैवात्मनाऽऽत्मानं पश्यन्नात्मनि तुष्यति।।6.20।।

1 HIGHEST PERCEPTION
Yogi's quietitude advanced
In the restrained flow of trance
Streams to Oceanic glance.

2 YOGIC TRANSLATION
Mine and His
Need be quietly permeated
For bliss.

3 SATISFACTION IN MEDITATION
In the meditative caress,
Lot the objective screams lull
To wake in Bliss embrace.

4 INTERIORIZATION
Close the lid
Of this self to lead
To the 'the Self'.

5 DHYAN YOG
Meditative quietitude,
Transcends the louds of objective attitude
Explores bliss of Mute.

Verse 21

Beyond the senses' sense
The intuitive wisdom transcends
To grasp the Infinite bliss
Never wavers, gets ever established.

1 ETERNAL STATE IS NATURAL
Disunion gained
From any union with pain,
Innately installed in Bliss.

2 WISDOM OF PEACE
Once the organ's sense divorced,
Non – organ perception metamorphose
Into bliss wings.

3 UNWAVERING BLISS
The weak wick's glow
Wavered; till dawned at window
Un wavering sun.

4 TRANCE
Perpetual ecstasy
Body's perception beyond body
Is 'Samadhi'

सुखमात्यन्तिकं यत्तदबुद्धिग्राह्यमतीन्द्रियम्।
वेत्ति यत्र न चैवायं स्थितश्चलति तत्त्वतः।।6.21।।

5 GYAN
All is non- Knowledge,
But, that which unveils the covered
Bliss of Self-knowledge.

6 MUNDANE RELATIVITY
In Unveiling Reality
Should all the dualities
Be faded.

7
Man is,
As the God is,
All-Bliss.

Verse 22

Thus gaining zenith
Established in it,
He never believeth,
Of the superior bliss
Unmoved by heavy grief.

1
Purest bliss
But for is non adherent
To grief.

2
Reality, once perceived
Dualities of joy and grief
Never further deceived.

3 I'M SOUL
Body so uninstalled
I'm not body now
In consciousness at all.

4
The conscious bliss
Hoisting its flag on zenith
Waver on unwavering pole.

5 I'M SOUL
Where body executes,
For soul, surrendering own abuse,
Is bad bargain's best use.

6 RIGHT USE OF SENSES
Senses transcend
On the untrodden, tend
Never to return.

यं लब्ध्वा चापरं लाभं मन्यते नाधिकं ततः।
यस्मिन्स्थितो न दुःखेन गुरुणापि विचाल्यते।।6.22।।

Verse 23

Once severed from Union with grief
Let it as Yoga be perceived
Yoga be resolutely practised
Duteously without drift.

1 SEVERED GRIEF FROM LIFE
Throbs of worldy carbuncle
Incised with resolute scalpel
Leaves no mundane scar.

2
Not a worrier in you
But a warrior resolute
Resolved all.

3 BEYOND SHADOW OF RELATIVITY
Yoga conceives
Even under grief's eaves
The sky of Bliss.

4 STEADY MIND
Within pollens' calm
The determined butterfly remained
Untouched by storm.

5 YOGA - IN LORD'S WORDS
The absolute Resolute
Into relative world intrudes
Unites with the Absolute.

6 YOGA DEFINED
Body – mind sieved,
Through practice, grief thus drained
Soul bliss remains.

Verse 24

Desires and its desired incentives
With no reserve be abandoned
And flocks of senses, all about
By the mind alone be won.

1 MEDIATION THOUGHTS
Solo mind
Has strongest lightest wings
To reach the Soul.

2
None, but except
The desire of Desirelessness
Is the desire He accepts.

Eaves= over hanging thatched area

तं विद्याद् दुःखसंयोगवियोगं योगसंज्ञितम्।
स निश्चयेन योक्तव्यो योगोऽनिर्विण्णचेतसा।।6.23।।

सङ्कल्पप्रभवान्कामांस्त्यक्त्वा सर्वानशेषतः।
मनसैवेन्द्रियग्रामं विनियम्य समन्ततः।।6.24।।

3 PREREQUISITE
Yogic mind has nothing
As wants and its longings
Is blessed with everything.

4
The slaves of empty desires,
Can never be the Sire
Of Fullness empire.

4
Wanting mind
Ever and ever finds
The Unwanted.

5 MEDITATION
Quieten! Desires' din
And Hark ! fulfilled harmony
Of eternal melody within.

Verse 25

Little by Little, be attained,
The Poise through the brilliance
Mind be established in the Self
Freeing from anything else.

1 SAMADHI- TRANCE
Just lock Thought flow
This knocks the Poise door
Simply enters halt mo.

2 PERSEVERENCE
Possessed of patience
By degrees attains
Non possessed state.

3
In flooded mind, the wisdom
With toil-free quietness as flotsam
Gradually touches the shore.

4 'TYAGA' - RENOUNCING.
In the Kingdom of Peace
What we call 'Nothing'
Possessed Everything.

5 STAGE OF NO IMPATIENCE
Fastness astrays
Soul in gradualness permeates
Transcendents and stays.

6 ULTIMATE BLISS
In the fullness of spring
With fragrant bliss a Thinker thinks
Not of Soil, manure, tilling.

शनैः शनैरुपरमेद् बुद्ध्या धृतिगृहीतया।
आत्मसंस्थं मनः कृत्वा न किञ्चिदपि चिन्तयेत्।।6.25।।

Verse 26

Whenever unsteady mind wanderth away,
And what ever maketh it astray
Shouldst the Yogi withdraw back
From those distracting tracks
To the Sway of 'the Self'.

1 UNGOVERNED MIND
Unbridled steed,
With unruly wild speed
Wins no race field.

2
Exerting fickle of Mind,
are in idleness, on the dole
Unmoved mind, dynamic to soul.

3 STEADY THOUGHT
Non wandering–Mind
Is at all no 'Mind'
But Conscious- Self.

4 SHAPE TO SHAPELESSNESS
Matter shapes the Mind,
In Non- matter , the thoughts find
Mind dissolving into 'Self'

Verse 27

Supreme Bliss verily comes
Where Yogi is one with Brahmn,
Whose mind is deep in peace
Spur to lust is stilled
All free from the impurities.

1 STEADINESS
Non –wandoring Mind,
Is at all No mind
But the 'Conscious – Self'.

2 DISCOVERY
Innor oxcursion
Of mind knocks the door of consciousness
Enters Brahm state.

On the dole=jobless.

यतो यतो निश्चरति मनश्चञ्चलमस्थिरम्।
ततस्ततो नियम्यैतदात्मन्येव वशं नयेत्।।6.26।।

प्रशान्तमनसं ह्येनं योगिनं सुखमुत्तमम्।
उपैति शान्तरजसं ब्रह्मभूतमकल्मषम्।।6.27।।

3 YOGIC JOURNEY

From Stuffy mind
To the introspective thoughtlessness
Is inner voyage.

4 VEILING THE SELF

Assigned to craving wish
The mind with spurs of blemish
Makes the Soul eclipsed.

5

In 'I' and mine
Lie all the fuss of 'my' mind
Rest all is Bliss.

Verse 28

Ever collecting himself thus,
Yogi freed from impure lust,
Attains Supreme–contact with ease,
The Eternal bliss, it is.

1 GEETA

Wordless scattered words,
I picked, collected and took
Turned into blessed book .

2

Scattered wool of noon
In eve gathered thus monsoon,
Blessed heaven on Earth.

3 EASY REACH

The Eternal boundless friend,
Declared Himself to the Unbound Yogis
Easy , at hand.

4 THE GOLD – THE YOGI

Freed of impure, the core
Ever Collected from corrupt ore
The nugget in itself pure.

5

In the quest
Of pure; through pure conquest
Yogi reaches the Purest.

6 EASY

He made easy task
Only, Lord hath asked
Leave binding tasks.

युञ्जन्नेवं सदाऽऽत्मानं योगी विगतकल्मषः।
सुखेन ब्रह्मसंस्पर्शमत्यन्तं सुखमश्नुते।।6.28।।

EQUAL VISION OF YOGI

Verse 29

Having filled with yogic vision,
Who perceives everything as Even
In all-beings Me, the Supreme Soul
In Me, all-beings he doth Behold.

1 DIVINE VISION
The Absolute; the Relative
One within the other
Be perceived.

2
Me, he, it, they
Equally we change role in play
Of timeless Time–space.

3 DIVINITY AT HAND
Holiest was Farthest
Till, through Yogic lens' parallel rays
Equalled on 'the closest'.

4 *OMNIPRESENCE*
The Infinite in us
To connect, required very first
Feeling the Divine all about.

5 *EVENNESS*
Yogis equal eyes
Journey Into Infinite more n more,
Find Him to the fore.

Verse 30

Everywhere, who doth perceive 'Me'
And everything in Me who doth See
Sight of Me; who doth never loose
Nor him, I ever overlook.

1 DIVINE LIVING
Where living reality
Breath and throb for Entirety
Cohabit with Divinity.

2 *SELF-SURRENDERING*
The level of Being,
When transcends into the Non-Being
Universal existence it brings.

सर्वभूतस्थमात्मानं सर्वभूतानि चात्मनि।
ईक्षते योगयुक्तात्मा सर्वत्र समदर्शनः।।6.29।।

यो मां पश्यति सर्वत्र सर्वं च मयि पश्यति।
तस्याहं न प्रणश्यामि स च मे न प्रणश्यति।।6.30।।

3 MUTUAL RELATIONS
Thought remains mere thought
to enliven it, consciousness be brought
To reciprocate with the Lord.

4
Lost in Him
Should be though lost to the world,
Found Each-other*.

5 TOUGHT
A divine lover on–window.
Found; The Divinity through every window
Of His omnipresent love.

Verse 31

May life come in whatever way
Duteously with Me who doth stay
And in all beings, 'My abode' who doth see
Within 'Me' dwellth always.

1
Established 'one' in all
Yogi contemplates 'All' in all
Yogi thus finds the Divine.

2
Once 'I' and 'You' subside
Then Only He, the Lord remains
In which tiny 'i' resides.

3
The consciousness of person,
If established at Vast horizon
Masters all Creation.

4
Only the Vast vision,
Zeroes to the unbroken
Divine-union.

5
Not the thought about God
But the God in all thoughts
Is fullness, He brought.

6
Matter's slave concern,
Be diffused in 'One' perception
To master His Oneness.

**Lord and Bhakt (devotee)*

सर्वभूतस्थितं यो मां भजत्येकत्वमास्थितः।
सर्वथा वर्तमानोऽपि स योगी मयि वर्तते।।6.31।।

7
O slumber of Existence !
Into the Ecstasy of Non existence
Sublimate ! to exist in Him.

Verse 32

Who, with ownself by comparison
Perceiveth everything by Even-vision
Be it pleasure or misery
O Arjun ! is deemed the highest Yogi.

1 YOGIC OFFERTORY
Worshipper to the Worshiped
Once offers all the diversities
What else this Yogi needs.

2 ENTIRENESS
Likeness of Yogi's own,
Innately holds alike all things
Beholds life in totality.

3
More and more 'He'
In diverses and others, I see
Explored more God in me.

4 GOD UNION
The thinking and feeling freedom
Getting even with Eternal wisdom,
Perfects to 'the Perfect Being'

5 YOGI
In whom Even prevail
That Absolute is full n relative as well
He in the Highest dwells.

आत्मौपम्येन सर्वत्र समं पश्यति योऽर्जुन।
सुखं वा यदि वा दुःखं सः योगी परमो मतः।।6.32।।

LORD'S PROMISE ON YOGA

Verse 33

Arjun Said –

What Thou havest taught
This Yoga of even-vision
Its endurance stead fast
O Madhusudan ! I see not
Because of my wavering thought.

1 SHALLOW SEARSH
On Wavering surf
Not the ocean be blamed
For not finding gems.

2 INTERROGATING DEVOTION
Blind-faith masks
And corrupts seeker's link
So logically Arjun asks.

3 GOOD LEARNER
Ideal disciple doubts
Not the Teachings, but all about
Own skill to sharpen.

4 THE UPRISE
Occasional flashes take up
To momentary knowledge make ups
Need long endurance to wake up.

Verse 34

Arjun continues-

For the mind is restless enough,
Strong, tumultuous unyielding rough,
To master this, as the wind is
O Krshna ! I consider it tough.

1 CAUTIOUS PRACTICE
Yogic mind reminds,
The wavering influence on mind
To cultivate even-mind.

2 SELF ASSESSMENT
While Own-self warned,
Of the enmity within stubborn
Is first leap to achieve.

योऽयं योगस्त्वया प्रोक्तः साम्येन मधुसूदन।
एतस्याहं न पश्यामि चञ्चलत्वात् स्थितिं स्थिराम्।।6.33।।

चञ्चलं हि मनः कृष्ण प्रमाथि बलवद्दृढम्।
तस्याहं निग्रहं मन्ये वायोरिव सुदुष्करम्।।6.34।।

3 CALMNESS FIRST
The wind, puff, breath, Pranayaam,
The Mind, Sense, thought, meditation, trance
Let evolve to Conscious Calm.

4 GEETA
Had Arjun had no doubt
Divine words of the Divine
Would not have come out.

5 SENSES GOVERNED MIND
In the storm of 'senses'
Mind flies berserk non-vigilant
On palsied pinions.

6 PRY
It's not just curiosity
It's to cure, to make pure
Mankind from Impurity.

Verse 35

The Blessed Lord said-

For wavering is Mind
O Arjun ! its control is tough
But by practice and dispassion
It's possible to curb.

1
Mind wanders of demands,
Should these demands not command
For mundane bonds.

2 YOGIC PRACTICE
Non-attachment gets clinged
To Him, Whom nothing clings
This practice frees from things.

3
With restrained restraint
Mind thus devoted and trained
This Mind stilled is Self-gained.

4 YOGA
Strong yet short lived
Senses die once soul is perceived
Yogic practice brings this Bliss.

5 DEPRIVED OF NOTHING
though possessions subdue
In practice nothing deprives you,
Unless adhere to.

6 ELEVATION
Practice and Detachment,
Each Strengthen hand in hand
The steady sublimity.

असंशयं महाबाहो मनो दुर्निग्रहं चलं।
अभ्यासेन तु कौन्तेय वैराग्येण च गृह्यते।।6.35।।

7 UNSTRAINED SELF-DENIAL
Practice and practice brings
Unrestrained renouncing of all things,
Of own accord drop off.

Verse 36

Lord Krishna Said –
Here I dost opine,
Yoga ist difficult for unruly mind,
But the Self controlled, striving can
By proper means obtain.

1 SANG-FROID
Right mean is self control
Right path too is self control
Self control is the Goal.

2 YOGIC FIRE/ MUNDANE BLAZE
Yogic bliss is flame unbroken,
Short-lived are seeming inferno of mundane
Soon get extinguished.

3 DISPASSION ITSELF IS DIVINE
Rise ! even above heaven's charm,
Dispassion be practiced Lord appealed
As Mean of Eternal Calm.

4 REGULAR YOGA
Even damp fuel wood in altar,
In daily Sun of the Endeavour,
Ignites Yogic fire.

5 MEDITATION FLAME
In mind's tranquil ignition,
Inextinguishable flame of soul,
Consumes fire of sensual perception.

6 ONLY ABSTINENCE WOULDN'T DO
'Non-attached 'not by restrains
But being subject of higher contentment
Disciplines to rule 'the Self '.

असंयतात्मना योगो दुष्प्राप इति मे मतिः।
वश्यात्मना तु यतता शक्योऽवाप्तुमुपायतः।।6.36।।

Verse 37- 39

Arjun Asked again

Though possessed of faith,
But for lacking efforts yet
Whose mind gets astrayed
And in Yoga not perfected
O Krshna ! what's his fate ?

Deluded on the road to Brahmn
With no base and sidetracked even
O Krshna ! from both thus fallen
Like a rent cloud
Doth he not succumb?

There is none, truly
To dispel doubts save Thee,
O Krshna ! banish doubts in me.

1 A MUST
Stepped into conscious move,
One could alone succeed who
prerequisites knew.

2 ARJUN'S ASKANCE
Doubts do Sacredly submit
As Serious efforts beyond the Finite
Striving for the Infinite.

3 TIME CHAIN
In its pursuit each today,
With Perfection linked chain of yesterdays
By acts and thoughts intact.

4 SEEKER'S QUERY
Effortless faith,
Faithful efforts or both,
What's the road?

अर्जुन उवाच
अयतिः श्रद्धयोपेतो योगाच्चलितमानसः।
अप्राप्य योगसंसिद्धिं कां गतिं कृष्ण गच्छति।।6.37।।

कच्चिन्नोभयविभ्रष्टश्छिन्नाभ्रमिव नश्यति।
अप्रतिष्ठो महाबाहो विमूढो ब्रह्मणः पथि।।6.38।।

एतन्मे संशयं कृष्ण छेत्तुमर्हस्यशेषतः।
त्वदन्यः संशयस्यास्य छेत्ता न ह्युपपद्यते।।6.39।।

5

Any effort of past
Any moment of faith is not lost
Every step steps to cross.

6 *YOGIC MODERATION*

Less is more astrayed
Or more is more off the track
What counts in efforts and faith?'

7 *QUESTIONED ARJUN*

Various epochs in between
The Ignorance-wisdom and its conscious links
What goes waste, who wins?

8 *ARJUN'S QUESTIONING*

Learner efforts to hear
An hearer is faithfully eager,
Why how, what, thus appear.

9 *REALIZING THE OMNISCIENT*

One thing I know
That He alone knows,
This makes me know.

10 *ASKING THE LORD (IN GEETA)*

Pertinent question of Man
To the Lord, fruitfully extends
Answer to whole mankind.

11 *SUBLIMITY/ DELUSION*

Vapours from mud are meant
To rain the bliss over excellence,
But cloudy thoughts rent.

12 *GEETA FOR ALL TIMES*

Where Disciple knows-
'His Master Knows', thus wisdom flows
Beyond that Disciple it goes.

13 *'ARJUN'S QUESTIONING'*

A pauper knowing Him
All-wise, for treasure asked Him
To learn to the brim.

14 *MOKSHA PATH*

On face of Lord, All-wise
Fate, fear, fault, faith dissolve
Salvation to solve.

Verse 40

The Blessed Lord Said –

O Parth ! No destruction he suffers
Nor Here nor Hereafter,
A doer who acts upright
Dear ! Falls not into evil plight.

rent = split

पार्थ नैवेह नामुत्र विनाशस्तस्य विद्यते।
नहि कल्याणकृत्कश्चिद्दुर्गतिं तात गच्छति।।6.40।।

1 GOOD ACTS TREASURED
Every little practice learned
Every bit of purity earned
Its –my gain in every turn.

2
Failures as well amount,
All good acts get treasured in account
The Divine Assurer counts.

3 ULTIMATE ASSURANCE OF LORD
For persisted act of virtues
In spite of many falls and pursuits
All souls finally rescued.

4 FATE
Pure tomorrow is ensured
By today and all yesterdays as doer
Gathering all ages true treasures.

5
Though sincere even if failed
Godliness reassures what's today withheld,
All persevered acts prevail.

6 YOGIC DRIVE
Sublime Yogic employs
His all sense cravings and rejoice
Into hunger for soul-joys.

Verse 41

Attaining virtuous height
Even he, who so ever strayed from Yogic insight,
Living for many years, a pious life
Is reborn in prosperous home, upright.

1 VIRTUES CARRIED FORWARD
Through births the pure deeds,
To further purer, the purity increased
To the Purest it leads.

2 EVOLUTION / SUBLIMITY
Birth by birth, plane by plane
To the Higher consciousness soul transcends
Finally the 'Absolute' is attained.

3 ADVANTAGE OF SANCTITY
Unstained life of even ignorant
Rebirth chances to purify his existence
Thus he attains.

4 RIGHTEOUS ECHELONS
Blessed and prosperous place,
Blessed birth by birth to further bless
Self with blessedness ahead.

प्राप्य पुण्यकृतां लोकानुषित्वा शाश्वतीः समाः।
शुचीनां श्रीमतां गेहे योगभ्रष्टोऽभिजायते।।6.41।।

5
Desired to be Desireless,
Once this only desire is left
Accomplishes.

6 IMPERFECT YOGIS ARE CHANCED
Physical body is access,
Opens for Yogis astral world gateways
Birth by birth in steps.

Verse 42

Or he takes his birth,
Sure in family of enlightened yogis
Though, Actually such a birth
Is very rare on the Earth.

1 LORD'S BLESSINGS
Advantages bless us
Lord fulfills Himself thus
And fulfills His opus.

2 CARRIED FORWARD VIRTUES
Deeds, thought never are lost,
Wisdom, virtues are continuity of the past
As Lord's reward.

3 EXPECTANT LORD
With enlightened pedigree,
Lord hath honoured entrusting a decree
Of great hope in me.

4 VIRTUOUS REBIRTH
Leaving mortal coil, the Ego-virtue
In conductive form manifest accrued
Pilgrimage thus continue.

Verse 43

Same level of conscious virtue
What his former body knew*
Here he regainth anew.
*By virtue of this, O Son of Kuru** !*
For Perfection he does utmost do.

अथवा योगिनामेव कुले भवति धीमताम्।
एतद्धि दुर्लभतरं लोके जन्म यदीदृशम्।।6.42।।

तत्र तं बुद्धिसंयोगं लभते पौर्वदेहिकम्।
यतते च ततो भूयः संसिद्धौ कुरुनन्दन।।6.43।।

1
Through ages the Physical age,
As infant's wisdom or childish aged cage,
Journeying on virtue's pilgrimage.

2 NO TOIL IN VAIN
In journey of God-Consciousness
Those traversed milestones are deathless,
Steps are also deathless.

3 YOGI'S REDISCOVERY
Acquired in former life's practice
Preserved as inherited to call- 'Born Yogis'.
Rebirth revised it with ease.

4 REAL TREASURE
Prior births' solvent
Credited for salvation to claim
In immortal astral bank.

5 SERENE GROWTH
Virtuous pollens of Wisdom
Detached from mother-garden do blossom
Yield further virtuous pollens.

6 NEXT BIRTH OF YOGI
Past live's wisdom
Of yogi germinate in astral cerebrum
Blossom in next environ.

*previous birth, **Arjun. Solvent=credit worth.

Verse 44

By that former birth's practices itself
Automatically advances on Yogic path in the Next,
Even such aspirant of Yoga,
Passes beyond ritualistic text.

1 PRACTICE
Tho' gardener wrote of rose
In flowery verses and lengthy prose
Essence he could n't compose.

2 EVOLUTION OF PERCEPTION
First seeing is believing,
Then, what mind's eye perceives, I view
Believed, finally, becomes true.

3 BEYOND RITUALISTIC PRINCIPLES
Wordless past praxis strives
For wordless realization to cite,
Need no word.

4 EXOTIC PATH
Wordy chanting , a parrots mind
on water with ritual pen I sign
Seeking Union, I lack behind.

पूर्वाभ्यासेन तेनैव ह्रियते ह्यवशोऽपि सः।
जिज्ञासुरपि योगस्य शब्दब्रह्मातिवर्तते।।6.44।।

5 YOGI'S SELF MOTIVATIONAL INSTINCT

Instinctive Today is shaped
By many yesterdays' striving steps
Thus, self-motivated surpasses maps.

6 A YOGIC LIFE

Born aligned to Self-control,
On ritual texts need not to enroll,
To decode the Supreme soul.

Verse 45

But, following path, the Yogi, diligent,
Is purged of all Sins, Karmic taints,
Perfected through many births, then
Attains The Supreme instant.

1 INSTANT LIBERATION

Many births strived to finish,
At finishing point, the Time ceased,
Turning to Timeless bliss.

2 YOGIC PRACTICE, THE KEY

Rust and dust fastened and blocked,
Engineered, levered, endeavoured, hammered
Thus purging freed, unlocked.

3 MEDITATION

O Mind! Rise to threshold
To transcend into realm of 'Yog'
to consciousness of Soul.

4

Through births same Mind rockets
With any noble or evil fuel of traits
Is programmed to find depth.

Verse 46

To the ascetic, to the wise empiricist
Even to fruitive act performist
The Yogi is deemed superior
Be O Arjun ! a Yogi; Therefore.

प्रयत्नाद्यतमानस्तु योगी संशुद्धकिल्बिषः।
अनेकजन्मसंसिद्धस्ततो याति परां गतिम्।।6.45।।

तपस्विभ्योऽधिको योगी ज्ञानिभ्योऽपि मतोऽधिकः।
कर्मिभ्यश्चाधिको योगी तस्माद्योगी भवार्जुन।।6.46।।

1

Best of whole lot
Labyrinth of seeking paths to Lord,
Is science and art of thoughts.

2 NOBLEST PATH

Strains worked up in worldly cage
Remained worked up in wordy texts
But workable is inner knowledge.

3 THE RAJPATH-DIRECT PATH

Reasoning renunciation action
All are good but a by path
Yoga a shortest highway.

4 MEDITATION-THE BEST WAY

Above noble thoughts and acts
From man the best, Lord expects
'Well-thought thoughtlessness'.

5 GLORY OF YOGA

Purity, charity, duty do refine
Take longer time and are confined
Yoga is fullest glory of Mind.

Verse 47

Among all classes of Yogis,
Whose 'Self' is immersed in Me,
Who worships Me in full faith
I hold him fully united,
As the devout highest.

1

Nor just path of sense
Nor wisdom but inmost Self
Attains God- Consciousness 'fullest'.

2 FULLEST GOD-CONSCIOUSNESS

To my faith, Lord assured
Fullest Divinity that existed ever
Is sure now and here.

3

Bared of body–ego, the soul
Is cared by the Supreme Soul
As if own-Self owned.

4 GOD IN YOU

Stature of Soul is scaled
By density of faith which dwells
God conscious pixels.

योगिनामपि सर्वेषां मद्‌गतेनान्तरात्मना।

श्रद्धावान्भजते यो मां स मे युक्ततमो मतः।।6.47।।

5 EARNED INNOCENCE

Infant babbling may outshine,
The utterly childish world of Aged design
Being uncorrupt astral treasure.

CHAPTER SEVEN

Matter and Spirit ; Prakriti and Purusha

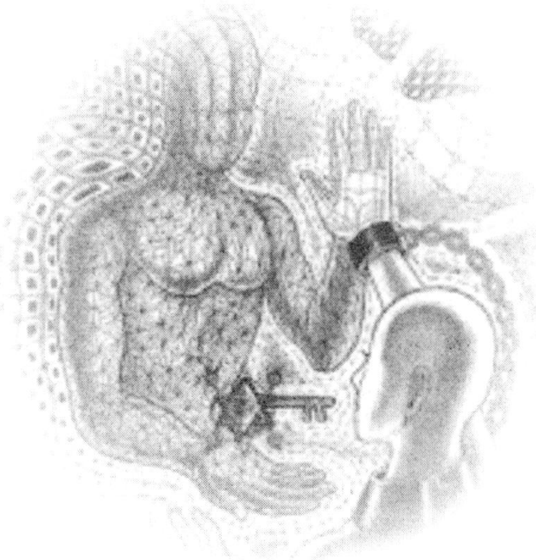

Presumptuous devoted robots,*
Imagine practice and techniques as goal
Fail to commune with Lord.

* Customary

No true devotee is ignored

No matter what form he adored

The Supreme approves the core.

Chapter Seven

HOW THOU CANST DO

Verse 1-2

The Blessed Lord Said –

Absorbing the mind in Me O Parth !
Taking refuse in Me, on Yoga-path
How thou shalt, without doubt
Know Me; that thou dost hark !!

Unto thee I shall now declare
In full phenomenal knowledge as well
Noumenal knowledge ; which being known,
There remainth none to be known further.

1 WORDS OF LORD TO DEVOTEE
The Unknowable Own-self ope,
Before ignorant duteous devout with hope,
In him God be un enveloped.

2 YOGA
Yoga is a path, a vision
Surrender and refuge are the means
To the Divine destination.

3 RELATIVITY
Time-place-thought couldn't intercept
Where Poise perseveres in these states
God-Consciousness is fullest.

4 CUSTOMARY PRACTICES
Presumptuous devoted robots,
Imagine practice and techniques as goal
Fail to commune with Lord.

मय्यासक्तमनाः पार्थ योगं युञ्जन्मदाश्रयः।
असंशयं समग्रं मां यथा ज्ञास्यसि तच्छृणु।।7.1।।

ज्ञानं तेऽहं सविज्ञानमिदं वक्ष्याम्यशेषतः।
यज्ज्ञात्वा नेह भूयोऽन्यज्ज्ञातव्यमवशिष्यते।।7.2।।

5 LORD'S GEETA
The Maker's own make
Theory of all theories Lord spake
Practically all to awake.

6
Many texts talk of Him,
Geeta chanced me, hear from Him
Supreme words of the Supreme.

7 'THE SUPREME PREACHER'-GEETA
Where both have ideal keenness
Teacher fullest and Taught emptiest
Complete pour completely grasped.

8 KNOW THE LORD FULLY
Distinct Mind, intellect techniques
Potentiate seeker to evolve doubly quick
From Limited to fullest Infinite.

9
Essence of pollen is quest
Of having within itself, the richest
Nectar unto the fullest.

10
'I know is but none' –
Is only vastest knowledge of the wisdom,
Needs be known, to know.

Verse 3

Someone amongst the thousands,
One perchance strives perfection to attain,
Among those true seekers, even
Only one perchance know Me as I am.

1 LORD HELPS
From common attentions, I withdrew,
That drew attention of the Lord, drove who,
On path of rarest few.

2 CATCH MESSAGE
To rise from error to Truth,
Lord blessed instinct commonly to avail
Save rarest, All commonly fail.

3 BIASED PATH GOERS
Perfects are those, having drive
To be amongst perchanced to strive,
Between aspirant and realized lives.

4
Lord equally blessed - 'Rising urge'
All commonly bartered it with pottage.
Rarest strived for the Knowledge.

मनुष्याणां सहस्रेषु कश्चितद्यतति सिद्धये।
यततामपि सिद्धानां कश्चिन्मां वेत्ति तत्त्वतः।।7.3।।

5 LORD'S DECLARATION
Who strive at final aim,
My words induce to seeker's claim
'To know Me as I am.'

6 REDISCOVER
God is not to be earned
'Tis deposit in every soul' – when learned
Instantly God is realized.

PRAKRITI-DUAL NATURE

Verse 4-5

Earth, water, fire, air, space
Mind, Intellect and false ego
My eightfold energy –Nature cleaved,
Beside this inferior nature
O Arjun ! Higher Nature of Mine perceive,
Which is very life's element – 'Jiva'
With which very Cosmos lives.

1 THE CREATION
Lord's holistic nature is expressed,
In the spaces occupied or spaces unspaced
Thus plurality created interlaced.

2
Non-real are Non transcendental,
But are support-factors of real Ethereal
To transcend unto Eternal.

3 SPIRITUAL STRUCTURE
Permutation, permeation of matter ions,
Vitalized by comingled thoughtrons n'lifetrons
Create immutable astral constitution.

4 THE SUPREME DOER'S DEED
Unto non-eternal inert world,
Dynamizing with spirit, the non vitals
Unchangeable is put in changeable.

5
Inferior elements have limits,
Yet are foundation vibes created to build,
Infinite edifice for the Spirit.

6 MEDIUM TO ACHIEVE
Matter elements be perceived,
As blessed support for Non-matter ' Jiva'
As a medium to achieve.

भूमिरापोऽनलो वायुः खं मनो बुद्धिरेव च।
अहङ्कार इतीयं मे भिन्ना प्रकृतिरष्टधा।।7.4।।

अपरेयमितस्त्वन्यां प्रकृतिं विद्धि मे पराम्।
जीवभूतां महाबाहो ययेदं धार्यते जगत्।।7.5।।

7
Matter by nature vibrate, circulate
Non matter by Nature have intuition, instincts, acts
To elevate, sublimate, transcend.

Verse 6

These dual element Nature; understand !
Are the womb of all beings
So, I am the commencement
Also for entire Universe, the end.

1
Argil, the Potter shaped
In different shapes of pots, toys, puppets
Clay claimed again All-clad.

2
One cause of all causes
Caused high-low nature work in embrace
World's all diversities to manifest

3 ONE WOMB
Basic clay with specific sojourn
The soul, embraced tho' segregate, is born
Further to proceed to bourn.

4
Waves and tides
Rise and do surf
Cann't stay enough.

5 EXPRESSION OF LATENT
Latent dynamism of life force
Can not be expressed if kept divorced
From evident matter source.

THE SUSTAINER OF CREATION

Verse 7

O Arjun ! O conqueror of wealth !!
Supreme beyond Me, none existth else,
All and all are strung to Myself
Alike string on thread, the pearls.

Bourn = journey's destination. Argil = Clay of potter

एतद्योनीनि भूतानि सर्वाणीत्युपधारय।
अहं कृत्स्नस्य जगतः प्रभवः प्रलयस्तथा।।7.6।।

मत्तः परतरं नान्यत्किञ्चिदस्ति धनञ्जय।
मयि सर्वमिदं प्रोतं सूत्रे मणिगणा इव।।7.7।।

1 ONE STRING
Lord, the one common Consciousness,
By nature equally carried to different selves,
He holds all them intact.

2
Humans, Rocks, Roes, Racemose , Rose,
Rabbits, Robots, every bit He compose
All strung garland of Cosmos.

3 LORD'S IMPLICATION
The pearls in the necklace,
Are regularly regular all alike nonetheless
Core held unseen through thread.

4 HE IS HIS OWN CAUSE
The Infinite evolves Himself,
Causes all Beings and Non Being selves
Causes Himself by Himself.

Verse 8-9

In water, the sapidity I am,
In the Sun and the Moon, radiance,
I am Aum in all vedic texts,
The Sound in the Space,
In men, the manfulness.

Sacred fragrance in Earth I 'm
Vivid Brilliance in fire I'm
Life itself in all existence
Of All ascetics, I'm Penance.

1 ALL IN ALL BEINGS
He, the everything in Everything,
He ist the Being in all beings
Also Being of Non-beings.

2
All energies and all essence,
As God consciousness the cosmos sustains
Through dreamer and doer men.

3 THE ENLIGHTENMENT
Meditates on Unknowable - a Yogi
The knowing, Knower, Known he could see
In one perception of ecstasy.

4 PRANAVAH
Virat whispers into every quantum
In the din of space, silence of Lord's hum
Is sonic manifestation 'Aum'.

रसोऽहमप्सु कौन्तेय प्रभास्मि शशिसूर्ययोः।
प्रणवः सर्ववेदेषु शब्दः खे पौरुषं नृषु।।7.8।।

पुण्यो गन्धः पृथिव्यां च तेजश्चास्मि विभावसौ।
जीवनं सर्वभूतेषु तपश्चास्मि तपस्विषु।।7.9।।

5
Frequencies those pervade space
To substantiate Creation, many ways express
Around soundless Hum – 'Aum' the Base.

6 ALL-PERVADING LORD
Infusing Himself into the Matter,
As Divine non-matter of peculiar Nature,
Creator made everything so Divine.

7
Manhood is God in man,
Without divinity Man would be no man,
'Man is Divine' thus Lord proclaims.

8
In matter more than 'Matter'
That exists is God owned 'Non-matter'
In which He innately occurs.

Verse 10-11

O Parth ! I am thus be cognized,
Of all beings, the Eternal seed
I'm wisdom of the wise
And splendour of the Splendid

Of the strong I'm strength
Devoid of passion n attachments
In Beings O Arjun ! I'm Desire
Which is not opposed to Dharma.

1 ONE ORIGIN
Ancient of ancient seeds,
Newest of recently, evolved pedigrees
Through its seeds, Eternal-seed feeds

2 HIS WISDOM ALONE
Vital Grey, His tool*
Through which Divine expresses His plan
Lest mortal coil is fool.

3
Lord's all Creation's source,
Caused changes in the Ever-changing course,
With unchanged continuity of Vital force.

4 DIVINE PRESENCE
Every essential of nectarine sap,
In furrows of vault cap, fishes of Biceps
Many ways the Divinity expresses.

* Brain

बीजं मां सर्वभूतानां विद्धि पार्थ सनातनम्।
बुद्धिर्बुद्धिमतामस्मि तेजस्तेजस्विनामहम्।।7.10।।

बलं बलवतामस्मि कामरागविवर्जितम्।
धर्माविरुद्धो भूतेषु कामोऽस्मि भरतर्षभ।।7.11।।

5 THE CREATOR
The Former of 'soul yield'
Is great farmer of the thought n deed
Plants in heart – hand, seeds.

6 THE DIVINE INTIMACY PLANTED
Seeds the Divine Expert
Into seeming vitals and seeming inert,
His own Soul as soul-mate.

7 SPIRITUAL ECO CYCLE
Plants from seed emerge
On Gardener's plan saplings to urge
Back into seed to merge.

8 SEED TO SEED JOURNEY
Once origination process does begin,
Naturally moves to sublimity of Eternal Being
Which is originally 'The Origin'.

9
Only desirable Desire is
Which that very Sire hath agreed
Desire to be desire-free.

10 RECIPROCATE LORD'S GRACE
Only one Divine touch,
Plants in the Bhakti, the Shakti as much
(as to) Love Him as He does.

11 THE EVER CHANGING CREATION
Ever changing imbroglio
Instilled into go and ego at every mo
Is Un-changeable's show.

12 DHARMA
The Desire in itself lust
But desire What's desired from us
Is a 'Consigned Sire's Trust'

13 STRENGTH OF THE STRONG
The desire of the Un-possessed
Is the instilled wish of the God head
Strength that keeps Non-attached.

Verse 12

All the traits that manifest,
*As Divine, Terrene, Malign states**
Know thou ! from Me emanate
I'm not in them, they are in Me yet.

Imbroglio = Confusion (World) * Sat, Raj, Tam Gunas

ये चैव सात्त्विका भावा राजसास्तामसाश्च ये।
मत्त एवेति तान्विद्धि नत्वहं तेषु ते मयि।।7.12।।

1 *DIMENTIONS OF TEMPERAMENTS*
Infinite Consciousness is the Absolute
Upon which lower impulses, constitute
apparent effect but Untruth.

2
Mud, foam, waves, pearl-dews
Attributive phenomena of manifested issues
Reveal not essentials of 'the Blue'.

3
Infinite varieties of feelings ideas
Of finite impulsive acts are Mayas
All aloof, He doth cause.

4
Impulse of relative states
Of man from the Absolute emanate
Remains He Unaffected, separate.

5 *NEUTRAL SPIRIT OF LORD*
Attributive vernal trend
Of blooms in every bit of its pollens
Have colourless essential essence.

6 *TRAITS*
The three relative moods
All basic traits from the Absolute
All waves of Ocean-o-Truth.

THE WAY BEYOND MAYIC WORLD

Verse 13

Nature, composed of traits Three,
Deludes the whole world
This world does not perceive Me
Who am beyond these traits and Immutable.

1
Dazzled by hypnotic gleam
Of infernal fire of delusive cosmic dreams
O Vision ! perceive 'source beam'.

2 *WORLDLY PLEASURE*
I burnt hands in inferno;
About flame I did not know
Which, inmost glow.

3 *DELUSIVE WORLD*
First dazzled and amazed
Then this infernal fire scorched and blazed
Ask ! internal flame to bless.

4
From triple nature of world
To transcend beyond dimensions of whirls
Churn (your) world reach Beyond World.

त्रिभिर्गुणमयैर्भावैरेभिः सर्वमिदं जगत्।
मोहितं नाभिजानाति मामेभ्यः परमव्ययम्।।7.13।।

5 SOUL

In changeable, what changes not,
Is little of Himself, the Immutable part
Instilled unchanged by Lord.

Verse 14

Maya, the cosmic illusion of Mine
Indeed is Divine;
In triple material traits imbued
Is difficult to be subdued.
In Me who take refuge
From illusion they alone are rescued.

1 ONE SOURCE

All matter, Non-matter energy states,
Are emanations from one Divine Godhead,
Natured to lower natures, deluded.

2 MAYA

Cosmic hypnosis, Maya is rope
Bound to it, can't help that galloped
Alone Unbound is the Hope.

3 THE DIVINE PATH

Maya, the imminent ego
Has ever changing existence, though
May transcend to Divinity, 'All above'.

4 ALONE SAVIOUR IN JOURNEY

Divine sail at Compass's mayhem
In storm Divine soul strays from aim
Save! Lord's Refuge at helm'.

5 SOUL-BODY ENTITY

Where matter 's vitalized essentially,
Conditioned Soul is conditioned ever eternally
Not overcomes material entity.

6 ALL DIVINITY

Maker's Maya never divorced
Maker's Divinity in ever changing course
Pervaded by Never-changing forçe.

7 TAKE REFUGE

With abraded knees, bled elbows
In mayic play unto lap child goes
The rest , Mother knows.

दैवी ह्येषा गुणमयी मम माया दुरत्यया।
मामेव ये प्रपद्यन्ते मायामेतां तरन्ति ते।।7.14।।

Verse 15

The doers of wrong deeds
Whom, the Ignorance lead
Whose wisdom, the Illusion sneaks
Follow the ways demonic
Not Me do they seek.

1 WHAT'S EVIL (TAMO GUNA)
Credents created by the Supreme,
In contrast to carve the Creator's dream
Further wrongs Miscreants' whim.

2 THREE TRAITS OF DESTRUCTION
Creator assigns destruction to transform
Destruction consigned by the man alarms,
The demonic destruction designs harm.

3 DEVOLUTION
Who have deluded themselves,
Indulge themselves as mass of flesh
This is sin in itself.

4 WHAT'S GOOD (SATO GUNA)
Lord planted a plan-Divine
Unto All beings to evolve and refine
Ignorance-blinded declined.

5 RATIONAL INTELLECT
Instinct instilled in Intellect
As Natural plan good-bad to discriminate
There by the man perfects.

Verse 16

Four types of people of virtue,
O Arjun ! worship Me and pursue
Are Afflicted, the questers of wisdom,
The seekers of mammon
And the Enlightened persons.

Sneak = Steal.

न मां दुष्कृतिनो मूढाः प्रपद्यन्ते नराधमाः।
माययापहृतज्ञाना आसुरं भावमाश्रिताः।।7.15।।

चतुर्विधा भजन्ते मां जनाः सुकृतिनोऽर्जुन।
आर्तो जिज्ञासुरर्थार्थी ज्ञानी च भरतर्षभ।।7.16।।

1
Unfulfilled naturally seek refuge,
And Achievers of fulfillment are who
Through desire-less worships pursue.

2
Modes to attain bliss
Differ to noble seeker's mind and worship
Likewise, The Giver bestowth gifts.

3 *FOUR MODES OF WORSHIP*
Be it grieving, or relieving way
For believing, for perceiving I pray
For 'Non-thing', Everything I lay.

4 *ALL RIGHTEOUS WAYS*
The worships in quest
Of gain in here, attain in Next
Highest way to the Highest.

Verse 17-18

All worshippers are Noble indeed,
Ever united, devoted to Me, I deem
Of these the Wise, exceeds;
Me, that wise doth steadily love
I too love Him all above.

Among all these nobles, the Sage
I consider truly as My very Self
In Me alone he unwaveringly holds,
Sets Me, as his Supreme Goal.

1
True prayers surrender to Lord
A noble refuge to fulfill man's demand,
Yet undemanding prayers fulfill Both.

2 *MUTALITY*
All prayers are though noble,
The Enlightened sages have love shackles
Bind worshipper with the Worshipped.

3 *THE BEST WORSHIPPER*
Demanding Nothing, None he expects
Carry with prayers himself to oblate
For love, the Love reciprocates.

4 *ALL HIS GRACE*
Let my worship be
Expression of joy that He
Put into me a worshipper.

तेषां ज्ञानी नित्ययुक्त एकभक्तिर्विशिष्यते।
प्रियो हि ज्ञानिनोऽत्यर्थमहं स च मम प्रियः।।7.17।।

उदाराः सर्व एवैते ज्ञानी त्वात्मैव मे मतम्।
आस्थितः स हि युक्तात्मा मामेवानुत्तमां
गतिम्।।7.18।।

5 REFUGE
Among droplets is the 'One'
Whose unbound surrender reached and won
Unbound status of Ocean.

6 UTMOST GOAL
Noble prayed for his pain
And he again worshipped for nothing
the Noblest aimed.

7 NO DEPRIVEMENT
Enlightenment infuses the Being,
With fullness of fulfillment to the brim
Perfecting to very self of Supreme.

8 NOBLEST WORSHIP
To be' Have-nots' from the Haves
To be slave-of-Lord and slave-o-slaves
Dearest to the King of kings.

9 EGOLESS
Where wisdom of the wise
From individual to Total Oneness rise,
The Virat owns the Man-sized.

10 OMNIPRESENT DIVINITY
Equal everywhere is the Supreme
But the Supreme manifests His omnipresence
On what man gives Him.

Verse 19

After many births end
Finds Me the Enlightened,
Realizing that 'all this is Vasudev';
Such a great soul is very rare to have.

1 VASUDEV – ALL OVER
Thews, Throne, Thorn, Thought, Texts
Everything is His theme, the Lord concluded
Nothing is 'man-made'

2 ONENESS IS KNOWLEDGE
Many births' opaque vast studies,
Synopsized this ignorance, into un-blurred vision
'I am one with 'ONE'.

3 DIVINE EVOLUTION
Of world-dwarfs, above all
What a man alone is naturally installed
Is chance to rise tall.

4 GOAL OF EVOLUTION
Man studied Scripture
Fulfilled but, against Nature
Till man lives that scripture.

Thews = Power

बहूनां जन्मनामन्ते ज्ञानवान्मां प्रपद्यते।
वासुदेवः सर्वमिति स महात्मा सुदुर्लभः।।7.19।।

5

After many births of wise
Realized in him the man dies
A Vasudev in him arise.

6 GUIDELINE TO THE WISDOM

Knowledgeable man be not
Contented by rising in thought
Lift ! own being to the God.

7

Perceiving All-pervading Consciousness,
Is agianst pseudolife hypnotizing the 'Self'
Thus rarest is Blessed.

THE SUPREME

Verse 20

Whose wisdom is looted away by lust,
Go to demigods and godules
Led by their own bias
Follow this or that rites and rules.

1

Lesser desires fulfilled
By lesser gods have a lesser worth
Misguide for very many births.

2

Desires are springs of thoughts
Splashing continuously to flood mental part
Distorting rays of Truth apart.

3

Wasted in lesser pursuits
Alas ! futility of many births not understood
Bias discriminated not the Truth.

4

Demigods and deities indeed
Fulfill the desire to desirous needs
Astrays from being Desire-less.

5 LUST

Where desires minister kingly bosom,
Where lesser bias cloud the empire of wisdom
King surrenders to Thraldom.

* Slavery

कामैस्तैस्तैर्हृतज्ञानाः प्रपद्यन्तेऽन्यदेवताः।
तं तं नियममास्थाय प्रकृत्या नियताः स्वया।।7.20।।

Verse 21-22

Whichever form of deity
With faith, worships the devotee
'Ts I who place in that very deity
His unflinching fealty.

With such a faith endowed
From a particular deity he seeks favour
Obtains fulfillment of desires
Which actually Me alone bestow.

1 THE SUPREMACY
Even if lesser god's adored
The Supreme heeds, wish to endorse
For, He is Ultimate source.

2 GARDENER
Any crop, any faith seed,
Krshna, alone waters more faith in field
Of faith, for purest yield.

3 THE SUPREME IS FAITH GIVER
To symbolical deity with great faith
Even lesser worships, from the Supreme get
For that deity greater faith.

4
Worships and the worshipped are not
But Supromacy tunod to bhakt's thought
The Supreme attunes to that form.

5 ONE SOURCE OF FAITH
Worshipping idols worshipping altar
With Divine illusion or Divine discretion,
alter
Maker makes my faith unwaver.

6
In any worship, the faith
Has one alone source of faith's depth
So no intolerance, no sects.

7
Any hymn of any theme
To 'anyone' for any desire, any dream
Finds response from the Supreme.

8
No true devotee is ignored
No matter what form he adored
The Supreme approves the core.

Fealty = loyalty

यो यो यां यां तनुं भक्तः श्रद्धयार्चितुमिच्छति।
तस्य तस्याचलां श्रद्धां तामेव विदधाम्यहम्।।7.21।।

स तया श्रद्धया युक्तस्तस्याराधनमीहते।
लभते च ततः कामान्मयैव विहितान् हि
तान्।।7.22।।

Verse 23

But the little knowing man accrues
Verily limited and transient fruits.
Lesser worshipper , go unto them
But My devotees unto Me, come.

1
On the path of faith,
Many godules with mere milestones attract
May delude as the Ultimate.

2 BENIGN APPROACH
Man's complex rites belittled
The gain; though simple worships are simple
Simply big as Supreme.

3
The pursuit of finite gains,
Have blunted all worships in vain
In quest of the Infinite.

4
Personal desires, personal godules
'Ts purpose, Lord most purposely refutes
Realize ! far more than fruits.

5 SUPREME SOURCE
Star's dreaming glow borrows
Its sheen from Sun's Luminescence kudos
The Enlightened worship knows.

Verse 24

The unwise understands
Of Me, the Unmanifest;
As the limited human embodiment;
And cannot ken
I'm Unchangeable Supreme

अन्तवत्तु फलं तेषां तद्भवत्यल्पमेधसाम्।
देवान्देवयजो यान्ति मद्भक्ता यान्ति
मामपि।।7.23।।

अव्यक्तं व्यक्तिमापन्नं मन्यन्ते मामबुद्धयः।
परं भावमजानन्तो ममाव्ययमनुत्तमम्।।7.24।।

1 THE ADVENT

The Divinity remains Unmanifest
'Ts coming diffuses from transcendent skies
Thus appears He Man-sized.

2

Feelable glory of the Manifest,
Is not all in all about Unmanifest
Who is All and in all.

3 COMING OF THE LORD

Transcendental form taken
By the Imperishable Unmanifest is Descent
As the Earthling, mistaken.

4 AVATAAR

Fundamental human concept
Is aimed at Eternal through transitory quest
Of Unmanifest in the Manifest.

YOGA - MAYA

Verse 25

The Unwise never perceive Me,
Veiled by My delusive energy
So knows Me not, this beguiled world
Who am Unborn, Imperishable.

1 WISE-PERCEPTION

The man –Sized eyes of man
Can visualize only with wisdom's lens
Through opaque Maya, the transparence.

2 WORSHIP

Worships be in His quest,
In pursuit of some objective gain,
Worships are in vain.

3 WISE QUEST

Purer is the wiser quest
Shapeth the transcending purest
Unmanifest,
To reveal as the Manifest.

4 THE ADVENT

Through His shapeless pep
His Supremacy doth shape, deshape, reshape,
Unto Shape, the Unmanifest haps.

Verse 26

I know the Past Beings,
As well the present happenings,
And Beings yet to come;
O Arjun ! but knowth Me none.

Pep = Energy/ vitality Hap = Chance

नाहं प्रकाशः सर्वस्य योगमायासमावृतः।
मूढोऽयं नाभिजानाति लोको मामजमव्ययम्।।7.25।।

वेदाहं समतीतानि वर्तमानानि चार्जुन।
भविष्याणि च भूतानि मां तु वेद न कश्चन।।7.26।।

1
Time manifest in relative world
And is time-bound to the planets' whirls,
In Unmanifest it's timeless.

2 KNOWS ME NONE
He, who knows,
That he knows none
That 'none-knowing, knows the most.

3 INFINITE TIMELESSNESS
From the beginningless Beginning
To the Endless End the Lord did plough
Yielded Time seed of 'Ever-Now'.

4 TIME BOUND WORLD
Dwelling in the Eternal Present
The Supreme deluded world with Time-spell
Immortal Present became dead past.

5 THE EVER PRESENT STATE
Unto timelessness, the Time
Dissolve the past and future sublime
Into Eternal Infinite Present.

Verse 27

O Arjun ! All the beings,
Born with contrasts those commence
From the longings and the loathing,
Are subject to delusion intense.

1 WISDOM-PATH
In relative world opposites' feud
Once Dissolved contrasts, can't delude,
In that relativity appears Absolute.

2 THE SCOPE
Not Own Divinity, at birth
Lord gave ignorance and delusion first,
But resourced to rise from worst.

3 BODY IGNORES SOUL
Body is born to brew
Impulses of the physical duel,*
Consuming Spirit as fuel.

4 UNKNOWN TO INNER SELF
Embodiment of Duality
Remained Ignorant to treasured astral
entity
Loses his Divinity.

*Loathing = abhorrence. * Likes-Dislikes*

इच्छाद्वेषसमुत्थेन द्वन्द्वमोहेन भारत।
सर्वभूतानि संमोहं सर्गे यान्ति परन्तप।।7.27।।

5 DELUSION REFRACTION

From embodied Dew grow
Many dualities coloured in a rain-bow
Its absolutely transparent though.

Verse 28

But those men of virtuous deeds
Whose sins ended, who are freed
From delusions of pairs of contrast,
Worship Me in vow steadfast.

1 BLEMISH

Deed meets outer instinct
Acts committed not to what's within
That alone deed is sin.

2 THE INTENT

No soul is conditioned to Sin,
Only it's resolve of deed that determines
to reach Supreme.

3 COMPLEX TRIO

Soul may be caged
within the body-mind's delusion edge
Or with the mind-soul's pledge.

4 SUCCESS STORY

Virtuous deeds shape deeds
These deeds further bring more virtues
Own Karma aims to meet.

Verse 29

The freedom, those who,
From decay and death, pursuit,
And in Me take refuge,
They know the all inclusive Absolute
As well Karma's Truth.

1

Unto Immortal refuge who toil
Toil to get rid of Mortal coil
Could know the Unknowable.

2 THE SOUL CONTROLS

Surrendering the whole
The dying breaths before deathless soul
Is on surrenderee's control.

येषां त्वन्तगतं पापं जनानां पुण्यकर्मणाम्।
ते द्वन्द्वमोहनिर्मुक्ता भजन्ते मां दृढव्रताः।।7.28।।

जरामरणमोक्षाय मामाश्रित्य यतन्ति ये।
ते ब्रह्म तद्विदुः कृत्स्नमध्यात्मं कर्म
चाखिलम्।।7.29।।

3 SPIRITUAL EVOLUTION
Breath, Bread and brain
seeming existent, their continuity are drained
So aim ! at what remains.

4
Diligently attuned strings
Tooled up in free hands, the violin
Played melody among din.

5
All things all non-things
Surrendering even reasons of reasoning
*-ope to **realm of Realizing.***

Verse 30

Those who are certain
Of Me as element of all material
And as essence of all spiritual realm
And as effulgence of Yagna-sacrifice;
With Divine, their minds unified
Consciously know Me, even at demise.

1
Conscious Lord who perceives
In matter – Non matter, in active – in passive
Him the death never deceives.

2 REBIRTH
Ego disembodied called 'death',
Leaving sub conscious desires on blueprints of Karma
Finds bodily prison's new term.

3 IDEAL PASSING
The death is life in Death
Where battle of breath at final gasp,
Hath continuous God Consciousness.

4 LIBERATION
All lessons he has learned
For the world was created to teach,
His exit has no return.

साधिभूताधिदैवं मां साधियज्ञं च ये विदुः।
प्रयाणकालेऽपि च मां ते विदुर्युक्तचेतसः।।7.30।।

5 DESIRES

The desire is infinite
But it's fulfillment has its limit
So its obstacle to Infinite.

6

The man dies,
But deathless God in him is survived
By conscious God in the next.

CHAPTER EIGHT

Attaining Moksha, the Imperishable state

The worshipper should possess
A warrior within, and warrior should progress
As worshipper, to perfect success.

Toiled a poor pauper

In course dying as lord of matter

Remained a pauper.

Chapter 8

THE MANIFESTATION OF SPIRIT

Verse 1-2

Arjun asked –

O Person Supreme !
What's that Brahmn?
What is Spiritual realm?
What's that Karma?
What is manifested physical realm?
And what's that demigods means?

Who is spirit flame of Yagna Sacrifice?
How in this very body reside?
How can Thou be realized
By the Self-controlled at demise?

1 LORD'S REPLY
It's just and appropriate
To respond to queries of man's quest
for Unknown and the Unknowable.

2
Arjun asked and asked
Lord's response is vaster than vast
for man-kind at large.

3 DISCRIMINATORY GUIDANCE
This frame has many frames
Some expand, some shrink at the same
Lord guides at frameless aim.

4 ARJUN ASKED
My infant query
Is brilliance of Thy glory
Of man's evolution theory.

किं तद्ब्रह्म किमध्यात्मं किं कर्म पुरुषोत्तम।
अधिभूतं च किं प्रोक्तमधिदैवं किमुच्यते।।8.1।।

अधियज्ञः कथं कोऽत्र देहेऽस्मिन्मधुसूदन।
प्रयाणकाले च कथं ज्ञेयोऽसि नियतात्मभिः।।8.2।।

5 NEXT OF KIN – LORD

My faith looks at Him
His faith about my faith, looks at me
Thus is eternal kinship.

6 BLESSED DEATH

Many qualms in life
Of ignorant are, By death if realized
Grant 'grand exit' from life.

7 ETERNALLY LIVING

Deadly death never ordeal,
Conscious Discipline, with Lord, has a deal
At death, life to reveal.

8

Who controls contrast pairs,
About all mortal fears who is aware
The Death, with immortals share.

9 THE VOYAGE

Death from thus very sojourn
Sails on new sea as a new-born
Continues till achieved 'bourn'

10 SELF-CONTROL

Mastering the Self
Masters the Master
As well.

11 BE NUMISMATIST

He Treasures coins of self-control
At surrender of breaths, pays the toll
At crossing border of Body-soul.

Verse 3-4

The Blessed Lord said –

Imperishable supreme self is Brahmn,
Whose essential nature is spiritual realm;
Creative cause that comes
With matter manifests is 'Karma'
What constitutes mutable is physical realm,
Demigods form astral existence of the Supreme
I'm spirit flame – the Yagna
O Arjun ! that dwells in every one.

Bourn = Ultimate goal   Numismatist = Coin Collector

अक्षरं ब्रह्म परमं स्वभावोऽध्यात्ममुच्यते।
भूतभावोद्भवकरो विसर्गः कर्मसंज्ञितः।।8.3।।

अधिभूतं क्षरो भावः पुरुषश्चाधिदैवतम्।
अधियज्ञोऽहमेवात्र देहे देहभृतां वर।।8.4।।

1 MATERIAL REALM

Toiled a poor pauper
In course dying as lord of matter
Remained a pauper.

2 KARMA

Lord's creative nature creates,
Creature's 'Karma', which Divinely elevates
All else is toil and sweat.

3 ALL PERVADING

Every of elements and entities
By His essential nature The Creator enriched
With His flame nitched.

4 FEEL THE UNFEELABLE

Every element is mutant
It contains certain immutable non–element
Sense that Eternal essence.

5 EVOLUTION

The Immutable is not mute
Blest changes in world of vicissitude
Changes in changes to improve.

6 KARMA OF ADVANTAGE

Presiding demigods dwell
In perishable world as phenomenal self
Should advance to spiritual advantage.

7 PROMINENCE OF FREE WILL

In Every-being room
Physical, astral, supreme freewill to loom
But for who masters whom.

8

The Self-chosen nexus
Of the Self with delusory not-self, thus
Discriminates divinity of Ever-conscious.

YOGI

Verse 5

Lastly, when the body 's abandoned
At that mo who remember Me alone
My Supreme Being he doth reach
Its all true beyond skepsis.

1 WHERE DEATH IS GAIN

Vicinity to Lord, amounts
Vanity of existence could n't eke out
Validity of Death at death.

2 ATTACHMENT

The God's dream who cherish
Physical form as body dream when perish
Wakes in dreamless bliss.

Vicissitude = variation. Loom = overshadow, dominate eke out = fill

---

अन्तकाले च मामेव स्मरन्मुक्त्वा कलेवरम्।
यः प्रयाति स मद्भावं याति नास्त्यत्र संशयः।।8.5।।

3 LORD'S PROMISE
Selfless self put to test
Thus innately unattached life fades
Unto assured awakening death.

5
All time pal in core
At demise devotee explores
Same lord to the fore.

4 TRUE PERCEPTION
Disciplined life what pursued
Through discipline of death, reach to Truth
As Truth can't be two.

Verse 6

In Whatever state of mind
His body whoever doth quit
He attains the state, he is inclined
O Arjun ! for his persistence in it.

1
Thoughts never go waste,
Carry prints on soul at the death
Carried to the next.

2
For here as he thinks,
Writes same destiny in death's ink
Making here-after links.

3
Habitual channels of this vault,
Same thoughts, the death would recall,
To determine the next halt.

4
Thoughts and deeds shape
As free choice in final vector map
Guide next pilgrimage.

Verse 7

So, think of Me O Arjun ! ever more
Also duty of fight be carried out
Surrender unto Me thy mind, thy lore
Thus thou shalt come to Me, no doubt.

यं यं वापि स्मरन्भावं त्यजत्यन्ते कलेवरम्।
तं तमेवैति कौन्तेय सदा तद्भावभावितः।।8.6।।

तस्मात्सर्वेषु कालेषु मामनुस्मर युध्य च।
मय्यर्पितमनोबुद्धिर्मामेवैष्यस्यसंशयम्।।8.7।।

1

Prayer and warfare
Worthy light and earthy fight in you
All together Lord approve.

2

The Divine Surrender decides
The purity of duty in sizing fight
All wrongs to right.

3 REALIZATION – LORD'S WORDS

My blessed beams
If project in mind as oriental theme
Awake you in dreamless realm.

4

The worshipper should possess
A warrior within, and warrior should progress
As worshipper, to perfect success.

Verse 8

O Arjun ! O Parth !!
Keeping fixed the thought
By meditation made steadfast
Undeviated from the path,
Is sure to reach the Effulgent Lord.

1 STEADFAST WILL POWER

Worm thinks n thinks to fly
This conative thought made wings to arise
Transforms in the same life.

2 CONSTANT WORSHIP

The unbroken and steadfast
Flow of contemplative thought, stagnate not
Ultimate channel to the Lord.

3 ANCIENT HOME

A Sojourner be not possessive
To travels' earnings and learnings delusive,
Be fixed on the Native.

4

Endlessly remembering Him
At the end of life, reveals the Truth
Ending at Endless Supreme.

अभ्यासयोगयुक्तेन चेतसा नान्यगामिना।
परमं पुरुषं दिव्यं याति पार्थानुचिन्तयन्।।8.8।।

Verse 9 -10

Whoever bringeth to the consciousness
The Supreme as All-knowing Omniscient
As the Ancient of the ancients
All Who disciplineth, all Who sustainth
Beyond perception as subtlest of the elements
The dark Who transcends like Sun, the Effluent;

At the time of death
With unshaken mind who fixes
By yogic force, with full faith
And condenses who his flame-breath,
Between twin eyebrows by Yoga
He attainth this Divine God-head.

1

As well, I'm ancient
O Most Ancient ! but my ignorance
Kept me an infant.

2 MEDITATIVE EYES

In Imperceptibility of blurs
Mind's eye could single out clear
Beyond the physical Universe.

3 SHIV'S VISION OF YOGA

When Yogic eye grows
Above physical images * between two eyebrows
The Unknowable, glows.

4 THE DAWN

Lord affirmatively said
May not ignorance make you afraid
Of the Light I blessed.

5 YOGIC REALIZATION

Gross, subtle –all lifetron
All energies focus into thoughtron
To be one with ONE.

6 ETERNITY OF VISION

Dead in the mundane eyes
Dazed by vestigiality could not realize
Mind's eye never dies.

**visible through body eyes.*

कविं पुराणमनुशासितार, मणोरणीयांसमनुस्मरेद्यः।
सर्वस्य धातारमचिन्त्यरूप, मादित्यवर्णं तमसः
परस्तात्।।8.9।।

प्रयाणकाले मनसाऽचलेन, भक्त्या युक्तो योगबलेन चैव।
भ्रुवोर्मध्ये प्राणमावेश्य सम्यक्, स तं परं पुरुषमुपैति
दिव्यम्।।8.10।।

7

The physical existence takes leave

Its dust and ash return into native

Spiritual –remains, Yogis perceive.

8 SOUL'S PATH

Where life's vitality exhausts

If eternal consciousness is not lost

That obviously is Yogic path.

METHOD TO ATTAIN

Verse 11

That which, Vedic seers learn
As the immutable Absolute state
That which, renunciants of passion earn,
For such perfection, who live life chaste,
The process to attain that
Unto thou in brief, I'll relate.

1

Born to be true

That makes a run way in you

To take-off to the Absolute.

2

True is any path

Which seeker treads to seek the Truth

Makes it a true path.

3

Where lust have little space

Get the maximum chance for greatest access

Into path of Ultimate success.

4

Words, worships and will,

Many more human ways those reveal

Fulfilled God's will.

5 RENOUNCEMENT IS NATURAL

Shedding petals winsome,

Is the natural renunciation of natural blossom

Perfecting for the fruition.

यदक्षरं वेदविदो वदन्ति, विशन्ति यद्यतयो वीतरागाः।
यदिच्छन्तो ब्रह्मचर्यं चरन्ति, तत्ते पदं संग्रहेण प्रवक्ष्ये।।8.11।।

Verse 12 -13

Closing all the senses' access,
Mind in the deep who fixes
And the flame-breath in cerebral-dome
Putting himself into yogic practices,
Uttering sonic Manifestation 'AUM'
His Mind in Me keeping dipt,
Attains the Absolute, when the body he quits.

1 OCEAN OF MEDITATION
Through the waves in hush,
Dome beams of Sun just not surf
Penetrate into the benthos.

2 SAMADHI
Where mind confines, not roams
Further if refines by uttering 'AUM'
Finds soul at Home.

3 MEDITATING – 'AUM'
Hush ! the senses those thrum
Then meditate on 'AUM', universal vibrating hum,
To harmonize with Brahm.

4 SHUT GATES TO EXTERNAL WORLD
Dust storms and pathos
Enter through doors, so be closed
Let Sun knock the windows.

5 AUM
Music of Absolute silence
Which whispers into soul; that eternal melody
'AUM' is Lord's Sonic Advent.

6 RENUNCIATION IN LIFE
Even before the death owned
One who disowned his little owns
To the Deathless, has grown.

Verse 14

Yogi, who, with mindful mind on Me
Thoughts, on and on reclined on Me
O Parth ! he simply finds Me.

Thrum = unskilled play of instruments.

सर्वद्वाराणि संयम्य मनो हृदि निरुध्य च।
मूर्ध्न्याधायात्मनः प्राणमास्थितो योगधारणाम्।।8.12।।

ओमित्येकाक्षरं ब्रह्म व्याहरन्मामनुस्मरन्।
यः प्रयाति त्यजन्देहं स याति परमां गतिम्।।8.13।।

अनन्यचेताः सततं यो मां स्मरति नित्यशः।
तस्याहं सुलभः पार्थ नित्ययुक्तस्य योगिनः।।8.14।।

1 CONTINUANCE
The duteous routine
Of mechanical worships of machine
Never win.

2 HYMNAL BEAT
His soul into mine, the Supreme
Fills everyday every mo to the brim
Should overflow as hymn.

3 UNINTERRUPTED PRAYER
Awaken through matin to compline
Constant vigil reclined to the next matin
Revealed what's hidden within.

4 INCLINATION
Very many ways to reach
Constant remembrance is an inclined street
Where destination rolls to meet.

Verse 15

My great devotees
Having obtained Me
The Supreme state having achieved
Never take birth in abode of grief
The world which is short-lived.

1
Having dipt in ecstasy
Never toil, in mortal coil, the Yogis
For mere mass of pottage.

2
In world of cosmic dream
Where dreamless blessedness take origin
'Ts inception of Conscious Supreme.

3 REBIRTH CHAIN / MOKSH
Mortals are mortal pseudo,
Their Immortal form once they know,
To mortal world never go.

4 STATE OF REALIZATION
In middle of dream,
Conscious trance awakened me in realm
Of reality of Supreme.

Matin = morning prayer, Compline = last prayer at night.

मामुपेत्य पुनर्जन्म दुःखालयमशाश्वतम्।
नाप्नुवन्ति महात्मानः संसिद्धिं परमां गताः।।8.15।।

5 BEYOND WORLD OF SORROW
Soul is gravitated by ego,
Is conditioned to journey, to and fro,
Levitated-ones cross the woe.

MUNDANE CYCLE

Verse 16

Brahma's different cosmic planes
Yet not free, are places of rebirth chains,
But My abode once who attainth
O Arjun ! never taketh birth again.

1 WORLDLY DESIRES
Dreamers' run on thought road
In various circles in circumambulatory mode,
Fly not to Conscious Abode.

2 BEYOND GRAVITY OF BODY
Body conscious ego be ignited
With soul conscious fire to be established
Beyond its gravity to rocket.

3 LIBERATION FROM REBIRTH
From gravity of mundane
Soul rocketed in to super conscious plane
For no return, no change.

THE LIBERATING WAY

Verse 17

True knowers comprehend;*
'In a thousand aeons
Brahma's one day endth
As well a night of Brahma
Endth in aeons thousand' -
This day-night they understand.

*Yogis.

आब्रह्मभुवनाल्लोकाः पुनरावर्तिनोऽर्जुन।
मामुपेत्य तु कौन्तेय पुनर्जन्म न विद्यते।।8.16।।

सहस्रयुगपर्यन्तमहर्यद्ब्रह्मणो विदुः।
रात्रिं युगसहस्रान्तां तेऽहोरात्रविदो जनाः।।8.17।।

1 MY SMALL DAY
Knock of sun ray
Earth planet appreciates as day
What's for Sun itself?

2 CLOCK OF RELATIVITY
In the mind what dwells
That lengthens or shortens the Time scale,
To run or snail.

3 LORD'S CLOCK
In timeless conception
What is arithmetically counted 'at once'
Man timed it an aeon.

4 IMMORTALITY
Even Death has its death
In a wider noose will be trapped
Into Immortal-Time Lap.

5 RELATIVITY OF TIME SCALE
In the Creator's Infinite dial
Man sized clock picked one while,
Timed day–night cycle.

verse 18-19

At the dawn of Brahma's day
All manifest from the Unmanifested state
At dusk of Brahma's Night
All creation dissolves in that Unmanifest.

Again and Again at dawn
This throng of beings is reborn
And O Parth ! again Night falls
They all helplessly dissolve.

1 ORIGIN OF EXISTENCE
All Creation is but
A Pot-ness expansion dawned by big thud,
From condensed Unmanifest mud.

2
The Unmanifest, though is hidden
Doesn't mean the non-existent condition
But 'ts dormant one.

अव्यक्ताद्व्यक्तयः सर्वाः प्रभवन्त्यहरागमे।
रात्र्यागमे प्रलीयन्ते तत्रैवाव्यक्तसंज्ञके।।8.18।।

भूतग्रामः स एवायं भूत्वा भूत्वा प्रलीयते।
रात्र्यागमेऽवशः पार्थ प्रभवत्यहरागमे।।8.19।।

3 EVERY BEING IS ETERNAL
All the ancient days sum
To the Infinite endless days to come
Eternal Today thus termed.

4 CARRY FORWARD
Not capable to disinherit
The bundles of the merits and demerits
Unto all next worlds carried.

5 ONE ETERNAL THOUGHT-CURRENT
Thought-process earlier made
Since days of genesis have added
Into Beings' intellect.

6 SOUL
In string music rests
Thus playing violin manifests
'Ts helpless soul, lest.

Verse 20

But truly there existth
Beyond those unmanifested
The Absolute nature, that remainth as it is,
While all beings are extinguished.

1 CYCLE
From Unmanifest seed of genesis
Hath caused Itself into the manifest
Again for dissolution, quest.

2 THE UNMANIFESTED SOURCE
Beyond hide and seek plays,
So called birth-death's cyclic race
Remains One undying grace.

3 THE UNMANIFESTED SUPREME
The Maker on potter's wheels,
Makes shapes, sherds, shades, shells, shields
Own-self never revealed.

4 THE SUPREME
The Unmanifest manifests in sojourn,
But one eternal Unmanifest in its turn
Has nor coming nor return.

5 REALITY
What seems existent
Is never so ; what eternally remains
Doth exist, seeming non-existent.

Sherds = broken pieces of pots found in excavation.

परस्तस्मात्तु भावोऽन्योऽव्यक्तोऽव्यक्तात्सनातनः।
यः स सर्वेषु भूतेषु नश्यत्सु न विनश्यति।।8.20।।

Verse 21

The Unmanifest and Immutable as told
Is thus called the Supreme goal
That's My Supreme Abode, who restore
The rebirth, they have no more.

1 THE VIRAT
Where matter matters not
Where 'gross' dissolves fullest into microcosm,
In that, manifests the Vast.

2 ETERNAL DAY
Rise ! above skyline zone
Where east-west dissolve in imperishable Horizon
The Nightless day to own.

3
Changing the Changeable
Slow and Slow becomes transcendable
To attain the Unchangeable.

4
Where the Subtlest vastly embraces
It's warmth melts delusion into Consciousness,
Blunts all gross experiences.

Verse 22

Supreme personality of Godhead,
Within whom all beings dwell,
By whom all is pervaded
Could alone be attainable
O Parth ! by Bhakti unalloyed.

1
The Purest of the pure
Which subtly dwells in every core
Alone purest devotion explores.

2
Here – hereafter crowd,
Is crowded and shrouded with God alone
To unalloyed Bhakti its known.

अव्यक्तोऽक्षर इत्युक्तस्तमाहुः परमां गतिम्।
यं प्राप्य न निवर्तन्ते तद्धाम परमं मम।।8.21।।

पुरुषः स परः पार्थ भक्त्या लभ्यस्त्वनन्यया।
यस्यान्तःस्थानि भूतानि येन सर्वमिदं ततम्।।8.22।।

3 CONSCIOUS DESCENT
Serene awareness gains worth
Of the Unmanifest to project forth
As the manifested Truth.

4 'DEVOTION'- BEYOND GRAVITY
The whole-souled Soul
With its unalloyed fuel rockets to Goal
As destination of no return.

Verse 23

O Arjun ! now I narrate,
That very departing state
In which Yogis go never to return
As well the very state
They pass away to come back.

1
In steps, inclined gait
Run in gyrii in the circular race
While the Straight go straight.

2
Seekers in their turn
Either do yearn path of return
Or earn path of no return.

3 TWO HOLY PATHS
Both take to the Supreme,
One path takes me closer to Him,
Other dissolves into Him.

4 SALVATION FROM REBIRTH
The point of no return
In cyclical mode since I had begun
Need a mode turn.

5 LONELY PATH
Time gave me choice,
Busy to and fro, I stepped otherwise
Untrodden gave me height.

Verse 24

Pursuing auspicious path at demise
Which the enlightened fire presides
And path of daytime, path presided by deity of bright fortnight
Or six months of Northern solstice
Yogis through these Yogic
Paths to Brahmn reach.

यत्र काले त्वनावृत्तिमावृत्तिं चैव योगिनः।
प्रयाता यान्ति तं कालं वक्ष्यामि भरतर्षभ।।8.23।।

अग्निर्ज्योतिरहः शुक्लः षण्मासा उत्तरायणम्।
तत्र प्रयाता गच्छन्ति ब्रह्म ब्रह्मविदो जनाः।।8.24।।

1
A worthy life so named
An auspicious finish, has to have claimed
To attain worthy aim.

2
On the oriental threshold,
In cycdes of day-night of soul,
May eternal dawn unfold.

3 KNOWLEDGE WORKS
The flame-light-Sun preside
The path of very Soul, to decide
The dynamity of the demise.

4 YOGIC LIVING
An invisible torch within,
Accrued more flames in Yogi's living
And death blest all illumine.

5 LIBERATING ENLIGHTENMENT
Traveler Sun blest worth,
Auspicious end to travelers of the Earth
To go beyond rebirth.

6 WORTHY DEATH
My working thought
At this workable end has brought
To me worthy path.

Verse 25

Goer in smoke and night
In the dark moonless fortnight
While the sun travels southern, those six months
In presiding Lunar light in turn
Having blessed with the heaven
But that Yogi again returns.

1 LUNAR FORTNIGHTS WITH IN
Mind's miniature universe
Has waxing and waning urge,
To immerse or to emerge.

2 DELUSION TO CONSCIOUSNESS
Body conscious attires
In the altar of soul, once consumed entire
Torches path of soul.

3 DELUSIVE MIND
An Altar without fire
Is full of smoke that obscure
And corrupt the entire.

4 IGNORANTS
Goer of the Darkness
Dazed by light of Immortal consciousness
Can't break mortal bondage.

धूमो रात्रिस्तथा कृष्णः षण्मासा दक्षिणायनम्।
तत्र चान्द्रमसं ज्योतिर्योगी प्राप्य निवर्तते।।8.25।।

5 REBIRTH CYCLE
Darkness further dooms
More shapes of darkness to assume
In the dark womb.

6 PRESIDING PATH /DECIDING PATH
The light makes shades
Same 'light unmakes as well the shades
Beam's deviation makes difference.

Verse 26

Exiting ways are two
Reckoned as eternally true-
Light leads to redemption
while dark paths repeat returns.

1 STEADY PATH OF LIGHT
In the darkest night
Of many journeys, is blessed with light
Of polar star to guide.

2 CHANCE
The Destiny halved equal
Darkness and light in their vicious cycles
Turn ! probables into possible.

3 ALL REACH
Where ever I roam
In dark or day, all through the paths
One day reach home.

4 TWO PATHS
Extroversion and temptation
Introversion inner revolt for higher aspiration
Eternally tugged war of vision.

शुक्लकृष्णे गती ह्येते जगतः शाश्वते मते।
एकया यात्यनावृत्तिमन्ययाऽऽवर्तते पुनः।।8.26।।

Verse 27-28

Who understands two paths
Such Yogi is never deluded O Parth !
Therefore O Arjun ! in Yoga
At all time be steadfast.

Yogi, having known 'very That';
About fruits of Study of veds
And Yagna, charity, penance,
Rising beyond all merits
The Supreme-Origin Yogi meets.

1 THE KNOWING
To know of untruth
Is the first precious glimpse of Truth.
Route beyond all routes*

2 STEADFAST TO UNITE
All Ungodly eddies
Together can't obstruct river of Yogi
Meet ocean reaching estuary.

3 PATH OF MOKSHA
Penance, Procedures and texts
But are non-knowledge and go waste
Till brim over the soul.

4
Gross melts into fine
And knowledge into realization of mind
The Highest self to find.

5 PATH GOER
Steadfast man is known
To never ever get astrayed on path
He makes path of own.

6 MOKSHGAMI
Re identified on path of return
Once identifies self as 'unidentified traveler'
Walks on path of no return.

7 REALIZATION
Not the addition in knowledge,
But the absence of Non-Knowledge,
Discovered existent knowledge.

8 KNOWLEDGE, ITSELF THE SOUL
Soul is compressed knowledge, is
Synonym of the pure knowledge, the gnosis,
In itself Ultimate bliss.

* Methods estuary = where river meets ocean

नैते सृती पार्थ जानन्योगी मुह्यति कश्चन।
तस्मात्सर्वेषु कालेषु योगयुक्तो भवार्जुन।।8.27।।

वेदेषु यज्ञेषु तपःसु चैव, दानेषु यत्पुण्यफलं प्रदिष्टम्।
अत्येति तत्सर्वमिदं विदित्वा, योगी परं स्थानमुपैति चाद्यम्।।8.28।।

9 *MEDITATION – DIVINE SECRET*

A single pointed mind
On the way to imperishable goal, finds
His Single-pointed goal.

CHAPTER NINE

Right methods of Royal Knowledge: Raj -yog

None the mystery none secret,
All knowledge is knowable with ease
All knowing Lord promises.

It's faith alone,

Evolves and makes spirit of Lion

Of mere mass of man.

Chapter Nine

EASY WAY TO GOD

Verse 1

The Blessed Lord said –

To thou, who dost not cavil
Now I shalt reveal
Most secret and profound science,
Knowing which thou wilt
Be relieved of world's evils.

1
Non-envious alone is sacred
With mind dovetailed to pacific depth
To suit depth of secrets.

2 PURE MIND
To my clouded quiz
Simple rain of solution is His
That's uncorrupted sky's bliss.

3 KNOWLEDGE
Only to ope doors
Every dim of room limns to the fore,
Secret remains secret no more.

Verse 2

This very Knowledge is
Kingly science, the Royal secret
And Highest and purest is this
Brings perception of Truth, straight,
In Dharmic means its perfect
Its eternal, performed with ease.

इदं तु ते गुह्यतमं प्रवक्ष्याम्यनसूयवे।
ज्ञानं विज्ञानसहितं यज्ज्ञात्वा मोक्ष्यसेऽशुभात्।।9.1।।

राजविद्या राजगुह्यं पवित्रमिदमुत्तमम्।
प्रत्यक्षावगमं धर्म्यं सुसुखं कर्तुमव्ययम्।।9.2।।

1 EASE OF KNOWING
How wiser is the All-Wise
In formatting thoughts, which is otherwise,
Be perfected to realize.

2 MYSTERY
None the mystery none secret,
All knowledge is knowable with ease
All knowing Lord promises.

3 ROYAL SCIENCE- RAJ YOGA
Where knowledge avails
Comprehension of the Pious with in it,
Science is available to the Self.

4 INNER PERCEPTION
Only firm faithful pursuit
In din of Ignorance, the intuitive mute
Is easy way to the Absolute.

Verse 3

In this Dharma who have no faith,
Attain Me not, O Scorcher of foes !
But to path of world fraught with death,
Again and again he goes.

1 MEN OF EXTROVERSION
For worldly world who fought
Beyond this world he attains not,
Gets rebirth, with death fraught.

2 FAITH
With Him a virtuous bond,
Its ever eternal strong
Lo ! this faith O Vagabond !

3 CHANGEABLE WORLD
Aiming at changeable state
Any change to previous brings death
Every change tastes birth, next.

4 DEVOLUTION THOUGHT.
Lord created heavens and heavens
Bonded with faith the heaven on Earth,
Here perfidity is alien.

Perfidity =faithlessness.

अश्रद्दधानाः पुरुषा धर्मस्यास्य परन्तप।
अप्राप्य मां निवर्तन्ते मृत्युसंसारवर्त्मनि।।9.3।।

5 CROSSING THE BAR
The faith is the boat
To cross impassable gulf of world
A faithless can't board.

6
It's faith alone,
Evolves and makes spirit of Lion
Of mere mass of man.

ALL-PERVADING LORD YET ALL ALOOF

Verse 4-5

In My Unmanifest aspect
By Me whole existence is pervaded
All beings in Me dost reside
But in them I dost not abide.

Nor do Beings really exist in Me
My Divine mystery see !
Nor doth My Self in them lodge,
Yet I alone am All-Being's efficient cause.

1 MEETING POINT
Lord 's a circle Infinite
With infinite number of Finite
Centers every where to meet.

2 'TRUTH REALIZED
More the Unmanifest vitalized
More the manifested world is realized
-To be false.

3 HE IS HERE
God is Infinite instinct
Perpetually imbued in all brief things
Yet God is distinct.

4 SEARCH OF OMNIPRESENT
In the finite Manifest,
There is a definite Infinite quest
Of pervading Unmanifest.

5 WORLDLY DELUSIONS
The Real pervades as Divine,
Into unreal apparently, which designs
As real redefined.

6
Ethereal products the Maker makes
But all unreal by-products we take
As real, making mistake.

मया ततमिदं सर्वं जगदव्यक्तमूर्तिना।
मत्स्थानि सर्वभूतानि न चाहं तेष्ववस्थितः।।9.4।।

न च मत्स्थानि भूतानि पश्य मे योगमैश्वरम्।
भूतभृन्न च भूतस्थो ममात्मा भूतभावनः।।9.5।।

7 YOGIC POWER
Many changeable shapeless shapes
By immutable energy of the conscious sap
Melt into unnamable origin-less.

8 GOD REALIZATION
Where Opacity turns transparent
Yogi's transcendence brings Lord at once
Immanent and transcendent.

9 IMPERCEPTIBLE PART
With unexhaustive godly features
God expanded Self, into gross creatures
With own subtle substructure.

10 THE ABSTRUSE
All with God imbued,
Is subjected to ungodly world that deludes
What a mystery brewed.

Verse 6

Blowing all about as the mighty wind,
Always rest in space of the welkin
All beings, you know!
Rest in Me, even so.

1
Gross gets support of subtle
As non-self of the Self, Unreal of Real,
Yet Gross can't condition Subtle.

2 PARADOX OF CREATION
The Creator of gross–subtle
Puts subtle in all gross as vital
Which never gets entangled.

3 GOD IS ALOOF
In biggest Manifest space,
Many God-made apparent things rest
But this Unmanifest keep detached.

4 AEOLIAN CREATION
The Sky never shifts
Although cloud and wind make drift
Thus Mutables in Immutable exist.

यथाऽऽकाशस्थितो नित्यं वायुः सर्वत्रगो महान्।
तथा सर्वाणि भूतानि मत्स्थानीत्युपधारय।।9.6।।

Verse 7-8

O Kunti's Son !
At the end of aeon,
All beings dost return
Into My cosmic nature,
And aeon that begins next
All, again I create.

Revivifying My very Nature
I again and again send forth
Multitudes of the creatures,
All subject to Nature's force.

1 FOREVER AND A DAY – KALP
All the yesterdays end
Into halted today of timeless aeon
New today, the Creator then commence.

2 WE, BEYOND TIME
Time nor ends nor commence
The Eternal soul is so infinitely timed
We are in eternal present tense.

3 ALMIGHTY'S PLAN
Why wish to conclude,
While His will is to commence,
All lie at His end.

4 CHANGING KALP
Every end has
The endless eternity, That blessed
The beginning of Infinity.

5 CYCLICAL CREATION
Time, Space and Beings
Into timeless spaceless Nature shrink,
Again unfurl from very Origin.

6 HIS WILL
I'm one Small multiply
From compressed energy into phenomenal size,
Lord's will thus revivifies.

7 THE ULTIMATE
The Supernature is so uniform
It concludes all forms into formless
Ends where it started from.

सर्वभूतानि कौन्तेय प्रकृतिं यान्ति मामिकाम्।
कल्पक्षये पुनस्तानि कल्पादौ विसृजाम्यहम्।।9.7।।

प्रकृतिं स्वामवष्टभ्य विसृजामि पुनः पुनः।
भूतग्राममिमं कृत्स्नमवशं प्रकृतेर्वशात्।।9.8।।

Verse 9

All these deeds
O Arjun ! Cannot entrammel Me, indeed,
I'm ever detached thus
Witnessing like one unbiased.

1 BIASED WORLD
'World' for it carried
Is called so, for its dualities
Lest, is Godly deed.

2
From Egocentric lustful deeds,
To the Egoless non attached feat is journey
Of Mind to the Self.

3 MATERIAL WORLD AND LORD
Though involved is Referee's feat
Never is engaged in player's game -deeds
Neutral to victory or defeat.

4
The Unbias deeds of Lord
Are the pious deeds of Lord, for
His Non-attachment to fruits.

Verse 10

As I dost direct
Mother Prakriti doth create
The Animate and inanimate
*Thus, the world cycle alternates.**

1 NATURE SEEMS DOER
Supreme Doer is the cause
Of the Nature, among its flaws
To implement Doer's laws.

2
Mother Nature's naturality
Is naturally borrowed and achieved from
All pervading Divinity.

3
Of the Energy, the Unseen
Of all the things and non things
He is the origin.

4 CREATOR'S WORKING HAND
Creating 'Nature' the Creator proposed
In matters of all matters; in auto-mode
The Nature to dispose.

Entrammel = entangle. **of creation and dissolution.*

न च मां तानि कर्माणि निबध्नन्ति धनञ्जय।
उदासीनवदासीनमसक्तं तेषु कर्मसु।।9.9।।

मयाऽध्यक्षेण प्रकृतिः सूयते सचराचरम्।
हेतुनाऽनेन कौन्तेय जगद्विपरिवर्तते।।9.10।।

5
The Action-free Supreme creates*
The Nature, His power He delegates
To the Nature to act.

Verse 11-12

When in Human form I descend
Disregard Me, the lack-brains
Unaware of My transcendental nature
As the Creator of all creatures.

Bewildered by delusion Those who,
Of vain vision, vain action, reason too
Are attracted by demonic, atheistic view.

1 AVTAAR
The Unmanifest is farthest
His Human form is though closest
Is Closed to deluded quest.

2
The Absolute existence I feel,
Most dynamic in Human form it reveals
Where visibly He exists.

3 AVTAAR
Human incarnation messaged thus,
The Infinite could not limit His opus
Truly became one of us.

4
Man actually sees
The Shapeless Absolute Lord through these
Man –Shaped phiz.

5
With their opaque insight
*Very transparent** Maker of their eyes*
Dazzled fools never visualized.

6 DELUSIVE CYCLE
The undesired desires
Lead to undesired actions to acquire
Baser nature and lesser desires.

* Not bound to Action (Karma) **Obvious

अवजानन्ति मां मूढा मानुषीं तनुमाश्रितम्।
परं भावमजानन्तो मम भूतमहेश्वरम्।।9.11।।

मोघाशा मोघकर्माणो मोघज्ञाना विचेतसः।
राक्षसीमासुरीं चैव प्रकृतिं मोहिनीं श्रिताः।।9.12।।

7 NON-BELIEVER
Who derides pure flame
Not as incarnated fire but ignited sham
Only Ash that fool claims.

8 DEMONIC – REBIRTH
Thrust again and again,
Into Flesh until man comprehends
The flesh is all vain.

9 ATHEIST
He derides Lord
This decides in itself he,
Denies not, the Lord.

10 I DERIDE MYSELF
My delusion derides
The Man sized coming, to make man pride
Of His man-size.

11 ATHEIST
An atheist concept
As the God's puppet, he disrespect
Through his hidden faith.

Verse 13-14

Partaking the divine nature in Me
O Parth ! Great souls revere Me
With undeviated mind to Me
Knowing Me, as eternal source of all life,
Constantly dipt in me,
Firm in vow, fixed in Me
Bowing low glorify Me
With Love deify Me.

1 A WORSHIPPER
God has truly put
Little bit of God in him
That alone worships Supreme.

2 PROPER PLACE
Blest breath and dipt thoughts
Are dovetailed first with the God
Rest fall in lesser slots.

महात्मानस्तु मां पार्थ दैवीं प्रकृतिमाश्रिताः।
भजन्त्यनन्यमनसो ज्ञात्वा भूतादिमव्ययम्।।9.13।।

सततं कीर्तयन्तो मां यतन्तश्च दृढव्रताः।
नमस्यन्तश्च मां भक्त्या नित्ययुक्ता उपासते।।9.14।।

3 ABSORBED IN LORD

His Blest prayers are those,
Which know not for loud echoes
Dipped in whispers so close.

4 ABSORBED AND FIXED MIND

Emptying from things,
Filling it with Divinity of Non-things
All fulfillment brings.

5 PARTAKING DIVINITY

In surfing slaps, the flotsam
Absorbing deeper into it, the Divine wisdom
Settles in serene bottom.

Verse 15

Offering Gyan-yagna, the Wisdom
Also worship Me some.*
As Distinct, as well as Manifolds
Regarding Me also as One, they extol.

1 MANY-FOLD

Offering through many-ways,
Man worships many divine visages
All end up in 'ONE Blessed'.

2 ONENESS

Distinct worships, Distinct names
Conclude in phenomenal multiple attempts
Finally One Flame, very same.

3 EVOLVING KNOWLEDGE

Through many learnings he extols
First learning God exists in All
Then All existence is God.

4 The 'ONE' - TRUTH

Pluralistic of opposing mirrors
Where the Infinite multiplicity appears
While One ray truly enters.

*Some others (Gyani)

ज्ञानयज्ञेन चाप्यन्ये यजन्तो मामुपासते।
एकत्वेन पृथक्त्वेन बहुधा विश्वतोमुखम्।।9.15।।

Verse 16

But 'ts I who am
The rite, sacrificial Yagna I'm
I'm offering to the paters
*I'm the healing herb**
The Sacred chant –mantra I'm
Also I'm fueling Butter
I'm oblation and am fire of altar.

1 DIVINITY EVERYWHERE
The Gem, its mine,
Its raw, 'ts cut, glow, shine, design
Borrows everything from Divine.

2
Where the action consists
Of Divine essence constituting every bit
Such happening is worship.

3 ALL – HIS
Devotee, his devoted oblations,
Worships,words,rites, hymns, texts, petitions
*Mutual Gifts** all Lord's donations.*

4 GOD IN ALL CONSTITUENTS
The walker, the walk and aim,
God the means, métier, medium, lane.
Discretion, vision and flame.

5 YAGNA – SACRED ACTION
Obliged oblating worshipper
In turn honours Lord as the Giver
As Offering itself n the Receiver.

Verse 17

The father, the Mother I 'm Ancestor
Of this 'Jagat' I'm supporter
I'm knowable cosmic 'AUM' pure
Also Rik, Sama, Yajuh vedic lore.

**used as consumable in Yagna. Metier =profession/Nature.   **oblations(in turn) to Lord.*

अहं क्रतुरहं यज्ञः स्वधाऽहमहमौषधम्।
मंत्रोऽहमहमेवाज्यमहमग्निरहं हुतम्।।9.16।।

पिताऽहमस्य जगतो माता धाता पितामहः।
वेद्यं पवित्रमोंकार ऋक् साम यजुरेव च।।9.17।।

1 INFINITE KINSHIP
The world timed all relations,
Ultimate binding with that ONE
Has no Time's invasion.

2 SONIC POTENTIAL –AUM
The Unknown is known
When He becometh Knowable through 'Aum'
Vibration that every soul owns.

3 KNOWING 'AUM'
The Soul elixired with 'AUM'
Immerges into one vedic theme,
Reality of Supreme.

4 INFINITE KINSHIP
The Supreme is Origin,
Of All kindred pedigree of changing paters,
He's ever next of Kin.

5 SONIC MANIFESTATION
Container differs from content
Worldly din is different from Conscious silence
Of 'AUM' contained in existence.

Verse 18

I 'm sustainer, the Ultimate Goal
I'm Master, Most intimate to uphold
I'm Maker, destroyer and Basis
I'm Observer, Refuge and dwelling seat
I'm Nidhanam and eternally Ancient seed.*

1 ONE DIVINE
Being Ignorant to Divinity,
In the dreamy screen on the reality
World seems of plurality.

2 GOD, THE BOSOM FRIEND
May I not fall !
For He and me are witness
Of being Mutual pal.

3 LORD THE WITNESS
One Conscious Supreme
Observes every blueprint of delusive extremes
Of every cosmic dream.

4 AGELESS SEED
At infinity I gazed
That made me Infinitely amazed
That I'm very That.

* Nidhanam = Final-treasure, where all souls in their subtle form dissolve.

गतिर्भर्ता प्रभुः साक्षी निवासः शरणं सुहृत्।
प्रभवः प्रलयः स्थानं निधानं बीजमव्ययम् //9.18//

5 NIDHANAM
Being end of all origins
Being all beings earths and welkins
Infinite is finites' infinite kin.

Verse 19

O Arjun ! I 'm heat and
Bestow or withhold rains.
Immortality also Death I am
Both the Existence and I 'm the Non-existence.

1 THE WEATHER, HE IS
As blessed or ablazed sun,
The Unmanifest avails reason, in turn
And manifests Himself as season.

2 POTENTIAL TO RISE
Immutable creates mutable
With immortal potential to rise out of mortals
To change into changeless self.

3 HIS INSTRUMENT, SUN
Conditioned to be phenom
As existent tool of Energy that's Noumenon
A planet phenomenalized as 'Sun'

तपाम्यहमहं वर्षं निगृह्णाम्युत्सृजामि च।
अमृतं चैव मृत्युश्च सदसच्चाहमर्जुन।।9.19।।

RIGHT WORSHIP

Verse 20-21

Vedic ritualistics by 'some' rites*
Cleansing themselves from vice
Praying way to paradise
Worshiping Me by Yagna-sacrifice
They sublime to heaven's height
And enjoy the celestial delights.

But after these heavenly mirths
At ceasing of Good 'Karma' worth
They again return to mortal Earth
Thus Vedic rites who follow
Between heaven and mundane
Travel to and fro.

1 RITUAL PERFORMANCE
Elixired with vedic disciplines
Mortal immorality getting cleansed of sins,
The moral immortality wins.

2 SPIRITUAL RITES
Most sacred are the rites
Those right all wrongs of lesser height
To the Supremest abide.

3 RITUALS
Rites are scriptural,
Rightly by inches rise to spiritual
To reach the Very Real.

4 RITES FOR HEAVENLY ABODE
Not for Supreme but gifts
Though astral level the rites do meet
But for inevitable exit.

5
Scriptural rituals in dream
Dreaming of further unrealistic realm
Keeps from the Supreme.

6
Texts, if work as maps
To celestial gifts then those astray
From 'Destination-Self'

**who study three veds (as mentioned in verse 17/Ch9)*

त्रैविद्या मां सोमपाः पूतपापा
यज्ञैरिष्ट्वा स्वर्गतिं प्रार्थयन्ते।
ते पुण्यमासाद्य सुरेन्द्रलोक
मश्नन्ति दिव्यान्दिवि देवभोगान्।।9.20।।

ते तं भुक्त्वा स्वर्गलोकं विशालं
क्षीणे पुण्ये मर्त्यलोकं विशन्ति।
एव त्रयीधर्ममनुप्रपन्ना
गतागतं कामकामा लभन्ते।।9.21।।

7
Unintelligent seeker abide
To flotsam desires of surfing rites
Suffer flood of rebirth-tides.

Verse 22

With All devotion who worship
Unto Me, who are ever dipt,
I secure what they possess
What they have not, I bless.

1 FULL DEVOTION
Plenty, with no paucity
Open more and more potency
To perfect 'The Totality'.

2
Being one with the 'ONE'
Always possessed have won
That very ONE.

3 AT HIS WILL
My imperfect hand is,
Hand in hand with the Perfect God
Unworried of gain or guard.

4 BHAKTI
To the Lord Subdued
Brought more and more devotion true
Of Lord to you.

5
The surrendered man
Has no worry to guard or gain
Lord promises to maintain.

Verse 23

Who worship other gods and credo
But with full faith endowed
Even they, worship Me alone, just
In no true understanding, but.

अनन्याश्चिन्तयन्तो मां ये जनाः पर्युपासते।
तेषां नित्याभियुक्तानां योगक्षेमं वहाम्यहम्।।9.22।।

येऽप्यन्यदेवता भक्ता यजन्ते श्रद्धयाऽन्विताः।
तेऽपि मामेव कौन्तेय यजन्त्यविधिपूर्वकम्।।9.23।।

1

Silence, whispers or din,
But with faith; bypassing the mean
Is heard and esteemed.

2 *WORSHIP HEARD*

A Song is song,
Till learning of leaning, rights all wrongs
Making song more than song.

3 *ALL PRAYERS BUT FOR ONE*

Labyrinthine ways universally occur
In silence of folded hands, in pealing words
In any faith never diverge.

4 *DEVOTION*

'Ts heart
Nothing else
Which is heard.

5 *YOGA*

Without second, He, the One
Accepts any faith, devotion petition, orison
Into His silent Union.

6 *LESSER APPROACH*

With the primitive procedures
They achieve the petty lesser world
Of chain of rebirth.

Verse 24

Only object Enjoyer indeed I 'm
And Lord of Yagna-deeds I 'm
Till who know not My true essence
They fall to rebirth, hence.

1

Should devotee master worship
For joy of Master-Enjoyer, the Lord
For my Joy's all His.

2 *SIMPLE FAITH*

Lesser paths, lesser names
Reach no where; but great aim
Itself to simple Bhakt came.

3 *PETTY WORSHIPPER*

With lesser bid
Lesser potential is invoked, instead
To return to worldly limits.

4 *DAILY STEPS TO REDEMPTION*

My infinite pasts
Added my daily joy unto Supreme Enjoyer
To gain Timeless future.

अहं हि सर्वयज्ञानां भोक्ता च प्रभुरेव च।
न तु मामभिजानन्ति तत्त्वेनातश्च्यवन्ति ते।।9.24।।

Verse 25

Striver of demigods, deities,
And who seek ghosts and spirits
Go to their particular ambits
Worshipper of ancestors go to manes
Me, My devotee alone attains.

1
Lesser the worship
With all its stretch, have short leap
Short to reach the Supreme.

2
Lord assures sure success,
It's we to aim Supreme goal
No lesser compromise.

3 PRECISE WORSHIPS
Short and rightly prayed
Are the complete and shorter ways
Over long anthems strayed.

4
Naturally, the Nature
And thought would chisel and sculpture
My reach into future.

5
The imperfect worship
Will not bring imperfection to Divine Lordship
But Human 'll be imperfect.

Verse 26

Whoever unto Me
With serene devotion offers
A leaf, even flower
A fruit or water
I do accept the very
Reverent offering of devotee.

यान्ति देवव्रता देवान् पितॄन्यान्ति पितृव्रताः।
भूतानि यान्ति भूतेज्या यान्ति मद्याजिनोऽपि माम्।।9.25।।

पत्रं पुष्पं फलं तोयं यो मे भक्त्या प्रयच्छति।
तदहं भक्त्युपहृतमश्नामि प्रयतात्मनः।।9.26।।

1
The poorest belongings
With purest longing to Him
Are most precious offerings.

2
His matter, His mundane,
Every thing, every non-thing is His
My part – my reverence.

3
Serenest offering
Is with certain small things
But with certain love.

4 BHAKTI – MATTERS
It's not just honey
but the honey honeyed with reverence
Elixirs votary with His Grace.

5 LORD'S SCALE
Not the size of offering
But the size of faith, the votary had
Magnifies offerings he made.

Verse 27

Whatever one acts
Eats, oblates or donates
O Arjun ! also the penance be
Done, as offering unto Me.

1
When all the doings
Are done in the spirit of offerings
Reach the Supreme Doer.

2 DONATION
In account of life-spans
Giving away transaction; into my Balance
Credits high interest of Lord.

3 OFFERING ALL TO HIM
Ope hands stretched low
Oblating offerings have more magnitude
Over raised folded hands empty.

4
Handful of routine words
This prayer offered to Him as child offers
Toys to the Father.

5
In the spirit of offering
To the King of kings everything
Is princely before Him.

यत्करोषि यदश्नासि यज्जुहोषि ददासि यत्।
यत्तपस्यसि कौन्तेय तत्कुरुष्व मदर्पणम्।।9.27।।

Verse 28

With such renunciation in mind,
Thus no fruit of Karma can bind
With good or evil deeds;
In this way one will be freed
And come to Me, indeed.

1 SURRENDERING ACTIONS
The Karma bound –Destined,
Renouncing everything unto Him, will win
Emergence from the Sin.

2
Renouncement in mind
And karmic hands emptied of fruition; find
The Lord enshrined.

3
Not from the Action
But renouncing cravings for fruits
Is expression of renunciation.

4 UNBINDING KEY
Ever in binding mode
The Action bound to mundane, be bound
To the Lord, to decode.

5 PURE ACTION
Any sincere deed
From fruition; attention freed
Is liberated and complete.

6 LORD'S WORDS
Renouncing fruit
Ripens his untrodden route
To Me, the Absolute.

Verse 29

I'm partial to none
I envy no one
Towards all I'm equal
But My devouts are my pal;
Who worship Me with love,
Are in Me, I 'm in them as well.

शुभाशुभफलैरेवं मोक्ष्यसे कर्मबन्धनैः।
संन्यासयोगयुक्तात्मा विमुक्तो मामुपैष्यसि।।9.28।।

समोऽहं सर्वभूतेषु न मे द्वेष्योऽस्ति न प्रियः।
ये भजन्ति तु मां भक्त्या मयि ते तेषु
चाप्यहम्।।9.29।।

1 ALL INVASIVE GRACE
No one should see
The Blind-end near or far to plea
For the Divine mercy.

2 MUTUAL BOND
As much I ope
My love, to permeate into Him
His Self permeates into me.

3 DEVOTEES/ NON DEVOTEES
Through equally blessed the rain,
The Unbiased clouds on tilled farm relent
Better than the barren.

4 THE OMNIPRESENT
He pervades all
He is interfused in devout as pal
(is) but ancient friend of all.

5 INTO EACH OTHER
Thought force of Love
Raises closer and closer to total Oneness
Of contemplative peak above.

Verse 30

Even a gross sinner involved
In My devotion, away from all else
Because of his righteous resolve
May be counted among the Blessed.

1 ASSURED
The devotional process,
Inspite of many labyrinthine ways
Always gets success.

2 TRANSFORMATION
Lord condemns the sin
Not the sinner, who can win
Itself the Sin.

3 POTENTIAL TO COME BACK
Words of Lord assure
Here souls are not lost forever
Heritage of soul may recover.

4 UNDEVIATED DEVOTION
Not the lot of mind
But the single beat of single heart
Meets the 'Lord'

Relent = yield

अपि चेत्सुदुराचारो भजते मामनन्यभाक्।
साधुरेव स मन्तव्यः सम्यग्व्यवसितो हि सः।।9.30।।

5 NOBLE DECISION
A culprit in the pit
Alone with sublime resolution someday
May meet perfect summit.

Verse 31

He will become virtuous fast
And sure attain peace that lasts.
Know Just declaration O Arjun !
My devotee is never ruined.

1 MAN'S RESOLUTION
Even for sins thronged
Man is made so perfect and strong
To right all wrongs

2 ADVENT RESOLVE
Resolution to be right
Is no success route to the peace,
Its peace in itself.

3 VIRTUES DIE NOT
Though bodies die
But devout with devotions is ever survived
By right steps of resolve.

4
At war with sins
In a strong resolve that brings
The long lasting Peace within.

5
From any muddy land,
Virtuous steps of ardent footings of man
Begin the very pilgrimage.

Verse 32

For taking refuge
In Me O Parth !
Women, Vaishya, lesser or sinful birth
Even they can attain the Supreme worth.

क्षिप्रं भवति धर्मात्मा शश्वच्छान्तिं निगच्छति।
कौन्तेय प्रतिजानीहि न मे भक्तः प्रणश्यति।।9.31।।

मां हि पार्थ व्यपाश्रित्य येऽपि स्युः पापयोनयः।
स्त्रियो वैश्यास्तथा शूद्रास्तेऽपि यान्ति परां गतिम्।।9.32।।

1 DIVINE SHELTER

It's man-made noose,
In soulful realm inequality is refused
No fragments in His refuge.

2 UNBIAS LORD

Warm worships vapour up
Of river, rocks, soil or Main
Clouds bless equal rain.

3 ONLY REFUGE THROUGH DEVOTION

With grass mud I thatched
But found a refuge within to rest
Where He doth rest.*

4

Nor the congenital averse,
Lord sees, nor the acquired commerce
Alone, the soul immersed.

5 CHILDREN OF SUPREME KINGDOM

In eternal family tree
In reality, there is no relativity
Coheir the Absolute equally.

Verse 33

In context how easy then,
For Born-pious, Brahmans,
And High saints to attain,
Having (even) obtained
Brief lived, grief lived mundane,
Adore Me ardent.

1 FOR PIOUS IT'S EASIER

What's simple for laden evolutes
For spontaneous Pious its spontaneous route
To access the Absolute.

2 EASY TO ATTAIN

Deluded wicked called it hell,
This is no world but God himself
Only pious perfect beheld.

3 UNLADEN TRAVEL

In the short sojourns,
Be traveler selective in what to earn
For unladen back home ease.

4 PERFECTION IS SUCCESS

Even Sinful retrace Home
How perfect should be journey for perfects
Who are born phenom.

*The Lord. Phenom = Authority (sages).

किं पुनर्ब्राह्मणाः पुण्या भक्ता राजर्षयस्तथा।
अनित्यमसुखं लोकमिमं प्राप्य भजस्व माम्।।9.33।।

Verse 34

You be My devotee
Unto Me let mind be fixed
Offer Me obeisance and worship
Having thus united your whole
Taking Me as Supreme Goal
You shalt be Mine own.

1 MEDITATES AND UNITES
Mind full to the shore,
Makes own ocean to further drown the mind
Divinity fills thus, core.

2 BHAKTI
Your Little self,
By Breaking everything else,
Fix in canvas of 'Self'.

3 REDEMPTION
Drop by drop slow
Let this droplet unto ocean flow
Dissolve to evolve to ocean.

मन्मना भव मद्भक्तो मद्याजी मां नमस्कुरु।
मामेवैष्यसि युक्त्वैवमात्मानं मत्परायणः।।9.34।।

CHAPTER TEN

Omnipresence of the Supreme

His love for us
Has blessed very insight into us
How to Love Him.

My devotion is His relish

My love is my way of worship,

My insight is His Lord-ship.

Chapter Ten

THE UNBORN AND FORMLESS

Verse 1

The Blessed Lord said –

O Arjun ! hark !!
More of My Supreme Remarks
Wishing thy highest good I further voice
To thou, who listenth Me with rejoice.

1
Happiness is devout's art
That delights the Supreme to further impart
More of Divine part.

2
Let us attune all ears,
To whispers of Lord with eternal echo
Divine calmness to treasure.

3
Once bliss calls
Listen ! opening doors by God as pal,
Where there were only walls.

4 WELLWISHER LORD
With devotion listen !
Lowering the din of all delusions
Heed ! Lords' concern.

5
Perfectly blessed is, who
Truly listens to God's words, God's mute
Thus perfecting own virtues.

Verse 2

Nor ethereal hosts nor earthly Rishis,*
Know My uncreated Genesis
For Devas and Rishis too
In Me, have an Origin.

**Spiritual sages.*

भूय एव महाबाहो श्रृणु मे परमं वचः।
यत्तेऽहं प्रीयमाणाय वक्ष्यामि हितकाम्यया।।10.1।।

न मे विदुः सुरगणाः प्रभवं न महर्षयः।
अहमादिर्हि देवानां महर्षीणां च सर्वशः।।10.2।।

1 RELATIVE TRUTH
Reformed and Reformers know
Sustaining forms of the formless Truth,
As step to know Absolute.

2
From womb of Origin-less,
Celestials and Created-beings are born
Have limits, this be known.

3
Ever the Absolute
Is the conscious object that perceives
Beyond the subjective Truth.

4 THE OMNISCIENT
The Earth even when etherealized
Will come up with the reality, realized
The All-knowing Lord alone knows.

Verse 3

He, who among the mortals
Knows Me as Unborn, beyond Origin
Knows Me as Supreme Lord of worlds
Is liberated from all sins.

1
Conditional souls change frames
Supreme hath many forms many names
Yet Unconditional, Unborn ever same.

2
Among things and non-thing stuff,
Knows, 'He is ahead', is Known enough,
To be freed of All sins.

3
Reformed and Reformable stuff
Evolved of the Virat, are lesser ever
To That Uncreated Creator.

4
Transcending to Serenest of serene,
Constitutional position of Immunity he wins
From contamination by sins.

यो मामजमनादिं च वेत्ति लोकमहेश्वरम्।
असम्मूढः स मर्त्येषु सर्वपापैः प्रमुच्यते।।10.3।।

LORD'S NATURE

Verse 4-5

Intellect, wisdom, non-delusion and pardon,
Honesty, self-control, self-compose, Joy-sting.
Birth-death, fear-courage non violence equality,
Contentment, Penance, beneficence, fame and infamy.
These states of beings
From Me alone, all spring.

1
God goaded Bad and Good
So the man is natured out of crude
All in His blessed mood.

2 ONE SOURCE
All contrasting potential in man,
And density of triple Gunas in destiny pattern*
Alone, the Lord ordained.

3
Plurality is mind's course,
Caused to its efficiency with varied force
Ever has one Supreme source.

4 PATH OF DISPARITY
Journeying in contrasts two
Rejecting a few, gathering refined few
At last find second-less Truth.

**Triple Nature Traits-Divine=Sat/ Terrene=Raj/ Malign=Tam.*

बुद्धिर्ज्ञानमसंमोहः क्षमा सत्यं दमः शमः।
सुखं दुःखं भवोऽभावो भयं चाभयमेव च।।10.4।।

अहिंसा समता तुष्टिस्तपो दानं यशोऽयशः।
भवन्ति भावा भूतानां मत्त एव पृथग्विधाः।।10.5।।

Verse 6

Seven great sages, further more
*Ancient primeval four**
*And Manus***, progenitor of mankind,*
Endowed with creative strength of Mine,
From whom all creatures are born
All are born out of My Mind.

1
I'm child of thought,
Manifested yesterday in Mind of Lord
Thus Today's mankind is brought.

2
All men, all possible men
All gods, all possible gods emerged
As Supreme's creative urge.

3
Out of oceanic Supreme
Born vapours of cloudy and sunny theme
Thoughts stream again to ocean.

4 'PROUD' - PURE ANCESTORS
Unto chains of fathers, serene
Son's blur through their transparence has seen
The Serenest, most Ancient Supreme.

Sanat , Sanandan, Sanatan, Sanatkumar.* * 14 Manus.*

महर्षयः सप्त पूर्वे चत्वारो मनवस्तथा।
मद्भावा मानसा जाता येषां लोक इमाः प्रजाः।।10.6।।

WISE WAY TO ADORE

Verse 7 -8

Who truly knows all about,
My divine kudos and Yogic clout,
Unite to Me as Unshakable devout;
This is beyond doubt.

From Me all creations arise,
For everything I'm the source
With this realization, the Wise
Me, with all his heart, adores.

1 TRUE KNOWLEDGE
It is highest Summit,
Of all learning, leaning, lettering is
To perceive Supreme Spirit.

2 DIP INTO
Mindful worships not a few
All are empty; till emerges the view,
True knowledge to immerse into.

3
Man can alone know,
Worships or worshipped one when endowed,
With surrendered conscious love.

4 BHAKTI
A Bhakt knows,
For the Lord, his wise-stand is
That he bows.

5 OMNIPRESENT LORD
To know this is enough –
All matters and Non matters are puffed
With one Divine stuff.

6 CONSCIOUS WORSHIP
True worshipper finds not
His ego identified by prayers to Lord
Identified himself in the Worshipped.

7 TRUE DEVOTION
My path to adore
Is an unshakable soul more and more
Transfixed to Lord's Grandeur.

Clout=Power

एतां विभूतिं योगं च मम यो वेत्ति तत्त्वतः।
सोऽविकम्पेन योगेन युज्यते नात्र संशयः।।10.7।।

अहं सर्वस्य प्रभवो मत्तः सर्वं प्रवर्तते।
इति मत्वा भजन्ते मां बुधा भावसमन्विताः।।10.8।।

Verse 9

Their thinking dipt in Me
Their being they submit to Me
Proclaiming Me ever, Enlightening each other
My devouts find bliss and rapture.

1 TALK OF GOD
Bhakti sown on wholehearted earth
Cared, watered with more Bhakti, is worth
Fructify more seeds to dispense.

2 THE VOICE
'Ts manner of soul,
Not just the matter of discourse, done
Reflects through course of tongue.

3 DISCUSSIONS/SHARING KNOWLEDGE.
The mud threatening a slip
Mutually watching with hand in hand grip
Strengthening each other, All reach.

4 TALK OF GOD
Dipt mind should rise
On horizon of soul as speaking eyes
Every sense as Bhakti's voice.

5 MUTUAL LEARNING
Books are silent, can't discuss,
Let all strayed letters converge, bringing us
Together at Divine Focus.

मच्चित्ता मद्गतप्राणा बोधयन्तः परस्परम्।
कथयन्तश्च मां नित्यं तुष्यन्ति च रमन्ति च।।10.9।।

Verse 10 -11

Devoted ever constantly,
With Love, who worship Me
I give them the insight
By which they come to Me.

For them, My sheer compassion,
I, being Dweller of their bosom
By the Luminous lamp of wisdom
I banish murk, born of oblivion.

1 GOD AND DEVOTEE
Reverential flow to the God,
Is Ancient nature, naturally brims over
Mutually overflows between two.

2
His love for us
Has blessed very insight into us
How to Love Him.

3 GOD'S GRACE
Lightening needs none the light
For the cloudiness of the dark cloud
To illumine murk of cloud.

4
Who loves one's Beloved,
With constantly everlasting love
Opes door to the Beloved.

5
My devotion is His relish
My love is my way of worship,
My insight is His Lordship.

6 GRACE ALONE
Mental efforts nor matter's race
But with conscious devotion, through ages progress
Achieved alone, by the Grace.

तेषां सततयुक्तानां भजतां प्रीतिपूर्वकम्।
ददामि बुद्धियोगं तं येन मामुपयान्ति ते।।10.10।।

तेषामेवानुकम्पार्थमहमज्ञानजं तमः।
नाशयाम्यात्मभावस्थो ज्ञानदीपेन भास्वता।।10.11।।

EAGER DEVOTEE

Verse 12 -13

Arjun Said –

Self evolved Supreme purifier! Original Deity !!,
Thou art Supreme Spirit, Supreme Abode, Uncaused.
The Eternal, God of gods and all pervading Beauty,
Divine seer Narada, Asit, sage Deval, Vyas
Hath thus described Thee
Now Thou Thyself tellest me.

1 ANCIENT SAGES AND SEERS
Even these author-seers
Are authored by the Supreme Authority
Made them Knower of Truth.

2 DIVINE KINSHIP
Nor the academic succession,
Nor worldly confusions nor worldly persuasion
Alone 'Grace' transcends relation.

3 ABSOLUTE IS KNOWABLE TO MAN
The Unknown; man could witness,
Sages solved the Unknown into knowable text
(Here), Lord Himself validates.

4 GEETA
Unknown Unknowable Mystery,
Sages toiled for ages to foresee
(here) Lord revealed simply before Devotee.

5 DARSHAN
All texts turn texture-less,
When wonderment of the 'Supreme Wonder' unveils
Even a bit of Himself.

परं ब्रह्म परं धाम पवित्रं परमं भवान्।
पुरुषं शाश्वतं दिव्यमादिदेवमजं विभुम्।।10.12।।

आहुस्त्वामृषयः सर्वे देवर्षिर्नारदस्तथा।
असितो देवलो व्यासः स्वयं चैव ब्रवीषि मे।।10.13।।

Verse 14

What Thou havest told,
O Keshav ! verily I uphold
O Lord ! nor Devas nor Demons
Could fathom Thy Manifestations.

1
Faith in the core,
Though satiates, yet is starved more,
Knower's thirst to know more.

2 KRISHNA
Nor gods nor anti-godlins could
Know, the Manifestation of the Absolute
That a blessed man understood.

3 GRACE OF GOD
Nor the Beast,
Even nor who claimed the Bests
Reached but alone 'the Blessed'.

4 EGO CAN'T SEE AVTAAR
Extremes of demigods, demons
Blur coming of the Absolute as
phenomenon,
Manifests not in such man.

Verse 15 -16

O Lord ! and O Origin
Of all heaven n all beings !
O Lord of lords ! O Divine Self !!
Verily Thou knowest
Thyself by Thyself.

To me now in details
With no reserve tell !
Of Thy Divine potential
By which Thou dost dwell
In these worlds and
Sustain as well.

सर्वमेतदृतं मन्ये यन्मां वदसि केशव।
न हि ते भगवन् व्यक्तिं विदुर्देवा न दानवाः।।10.14।।

स्वयमेवात्मनाऽत्मानं वेत्थ त्वं पुरुषोत्तम।
भूतभावन भूतेश देवदेव जगत्पते।।10.15।।

वक्तुमर्हस्यशेषेण दिव्या ह्यात्मविभूतयः।
याभिर्विभूतिभिर्लोकानिमांस्त्वं व्याप्य तिष्ठसि।।10.16।।

1
In ornaments that embellish,
The stuffed essential metal is Gold
As Lord in every soul.

2 HIDDEN KNOWLEDGE
Lord knows that He knows
But Mortals think that they do not know
They know, Although.

3 ARJUN'S PLEA
Let into my little lore
Thy blessing, Thy words, power, grandeur
Infinitely be explored.

4 OMNIPRESENT LORD
Knowing this is enough –
He's essence of essence, stuffed
In everythings, every nonthings.

5 LOOK AT HIM
Every curious thought
Hath some puzzles and some knots
For none but the Lord

6 REALIZATION
My dark sightedness fail
To see Luminous Being that dwells
Till the Dweller lits lamp.

Verse 17

O Krshna ! O Great Yogi !!
In order to know Thee,
How shall I even meditate
In what forms and what aspects
O Blessed Lord ! Thou be conceived by me.

1 HOLY MIND QUESTIONS
Holy thoughts need a subject,
Be it Divine n sacred to contemplate
But what is that?

2 MEDITATION OBJECT
By little self, through self,
Into higher and higher inner self,
Man realized the Supreme Self.

3 ATTRIBUTORY LORD
To figure out the Absolute
To worship Him and pay salutes
Meditator conceives through Attributes.

4 MEDITATING BEYOND WORLD
Journeying this mortal coil,
By the Unification of subject and object,
Conceives through toil-free toil.

कथं विद्यामहं योगिंस्त्वां सदा परिचिन्तयन्।
केषु केषु च भावेषु चिन्त्योऽसि भगवन्मया।।10.17।।

PHENOMENAL EXPRESSION

Verse 18

O Janardan ! tell me again
More, at a great length
Of Thy glory and yogic strength
Because listening Thy nectar- speech,
Never shall I be quenched.

1 KEEN SUBMISSION
Devout's keenness is blessed
By learning that 'quest of the Unsaid'
Is in humble request.

2 CONTINUE TO LEARN
Pure listener digest
With more appetite, the purest knowledge
Keen further on quest.

3 LORD BLESSED TALK
A drop of nectar
With Divine words once elixirs core,
Brings relishing lore.

4 SATSANG – 'FIRST RIGHT STEP'
Fascinated to Listen more,
Of the Truth, in All True discourse,
Is beginning of Godly course.

Verse 19

The Blessed Lord said –

O Arjun ! O Best of Kuru'!!,Now
I will declare to thou,
My Glory but only prominent few,
For My Glory is endlessly huge.

1 BLESSING GEETA
The Blessed Lord's Blessed lessons
Are repeated at times to the blessed one,
Until fully learned.

2
The Unknown is knowable little
A God fully known is no more God
Becomes finite like us.

विस्तरेणात्मनो योगं विभूतिं च जनार्दन।
भूयः कथय तृप्तिर्हि श्रृण्वतो नास्ति मेऽमृतम्।।10.18।।

हन्त ते कथयिष्यामि दिव्या ह्यात्मविभूतयः।
प्राधान्यतः कुरुश्रेष्ठ नास्त्यन्तो विस्तरस्य मे।।10.19।।

3 LITTLE BUT PERFECTION

'Ts not the fullest
Knowing whatever, be it purest,
Sure, this little perfects.

4 FINITE WISDOM

The finite mind of devout
Just could know about God
Though, not know the God.

5

Will to know
Is highest knowledge; and that will is-
'Should man know Him'.

Verse 20

I'm the very Self
In all creatures dost dwell.
I'm their origin, middle and
End of all beings as well.

1 ALL ETERNAL

The One Immortal
Is seated in every mortal, mutable
And It's eternally Immutable.

2 THE CREATION

In every mould,
Lord enters as Manifestation in all
As Soul of all souls.

3 ONENESS

All multiplicity dissolves
For His created, when the Creator calls,
'He is All in all.'

4 THE INFINITE IS ORIGIN OF ALL

All the timed finites,
Are the manifestation of the Infinite
Whose entity is Timeless.

अहमात्मा गुडाकेश सर्वभूताशयस्थितः।
अहमादिश्च मध्यं च भूतानामन्त एव च।।10.20।।

Verse 21-23

Among the Adityas, Vishnu I'm*
Among the Luminaries, the Sun radiant
Among Marut's, Marichi I'm
Among asterisms, the Moon I'm

Among Vedas, the Sama-Ved I'm
Among gods, demigods, Indra I'm
Of the Senses, the Mind I'm
Of the Creatures, the Conscious I'm

Among all the rudras, I'm Shankar.
Among Yaksh-Rakshas, I'm riches, Kuber
I'm fire god among Vasu'
Of the mountains I'm Sumeru.

1
The Nature completes itself
Borrowing divinity from the Divine-Self,
More the divinity, the Best.

2
Same Essence of the Absolute,
Be identified through distinct attributes
His Vastness in every minute.

3
Vedas are Devas true,
And Devas are Vedas too,
Being, in the Divine, imbued.

4 THE ALMIGHTY'S PRESENCE
Who enlivens life, He
Who luminates light, fills music with melody,
Also consciousness of Pysche.

5 ALL THE BESTS-HE OWNS
Lord's divine expression,
Is ever best intensified in His vision
Making own Infinite expansion.

6 CREATOR OF GROSS TO REFINED
He creates, He concludes
Maintains subtle Parenthood
In World, objectively crude.

**Twelve born of Aditi.*

आदित्यानामहं विष्णुर्ज्योतिषां रविरंशुमान्।
मरीचिर्मरुतामस्मि नक्षत्राणामहं शशी।।10.21।।

वेदानां सामवेदोऽस्मि देवानामस्मि वासवः।
इन्द्रियाणां मनश्चास्मि भूतानामस्मि चेतना।।10.22।।

रुद्राणां शङ्करश्चास्मि वित्तेशो यक्षरक्षसाम्।
वसूनां पावकश्चास्मि मेरुः शिखरिणामहम्।।10.23।।

7 BENEVOLENT THOUGHT IS GOD
Among many eddy currents
Pacific Marichi with its divine essence
Is Himself Lord, most benevolent.

8 GOOD THOUGHTS ARE LORD HIMSELF
The Sacred thought,
That brought the soul to God
Is 'he himself, the Lord'.

Verse 24 -26

O Parth ! Thus understand Me
Among Priests, I'm chief Brahaspati
Among Generals I'm Skand
Among water-bodies I'm Ocean.

I'm Bhragu among Ascetics,
I'm 'AUM' among phonetics
I'm Japa-chanting of ritual practice
The Himalayas, Among static things.

Among celestial sages, I'm Narad
*Among all trees I'm the peepal**
Among songsters I'm Chitrarath
Among perfected seers I'm Kapil.

1
Wisest, vastest, holiest
Among all which He created as Perfect,
Best is He Himself.

2 AUM
All energy sounded AUM
Eternally the word made God, its Home
With God it became God.

3 THE MAN – THE SUPREME
Formless , shapeless transparent
Takes shape, taken out of the main
Manifests in the Frame.

4 'AUM'-SONIC DIVINITY
Many thoughts, Many word-symbols
Made conceivable in the finite world
'AUM' is Eternal Phonic–idol.

**ficus religiosa*

पुरोधसां च मुख्यं मां विद्धि पार्थ बृहस्पतिम्।
सेनानीनामहं स्कन्दः सरसामस्मि सागरः।।10.24।।

महर्षीणां भृगुरहं गिरामस्म्येकमक्षरम्।
यज्ञानां जपयज्ञोऽस्मि स्थावराणां हिमालयः।।10.25।।

अश्वत्थः सर्ववृक्षाणां देवर्षीणां च नारदः।
गन्धर्वाणां चित्ररथः सिद्धानां कपिलो मुनिः।।10.26।।

5 JAPA
Godly thoughts he repeats
With blessed best ease the japist meets
His very goal in beads.

6
The perfection in Perfected beings
Shaped in physical, astral or causal thing
Lord governs its thorough - going.

7 PEEPAL TREE
Season by season the Fig ,
Through falls figures out and depicts
Shootlet is Ancient Big.

8 FOR 'JAPA' IS GOD
A devotee repeatedly chants,
It's no godly act but God in itself,
Brings the Lord at hand.

9 REPEATING THOUGHTS OF LORD
Matter of mortal confines
Chiseled by repeated Thought, carved shrine
The indwelling soul to sublime.

Verse 27 -29

Know Me, among steeds,
*Uchchashravas, born of Nectar**
Airawat, among elephant species
I'm, among men, the Emperor.

Of weapons I'm vajram, divine,
I'm Kamdhenu, among the bovines
*I'm Kama**, procreation tendency*
Among serpents I'm Vasuki

Of celestial Nagas, the Shesh I'm
Among aquatic, the Varun I'm
Of ancient paters, I'm Aryam
*Among celestial authorities, the Yama.****

*Nectar taken out of Ocean-churning **God of Love (Cupid) ***God of death

---

उच्चैःश्रवसमश्वानां विद्धि माममृतोद्भवम्।
ऐरावतं गजेन्द्राणां नराणां च नराधिपम्।।10.27।।

आयुधानामहं वज्रं धेनूनामस्मि कामधुक्।
प्रजनश्चास्मि कन्दर्पः सर्पाणामस्मि वासुकिः।।10.28।।

अनन्तश्चास्मि नागानां वरुणो यादसामहम्।
पितृणामर्यमा चास्मि यमः संयमतामहम्।।10.29।।

1 *HIS AMBROSIAL PRESENCE*

Whatever is Elixired
In this existence with nectar
Represents His Avtaar.

2 *PIOUS LIFE*

May Steed of thought divert
*The rider mind to the wisdom Airawat**
To rule with godly worth.

3 *VASTNESS*

Of the minute, the minutest
As well of the Great, the Greatest
All His Grace.

4 *ROYAL ENTITY*

As existed –Being
Being Son of the King of kings
I 'm prince or prince-kin.

5 *BEYOND SHALLOWNESS*

Only away from the coast
Churning of the ocean ever bless
With whatever best.

6 *ALL PRESENT LORD*

God is Omnipresent in man
None the man's finding in existence
Understand ! this Eternal trend.

Verse 30 -32

I'm Prahlad among demons,
'The Time' among the reckoners ,
Among animals, I'm King lion
And 'Garuda' among the birds.

The breeze among the Purifiers
I'm 'Rama' among warriors
I'm shark among Pisces
Among rivers I'm Ganges.

O Arjun ! I'm beginning and the End,
Also the middle, of all existence.
Of all sciences I'm Gnostic Truth
For debaters I'm logical proof.

Airawat is celestial elephant of Indra (sense)

प्रह्लादश्चास्मि दैत्यानां कालः कलयतामहम्।
मृगाणां च मृगेन्द्रोऽहं वैनतेयश्च पक्षिणाम्।।10.30।।

पवनः पवतामस्मि रामः शस्त्रभृतामहम्।
झषाणां मकरश्चास्मि स्रोतसामस्मि
जाह्नवी।।10.31।।

सर्गाणामादिरन्तश्च मध्यं चैवाहमर्जुन।
अध्यात्मविद्या विद्यानां वादः
प्रवदतामहम्।।10.32।।

1 ALL THE SOUL'S ALL TIME
Time is timed to finites
By momentary mind into many splits
Lest the Eternal clock, soul is.

2 TIME
Man's Ages are momentary
For God's Bigban; its span of relativity
Both with eternal Accuracy.

3 EQUALLY POTENT IN ALL
In Ganges the holy Divine
In jaws and paws He is ferine
Equally, in Human, refined.

4 THE SELF – EVIDENT SELF
He existed, exists and will
Before Genesis, after End and in Middle
Evanescent qualms, The Eternity's ripostle.

5 POTENTIAL TO RISE
A demon is not
All demon, but has part of God
Let it sublime as Prahlad.

6 TIMELESSNESS
Scale though differs
But moment in eternal Dial is same
For God, for hunter–game.

7 BEYOND BOOKISH SCIENCE
Confined in pages, the mind,
Once welled into Surge of the Brine,
Is Bathed by True Science.

Verse 33-35

I'm Aakar among syllables*
Of all compounds I'm dual
I'm everlasting time immutable
I'm omnipresent Dispenser,
And all-faced Face turned all over.

I'm birth, I'm all devouring death
And origin of all that wilt beget,
Of Feminine qualities I'm fame, fortuity
I'm reason, riches, rheotic, majesty
Mind's genius, mettle and mercy.

*Ferine=deadly, ripostle=quick reply. *'a'Aakar (of Sanskrit and Hindi) evanescent=short lived*

अक्षराणामकारोऽस्मि द्वन्द्वः सामासिकस्य च।
अहमेवाक्षयः कालो धाताऽहं विश्वतोमुखः।।10.33।।

मृत्युः सर्वहरश्चाहमुद्भवश्च भविष्यताम्।
कीर्तिः श्रीर्वाक्च नारीणां स्मृतिर्मेधा धृतिः क्षमा।।10.34।।

बृहत्साम तथा साम्नां गायत्री छन्दसामहम्।
मासानां मार्गशीर्षोऽहमृतूनां कुसुमाकरः।।10.35।।

Of Hymns I'm Brahm-saman,
Of poesy I'm Gayatri mantra
I'm Marga Shisha among the months
Among seasons flowery vernal season.

1

Books enlighten the dark
Words, quotes, lines are torch'
Vowel 'a' is first spark.

2 *THE TIME SCALE*

The finite scaled pure time,
By moment's perception in smooth run
Has one Infinite substratum.

3 *BIRTH AND DEATH, HE IS*

God is unsubject to things
Originates all, even Originates the Origin
Life of lest lifeless-livings.

4 *BLESSED ATTRIBUTES*

Filled, the empty manhood
With feminity, transformed man into new,
Man with godly virtue.

5 *TRANSFORMING INTO SPRING*

Burst out through buds
Are vernal colours transformed from sludge
God manifested out of mud.

6 *ALL GOD'S LANGUAGE*

All alphabets bade
In many timbre, tone, thoughts and texts
Have one spiritual taste.

7 *SUBSTRATUM OF ALL-TIME*

As intrinsic in each moment
He transcends into past, would be time
Making Totally the Present.

8 *FEMININE MANIFESTATION*

Alone the motherly worth,
In Him, conceives Eternity and give birth
To Divine attributes.

9 *FINDING PATH*

Mind's eye with visionary esteem
Picks some mantras, months, seasons and hymns
As best to reach Him.

Verse 36

I'm Gambling in fraudents
I'm Radiance of the Radiants
And Victory of the victor
I'm Resolve of the Resolute
I'm the Goodness in the good.

1
Vice, dice or nice
Divine Master designs trickster to realize
In all diverses He lies.

2 RESOLVE TO WIN MAYA
The Master gambler teaches disciples
Resolving main of man is able
To turn the dice-table.

3
Feelings lived in any attribute
Should experience the Self in relative world
The presence of the Absolute.

4 MAYIC TRICKSTER
One can't deceit
Trying so, one can't defeat
The Supreme winner.

5 ALL HIS ATTRIBUTES
The Maker of all contrasts
Is Bests of the best, worst in worst-parts
Those none can surpass.

6
Imbued in attributes
All this distinctions, God distributes
A difference, but all His.

Verse 37

*I'm Krshna in Vrisni race**,*
Arjun in Pandavs, 'Vyas' of the Sages
And Among the thinker poets
I'm Ushna, the seer great.*

1 GREATNESS
Krshna is full of Krshna
Exploring more of Krshna within and without
Makes Arjun, Vyas, Ushna.

2
He is Actor, and Act,
He is Activator and the Active state
All in its Best.

*Main = Dice-throw *Shukracharya, ** Yaduvansh.*

द्यूतं छलयतामस्मि तेजस्तेजस्विनामहम्।
जयोऽस्मि व्यवसायोऽस्मि सत्त्वं
सत्त्ववतामहम्।।10.36।।

वृष्णीनां वासुदेवोऽस्मि पाण्डवानां धनंजयः।
मुनीनामप्यहं व्यासः कवीनामुशना कविः।।10.37।।

3 GOD IN YOU

Krshna, Himself puts His-Self
Into warrior's fight, Thinker's insight, Sages light
To sublime all unto Him.

Verse 38

Of punishers I'm scepter,
I'm moral of victory-seekers
The silence of the secrets
And prudence of the Sage.

1 GOD'S PUNISHMENT

Many tiny scepters
Of God, chisel out the mould,
From worldly die, the soul.

2 VIRTUE IS GOD

Morality is weapon of God
Or the God in itself that shields
The victor in any war-field.

3 WORDLESS LANGUAGE

The silence and language
Who have decoded as perfect message,
Reached the secret of secrets.

4.

Knowingly or unknowingly
We all are striving for the Knowledge
Because it's in itself God.

5 LORD PUNISHES WEAKNESS

Sin is reflection of weak
Making strong the scepter of Lord, whips
The weakness to rid.

6 THE BLESSING PUNISHER

In any pain
See ! the Punisher planned,
Plan through pain.

7 MASTER'S MYSTERY

This Divine essence,
Prudence is silence, silence in prudence
Is real ethereal substance.

दण्डो दमयतामस्मि नीतिरस्मि जिगीषताम्।
मौनं चैवास्मि गुह्यानां ज्ञानं ज्ञानवतामहम्।।10.38।।

Verse 39

Moreover I'm the seed,
Of all that exist
Stabile or labile may those be
Can't sustain without Me.

1 REAL KNOWLEDGE
Knowing the Divinity
Is transcending finite world of plurality
To single out infinity.

2
The multiplicity of the whole,
Manifested in kinetic akinetic mould
Is breed of One Soul.

3 LINKED TO INFINITE
Brought out of the Infinite,
Total finites have unseen links
Vitalized by the same Infinite.

4 ONE SOURCE AND ONE SUSTAINER
Dynamic wave arose
From the Ocean grows and grows
Can't be parted from source.

5 FROM SEED TO SEED
From seed-state of Universe
Total causal bodies of world converge
Have vital link to merge.

Verse 40

My Divine stateliness
O Arjun ! in brief I have stated;
What I have declared
Is mere glimpse of My Infinite power.

1 IGNORANCE OF SELF
The infinite within every finite
Kept unexplored, transcends not the limits
Thus, defined as the Finite.

2 BEYOND WORDS
As wordless flower tells
Of spring's glory, majesty and spells
Krshna about His Self.

यच्चापि सर्वभूतानां बीजं तदहमर्जुन।
न तदस्ति विना यत्स्यान्मया भूतं चराचरम्।।10.39।।

नान्तोऽस्ति मम दिव्यानां विभूतीनां परंतप।
एष तूद्देशतः प्रोक्तो विभूतेर्विस्तरो मया।।10.40।।

3 THE SUPREME GOD
He, Himself hath shown,
Way of knowing Unknowable Unknown
Through glimpses that 're known.

4
Through temporary scenes
The Divine glimpse indicates the Unseen,
May be seen through little Seen.

5 CONCISE WORDS
For the ignorant
With Infinite numbers of 'Nows' He explained
-Infinite Eternal Present.

Verse 41

Whatever its in the Existence
With eminence, affluence and strength
Know it to be an advent
Of spark of My Radiance.

1 ONLY CRAFTSMAN
Man earned nor man made
Glory, nobility majesty man hath
Ever Lord's grace manifests.

2 SURRENDERING ACHIEVEMENTS
Man's glory acted
To dissolve into wonders of Most Glorious
Is glory perfected.

3 ALL 'HIS' QUALITIES
Attributes, so Divine
Found in realm of perishable Un-divine
Lord's presence here shines.

4
Greater thing on Earth
Though very little for His Splendours
Yet Lord counts its worth.

Verse 42

What purpose it avails
O Arjun ! to know these details?
Just know that in nutshell-
I dost sustain pervade the Entire
With Only one fragment of Myself.

यद्यद्विभूतिमत्सत्त्वं श्रीमदूर्जितमेव वा।
तत्तदेवावगच्छ त्वं मम तेजोंऽशसंभवम्।।10.41।।

अथवा बहुनैतेन किं ज्ञातेन तवार्जुन।
विष्टभ्याहमिदं कृत्स्नमेकांशेन स्थितो जगत्।।10.42।।

1 NO COMPLEXITY IS DIVINE

Text's formulae man's implex,
Let all conclude to the simplest
-The fundamental Simplicity.

2 PILGRIM

From Evident to the Hidden'
From vague glimpse to endless vision
Journeyed till i am 'He'.

3

Every bit of the whole,
With little bit of His whole
The Lord holds.

4 GROSS MELTS INTO FINE

Once one fact felt
He is and His is only Truth.
All other knowledge melts.

CHAPTER ELEVEN

Cosmic Form: The Vision of visions

'Ts me who fail,
Supreme visage is ever open unveiled
My veiled eyes can't avail.

On the war scene

The weapon of Divinity envisaged within

This alone can win.

Chapter Eleven

LORD REVEALS HIS COSMIC FORM

Verse 1-4

Arjun spake –

To Me Thou havest spoken,
Just, out of compassion
About the True Self, the secret wisdom
Thus banished my delusions.

Because O Lotus eyed Krshna !
From Thou I have listened-
The Origin and the End
Verily, of all the existence,
Also Thy endless Excellence.

O Supreme ! truly havest
Thou, thus described Thyself
O Purushottam ! I long to see yet
Thee in Thine Divine visage.

O Master ! O Lord of Yogis !!
If Thou dost know me
To be fit to behold it
Then please ! show me
Thine form Eternal Infinite.

मदनुग्रहाय परमं गुह्यमध्यात्मसंज्ञितम्।
यत्त्वयोक्तं वचस्तेन मोहोऽयं विगतो मम।।11.1।।

भवाप्ययौ हि भूतानां श्रुतौ विस्तरशो मया।
त्वत्तः कमलपत्राक्ष माहात्म्यमपि चाव्ययम्।।11.2।।

एवमेतद्यथात्थ त्वमात्मानं परमेश्वर।
द्रष्टुमिच्छामि ते रूपमैश्वरं पुरुषोत्तम।।11.3।।

मन्यसे यदि तच्छक्यं मया द्रष्टुमिति प्रभो।
योगेश्वर ततो मे त्वं दर्शयाऽत्मानमव्ययम्।।11.4।।

1 FINAL KNOWLEDGE

Once delusion is defeated
Very vision gets concentrated
On 'the Ultimate'.

2 COMPASSIONATE GOD

'Ts Master's compassion
Makes an ignorant a good listener
Now, to master teachings.

3 PERFECT KNOWLEDGE

Teacher's compassion has brought
More passion to learn in the Taught
For the practical perfection.

4 GEETA

One teaches one learns
But for the endless ages in turn,
The mankind earns.

5 ARJUN'S KEENNESS

Any good lesson,
Inherently look forward to the perception
Of realistic execution.

6 BE OPEN TO 'HIM'

Man's first opus
Through God's mercy to know the God
Then make God known us.

7 PETITION NOT THE CLAIM

No claim of mean desires
But humble, modesty, and reverence
To fulfill, the Lord admires.

Verse 5-7

The Blessed Lord spake-

Now opulence of Mine
O Son of Prathi ! Lo !!
Hundreds of thousands form divine
Multicoloured omnifarious also.

Behold ! Adityas and Vasus
The Rudras, Twin Ashwins, the Maruts
And many wonderous unknown hitherto.

Here and Now ! O Arjun eye !!
Whole Universe with moving things and stills
In My cosmic form unified
And see more to thy will.

1 INTIMATE DEVOTEE

To the will and hope
Of the closest devotee, Lord shrouds none
But to fullest, ope.

2 CLOSEST PERCEPTION

Mortal optical orb
On the farthest of vision be absorbed
Into nearest Divinity.

3 COSMIC FORM – THE VIRAT

His Virat visage
In the crowd of diverse crowded faces
Is one Unified grace.

4 THE VIRAT –COSMIC FORM

God is condensed cosmos
Also expanded dimensions of all subtle-gross
Multiple miniatured intact in One.

5 THE VIRAT – COSMIC FORM

Beyond Krshna's visage gross,
Multiframed totality compressed amassed
In Arjun's sight-canvas.

6 IDEAL DEVOTEE

Before transparent zeal,
None the mystery Lord conceals,
All transcendental form He reveals.

7 THE OMNIPRESENT

Let the observer before
Bring Universal form into core
What's already to the fore.

8 THE MANIFESTATION

That 'I know none',
This much knowing is humble petition
The Unknowable as kin comes.

9 DIVINE SIGHT – DIVYA DRISHTI

Where boundaries of little me
Dissolve into Total space, I see
'Ts all God beyond me.

10

'Ts me who fail,
Supreme visage is ever open unveiled
My veiled eyes can't avail.

पश्य मे पार्थ रूपाणि शतशोऽथ सहस्रशः।
नानाविधानि दिव्यानि नानावर्णाकृतीनि च।।11.5।।

पश्यादित्यान्वसून्रुद्रानश्विनौ मरुतस्तथा।
बहून्यदृष्टपूर्वाणि पश्याऽश्चर्याणि भारत।।11.6।।

इहैकस्थं जगत्कृत्स्नं पश्याद्य सचराचरम्।
मम देहे गुडाकेश यच्चान्यद्द्रष्टुमिच्छसि।।11.7।।

Verse 8

But thou can't visualize
Me with thy physical eyes
So I dost give Divine sight
Opulence of Yogeshwar, visualize !

1
Adapted to the dualities
Blended by world, Beyond I cannot see
Alone Maker makes me see.

2
Arjun's asking to behold
Is on words what Krshna had told
Ages of faith to uphold.

3 SIGHT OF INSIGHT
Eyes, mind nor the vision,
To visualize cosmic form of Kishan
Need a changed perception.

4 RECONGNIZE THE BLESSED LORD
Lord further blesses the Blessed*,
Beyond His textual and natural grace
By coming face to face.

Verse 9

Sanjay said (to Dhritrashtra)-

Having thus spoken,
The Yogeshwar, Lord Krshna
The Supreme Personality of God head
Opulent Divine- form to Arjun displayed.

1 BEST OF COMMENTATOR
The commentator in Sanjay,
Meets the quality of chaste unbiased voice,
For timeless Knowledge joy.

2 (DHRATRASHTRA – THE BLIND KING)
The Blind, in real sense,
Is blind who does not see consequence
Of being blind to conscience.

3 SANJAY
Chaste visionary no doubt
Involved in chaste description of God
Shares Lord's blessings as devout.

*Arjun

न तु मां शक्यसे द्रष्टुमनेनैव स्वचक्षुषा।
दिव्यं ददामि ते चक्षुः पश्य मे योगमैश्वरम्।।11.8।।

एवमुक्त्वा ततो राजन्महायोगेश्वरो हरिः।
दर्शयामास पार्थाय परमं रूपमैश्वरम्।।11.9।।

Verse 10-14

Arjun saw the weird opulence
Multifarious and marvelous presence
With limitless mouths, speaking wonders
With numerous wonderful eyes
Seeing everything with numerous sights
All too numerous to describe.

With numerous Divine patterns adorned
With many uplifted Divine weapons borne
With celestial garlands and wears
With Divine essence all over smeared
In every direction of the space
Omnipresent Divinity, all sides face.

Hundreds of thousands of Suns
In the sky, as if rose up at once
That would be like the shine
Of the Supreme radiance so Divine.

At that time Arjun saw
In His cosmic form, the Lord of lords
Unlimited expansion of the Universe
In one form yet all diverse.

Then Arjun filled with wonder,
Thrilled he began to offer
Obeisance to the Supreme
With folded palms addressed Him--

अनेकवक्त्रनयनमनेकाद्भुतदर्शनम्।
अनेकदिव्याभरणं दिव्यानेकोद्यतायुधम्।।11.10।।

दिव्यमाल्याम्बरधरं दिव्यगन्धानुलेपनम्।
सर्वाश्चर्यमयं देवमनन्तं विश्वतोमुखम्।।11.11।।

दिवि सूर्यसहस्रस्य भवेद्युगपदुत्थिता।
यदि भाः सदृशी सा स्याद्भासस्तस्य महात्मनः।।11.12।।

तत्रैकस्थं जगत्कृत्स्नं प्रविभक्तमनेकधा।
अपश्यद्देवदेवस्य शरीरे पाण्डवस्तदा।।11.13।।

ततः स विस्मयाविष्टो हृष्टरोमा धनञ्जयः।
प्रणम्य शिरसा देवं कृताञ्जलिरभाषत।।11.14।।

1 THE MOST INTIMATE

One Arjun in me,
Is closest to that Farthest and see
How strange is He.

2

No vaulty Grey could hold
Multiple visions in visions of the Whole
Needs no eye but soul.

3 SPIRITUAL VISION

Little more suns
And little more added heaven
Transcends into Virat vision.

4 DIVINE FRIENDSHIP

Finding all kins in friend
Is a God's intimate advent in exchange
Gets devout's obeisance.

5 GRACE

Totality compressed in One
Its no optic visual nor mortal phenomenon
Only 'Grace' magnifies Vision.

6 VIRTUES ACCUMULATED

Every sun routine sized,
Let add more glory more light
Then together all suns rise.

7

Multifarious marvel in 'One'
This form just not mental perception
More comprehension of soul's vision.

8 ASTONISHED ARJUN

When Divine Pal's love
Wonders a friend knowing His Ancient
Love
Is worshipable all above.

THE VIRAT

Verse 15 - 18

O My Lord ! I behold
All assembled gods Thy body holdth
And also various living tenants
And many sages and divine serpents
And Brahma, the Creator on Lotus I perceive
As well I behold Lord Shiv.

Wonder ! I behold again behold
Expanded and limitless many folds,
Bellies, eyes, arms and mouths
Thee everywhere, all about
Nor beginning nor middle nor the end.
Thy body is entire cosmos O Lord ! I ascertain.

Thee with crowns clubs and discs,
'Ts difficult my gaze to fix
For Thy radiance all around glare
Is incomprehensible blazing like sun and fire.

Thou are worth to best known
Imperishable ! whole Multiverse Thou dost own
The Eternal sanatan Thou dost sustain,
I opine – Thou art Endless Ancient.

1 FARSIGHTEDNESS
Cosmic form as Idol
The Infinite focused-vision could behold
Enshrining in perception, the Whole.

2 THE DIVINE VISION
The Vision of the visions
Widens to converge into very perception
One 's Whole, Whole 's One.

3 EVERYTHING IS DIVINE
Ether, ethereal and real
All are part of the Infinitesimal
Absolute and all Real.

4 DIVINE EXTRAVAGANZA
Dynamic form is autonomous
And Autonomous is also dynamic me,
Endless organs of cosmic dimensions.

Infinitesimal = extremely small.

5 MANIFESTATION IS NATURAL
Mind's circumference in Infinite cosmos
Churns out all unified divine and gross
Manifest as per cosmic laws.

6 ARJUN'S VISULALZING JOURNEY
From orbs, robes, weapons, jewels
Now, on Trine Divinity the gaze fixed
Thus journeyed to the Real.

7 LESSON FROM ARJUN'S DESCRIPTION
From all Low, all sublime,
Through births and births in cosmic design
Sight's insight be refined.

8
On the war scene
The weapon of Divinity envisaged within
Alone can win.

पश्यामि देवांस्तव देव देहे,सर्वांस्तथा भूतविशेषसङ्घान्।
ब्रह्माणमीशं कमलासनस्थ, मृषींश्च सर्वानुरगांश्च
दिव्यान्।।11.15।।

अनेकबाहूदरवक्त्रनेत्रं पश्यामि, त्वां सर्वतोऽनन्तरूपम्।
नान्तं न मध्यं न पुनस्तवादिं
पश्यामि विश्वेश्वर विश्वरूप।।11.16।।

किरीटिनं गदिनं चक्रिणं च, तेजोराशिं
सर्वतोदीप्तिमन्तम्।
पश्यामि त्वां दुर्निरीक्ष्यं समन्ता
द्दीप्तानलार्कद्युतिमप्रमेयम्।।11.17।।

त्वमक्षरं परमं वेदितव्यं त्वमस्य, विश्वस्य परं
निधानम्।
त्वमव्ययः शाश्वतधर्मगोप्ता
सनातनस्त्वं पुरुषो मतो मे।।11.18।।

9
Divine forms to serpentine worms
The whole in cosmic form is substratum
Of Entirety of the Entire.

10 VISION BEYOND TIME
Ancient of the ancients, Purusha
First spark of entire Entirety, very Truth
In multiversal form Arjun viewed.

11 THUS ETERNITY MANIFESTED
From timeless Time was made
The Earthy and ethereal space was still unmade
Ancient shapeless shaped Himself.

12 ARJUN'S VIEW
As true Guardian of Truth
As first among Ancients, last of New
The Unknowable; Arjun thus knew.

Verse 19-24

With nor beginning and nor middle,
Thou art with endless doom
Endless arms of endless potentials
The starry eyes of suns and moons
Throbbing flames from Thy mouth spume
Warming whole universe, Thy bloom.

Thou art the One spread
Through Skies, planets and all spaces
Beholding this terrible wondrous form
O Sovereign Soul ! the triune world is alarmed.

Demigods, godules enter in Thy forms
Some pray so overcome, with joined palms
The perfect seers and great saints
Reciting 'Swasti' in superb chants.*

**chants of peace and peace to all.*

अनादिमध्यान्तमनन्तवीर्य मनन्तबाहुं शशिसूर्यनेत्रम्।
पश्यामि त्वां दीप्तहुताशवक्त्रम् स्वतेजसा विश्वमिदं
तपन्तम्।।11.19।।

द्यावापृथिव्योरिदमन्तरं हि व्याप्तं त्वयैकेन दिशश्च सर्वाः।
दृष्ट्वाऽद्भुतं रूपमुग्रं तवेदं लोकत्रयं प्रव्यथितं महात्मन्।।11.20।।

अमी हि त्वां सुरसङ्घाः विशन्ति केचिद्भीताः प्राञ्जलयो गृणन्ति।
स्वस्तीत्युक्त्वा महर्षिसिद्धसङ्घाः स्तुवन्ति त्वां स्तुतिभिः
पुष्कलाभिः।।11.21।।

रुद्रादित्या वसवो ये च साध्या विश्वेऽश्विनौ मरुतश्चोष्मपाश्च।
गन्धर्वयक्षासुरसिद्धसङ्घा वीक्षन्ते त्वां विस्मिताश्चैव
सर्वे।।11.22।।

रूपं महत्ते बहुवक्त्रनेत्रं महाबाहो बहुबाहूरुपादम्।
बहूदरं बहुदंष्ट्राकरालं दृष्ट्वा लोकाः
प्रव्यथितास्तथाऽहम्।।11.23।।

नभःस्पृशं दीप्तमनेकवर्णं व्यात्ताननं दीप्तविशालनेत्रम्।
दृष्ट्वा हि त्वां प्रव्यथितान्तरात्मा धृतिं न विन्दामि शमं च
विष्णो।।11.24।।

Shiv's advent Rudras eleven,
Twelve Aditya's, the Suns
Eight vasus and seeking hermits
Twin ashwins and Patron spirits
All Maruts, the breezing power
Celestial songsters and fore fathers
Demigoblines, demigods, savages
All beholding Thou in awe-gaze.

O Mighty armed One ! Thee I sight,
In multiple faces cheeks teeth and eyes
With endless arms, bellies and thighs
Great terrible sights frightening the world,
And so too am I.

O Vishnu of fiery sight !
Radiant with many colours touching the skies,
The gaping mouth and dazzling eyes
Seeing all this I am terrified
I have lost my courage and poise.

1
Dualities of 'The Pure' blot,
All part, nor apart from the Lord
But relative not Absolute path.

2 OMNIPRESENT VASTNESS
In Universal temple, He's colossus
Dismayed devotee saw same, when focused
On soul of tiny dust.

3 A VISIONARY IS A DREAMER
Awakening from the dream,
Through immortal eyes of the Supreme
The vision, dreamer deems.

4 HIS OWN DUALITIES
God is and was
Ever dwelling in all contrasts
Short sighted I'm not Vast.

5 ARJUN'S VISION OF VISIONS
God is All God sized
His grace made realize the man-sized eyes
Godly size of man's sight.

6 KRSHNA
'Ts beyond mortal intellect,
Shaped Avtaar of unending Shapeless
Is not an object.

7 DYNAMISM OF LORD'S ARM

Handful of hands
Are dynamism at work of seeming
Quiescent
The Infinite arms extend.

8 FIRE OF LORD'S MOUTH

Dilemmas are consumed
And in Altar of wisdom, His voice ignites
The Fire to fire fumes.

9 DIVINE SUBSTRATUM

To judge yourself, you.
Stand by the Lord, then Him you view
-Not standing by yourself.

10 FRIGHTENED OF COSMIC FORM

My downsized mind perceived –
Totality of skies which trembled my earth,
Until my winged worth believed.

11

Not the awe-sick,
But the fearlessness hath right to pick
And enjoy the peace.

12 UNIVERSAL FORM OF LORD

Totality of visionary virtues
Together in multiple eyes and multiple views
Make one cosmic statue.

13 SOLE ENERGY OF UNIVERSE

Supreme Truth is universal womb
With its own light nurtures and warms
The True conscious bloom.

14 THE OMNIPRESENT PERCEPTION

My empty soul
Has all filled space with godly expansion
Sized to fill the whole.

15 AWESTRUCK ARJUN

When praying surrender meets
Few drops of honey of the Awe
Becomes ambrosial sweet.

Verse 25-31

Arjun continued to say –

O Lord of lords !
Having seen Thy Jaws with fearsome tusk
With deadly fires all around having burst
Four quarters are lost
O Abode of the Cosmos!
No poise I do find,
Be Gracious and be mild.

All allies of Dhratrashtra and his sons
Bhishma Drona, Karna and our chieftains
All are entering into Thy mouth of awe
Many are seen smashed in diastemata.

As the raging roar of the rivers
Rush to the ocean
Likewise all the victors
In Thy blazing mouth enter.

As the moths dash
Swiftly into fire ablaze
So also are creatures in haste
Into Thy mouth headlong race.

All the world, all over
Thy fiery mouth doth devour
Thou art licking with fierce beams
O Vishnu! scorching all worlds with prickly gleam.

O First of lords
So fierce in form
Who Thou art ?
May please I be informed.
Before Thee I bow,

As I do not know
Reveal to me Thy purpose
O Ancient ! be gracious.

1
Lord is 'Time' in Himself,
Is Eternal engulfs all in Timeless space
'The Time' as well.

2 LOST BEFORE THE SUPREME
Before halo of Eternity
Hollowness of momentary vanities
Merge it's span in Totality.

3
All discrete He created
All names –forms, all winners-loosers yet
Infinite hunger of Infinity ate.

4 NATURAL AFFINITY
The Ocean doesn't need
World's everything rush unto Lord hurried
As rivers rush in speed.

5 VISION OF THE TIME
In the Time space
Past and Future to the Timeless, paced
With Eternal - Today medley.

6 PILGRIMAGE
Enroute on pilgrimage
The manifests to own Paradise of the Unmanifest
Like moth to Flame, pace.

7 LIFE-THE WARFIELD
War in Kurukshetra*
Between fear and fearlessness
Is everyday fight still on.

8 THE ETERNITY
The present consumes future
And the Past devours the present
Making, Timeless Present tense

9 CHANGES ARE SUPERFICIAL
Eternal is the Existence
Repetition of changes is in raw elements
Done by Unchanging Changer.

10 THE VISION OF THE OBJECTIVE DESTRUCTION
He alone is real
All capable of having many unreal worlds
Where nothing is escapable.

11 BACK TO ORIGIN
The created multiplicity,
Rush to Oneness as its affinity
Towards the Totality.

12 BACK HOME
As the river's stream goes
Every diverse drop rush to divine source,
From which alone arose.

13 FEAR OF THE FEARLESS
None the Time-boon
Could make escape of the death doom
This dateless fate vexes Arjun.

14 DYNAMISM OF UNIVERSE
Destruction is constructive gain,
Into new creation ends the End
The Changer bringing continuous change.

15 REAL ASPIRANT – ARJUN
Seeker's mind when burns,
Even awe-struck or else, ever turns
The Truth to learn.

**the field of Mahabharat war.*

दंष्ट्राकरालानि च ते मुखानि दृष्ट्वैव
कालानलसन्निभानि।
दिशो न जाने न लभे च शर्म प्रसीद देवेश
जगन्निवास।।11.25।।

अमी च त्वां धृतराष्ट्रस्य पुत्राः सर्वे सहैवावनिपालसङ्घैः।
भीष्मो द्रोणः सूतपुत्रस्तथाऽसौ सहास्मदीयैरपि
योधमुख्यैः।।11.26।।

वक्त्राणि ते त्वरमाणा विशन्ति दंष्ट्राकरालानि
भयानकानि।
केचिद्विलग्ना दशनान्तरेषु संदृश्यन्ते
चूर्णितैरुत्तमाङ्गैः।।11.27।।

यथा नदीनां बहवोऽम्बुवेगाः समुद्रमेवाभिमुखाः द्रवन्ति।
तथा तवामी नरलोकवीरा विशन्ति
वक्त्राण्यभिविज्वलन्ति।।11.28।।

यथा प्रदीप्तं ज्वलनं पतङ्गा विशन्ति नाशाय
समृद्धवेगाः।
तथैव नाशाय विशन्ति लोका स्तवापि वक्त्राणि
समृद्धवेगाः।।11.29।।

लेलिह्यसे ग्रसमानः समन्ता
ल्लोकान्समग्रान्वदनैर्ज्वलद्भिः।
तेजोभिरापूर्य जगत्समग्रं भासस्तवोग्राः प्रतपन्ति
विष्णो।।11.30।।

आख्याहि मे को भवानुग्ररूपो नमोऽस्तु ते देववर प्रसीद।
विज्ञातुमिच्छामि भवन्तमाद्यं न हि प्रजानामि तव
प्रवृत्तिम्।।11.31।।

Verse 32-34

The blessed Lord said –

The Doomstime I am*
Destroying the world I aim
None the hostile warriors arrayed
But sans thou, they will die in coming days.

So rise up! With victor's fame
Let enemies be conquered
And enjoy the flourishing Empire,
By Me they are already slain
O Savyasachi ! mayst thou, but an instrument.

Droan, Jayadrath, Karna, Bhishma
Whom I have already doomed to die
Slay! them and more paladins
Fight ! fear not !! foes thou 'lt win.

1 GOD AS DESTROYER

'Ts God's summum bonum
On last graves are paved
Cradles of suns to come.

2 TIMES' POWER

Values, and wrongs and rights
Ever surrender before the Time's might
In due course of Time.

*Time of Death(Mahakaal)   Paladins = fighters   Summum bonum =highest Good.

कालोऽस्मि लोकक्षयकृत्प्रवृद्धो लोकान्समाहर्तुमिह
प्रवृत्तः।
ऋतेऽपि त्वां न भविष्यन्ति सर्वे येऽवस्थिताः प्रत्यनीकेषु
योधाः।।11.32।।

तस्मात्त्वमुत्तिष्ठ यशो लभस्व जित्वा शत्रून् भुङ्क्ष्व
राज्यं समृद्धम्।
मयैवैते निहताः पूर्वमेव निमित्तमात्रं भव
सव्यसाचिन्।।11.33।।

द्रोणं च भीष्मं च जयद्रथं च कर्णं तथाऽन्यानपि
योधवीरान्।
मया हतांस्त्वं जहि मा व्यथिष्ठा युध्यस्व जेतासि रणे
सपत्नान्।।11.34।।

3 LORD'S PLAN
His concept that thrives
To destroy is attitude of His Grace
Keeps universe survive.

4 RISE UP
The Supreme King is known
To make souls, the kingdom to own
Conditioned to rise to throne.

5 LORD'S PLAN
Wake up ! from nightmare,
Planned reality of the Supreme dream-maker
Is destined better.

6 ALL HIS INSTRUMENTS
The Ancient Unseen Hand
With active colours fills frames with names
As visible though, passive instrument.

7 I'M HIS INSTRUMENT
Into bamboo marrow
Krshna puffs consciousness in its hollow
Making flute with mellow.

8 SUPREME TIME-CYCLE
Lord's plan is plain
To slay, asks own diverse agent hands
Whom He, the Time had slain.

9 NATURE'S REFORMATION LAW
In the altar of renaissance,
On Names, forms, the Lord never depends
But Time's timed oblations.

10
Rise ! and defeat !!
Never the fear of the defeat,
Is winning feat that defeats

11 THE AGENT HAND
Hammering ego of fool
Mulls-over as framer of canvas, yet
Is the Carpenter's tool.

12
His sword and His arrow
I'm in war the peace tool of tomorrow
As well, wings of dove.

13
All bands, Brains, Brands, Braves
From All consuming Time, none is saved
Drained every craving, all haves.

14 THE REAL ENEMY*
Awakened man does go
With Lord and not with slave – ego,
Lord slain long ago.

*In context with Drona, Karan, Jaydrath.

Verse 35

Commentator Sanjay said –

After having heard
O King ! Lord krshna's words
Crowned-one Arjun trembled, all-feared
With folded hands worships offered
Falteringly spake Thus –

1 SANJAY'S DILEMMA

Worst part of war is
Far sight of unbiased mind's eye sees
Hope against hope of peace.

2 DHRATRASHTRA

If blinded good sense,
Is not invoked by far-seeing prudence
Inevitable providence is certain.

एतच्छ्रुत्वा वचनं केशवस्य कृताञ्जलिर्वेपमानः किरीटी।
नमस्कृत्वा भूय एवाह कृष्णं सगद्गदं भीतभीतः
प्रणम्य।।11.35।।

Verse 36-40

Arjun continued –

O Master of all senses!*
It's but meet
The world rejoices Thy paeans
And the world is in glee
Host of seers bow before Thee
While afraid demons flee.

O Limitless Ancient !
Even above Brahma's existence
O Ancient of the ancients !
O Universes' abode
And invincible source
Which beyond both-
The Manifest and The Unmanifest.

*Hrishikesh

स्थाने हृषीकेश तव प्रकीर्त्या जगत् प्रहृष्यत्यनुरज्यते च।
रक्षांसि भीतानि दिशो द्रवन्ति सर्वे नमस्यन्ति च
सिद्धसङ्घाः।।11.36।।

कस्माच्च ते न नमेरन्महात्मन् गरीयसे
ब्रह्मणोऽप्यादिकर्त्रे।
अनन्त देवेश जगन्निवास त्वमक्षरं सदसत्तत्परं
यत्।।11.37।।

त्वमादिदेवः पुरुषः पुराण स्त्वमस्य विश्वस्य परं
निधानम्।
वेत्तासि वेद्यं च परं च धाम त्वया ततं
विश्वमनन्तरूप।।11.38।।

वायुर्यमोऽग्निर्वरुणः शशाङ्कः प्रजापतिस्त्वं
प्रपितामहश्च।
नमो नमस्तेऽस्तु सहस्रकृत्वः पुनश्च भूयोऽपि नमो
नमस्ते।।11.39।।

नमः पुरस्तादथ पृष्ठतस्ते नमोऽस्तु ते सर्वत एव सर्व।
अनन्तवीर्यामितविक्रमस्त्वं सर्वं समाप्नोषि ततोऽसि
सर्वः।।11.40।।

Primal God ! the Original Purusha!!
Thou art all the final Refuge
Known as All knower, All knowable
O Form that never is lost
Pervaded by all the cosmos.

O Vital air ! O Agni, the fire !!
O Death ! O Moon !! O Water !!
O Prajapati ! O Divine Father !!
To Thee, my praises my paeans
My worships know no end.

O Boundless Power ! O Limitless Might !!
I bow to Thee in front, behind and all sides
All pervading Thou art
Thus, everything is Thou,
And thus All in All.

1 DRAINED BRAIN FOG
From innermost worrier
My inner Arjun looked at the Savior
And became warrior.

2 KNOWLEDGE OF GEETA
Visualizing the Form in His Voice,
Enshrined in fearless silence, the mellow rejoice
Silences demonic hollow noise.

3 THE DEVIL WITHIN
The Fear in me,
Is just feared; to see
The seer in me.

4 WONDERED DEVOTEE
My wonderment when meets
The True rejoice, in the praying spirit
Truth to the Truth speaks.

5
In the threatening chaos
Fearless seers enjoy the Divine cosmos,
Devil, in fear, is lost.

6 THE PERFECT CREATOR
He, the Perfect One,
Created and conditioned souls to evolve
Himself, being beyond Evolution.

7 ULTIMATE GOAL

Here ends the quest,
Where Manifested soul finds primal bond
With the Ancient Unmanifest.

8 ALL CONDITIONED SOULS

All modern cores
Are transcended by the Latest course
Of one most Ancient source.

9 EVERY PARTICLE IS TOTAL UNIVERSE

Totality of the Existence
Is housed in the Lord's Infinite
Again totality transcends every bit.

10 FIVE ELEMENTS OF BODY

Elements are just means
For Non-elemental conscious conditioned soul,
To achieve the Goal.

11 DEVOUT'S PRAYER

All diverse elements,
Enlivened by Him to the conscious essence
Revere His omnipresence.

12 MOST MODERN ANCIENT

The Ancient of ancients
In infinites past and infinites to come
Ever be neo Infant.

13 ORIGIN OF THE ORIGIN

'Ts own creative urge,
Of the Primal consciousness conditioned into womb
All later wombs to emerge.

14 EVOLUTION CYCLE

Wheeled on thought free Awareness,
From Unknown to knowable to Realized known
Cyclically journeyed the Existence.

15 LORD'S PRESENCE

Nothing exists sans
His essence everywhere as pure existence
Stationed in embodied elements.

16

All Pervaded by Supreme
Elements together elixired with life
Naturally inclines to Him.

Verse 41 -42

Arjun said again –

In the past I have
Addressed Thou Krshna ! pal !! Yadav !!
Unaware of Thy cosmic Halo
Whatever I behaved
In my madness or in Love
In fun while at play
Reposing, sitting or at meals

Sans = without

When alone or with pals
O Achyuta ! O Immeasurable !!
I beg forgive all.

1 AVTAAR
Even in His man-size
His universal form and glory-opulence
He maketh realized.

2 IGNORANT ARJUN –
Sensible of the world
But insensible to the Creator of world,
The potent world within worlds.

3 ARJUN'S OBEISANCE
God's grace bestows,
To man-sized friend, God-sized kinship close
Thus realized man, bows.

4
God blessed the blind,
Very close to him now, blind finds
The Omnipresent Divine.

5 KRSHNA ARJUN RELATIONS
Remnants of childhood games,
And engraved memory of the pet names
Brake never among friends.

6 EVER CLOSEST TO SOUL
Lord was ever intimate
With His childhood toys, names, pet
Alas! I realized so late.

सखेति मत्वा प्रसभं यदुक्तं हे कृष्ण हे यादव हे सखेति।
अजानता महिमानं तवेदं मया प्रमादात्प्रणयेन वापि।।11.41।।

यच्चावहासार्थमसत्कृतोऽसि विहारशय्यासनभोजनेषु।
एकोऽथवाप्यच्युत तत्समक्षं तत्क्षामये त्वामहमप्रमेयम्।।11.42।।

Verse 43

Father of all Thou art
Of animate and inanimate
Most worshipable Guru sublime
Unparallel in worlds Three,
O Lord of might Incomparable !
None may surpass Thee.

1 ONE SUPREME OF ALL

All the conditioned soul-mass
Also non-soul unconditioned for cause
Him none can surpass.

2 ORIGINAL RELATION

He is closest kin,
He is all kinship's origin,
All link unto Him.

3 HE IS ALL-LOVE

Lord – alone worshipable One
For worships of devotee, He bothers none
His love is not conditioned.

4 ALL MIRROR GHOSTS

Created His own image,
In the mirror of world, all mirage
None pars Original visage.

5 ANIMATE / INANIMATE

Every bit, every beat,
Has equal potential for the highest reach
Unto perfected Infinite.

पितासि लोकस्य चराचरस्य त्वमस्य पूज्यश्च
गुरुर्गरीयान्।
न त्वत्समोऽस्त्यभ्यधिकः कुतोऽन्यो
लोकत्रयेऽप्यप्रतिमप्रभाव।।11.43।।

Verse 44-46

O Lord ! O Adorable one !!
To implore Thy pardon,
So, my obeisance thus meet
Offerings at Thy very feet
Please bear my wrongs
That I have done,
Bear ! as father with his son,
As friend with his close
As lover to the dear most.

I am so gladdened
Thus, having gazed upon
A never-seen vision
At the same I am
O Lord ! fear-stricken
O God of gods ! O Universe's Abode !!
Thy mercy be bestowed !
To me bring familiar view
Again Of Thy form of Vishnu.

I long to see as before
Diademed, holding in arms four
Mace, conch, lotus, discus,
O Thousand armed ! Bodied Universe!!
In that very form reappear.

तस्मात्प्रणम्य प्रणिधाय कायं प्रसादये महमीशमीड्यम्।
पितेव पुत्रस्य सखेव सख्युः प्रियः प्रियायार्हसि देव
सोढुम्।।11.44।।

अदृष्टपूर्वं हृषितोऽस्मि दृष्ट्वा भयेन च प्रव्यथितं
मनो मे।
तदेव मे दर्शय देव रूपं प्रसीद देवेश
जगन्निवास।।11.45।।

किरीटिनं गदिनं चक्रहस्त मिच्छामि त्वां द्रष्टुमहं तथैव।
तेनैव रूपेण चतुर्भुजेन सहस्रबाहो भव विश्वमूर्ते।।11.46।।

1
What's next ? asked Him,
Replied Lord 'Repose!' , He being
The next of Kin.

2 ARJUN MAKES PROSTRATION.
Great archer with his prow
Bows to the Lord, for he knows
Lord's strength, in his bow.

3 PACIFIC FORM-VISHNU
Not as storm please !
O Helmsman ! Bless with navigating breeze
For sailing ease.

4
Man's perfect pursuit
In all its reach unto the Self
Seeks quieter-attitude.

5 OBEISANCE WITH EGOLESSNESS
Rising above ego-freaks,
May this pigmy realize the Vastness,
And bow to His feet.

6 LORD IS CLOSEST (ARJUN'S CONFESSION)
In my routine,
I realized not, He descends as kin
O Kin ! forgive my sin.

7 FEAR-STRUCK ARJUN
The Sun's very worth
And it's totality of grandeur is beyond
The stature of the hearth.

8 INNUMERABLE
Miens, forms, formless miens.
God head's expansions is Infinite,
I pursue to my limits.

Verse 47

The Blessed Lord said-

I havest graciously exercised
Mine own Yogic Might
O Arjun ! to reveal to thy sight
This Supreme Primeval form,
The Radiant and Infinite cosmos
Seen by none in the past.

1
Reflections unto my sight
I owe not but what I see
Reflects all Lord's mercy.

2
Every time Lord blessed
I perceived new mercy, felt new grace,
Alone through His grace.

मया प्रसन्नेन तवार्जुनेदं रूपं परं दर्शितमात्मयोगात्।
तेजोमयं विश्वमनन्तमाद्यं यन्मे त्वदन्येन न दृष्टपूर्वम्।।11.47।।

3 DARSHAN

Himself God never concealed
To the one, I-ness who concealed
Perceivable God revealed.

Verse 48

Save only thou, no mortal hast seen,
My This universal Mien,
Nor by charity, ritual , severe austerity
O Arjun ! nor by Vedas' study,
None canst see This.

1 HIS GRACE

Nor quest nor text
Nor worships but grace alone grace
Blessed the Supreme Visage.

2 ROBOTIC RITUALS

Mechanized practices,
Are the programmed channel in cyclical ways
Be aimed at centripetal grace.

3 SCRIPTURES

In the quest
Between text words in blanks
He, the Lord rests.

4 MEANS ARE NOT GOAL

Rigours, Rites, rituals
Are just propelling means, the vehicle
Be progressive ! to Final.

5

The Beads and deeds,
Are pious crawls those help to proceed
Need His Grace to speed.

न वेदयज्ञाध्ययनैर्न दानै र्न च क्रियाभिर्न तपोभिरुग्रैः।
एवंरूपः शक्य अहं नृलोके द्रष्टुं त्वदन्येन
कुरुप्रवीर।।11.48।।

Verse 49

Be not bewildered and alarmed
Beholding My Terrible form
Let dreads flee and heart with glee
Thy-desired form now, thou see !

1 FEARLESS DEVOTEE
Unafraid of roars
Containing vastness of Ocean; the shores
Know of pearls in core.

2
Fear not the master
The Great Master generously declares
To Master the fear.

3
God-fearing is dear
To the God and God doth ensure
Look beyond that fear.

Verse 50

Sanjay said to Dhratrashtra –

The Supreme Person, God head,
While to Arjun thus said –
His four armed form displayed,
At last again resumed form of Grace
And consoled this Man afraid.

1 BENEVOLENT LORD
Be faithful to Him
Because He is ever faithful
To 'Your faith in Supreme'.

2
God stirs up mind
By His Alien form, to blend into devotee
More of His Divine.

मा ते व्यथा मा च विमूढभावो दृष्ट्वा रूपं
घोरमीदृङ्ममेदम्।
व्यपेतभीः प्रीतमनाः पुनस्त्वं तदेव मे रूपमिदं
प्रपश्य।।11.49।।

इत्यर्जुनं वासुदेवस्तथोक्त्वा स्वकं रूपं दर्शयामास भूयः।
आश्वासयामास च भीतमेनं भूत्वा पुनः
सौम्यवपुर्महात्मा।।11.50।।

3 DARSHAN
'Show!' to trust I asked
The Lord trusted and revealed His Vast
How vast His trust was?

4 ADVENT OF GOD
Man sized coming of Lord
Is to make believe man, among odds
'Man is compressed God'.

Verse 51

Arjun said –

Thy gentle Human mien
O Janardan ! having seen
I'm restored to my own self
Now I'm composed serene.

1 AGITATION OF ARJUN
Truth of the Lord,
Is so transcendental beyond cosmic thoughts
Into comprehension befits not.

2
Arjun was hurt
Though Lord appeared, final Truth emerged
Above false comprehensive comforts.

3 AVTAAR
It behoves, it pacifies
Man-sized mind could perceive and eye
Descent of Lord, man-sized.

4
Anxiety is fed
By Faithlessness and anxiety fades
With beginning of true faith.

दृष्ट्वेदं मानुषं रूपं तवसौम्यं जनार्दन।
इदानीमस्मि संवृत्तः सचेताः प्रकृतिं गतः।।11.51।।

Verse 52-54

The Blessed Lord said –

The form, which thou havest seen,
Is hard to behold this mien.
For this very cosmic Darshan
Even gods ever yearn.

My this very form is disclosed
O Arjun ! O scorcher of foes ! !
Nor through rituals nor charities
Nor through vedic lore nor austerities.

Undivided Bhakti who own,
Canst I, of this Form, be known
And in reality I be witnessed
In Oneness, finally embraced.

1
Pure fire in eyes,
Melts worldly coats on every sight
Thus Divinity is realized.

2 DEVOTEE
His world one does see
Beyond the existence of world
Is world of devotee.

3
Conceals the Lord,
To the mindful minds of man
Reveals to heartful hearts.

4 SINGLE MINDED DEVOTION
To know that One;
Is the knowledge, of rest else
Should be oblivion.

Oblivion = Total forgetful

सुदुर्दर्शमिदं रूपं दृष्टवानसि यन्मम।
देवा अप्यस्य रूपस्य नित्यं दर्शनकाङ्क्षिणः।।11.52।।

नाहं वेदैर्न तपसा न दानेन न चेज्यया।
शक्य एवंविधो द्रष्टुं दृष्टवानसि मां यथा।।11.53।।

भक्त्या त्वनन्यया शक्यमहमेवंविधोऽर्जुन।
ज्ञातुं दृष्टुं च तत्त्वेन प्रवेष्टुं च परंतप।।11.54।।

5
Lord is undivided
So ever is His attention; in return
Cede ! undivided devotion.

6 STRENGTH OF DEVOTEE
Weakness of heart
For the Lord, is the strongest cement
Keep undivided reverence.

7 SINGLE MINDED DEVOTION
With the undivided heart
Hope of the Lord, to embrace devotee
Scatters not.

Verse 55

Who does action alone for Me,
He who surrenderth to Me with Love
From any attachment who ist free
From any enmity, who ist above
Certainly cometh to Me O Pandav!"*

**Arjun*

1 AWAKE!
To draw to Him
First learn to withdraw
From delusive dream.

2
Equipped with Bhakti
Weapons of Humanity, kill enmity
Thus win Divinity.

मत्कर्मकृन्मत्परमो मद्भक्तः सङ्गवर्जितः।
निर्वैरः सर्वभूतेषु यः स मामेति पाण्डव।।11.55।।

CHAPTER TWELVE

The Devotion: Bhakti-Yog

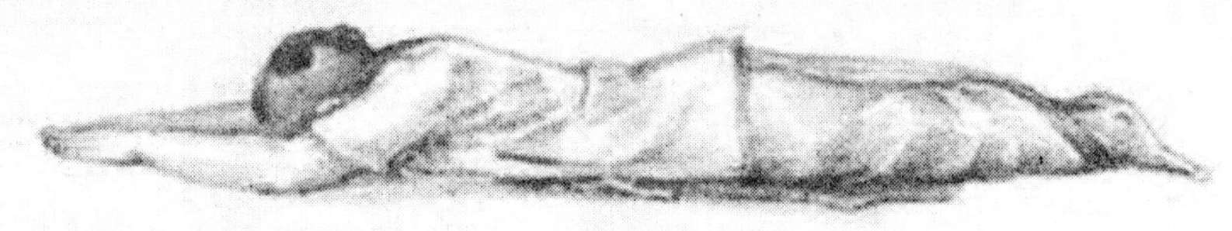

Surrendering at His feet,
At every step, the confined devotee meets
Grace of the Infinite.

He alone works pure

Who has nothing to secure

From the work.

Chapter 12

BHAKTI - DEDICATION

Verse 1

Arjun inquired –

They ever, who worship Thou,
Those steadfast ever immersed.
Others adoring the Unmanifested, those devouts
Who of these are better versed?

1
Not from false to Truth
But from Truth to All-Truth
The Real devotee pursuits

2 PATH ?
Whether wise-pursuit
Or the devotional surrender of the Subdued
Reached the Truth?

3 PUREST QUEST FOR PURE
The Adorable, I adore-
Which path, which means are pure?
'The purest' to secure.

Verse 2

The blessed Lord said –

Whose mind on Me, is ever fixed
Ever united to Me, who worship
Ever endowed with Supreme Faith
I consider them most perfect.

1 WORSHIPPER
I behave
Ever like Lord's slave
Richest haves I have.

2 PERFECTION STEP
Conditioning every breath
On the path of unconditional faith,
Is the perfect quest.

3
Waves of thought
Ever immersed in the Ocean of Lord
Perfect the dissolution unto Him.

एवं सततयुक्ता ये भक्तास्त्वां पर्युपासते।
येचाप्यक्षरमव्यक्तं तेषां के योगवित्तमाः।।12.1।।

मय्यावेश्य मनो ये मां नित्ययुक्ता उपासते।
श्रद्धया परयोपेतास्ते मे युक्ततमा मताः।।12.2।।

Verse 3-4

Worship with senses restrained,
The Unmanifest, Unthinkable, Omnipresent
Unchanging, the Stable, Eternal
The Imperishable, the Indefinable
With even-mindedness worship who;
And the welfare of all who pursue
Verily, attain Me those Yogi's too.

1 NIRGUN'S BRAHMN

Even-minded troth,
Perceives the Unmanifest as most Manifest
As Truth of Both.

2 YOGIC PATH - WALFARE

In the equanimous brain,
Senses restrained, turned to welfare intents
The Unmanifest descends.

3 SUPREME FAITH IN ABSOLUTE

I am blessed
For I believe the Supreme
Before I perceive Him.

4 PURE FAITH

The formed- Advent or Unmanifest
Are One under veils of renegade
Ever perceivable, lest.

5 ENTIRETY IS ONENESS

The World never conspires
If the wholeness of world manifests within
As the Unmanifest Entire.

6 YOGIC ATTAINMENT

All pervading Lord,
Meditatively worshipped into lore
The Formless intensifies in Core.

Verse 5

For those, whose mind
On the Unmanifest Lord, is inclined
Their advancement is arduous
Because for the Embodied-self its tough.

Renegade = Apostate (Unspiritual)

ये त्वक्षरमनिर्देश्यमव्यक्तं पर्युपासते।
सर्वत्रगमचिन्त्यं च कूटस्थमचलं ध्रुवम्।।12.3।।

संनियम्येन्द्रियग्रामं सर्वत्र समबुद्धयः।
ते प्राप्नुवन्ति मामेव सर्वभूतहिते रताः।।12.4।।

क्लेशोऽधिकतरस्तेषामव्यक्तासक्तचेतसाम्।
अव्यक्ता हि गतिर्दुःखं देहवद्भिरवाप्यते।।12.5।।

1 MAN'S WORSHIP OF NIRGUNA
For the shaped Mortal coils
To envisage the Shapeless Immortal
Needs greater toil.

2
For the Embodied it suits,
Finest of Impersonified God be understood
Naturally through attributes.

3
All pervading diffused Absolute
Difficult for the soul stationed in crude
Is perceivable through attributes.

4
In Entrapped mesh
Beyond nerves, the Embodied-mind perplexed
Hardly moves beyond flesh.

5 BHAKTI YOG
The soul compressed into attributes
Framed consciousness perceives well
The shaped Absolute.

Verse 6-7

But those who ever venerate Me,
Renouncing all actions unto Me
Single-minded who meditate on Me
Thus O Arjun ! who are absorbed in Me,
Ere long as Redeemer I redeem
Bringing them out of mortal ocean.

1 HE IS DOER
Seems I do,
But I don't, is the Highest view
To worship the All Doer.

2 SELF ANALYSIS
Devoted being in me,
Can't redeem, never the less if sees
But Devotee within.

3 BHAKTI
Surrendering at His feet,
At every step, the confined devotee meets
Grace of the Infinite.

4
Beyond Egocentric limitation
Once absorbed all into Supreme
Diffuses into Him.

ये तु सर्वाणि कर्माणि मयि संन्यस्य मत्पराः।
अनन्येनैव योगेन मां ध्यायन्त उपासते।।12.6।।

तेषामहं समुद्धर्ता मृत्युसंसारसागरात्।
भवामि नचिरात्पार्थ मय्यावेशितचेतसाम्।।12.7।।

5 WANDERINGS
Mental otherness wanders
With disintegrated goal blunders
Reaches nowhere.

6
Ever the Supreme
Here n here after, is keen to redeem
We delay, seems.

7 BHAKTI YOG
Absorption is real devotion,
Which is mutual diffusing phenomenon
Of 'one' into non-other One.

SURRENDER TO LORD

Verse 8

Mind be raised in Me, none else
Intellect be invested to Me as well.
Beyond doubt, then thou shalt,
In Me wilt always dwell.

1 NO I-NESS
Unto Lord the purged mind,
And parallelly dipt heart will find
The individuality dissolving into Divine.

2 GOD IS HOME
Ever to retain Lord,
Is the best bargain of living thoughts
To remain ever in God.

3
Freed mind and freed mindfulness
Also frees from slavery to senses
To King of kings it reaches.

4 LIVING IN GOD
Nor the God,
Nor the Home just a dwelling
Both together true feelings.

Verse 9

If thou art not able to fix,
On Me your mind unalloyed,
Then seek to reach
Me by repeated Yogic practice.

मय्येव मन आधत्स्व मयि बुद्धिं निवेशय।
निवसिष्यसि मय्येव अत ऊर्ध्वं न संशयः।।12.8।।

अथ चित्तं समाधातुं न शक्नोषि मयि स्थिरम्।
अभ्यासयोगेन ततो मामिच्छाप्तुं धनञ्जय।।12.9।।

1 YOGA
For calm interior
Shade off all qualms of exterior
Interior is already calm.

2 YOGA
The whole process
Is to awaken existing Godliness
Lying in hibernating state.

3 BODY IS SHRINE
Practice pursue
To enshrine soul anew
In every sinew.

4 YOGIC PRACTICE
Habit
Bit by bit
Could bid.

5
Thoughts abducted by mind,
Reach the lesser faculty of distraction
Practice win-back to sublime.

Verse 10

This Bhakti-yoga if thou canst not take
Be thou intent to work for My sake
In My work if thy Karma is engaged
Thou too wilt attain Supreme stage.

1 ACT FOR HIS CAUSE
Not the exhaustive efforts
But the daily toil for His sake
For Perfection is enough.

2 EASY PATH
Even external daily acts
If to Lord, as All Doer dedicated
Interiorize devotee to perfect.

3
Bud's innate scope
With ease petals slowly ope
Perfect nectar is hoped.

4
With God attuned
Even lesser work is opportuned,
To be Perfect-endeavor.

अभ्यासेऽप्यसमर्थोऽसि मत्कर्मपरमो भव।
मदर्थमपि कर्माणि कुर्वन् सिद्धिमवाप्स्यसि।।12.10।।

5
Work ! for the Lord
And let the world watch and record
Lord works for you.

Verse 11

Even if you are unable
To follow this very route
Then taking in Me refuge
Try to be self-controlled
Give up all action's fruits.

1
He alone works pure
Who has nothing to secure
From the work.

2 THE SELF-CONTROLLED
Masters of own mind
Master their work and master as well
The Great Master who works.

3 WORKING NOT IN REFUGE
In these mortal cages
Cycles of births toiling for ages
Alas! Earn no eternal wages.

4
To work is a privilege
By the Lord as mean to worship
If not attached to wage.

5 WORKING IN REFUGE
Sweat that wets the Earth,
Is not wage earning, in refuge but
Has oblation's worth.

6 IDEAL SURRENDER
Refuge, the Perfect Refuge
In it all work, wishes and all fruits
Transcendent totally to diffuse.

Verse 12

Better than mindless practice
Verily, is Gyan, the gnosis.
Meditation however is better than gnosis
Yet better than Meditation is
Fruit of action relinquished
For, its followed, promptly by the Peace.

अथैतदप्यशक्तोऽसि कर्तुं मद्योगमाश्रितः।
सर्वकर्मफलत्यागं ततः कुरु यतात्मवान्।।12.11।।

श्रेयो हि ज्ञानमभ्यासाज्ज्ञानाद्ध्यानं विशिष्यते।
ध्यानात्कर्मफलत्यागस्त्यागाच्छान्तिरनन्तरम्।।12.12।।

1 SPIRITUAL IMPLICATION
Mechanized physical acts
Should have correct grasp through intellect,
It reaches nowhere lest.

2 SPIRITUAL LADDER
Wandering with text
Pondering on it is further better next
Living in it, the best.

3 FRUITS OF ACTION
Wish of fruits
Not drop ripe, often get rotten
Poise of mind to pollute.

4
Seeded into devout
To learn to discern 'to renounce'
Peace quickly sprout.

5 MECHANISED DEEDS
A worship by rote
Can hardly ope that very route
What the worship should.

6
Imagination of fruits, ruins
Meditation assimilates to fruitless is so immune
To self-poise it attunes.

7 MEDITATION
Meditating wisdom is never mute
Seems sleepy though stoic giving-up attitude
Brings most dynamic quetitude.

BHAKT – BELOVED OF LORD

Verse 13-14

Who is free of envy
And to all full of mercy
Devoid of I-ness and possession
In pain and pleasure who is even
Lenient and Ever content yogi
Who is steady and sturdy;
With thoughts and sagacity
Who is dedicated to Me
Dear to Me, he is My devotee.

अद्वेष्टा सर्वभूतानां मैत्रः करुण एव च।
निर्ममो निरहङ्कारः समदुःखसुखः क्षमी।।12.13।।

सन्तुष्टः सततं योगी यतात्मा दृढनिश्चयः।
मय्यर्पितमनोबुद्धिर्यो मद्भक्तः स मे प्रियः।।12.14।।

1 DEAR TO GOD
With dispelled viles
At the same with assembled ideas high
Be! apple of His eyes.

2 GOD IS CAPTIVATED BY DEVOTEE
Moral and ethical tools
Frame this and next world, empower devotee
Over Supreme Ruler to rule.

3
Endeavored for Godliness
Yonder destination in a Yogi as such
Endear him to God.

4 DEAREST DEVOTEE OF GOD
Love is only worship
Of devotee in which Love is loved
Which Beloved God Loves.

Verse 15-16

By whom world is not ruffled
Who is not ruffled by the world
Free from pleasure, envy, scare, fear
To Me, he too is dear.

Free of mundane desires
In and out who is pure
Alert, above Pain above worldly care
Has given up all ventures
Thus devoted to Me, is dear

1
Among events of mundane,
Trusting Him uneventful who remains
Creates own heaven.

2 STOICISM
Joy is never pure
And sufferings never longer endure
Absence of both is cure.

3 PURITY HAS SIGHT
Purity transcends the whole
Beyond dazzling world it sees soul
Soul in turn sees God.

4 TI IE WORLD
Agitating the mundane
World's rebound agitation is gained
In mutual bargain.

Ruffle = agitate.

यस्मान्नोद्विजते लोको लोकान्नोद्विजते च यः।
हर्षामर्षभयोद्वेगैर्मुक्तो यः स च मे प्रियः।।12.15।।

अनपेक्षः शुचिर्दक्ष उदासीनो गतव्यथः।
सर्वारम्भपरित्यागी यो मद्भक्तः स मे प्रियः।।12.16।।

5 BE FREE FROM BAD

I sin
Even if, I do not win
Those dormant within.

6 STEADY INNER-CALM

Poise is so deep
That maddening storm can't bring whiff
To harmony, Yogis keep.

7 VIRTUOUS LIFE

Every true virtue
Is very dear to God in view
That nothing could woo(it).

8 NO EGOISTIC CLAIM OF DEEDS

All ventures are eternal
Without the commencement or any end
Independent of I, me and mine.

Verse 17

Who does, nor in content nor in contemn, indulge
One who keeps from grief and urge,
From good and evil who is free
Lovable to Me, is that devotee.

1 GOD-IDENTIFIED

Yogi keeps himself unidentified
By the relativity of cosmos, which defy
God identifies him Stoic.

2

The desire is Just
When it dedicates, but when it expects
Its all lust.

3 OMENS

Good and Evil confuse
Till the dualities of world diffuse
Into all auspicious muse.

4

Desires are unending thirst
Making desires most undesirable lust
Are to be curbed.

5 'A BHAKT'- SINGLE MINDEDLY ACTIVE

For Godliness is lively perceptive
Becomes most lively to Godliness
And to world, dead-nonreactive.

Whiff =puff Contemn=hatred.

यो न हृष्यति न द्वेष्टि न शोचति न काङ्क्षति।
शुभाशुभपरित्यागी भक्ितमान्यः स मे प्रियः।।12.17।।

Verse 18-19

Who is same to friend and foe
And in respect and insult also
Warmth and chill, pleasure and woe.
Who doth remain same
In fame and in blames,
Who has given up attachments
Poised and disposed to easy content,
Non-attached to matter tenements
With quietude, fixed in knowledge
Ever in devotions engaged
Such a very devotee
Also, is dear to Me.

1 YOGIC DEVOTION
Keeping himself unidentified,
With the relativity of cosmos, which defy
Yogic stoicism is deified.

2 BROADNESS
Bhakt's Bosom unbind-
Narrows not to estimate enmity, finds
On all wides embracing Divine.

3 VALUED LIFE
Existing value of man
Is valued by Creator's hope
Making him a man.

4 BALANCING ROPE
On the rope of contrasts
Acrobatic equilibrium in the dual cosmos
Equipoised the balance to cross.

5 SPECTATOR OF SCREEN PLAY
Ever-changing shadows
Of delusive screen by villains and heroes
Factual yogi knows.

Defy=challenge, Deify I worship / Praise.

समः शत्रौ च मित्रे च तथा मानापमानयोः।
शीतोष्णसुखदुःखेषु समः सङ्गविवर्जितः।।12.18।।

तुल्यनिन्दास्तुतिर्मौनी सन्तुष्टो येनकेनचित्।
अनिकेतः स्थिरमतिर्भक्तिमान्मे प्रियो नरः।।12.19।।

6 BEYOND FLESH IS DIVINE
Depth of poise in thought
Can never blister nor can frost
Which's only skin deep.

7 BLISS
Already at home with Krshna,
Is conditioned not by concrete possessions
But dwells ever in content.

8 EQUIPOISE
In world's wordy view
Censures are Praised, praises are Praised too
Though Silences transcendent mute.

9 SAINTLY POSSESSIONS
Elixired with God rapt
Not intoxicated by res, riches, realm
Keep himself aloof.

Verse 20

But, those who pursue and follow
The Eternal- Sanatan, I avowed
As declared by Me above
With all dedication endowed
In Me who are ever engrossed
My love to those, surpass.

1 DEAR TO GOD
Lovable is one of those,
Who unto God ever does engross
Krshna's words who follows.

2 SURRENDER THROUGH LOVE
Where Love does commence,
It has it's own but perfect end
Into the Lovable's hand.

3 DEVOTIONAL LIFE
This quality, otherwise
None the practice rule the devotional life
With Bhakti, the method dies.

4 BHAKTI
Love is all above
The only form in which, lovable Lord
Is loved.

At Home=comfortable Res = Property.

ये तु धर्म्यामृतमिदं यथोक्तं पर्युपासते।
श्रद्दधाना मत्परमा भक्तास्तेऽतीव मे प्रियाः।।12.20।।

5 GEETA

Only worth
In this and next world
Is His word.

6 BHAKTI YOG

Only Medium of spiritual nexus
For transcendental link among Lord n us
Is Devotion of Bhakt.

CHAPTER THIRTEEN

Field (The Body) and it's Knower

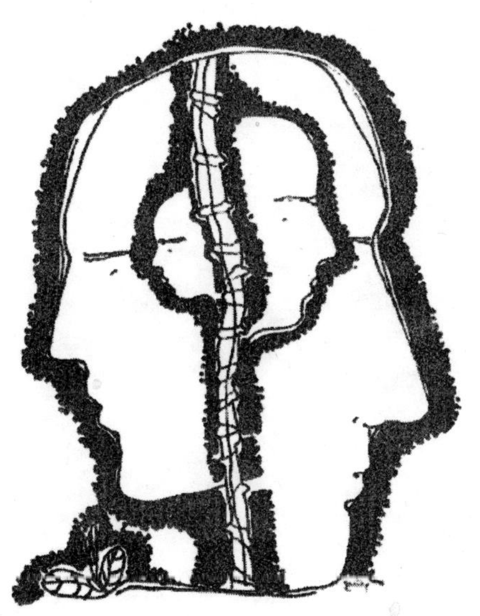

God is on my side –
Unto my learning, then God added
'There is no other side.'

The battle daily occurred

Against me, with all rattling the sword,

My weapon is His word.

Chapter Thirteen

BODY, THE FIELD

Preface* Verse

Arjun said –

"The matter and non-matter, the spirit,
The field and its knower in it,
The knowledge and knowable to know how
I crave to learn all about."

1 RESEARCH AND INTUITION
Knowledgeable and visible
Seeker searches through own learning level
The Unknowable and Invisible.

2
The knowledge itself
Is the highest privilege
To Perfect the knowledge.

3
Pleasure is body
Knowledge is the very soul
That is knowable goal.

**This verse is not chanted in some editions of Geeta to make the sum total to 700 verses and not 701.*

Verse 1

The Blessed Lord said –

This body is the field,
To whom this fact is revealed,
Sages call him knower of the field.

1 LEARNED LORE
Knowing matter layer
As distinct from spiritual non-matter
Is lore of the knower.

2
Universality in shield
Of expressed individuality of matter in field
To the knower is revealed.

3 ENVELOPE OF SOUL
Fathomed into matter
Found Phantom of the matter
Is pseudo epitome of soul.

4
In relativistic falsehood
Matter covers the Truth and deludes
Absolustistic Inner break through.

Verse 2

I know field and field's knowers
O Arjun ! I know the body and its owners
Distinguishing between fields and its knowers
Is True knowledge, I consider.

1 LORD IMPARTS KNOWLEDGE
Lord's own Lore
All-knower imparts into the sages' core
Highest knowledge thus explored.

2 GOD IMPARTS KNOWLEDGE
God will fail,
If All Knowing God doesn't tell
Little knower, in whom He dwells.

3 REAL KNOWLEDGE
If I know
That the Unknowable knows everything
I will know the Unknowable.

4 REAL KNOWLEDGE
God 's on my side –
Unto my learning, then God added
'There is no other side.'

प्रकृतिं पुरुषं चैव क्षेत्रं क्षेत्रज्ञमेव च।
एतद्वेदितुमिच्छामि ज्ञानं ज्ञेयं च केशव।।13.1।।

इदं शरीरं कौन्तेय क्षेत्रमित्यभिधीयते।
एतद्यो वेत्ति तं प्राहुः क्षेत्रज्ञ इति तद्विदः।।13.2।।

MATTER AND NON-MATTER

Verse 3-4

The field of action, it's attributes
And how does it constitute
What are defects and whence produced
Who the knower is and His sovereign
Briefly from Me listen !
What has been told by sages
In various chants in vedic text
And precisely reasoned analyses
And BrahmSutra's muses.

1
Body is field of defects
And is caused for the cause and effect
Many ways said this fact.

2 CYCLIC FIELD
None is produced
Without cause and the Effect has but
Caused the cause reproduced.

3 REDEMPTION
This field is unreal dream
We are all bodies, it falsely seems
Lesser this thought, redeems.

4
Body is field
It's must to know of field array
For inner soldier to sway.

5
In the field I sew
And I reaped all the same
No one else to blame.

6 INNER FIGHT
On My General's words
I in my own field battle
Ready to rattle the Sword.

Rattle=frighten for war.

क्षेत्रज्ञं चापि मां विद्धि सर्वक्षेत्रेषु भारत।
क्षेत्रक्षेत्रज्ञयोर्ज्ञानं यत्तज्ज्ञानं मतं मम।।13.3।।

तत्क्षेत्रं यच्च यादृक् च यद्विकारि यतश्च यत्।
स च यो यत्प्रभावश्च तत्समासेन मे श्रृणु।।13.4।।

Verse 5-6

Described briefly compact
Field, the Kshetra and modification of Kshetra
Are composed of Nature unmanifested,
The five cosmic elements, ego, mind, intellect,
The ten senses and five sense-objects
Desire, pleasure, pain and hatred,
All thus all diverse forces aggregate
And in body field with consciousness act.

1 EMBODIMENT
From Unmanifest grosser nature
Picked finer space, Earth, fire, water, air
Thus Inert formless comes overt.

2 CHAINS OF BIRTHS
For non-matter, the soul,
Diverse matters gather from the cosmic whole
Vehicle of soul thus roll.

3 DISTORED FIELD OF BODY
Shaped by the terrene elements
Vitalized by the Shapeless Divine essence
But Identified by malign I-ness.

4 BODY IS MATTER CLUSTER
Body has though name
It's aggregation of elements in frame
Animated in cosmic domain.

5
Unmanifested complex attributes
From causal to astral manifestation, evolve
Simplicity of soul to resolve.

ऋषिभिर्बहुधा गीतं छन्दोभिर्विविधैः पृथक्।
ब्रह्मसूत्रपदैश्चैव हेतुमद्भिर्विनिश्चितैः।।13.5।।

महाभूतान्यहङ्कारो बुद्धिरव्यक्तमेव च।
इन्द्रियाणि दशैकं च पञ्च चेन्द्रियगोचराः।।13.6।।

GNOSIS; THE WISDOM

Verse 7-11

Diffidence, No pretense, non-violence,
Pardon, Uprightness, to the Guru reverence,
Sanctity, firmness and temperance
Ego's absence, Indifference to the objects of sense,
Observance of the Evil and pains,
And sufferings, old-age, birth-death chains.

Non – attachment of self with mammon
Non identification of self with spouse, sons!
Equal amidst pleasant and Unpleasant,
By yogic practice of God-union
Unto Me with uncorrupt devotion,
Leading resort to seclusion
Abstain from company of worldly men,
Perseverance in Self-realization
In True-knowledge, a Divine Darshan
These all are True Knowledge,
What's opposed to it is Ignorance.

1 DISPOSSESSED BUT DUTIFUL
Possessed of God
Thinks of God in this dubious world
Keeping duteous to world.

2 SANCTITY IS FREEDOM
Purity has message
Decoded by the purest past sages-
'There is no bondage'.

Temperance=self-control

इच्छा द्वेषः सुखं दुःखं सङ्घातश्चेतनाधृतिः।
एतत्क्षेत्रं समासेन सविकारमुदाहृतम्।।13.7।।

अमानित्वमदम्भित्वमहिंसा क्षान्तिरार्जवम्।
आचार्योपासनं शौचं स्थैर्यमात्मविनिग्रहः।।13.8।।

इन्द्रियार्थेषु वैराग्यमनहङ्कार एव च।
जन्ममृत्युजराव्याधिदुःखदोषानुदर्शनम्।।13.9।।

असक्तिरनभिष्वङ्गः पुत्रदारगृहादिषु।
नित्यं च समचित्तत्वमिष्टानिष्टोपपत्तिषु।।13.10।।

मयि चानन्ययोगेन भक्तिरव्यभिचारिणी।
विविक्तदेशसेवित्वमरतिर्जनसंसदि।।13.11।।

3 VIRTUES AVAILED
Greatest virtues are worth,
A divine transcendence unto the next world,
Is simplest in this world.

4 I-NESS
This I, me, mine
Keeps me just one decision behind
Alas ! dead end I find.

5 EVOLUTION OF MIND
Mind with single mindedness
Evolved and Singled out a single step
Of 'One-ness'.

6 NON ATTACHMENT
Tangled tangy now,
With sap of virtues, gets ripe
Fruit falls from bough.

7
From Diffidence to the Truth
On ladder of knowledge with sublime virtues
Sages realize the Absolute.

8
Good and Evils so declared
Are our slaves, not we theirs
Being Eternal Father's heir.

9 MARCH ALONE!
I need no crowd
*My solitary struggle helps on untrodden**
Single minded March to 'One'

10 HE, THE 'HELMSMAN'
Simple way the Supreme
Drives me smooth on helm
Offering –'Yes I 'm.

11
A hush within you
Quietly rushes unto notice of God
Melody of your virtues.

THE KNOWER

Verse 12

Which 's to be known that
To thou I shalt narrate
Because with this knowledge
Immortality thou wilt taste.
The Supreme hast no beginning
Called nor a Being nor Non-Being.

Tangy =sour. **Untrodden path.*

अध्यात्मज्ञाननित्यत्वं तत्त्वज्ञानार्थदर्शनम्।
एतज्ज्ञानमिति प्रोक्तमज्ञानं यदतोन्यथा।।13.12।।

1 AMBROSIAL EXISTENCE
In the Livings which exists,
Is the Eternal Entity, knowing this
Realizes nectarine Gnosis.

2 THE MANIFEST GOD
Horizon seems with finite,
But on its way and walking to it
Makes known-- 'it's Infinite'.

3 THE CREATOR OF TIME
In the un-clocked continuance
Of Single –'Now' stretched into Present
The Eternity spanned moments.

4 A CERTAIN FACT
It's not probable
That I'm not the body feeble
But the same Immortal.

5
*Knower of body-field**
Is never born and never dies
Thus the Unknowable be realized.

6 CREATOR OF TIME
The Eternity with moments
Impregnated the womb of Timeless span
Thus the Unborn created 'Time'.

Verse 13-18

In the world He resideth
Enveloping all; the existth on all sides
With His hands, feet, eyes, ears
With His mouth and heads, (exist) everywhere.

Shining in all senses though
From the senses He is above,
Unattached to the Creation
Yet Mainstay, all to sustain
From all attributes He's free
Yet Enjoyer of all these freely.

Within and without He dwells
The animate and inanimate as well.
He is though imperceptible
Because of He is finely Unknowable.
He is far away distant
He is also very adjacent.

**Supreme Soul and sages souls*

Though He, the undivided, is not diversified
In all the existence, He appearth
He maintainth destroyth too,
He createth those forms anew.

He is Light of all light-shines
He 's said to be beyond darkness
In all hearts He is enshrined
He's knowledge, its object and goal of knowledge.

Blessed Lord said further –

The field, I havest narrated
The Nature of knowledge and its object
My devotee by this learning
Wilt enter into My Being.

1
Highest concept I can
Have of God in the whole existence
His tool I'm.

2
Man made the tools
And became himself tool of his tools
Till mastered as Master's tools.

3
Just not in the heart,
But in Hand, feet, mouth He dwells,
God is man's very Self.

4 ALL -PERVADING
There is no niche
Where Lord Himself hath not niched
Making Himself within reach.

**Three Gunas-Divine, Terrence, Malign.*

ज्ञेयं यत्तत्प्रवक्ष्यामि यज्ज्ञात्वाऽमृतमश्नुते।
अनादिमत्परं ब्रह्म न सत्तन्नासदुच्यते।।13.13।।

सर्वतः पाणिपादं तत्सर्वतोऽक्षिशिरोमुखम्।
सर्वतः श्रुतिमल्लोके सर्वमावृत्य तिष्ठति।।13.14।।

सर्वेन्द्रियगुणाभासं सर्वेन्द्रियविवर्जितम्।
असक्तं सर्वभृच्चैव निर्गुणं गुणभोक्तृ च।।13.15।।

बहिरन्तश्च भूतानामचरं चरमेव च।
सूक्ष्मत्वात्तदविज्ञेयं दूरस्थं चान्तिके च तत्।।13.16।।

अविभक्तं च भूतेषु विभक्तमिव च स्थितम्।
भूतभर्तृ च तज्ज्ञेयं ग्रसिष्णु प्रभविष्णु च।।13.17।।

ज्योतिषामपि तज्ज्योतिस्तमसः परमुच्यते।
ज्ञानं ज्ञेयं ज्ञानगम्यं हृदि सर्वस्य विष्ठितम्।।13.18।।

5
It makes sense
That God is aloof from all the senses
But it's godly essence.

6 UNCONDITIONING SENSES
Where mind is mute
To the conditioned effect of the attributes
Consciousness transcends to Absolute.

7
Deluded myopic blur,
Need far-sighted perception be cleared
To find Him near.

8
Sun knows no darkness
God enlightens light of soul same way
Which, though Ego veils.

9 IGNORANCE KEEPS HIM FAR..
With no peripheral spans
Unto many non-centred centres Lord expands,
To self-centred seems distant.

10 THREE GUNAS
Non attributive yet Divine,
God is all divinity in terrene,
And Hope in malign.

11 ALL PERVADING LORD
Though Unseen within and without
But needle is conscious of this
Unperceivable
The magnetic field all about.

12
Ignorance is the cataract
The light can't penetrate the eyes
To illumine the Self.

13
World of objectified light
Is illumined by God into perceptible rays
Light that lits any darkness.

14 ENLIGHTENMENT / BOOKISH LEARNING
To know what to know
Is the map, nor the journey nor go
Till I enter it's glow.

PURUSHA AND PRAKRITI (THE LORD AND NATURE)

Verse 19

Know ! the spirit, the living entity
And material Nature, The Prakriti.
Both are beyond genesis
And know! As produce of Prakrati's traits
All the attainments and ailments.

इति क्षेत्रं तथा ज्ञानं ज्ञेयं चोक्तं समासतः।
मद्भक्त एतद्विज्ञाय मद्भावायोपपद्यते।।13.19।।

1
Creator and His Creation
Spirited life and nature's material expansion
Both parallelly endless, Unborn.

2 NATURE IS MODIFYING MAYA
Undistorted Sun rays through
The natural refraction of the dew
Get into diverse hue.

3 ALL –ALOOF WITNESS
One Creator created
Many matter modifiers and non matter doers
He became Witness Himself.

4
Ocean, the Creator's calm
Prakriti* is the wave of storm
Shore to deform or transform.

Verse 20

The Nature is the cause
Of all material activities and effects
And Spirit, the Living entity is to experience
Delight's and plight's impact.

1 WORLD OF MATTER
Senses, objects, intellect
In their aggregate, Naturally not separate
Represent nature's effect.

2 PLEASURE AND PAIN IN LIFE
Light of Consciousness illumines
The material of objects and thought within
With shine and shadow of feelings.

3 SOUL IN THE BODY
Soul individualized by Name,
Is inferiorized to the Nature's frame
Conditioned to balm and bale.

4 WORLD OF SENSES AND BODY
Combination of deforms, reforms
Of senses interact, varied species to form
As effect of Nature's causative Norms.

5
Soul is perfectly Divine,
But while identified with the Body, Terrene
Tempered with malign.

**Material Nature (Maya)*

प्रकृतिं पुरुषं चैव विद्ध्यनादी उभावपि।
विकारांश्च गुणांश्चैव विद्धि प्रकृतिसंभवान्।।13.20।।

Verse 21

The Soul, living entity
Setting on to Prakriti's seat,
Experiences the qualities
Which are born of Prakriti
Thus, attached to Nature's qualities
Good or evil species it meets.

1 PRAKRITI
Soul prepares body
Or the Body through Nature tempers soul
Nature imposes its role.

2 SINS EARNED
*Where the mattered coil***
Conditions the soul enveloped by material toils
Destined to tragic spoils.

3 WORLD OF GOOD AND EVIL WOMBS
In this grey zone,
Not the fated but Acted field alone
Destines, what be owned.

4 VIRTUES EARNED
Affiliated to the Self
Modes* of nature to the Body – Soul Complex
Decode the world next.

5 DESTINY
Side by side
Good and Evil hand in hand reside
Deeds knock and decide.

Verse 22

In the body one who dwellth,
Is the Same Highest Self
Existing as detached witness
As Approver, sustainer and Lord Mahesh,
As transcendental Enjoyer inhabitth
Who is known as The Supreme Spirit.

*Three traits-Divine, Terrene, Malign. ** Body field.*

कार्यकारणकर्तृत्वे हेतुः प्रकृतिरुच्यते।
पुरुषः सुखदुःखानां भोक्तृत्वे हेतुरुच्यते।।13.21।।

पुरुषः प्रकृतिस्थो हि भुङ्क्ते प्रकृतिजान्गुणान्।
कारणं गुणसङ्गोऽस्य सदसद्योनिजन्मसु।।13.22।।

1 THINK BEYOND BODY
I'm not the frame
Bond free, boundless and the Same
Nameless, named protem.

4
Different but not indifferent
Representing Himself the Supreme
transcends
With His Equal Presence.

2 ETERNAL PAL
In me a friend
Even when my enmity hates myself
Eternity is hand in hand.

5 GEETA
The battle daily occurred
Against me, with all rattling the sword,
My weapon is His word.

3
Many men in one man
Who consents, who sustains, who witness
is One Unconditioned Great.

Verse 23

Whatever present life may be
*One who realizes Purusha's qualities**
And also threefold traits of Prakriti
He will earn his worth
To be exempted from rebirth.

1 WITNESS GESTURE
Being observer the Self
In the world of matter one who dwells
Is redemption in itself.

2 SALVATION / MOKSHA
At any moment
Not thru conditioned past but unconditioned present
Moment frees into Timelessness.

3 THE REALIZATION
*In domain of conditioning soot***
Who keeps from matter has understood,
Inner untainted Godhood.

4 REDEMPTION
From Things apart
Where Nothingness -fills empty heart
Thus never parts Lord.

*Protem=for time being   *True Nature of Supreme Self   **World of taints*

उपद्रष्टाऽनुमन्ता च भर्ता भोक्ता महेश्वरः।
परमात्मेति चाप्युक्तो देहेऽस्मिन्पुरुषः परः।।13.23।।

THREE PATHS

Verse 24

Lord is perceived by some
By meditation; and by some
By cultivation of Gnostic wisdom
And by others by fruitless Karma.

1
Soulful heart, mind, hand
Transform body-objects to transcend to goal
Of Soul of souls.

2
Creative dynamism or intuitive stillness
But to its perfections will tread
To evolve to the Perfect.

3 PATH
There is no lesser fit
Each path is fittest for the one
Who is walking it.

4 QUITETUDE
Not just the walking
But the stillness on path also reaches
Because stillness is a path.

Verse 25

Also, there are some who
*Ignorant of these yogic routes**
Worship, taking heed to other's view
If they regard heard-words as Supreme Refuge
Certainly transcend Death, they too.

1
Darkness of ages strewed
Betrayed, strayed – needed Ancient
Of ages' wisdom as refuge.

2 GYAN AND BHAKTI
Ignorance man-sized
Listening of light, stretch hands to rise
Evolve to Divine size.

3 A FAITHFUL LISTENER
His ignorance is none
Certainly remains no longer an Ignorant
Knowing 'how to Listen.'

4
Where Wisdom-speech
The Ignorance listens as shelter in words
Their worships reach.

**Paths of Meditation, wisdom or/and Karma Strewed = scattered.*

य एवं वेत्ति पुरुषं प्रकृतिं च गुणैःसह।
सर्वथा वर्तमानोऽपि न स भूयोऽभिजायते।।13.24।।

ध्यानेनात्मनि पश्यन्ति केचिदात्मानमात्मना।
अन्ये सांख्येन योगेन कर्मयोगेन चापरे।।13.25।।

5 'BE GODLY LISTENER'
I heard Godly words
Those words discovered in me a god,
That god alone worshipped God.

6
Good listener,
In spoken words should find-
'Who is behind?'

FIELD AND IT'S KNOWER

Verse 26

O Arjun ! whatever exists
Animate or inanimate yields
From union of Nature, the field
And Spirit, the Knower of field.

1 ADVENT
Any form of the formed
Is formed out of Formlessness
Of very Formless Consciousness.

2 THE LIFE
The Perfect One integrated
The scattered matter-field, and spirited
Thus the Integrator Lord created.

3 ADVENT
The Non-matter, Not formed
Manifests permeating into the matter forms
Thus All-Conscious Lord performs.

4 THE ELEMENTS OF COSMOS
Living Entity and inert mass
Super-imposed upon each other
Thus manifested phenomenal-cosmos.

Verse 27

He sees in actuality
Who sees the Supreme Existence in all, equally
And something Unperishing in perishing body.

1 DELUSION
Mortal darkness is blind
To visualize the Immortality behind
This daily dying designed.

2 I'M NOT BODY
When transcendentally made clear,
Who is divorced from seeable matter,
Is the actual seer.

अन्ये त्वेवमजानन्तः श्रुत्वाऽन्येभ्य उपासते।
तेऽपि चातितरन्त्येव मृत्युं श्रुतिपरायणाः।।13.26।।

यावत्सञ्जायते किञ्चित्सत्त्वं स्थावरजङ्गमम्।
क्षेत्रक्षेत्रज्ञसंयोगात्तद्विद्धि भरतर्षभ।।13.27।।

3 SELF-REALIZATION

When perception transcends
Unto mind's eye, sees intuitive view
Of realized Truth.

4 THE INSIGHT

One Closest hidden in us,
Was un-seeable through myopic apparatus
On Interiorize and focus.

Verse 28

Who is Conscious that 'Everywhere dwellth,
Equally the same Supreme Soul'
He destroys not Self by the self
Such conscious man attains Supreme Goal.

1

Equal vision has
An unseen strength to penetrate
Into Divine fact.

2

Shadow of Ego
In its way eclipsed the soul
Egoless equals with Divine Go.

3 SELF DESTRUCTION

This side, that side
My side, his side unequal bias-side,
Is suicide.

4 PARALLEL VISION

Biased converged focus to burn
Divergent rays scattered never to return
The Eternity, Equal rays earned.

5

The self never kills
The Self, when the very Real is revealed
Self is beyond Little-self.

Verse 29

He sees in actuality
Who sees all actions in entirety
*Are performed alone by Prakriti**
And actionless is inner Living entity.

*World of matter(Nature, field)

समं सर्वेषु भूतेषु तिष्ठन्तं परमेश्वरम्।
विनश्यत्स्वविनश्यन्तं यः पश्यति स पश्यति।।13.28।।

समं पश्यन्हि सर्वत्र समवस्थितमीश्वरम्।
न हिनस्त्यात्मनाऽऽत्मानं ततो याति परां गतिम्।।13.29।।

1

Keeping mute to all worthless
Of all actions-interactions of Nature's face
Soul is worthy witness.

2 THE OBSERVANT SOUL

The Soul is the soil
Where seed is the mortal coil
Bred, flourished and spoilt.

3 CREATOR-WITNESS

Supreme Doer puffs into matter
The Energy of Non matter for Nature's work
Making Ownself inert observer.

4 'INACTION' - AKARM

All Actions are interlaced
With Nature which overlay inert witness
The soul actively action-less.

Verse 30

When a man's vision
Beholds the Being's variations
As resting in the One
Beholds as Lord's expansion
He then merges with Brahmn.

1

Beyond the species
None the separated existence, who sees
Transcends to be Released.

2 ONENESS

World of multitude is none
But is unique for its expansion
Of the very 'One'.

3 RELEASED INTO BRAHMN

In this crowded patterns
When the elemental Oneness is learned
Never returns.

4 SPECTRUM

Divinity is not 'same hue'
But chromatic expansion over the Blue
Refracting through 'One dew'.

Verse 31

Being Unborn and without attributes as well
The Imperishable Self itself
O Arjun ! though in Mortal body dwells
Nor does anything nor entangles.

प्रकृत्यैव च कर्माणि क्रियमाणानि सर्वशः।
यः पश्यति तथाऽऽत्मानमकर्तारं स पश्यति।।13.30।।

यदा भूतपृथग्भावमेकस्थमनुपश्यति।
तत एव च विस्तारं ब्रह्म सम्पद्यते तदा।।13.31।।

1 I'M NOT BODY
Seems born, reborn
But in mortal whirl having brief sojourn
Soul is Eternally Unborn.

2 SELF-EVIDENT
For Nirguna soul its axiomatic
It has no attribute thus can not change,
And changeless can not perish.

3 MAKING OF COSMOS
Transparent Nirguna expands
Vividly in many hues on the canvas
Colourized thus attributory cosmos.

4 PERMANENT GOAL
Supreme spreads out as Soul
Freed to be identified as temporary
With same paramount love.

Verse 32

*As All pervading space**
Because of refined subtlety never gets soiled
Likewise the Soul is untouched immaculate
Throughout in the mortal coil.

1 OMNIPRESENT
Space is minutest
As well most spacious and widest
Like the soul pervades.

2 BEYOND FRAME
Akaash shaped into pot
When its shape is broken into shapeless
It expands unto Virat.

3 DETACHED
One alone Expanse of Space
Keeping aloof here pervades, here escapes
Like- wise the Soul upstaged.

4 MIND- BODY COMPLEX
Soul keeps mute
Among din of permutation of shaped mote
Among shapeless fleeting quotes.

Axiomatic=self evident *Ether/ Akaash Upstage=aloof Virat=Fullest expansion
mote=particle

अनादित्वान्निर्गुणत्वात्परमात्मायमव्ययः।
शरीरस्थोऽपि कौन्तेय न करोति न लिप्यते।।13.32।।

Verse 33-34

O Bharat !
As the One Sun illumines
The entire world
So the One Lord illumines
Whole field of Nature's whorls.

Who perceive with eyes of Lore
Distinction between World and Lord
And also method who know
Of liberation from Prakriti's ado
Unto Supreme they go.

1 DIVINE LIGHT SOURCE
Who dawns upon the Sol
As light of Sun that very Soul
Illumines the whole.

2 METAMORPHOSIS
Through very many cycles
Conscious larva released from the field
Winged to skies immutable.

3 INNER SUN
Sun's nature is light
Conscious eye has the nature of sight,
The darkness both fight.

4 INTUITION
The mind's eye here
First walk on path of fractal blur
Then perceives the Virat, clear.

5 EVOLUTION OF CREATION
One eternal night
On dark helios the Lord put light
Torched orb to the Sun.

6 GYANODAYA-WISDOM RISE
I see the Sun,
Like to perceive further through Yogic-Union
The Sun which dawns on Sun.

7 A PART –ALL APART
Light is Sun's proof
Consciousness similarly is Almighty's proof
But Both sources keep aloof.

8 LORE
The matter's glare blinds
Then wisdom brings opticity to opaque mind
Mind's eye confines to Divine.

Sol=Sun Fractal = Intuitional replica

यथा सर्वगतं सौक्ष्म्यादाकाशं नोपलिप्यते।
सर्वत्रावस्थितो देहे तथाऽऽत्मा नोपलिप्यते।।13.33।।

यथा प्रकाशयत्येकः कृत्स्नं लोकमिमं रविः।
क्षेत्रं क्षेत्री तथा कृत्स्नं प्रकाशयति भारत।।13.34।।

CHAPTER FOURTEEN
Three traits of Nature

All living beings
Of seeming difference, are Siblings
Of One Womb.

Add ! into pigmy man

In every birth more and more human

To rise to the God.

Chapter Fourteen

THREE TRAITS

Verse 1-2

The blessed Lord said –

Again I shalt phrase
The Gnosis, best of all knowledge
Knowing which all the sages
Have attained Supreme Perfection in the next..*
Sages fixed in this gnosis
And having attained My Being
Nor, are born at re-genesis
Nor at Dissolution get worries.

1
Those binding Nature's traits
To get liberated the Lord decodes track
On which sages tread.

2
The best knowledge
Is the knowledge which opens for all
The path of sages.

3 KNOWLEDGE IS KEY
Captive of powerful modes
Of the Nature, in captured detention
Need turn-key for redemption.

4 SAGES IN THE WORLD
Traps and nooses are made,
By the Prakriti ensnared on all spreads
The wise cautiously tread.

5 BLESSED PATH
The blessed knowledge
Blessed sages their foot marks in turn
Will bless coming ages.

6 REAL SCIENCE
That knowledge is best
Which makes a pilgrim out of traveler
And path, a pilgrimage.

7 KEEN TO LEARN
This prisoner
Be a seeker
To be Seer.

**after passing away.*

परं भूयः प्रवक्ष्यामि ज्ञानानां ज्ञानमुत्तमम्।
यज्ज्ञात्वा मुनयः सर्वे परां सिद्धिमितो गताः।।14.1।।

इदं ज्ञानमुपाश्रित्य मम साधर्म्यमागताः।
सर्गेऽपि नोपजायन्ते प्रलये न व्यथन्ति च।।14.2।।

Verse 3

This whole is My womb of Brahmn,
In which I emplace the germ
O Arjun ! making possible that
All-beings to germinate.

1

All living beings
Of seeming difference, are Siblings
Of One Womb.

2 THE GENESIS

A Kinetic God with own particles
Impregnated all inert matter with lifetron
That became dynamically vital.

3 SOUL-BODY COMPLEX

Total causal-womb
Causelessly caused seedling germ
As frontal of Brahmn.

4 ELEMENTAL CAUSE OF LIFE

Total matter is envelop
For living entity it has no worth
Lord's vital puff cause birth.

Verse 4

Whatever forms and features
In whatever wombs are produced
Prakriti is original mother
And I am seed-imparting Sire.

1

Each particle is womb
Once conscious seed bring forth dynamism
Life expresses in its bosom.

2 'THE PARENTHOOD'

Its great show
In the cradle of Nature, fathers grow
Who from godly sons borrow.

3 FIRST PARENT

For Ancient and Primal couple
Forefathers, paters and forthcoming fathers
All infants in Eternal cradle.

4 GODLY CREATION

On Nature's natural design
God Himself enshrines the Divine
Incarnating as man-kind.

मम योनिर्महद्ब्रह्म तस्मिन् गर्भं दधाम्यहम्।
संभवः सर्वभूतानां ततो भवति भारत।।14.3।।

सर्वयोनिषु कौन्तेय मूर्तयः सम्भवन्ति याः।
तासां ब्रह्म महद्योनिरहं बीजप्रदः पिता।।14.4।।

Verse 5

Material nature is designed
of three traits –Divine, Terrene, Malign
These three Gunas bind
Body with the Imperishable dweller.

1 CHAIN
Living Entity though transcendental
Is indifferent to world, where it dwells
Alas ! conditioned to its spell.

2 COMPLEX DESTINY
Conditioned by mental climate
Of traits between gloom and bloom
Decides indweller's fate.

*3 CONDITIONED BY THREE TRAITS**
On the transparent wall
Crayoned by worldly brush, moral and immoral
Composed the framed mural.

4 SPIRITUAL JOURNEY
In the pilgrimage within
Over terrene's grin, over malign's sin
The Divine battles to win.

Verse 6

O Sinless Arjun !
The Divine is the pious Guna
And because its taintless pure
It's luminous and lively to core
Yet hath bindings to happiness and lore.

1
Goodness also binds
Same as evil to vulgarity of mind
But the Goodness refines.

2 BONDAGE THAT FREES
The binding force purest
Is goodness that binds body – mind complex
That alone liberates.

3
Goodness is glowing jewel
In thought-life with it's blooming spell
Dazzles inside, out as well.

4
Malign and Terrene be shed
What remains need not earn for Self
Its Divine in itself.

*Gunas of Nature.

सत्त्वं रजस्तम इति गुणाः प्रकृतिसंभवाः।
निबध्नन्ति महाबाहो देहे देहिनमव्ययम्।।14.5।।

तत्र सत्त्वं निर्मलत्वात्प्रकाशकमनामयम्।
सुखसङ्गेन बध्नाति ज्ञानसङ्गेन चानघ।।14.6।।

5
The three modes are Siblings
Born of one womb of mental feelings
The Divine is regent-prince.

6
The Most knowable
Knowledge is that nothing external
Can be Eternal.

Verse 7

O Son of Kunti - Arjun !
Its Passion, The Terrene Guna
Born of attachment and lust
Embodied soul, it binds fast
To the work and fruitive result.

1 EVOLVING TRAITS
The earthy comes first
The Ethereal unto real come afterwards
This sublimation is worth.

2 MATERIALISTIC ACTIONS
A lust-bound trend
Endlessly earn and endlessly spend
Into Empty ledger ends.

3 CYCLE OF REBIRTH
Work done in the world
For this world alone, will get
The same world in next.

4
Passion adheres to lust
Fulfilled passion into vicious passion results
Binds to births – rebirths.

5 FRUITLESS ACTION
Work's egoistic motif
Reach no-where, till sublimity of the Action
Works, above fruits.

Verse 8

O Bhaarat ! O Arjun !!
But the delusion, the malign Guna
Born of the ignorance that err
Which binds the embodied soul
To maniac error, to torpor, to slumber.

रजो रागात्मकं विद्धि तृष्णासङ्गसमुद्भवम्।
तन्निबध्नाति कौन्तेय कर्मसङ्गेन देहिनम्।।14.7।।

तमस्त्वज्ञानजं विद्धि मोहनं सर्वदेहिनाम्।
प्रमादालस्यनिद्राभिस्तन्निबध्नाति भारत।।14.8।।

1

To the soul belong
The gnosis and bliss, which through ego wrong
For conditioned soul, rebirths throng.

2 GLOOMING DARKNESS

In the sunless life
The sleep in and out further deepens
Embedding in endless night.

3

Ignorance is self goal
Against ever-winner, now embodied soul,
Won by the ill-fortune.

4 MAN IN EVIL TRAIT

In the cocoon vallum
The vestal vessel-soul with vermiform wisdom
Never metamorphose from worm.

5 NO DIVIDENT EARNED

Being Unaware of higher purpose
Entangled birth by birth in lesser commerce
Keeping divine-business in loss.

6 KNOWLEDGE OF GEETA

Moonless darks on vault
Filled with meteor stream of fault
May end with eastern knock.

Verse 9

The Divine attaches to bliss
The Terrene attaches to work;
But shrouding the gnosis
The malign attaches to berserk.

1

The Mother-Nature prods
The living Entity with free accord
Among its triple modes.

2 'THREE ATTRIBUTES OF PRAKRITI'

When modes are well perceived,
Blessed with life fully lived or half lived
Get lifelessness when deceived.

3

Conduct is the dice
On world's board of snake and ladder
Wins transmuting by choice.

4 EVOLUTION

More the Goodness acts
Passionate work slowly transubstantiate
From artifact to the Perfect.

Vallum=earthly wall vestal = pure.

सत्त्वं सुखे सञ्जयति रजः कर्मणि भारत।
ज्ञानमावृत्य तु तमः प्रमादे सञ्जयत्युत।।14.9।।

MIXTURE OF GOOD AND EVIL

Verse 10

Now prevails mode Divine,
Having overpowered terrene and malign.
Now prevails mode Terrene
Having overpowered Divine and Malign.
Over Divine and terrene sometimes
Wins the mode Malign.

1 TRANSCENDING
The Determined and blessed
Through various modes of goodness
Reach Pure Krshna Consciousness.

2 CYCLE OF BLESSEDNESS
The Divine prominence produce
The bliss and gnosis as its by-product
Which viciously further contribute.

3 DOMINANT COLOURS
On the multi coloured canvas
Some colours fade some are glossed
Thus brush betrays gross.

4
Empowered by one attitude
Other modes became secondary and mute
Man, thus transmute.

5 MODE DECIDES DEALINGS
Any mode's prominence
With its marrow fouls or essence
Resolves duteous intent.

Verse 11

One may comprehend
The Divine, is prevalent
When from body's essence and sense gates
Light of wisdom radiates.

1 SPIRITUAL MAN
Who mastered senses
Perceives the feelings as Master of senses
Thus masters the Master.

2 SATTVIC PERCEPTION
Who shuns the senses
With wisdom turns the senses
Earns beyond senses.

रजस्तमश्चाभिभूय सत्त्वं भवति भारत।
रजः सत्त्वं तमश्चैव तमः सत्त्वं रजस्तथा।।14.10।।

सर्वद्वारेषु देहेऽस्मिन्प्रकाश उपजायते।
ज्ञानं यदा तदा विद्याद्विवृद्धं सत्त्वमित्युत।।14.11।।

3
Senses wound the Interior
Through wound once light of wisdom enter
'ts warmth heal conditioned soul.

4 'THE DIVINE' HAS TO COME
Cloudy vapours may veil
Light of the Sun, seem to prevail
Yet Dawn is inevitable.

Verse 12

When the Terrene trait comes up
Greed, need, lust develop
O Arjun ! also intense enterprise
As well restlessness with longings rise.

1 LUST
When materialized Ego
In search of more, stretches Elbow
Strangulates the embraced soul.

2 POVERTY AMIDST PLENTY
All Earthly enterprise
Concerned with more of Earthy to secure
Earns not bit of paradise.

3 ENDEAVOUR IN VAIN
Digging Earth's chest
With high rising wishes is just waste
All empty for the next.

4 LIMITS
Innately hands have chore
As the ocean have its entity in waves
But not to break Shore.

Verse 13

O Son of Kuru ! O Arjun !!
With rise of Malign Guna,
Ignorance-born stupor, berserk
Manifest also muddle and murk.

1 IGNORANCE
Captive of darks within
Identifies himself with Captor's whim
Keeps from wisdom, victim.

2 IMMORTAL TRAP
When consciousness is captive
Very purpose of entity is inactive
Life ends passive.

लोभः प्रवृत्तिरारम्भः कर्मणामशमः स्पृहा।
रजस्येतानि जायन्ते विवृद्धे भरतर्षभ।।14.12।।

अप्रकाशोऽप्रवृत्तिश्च प्रमादो मोह एव च।
तमस्येतानि जायन्ते विवृद्धे कुरुनन्दन।।14.13।।

3
When capability lacks,
To be identified as purpose, this lifelessness
From own Entity escapes.

4 DELUDED BY BELIEF
Murk of fanaticism chanced
Is the darkest among malign glance
For unrecognized murky stance.

5 NOT FOLLOWING GOOD
To Higher call, for him
Who is heedless slowly sinks
Here and here after mislinks.

FRUITS OF THREE GUNAS

Verse 14-15

One who lives and dies with
The Divine trait prominent
Then he does meet
Purest world of highest plane.

When one dies in materialism
Is born again among those with earthly acts,
Dying in trait of malign-worth
In the lesser species take birth.

1
Life in its worth
With plentiful Prakriti's mode or dearth
Destines next birth.

2
In vast terrene display
With its potential to life from midway
Man rise, fall or stay.

3
Man is free to pick,
Knowingly or unknowingly through own dealings
Heaven, this haven, or Hades.

4 THE FATE
The Amount of god within
Amount of being and amount of goblin
Decides what's destined.

यदा सत्त्वे प्रवृद्धे तु प्रलयं याति देहभृत्।
तदोत्तमविदां लोकानमलान्प्रतिपद्यते।।14.14।।

रजसि प्रलयं गत्वा कर्मसङ्गिषु जायते।
तथा प्रलीनस्तमसि मूढयोनिषु जायते।।14.15।।

5
All roots of divine,
Lie in the soil of soul to Spring
The Divine in mind.

6 EVOLUTION THROUGH BIRTHS
Add ! into pigmy man
In every birth more and more human
To rise to the God.

Verse 16

Fruits of good acts
Divine and chaste
Work of passionate acts
Result in distress
While fruits of malign acts
Is Ignorant craze.

1 BOUND TO FRUITS
Slave to outcome
How dare they wish to become
The Master of wisdom.

2 IMMORTALITY
The essence of inner dweller
Further elixired with the divine work
Blessed with Immortal nectar.

3 SELF –ANALYSIS
I should have sense
To perceive my own ignorance
To get rid of ignorance.

4 PERFECT PURSUANCE
A Noble pursuit
From terrene and malign trait transmute
Into divine for Divine fruit.

Verse 17

Arise the Knowledge, the gnosis
From traits of Divine deeds;
And from the terrene deeds
Sure, arises the greed,
And heedlessness, Ignorance indeed
Further illusions of stupid
Develops from malign deeds.

कर्मणः सुकृतस्याहुः सात्त्विकं निर्मलं फलम्।
रजसस्तु फलं दुःखमज्ञानं तमसः फलम्।।14.16।।

सत्त्वात्सञ्जायते ज्ञानं रजसो लोभ एव च।
प्रमादमोहौ तमसो भवतोऽज्ञानमेव च।।14.17।।

1 KNOWLEDGE OF THE EAST
On horizon of goodness
Discovered by oriental laboratory of sages,
(That) Sun dawns not to set.

2
On lost island deserted work,
Dipped in lifeless ocean, doped by Stupor
They work as lotus eaters.

3
Terrene deeds unearth,
With toilsome greed to earn more earth
Waste birth and rebirth.

4 PURSUANCE BY TRAIT
From bestial to Best
From shallow of unrest to Eternal rest
All are conditioned to quest.

Verse 18

Established in Divine
They go to sublime;
Who follow Terrene ways
In the middle they stay,
In malign acts who are found
They are degraded to loose ground.

1 KNOWLEDGE
May the wisdom earn
In its sky of vault, more sun
Get perpetually torched.

2
Hades, Haven or Heaven
Transformed in its evolving mutation
It conditions further sojourn.

3 FRUITS MAKE FATE
Conditioned by mortal coil
Disembodied soul roots in moral soil
Lest buried in immoral spoils.

4
Earthy dynamism go
Most dynamic for it keeps status quo
In journey of the soul.

TRANSCENDING NATURE'S GUNAS

Verse 19

Whoever as seer sees as only doer
the three traits of nature
And Further knows beyond even these traits
He attains Me and My state.

ऊर्ध्वं गच्छन्ति सत्त्वस्था मध्ये तिष्ठन्ति राजसाः।
जघन्यगुणवृत्तिस्था अधो गच्छन्ति तामसाः।।14.18।।

नान्यं गुणेभ्यः कर्तारं यदा द्रष्टानुपश्यति।
गुणेभ्यश्च परं वेत्ति मद्भावं सोऽधिगच्छति।।14.19।।

1 REAL COGNITION

A seer in his pursuit
Sees Nature as doer, is half truth
Till Seer perceives the Absolute.

2

Mixed traits of mould
Are free to condition the soul-
'The Seer state'.

3 ALMIGHTY

There is one eye
One hand one Doer
As well one Seer too.

Verse 20

Physical embodiment, which caused
Those, three traits of nature who surpass
From birth, death, decay and pain
Getting freed, the Immortality they attain.

1 CONSCIOUSNESS PILGRIMAGE

Stupor crawling in traveler
Consciously journeyed from dreamer
To waker to seer.

2

Beyond cause of change
The changing traits of Nature, who transcends
Become Unchangeable Entity.

3

This prison, the Nature brought
Conditions the soul to the modes of body
Be released by Soul-Entity.

4 BEYOND NATURE'S TRAP

Ocean caused flesh and gore
As flotsam in waves-surf, surge, corrode
Till it transcends to the Shore.

5 SUBLIME LIVING

Although in flesh and gore
If one is evolved in spiritual lore
Out does the trapping door.

गुणानेतानतीत्य त्रीन्देही देहसमुद्भवान्।
जन्ममृत्युजरादुःखैर्विमुक्तोऽमृतमश्नुते।।14.20।।

Verse 21

Arjun inquired –

O Lord ! what are the marks,
Of him who has surpassed
Beyond the three Gunas?
What is his behavior?
How does he transcends traits of Nature?

1 ARJUN'S KEENNESS

Inner seeking accord
Of Seeker, unveiled Own word-thoughts
Kept unvocalized by the Lord.

2 ARJUN'S QUESTIONING

Some questions were vital
So the Lord had to manifest in world
Make His words turn visible.

3 TWO BASIC QUESTIONS

True seeker's lore
First want to know the source
Lastly to know course.

4 'GEETA'S DISCOURSE

Among blinds of world
Who try to palpate the knowledge noble
Word's become seeable.

5 LORD'S REPLY

The Perfect Vision
Is ready to bless inquisitive questions
Of world's element of Delusion.

कैर्लिंगैस्त्रीन्गुणानेतानतीतो भवति प्रभो।
किमाचारः कथं चैतांस्त्रीन्गुणानतिवर्तते।।14.21।।

Verse 22-25

The Blessed Lord Said-

Who abhors nor the presence
Nor deplores the absence
Of the Divine, Terrene, Malign Guna,
Nature's three traits, O Arjun !

Remaining like one unconcerned
Unmoved by three traits' reactions
Who cognizes modes, naturally are alone lissome
Remain centred and firm.

With secured firm Divine plain
Who regards alike pleasure and pain
And also praises and blames
See equally a clod, a stone, a gem
To whom the dear and not-dear are the same,

Who is unchanged in laurels and libels
Friend and foe who treat equal
Personal doership who abstain
Its said the traits of Nature they transcend.

1 THE HARMONIZED
Who hate nor applause
The Cause, its effect and again its cause
Finely attunes with gross.

2 MODES OF NATURE
One of modes enslave
Which in life is prominent and grave
Likewise the man behaves.

प्रकाशं च प्रवृत्तिं च मोहमेव च पाण्डव।
न द्वेष्टि सम्प्रवृत्तानि न निवृत्तानि
काङ्क्षति।।14.22।।

उदासीनवदासीनो गुणैर्यो न विचाल्यते।
गुणा वर्तन्त इत्येव योऽवतिष्ठति नेङ्गते।।14.23।।

समदुःखसुखः स्वस्थः समलोष्टाश्मकाञ्चनः।
तुल्यप्रियाप्रियो धीरस्तुल्यनिन्दात्मसंस्तुतिः।।14.24।।

मानापमानयोस्तुल्यस्तुल्यो मित्रारिपक्षयोः।
सर्वारम्भपरित्यागी गुणातीतः स उच्यते।।14.25।।

3 EQUANIMITY

Being Equal he never craves
To have or not to have
Him the Earth can't enslave.

4

Modes of Nature caused effects
Who masters cause keeps unaffected
So nor longs nor hates.

5 WIN-WIN

Where matter, matters not
These modes of nature could not batter
With their bitters.

6 EQUANIMITY

World's uniform interpretation
In discretion even with diverses, come
To the unpossessed of possessions.

7 YOGI

With changing time
One holds the changes with unchanged
mind
He holds the Time.

8 GOODNESS

Even the goodness binds*
Loads of body-mind who sheds behind
All soul alone, he finds.

9 FIRMNESS

The unmoved surely moves
His world of three modes, and transmutes
His goodness into Godhood.

10

With mask on face
Man has potential be satan or saint
Equally occupy inner space.

11 BEYOND THE TRAITS OF ATTITUDE

A painted glass
Be made transparent and be washed
For transcendental view through.

12 FIRMNESS

With No alternative compromises
On that changeless goal he targets
Only changeless consistence goads.

*see also Chapter 14/verse 6

Verse 26- 27

For devotion without fail
He who surpasses three modes of material
Thus, comes to the Brahmn level.

For I am the basis
Of Infinite Brahmn
And basis of Absolute bliss
Immortal, immutable Dharma.

1 BHAKTI YOG
Man-sized lesser energy,
Has potential within his little entity
Sublime to Supreme Potency.

2
Brahmn in him blooms
In whom mortal modes has no room
Goes beyond mortal dooms.

3
Beyond the blank envelop
Offering everything, including the hope
Doors to destination ope.

4 PURE SERVICE
Into the daily joy
Pealing anthems, bells of shrines be employed
To bring devotion unalloyed.

5
Shedding off the loads
Of mortal entity of so called vital modes
To the immortality prods.

6 UNALLOYED DEVOTIONS
In Complex closures of gross,
The simplicity of close knit devotions
Opens openness of the Vast.

7 PERPETUAL DEVOTION
Consciousness with Godly lore
In the fill of ocean further pour
Fills the soul to shore.

8
Further devotion unalloyed
Brings purity with the Self to realize
Inner Immortality and Eternal joy.

मां च योऽव्यभिचारेण भक्तियोगेन सेवते।
स गुणान्समतीत्यैतान् ब्रह्मभूयाय कल्पते।।14.26।।

ब्रह्मणो हि प्रतिष्ठाऽहममृतस्याव्ययस्य च।
शाश्वतस्य च धर्मस्य सुखस्यैकान्तिकस्य च।।14.27।।

CHAPTER FIFTEEN

Purushottam ;The Supreme Being

In eternity, life is rooted
With eternal leaves of the vedic texts
In which this life, breaths.

The Sun is big altar,

Every altar has a Little sun

From One all beaconed.

Chapter Fifteen

VITAL TREE

Verse 1

The blessed Lord said –

Speak, the wise people
*Of the Bo fig, the Eternal Peepal**
With its roots uphill
And branches in this world.
As its leaves vedic hymns; they tell
Knower of this tree, is said
To be knower of veds.

1 VITALIZER-VED

In eternity, life is rooted
With eternal leaves of the vedic texts
In which this life, breaths.

2 KNOWLEDGE IS EVER AVAILABLE

Peepal is ever fruitful
But Vitally edible to you or not
Depends on you.

3 BODY – MIND COMPLEX

Crowned cosmic consciousness
Like inverted tree integrates itself with appendages
As Vital receptor of Knowledge.

4

Leaves all about collect
Light, flame-breath just like Vedic texts
Nourishing its own sap.

Verse 2

Spread of its bough
Is all over above and below,
Nurtured by the three modes,
Buds are sensory nodes
Which into world of Human go
Has extending roots
Into fruitive action originate.

**ficus religiosa (sacred fig)*

ऊर्ध्वमूलमधःशाखमश्वत्थं प्राहुरव्ययम्।
छन्दांसि यस्य पर्णानि यस्तं वेद स वेदवित्।।15.1।।

अधश्चोर्ध्वं प्रसृतास्तस्य शाखा, गुणप्रवृद्धा विषयप्रवालाः।
अधश्च मूलान्यनुसन्ततानि, कर्मानुबन्धीनि मनुष्यलोके।।15.2।।

1 EVOLUTIONARY

I 'm tree with boughs
By its own, expand above and below
Nourishing my Ego.

2 LIFE TREE

In the Peepal pattern
Urges of all higher lower to earn
Modes of Nature yearned.

3 WORLDLY EXPANSION

It's all spiritual
But with its budding potential
It enroots to terrestrial.

4 WORLDLY EXPANSION

World from infant stem grow
With its buds bursting above and below
As the secondary thoughts grow.

5

Like the main root
With budding of secondary off-shoots
Into earthly modes fasten.

Verse 3-4

It's true-form here, is not seen
As such its end and its origin;
And its root- foundation where it rests
Which is downwardly firmly annexed
With 'non-attachments' be axed,
Doing so, One must seek to gain
Having gone, none to return again.
And should also seek refuge
In that Most Ancient Purush,
Who, eons before, streamed forth
All the Creative vital force.

1 DELUSION OF WORLD

Multiple Ignorant Offshoots
Fall down into mud and grow huge
Confuse as main taproot.

2 UNWISE INSIGHT

Tree has manifested webs
Has Master taproot, seems unmanifested
In One common gaze.

न रूपमस्येह तथोपलभ्यते
नान्तो न चादिर्न च संप्रतिष्ठा।
अश्वत्थमेनं सुविरूढमूल
मसङ्गशस्त्रेण दृढेन छित्त्वा।।15.3।।

ततः पदं तत्परिमार्गितव्य
यस्मिन्गता न निवर्तन्ति भूयः।
तमेव चाद्यं पुरुषं प्रपद्ये
यतः प्रवृत्तिः प्रसृता पुराणी।।15.4।।

3 LIFE WEBS

Man is lost,
Because he feels himself free
In tangles of the gross.

4 SUBLIMITY

The Off-shooting Secondary Boughs
Of the life tree need be axed
For main stem to grow.

5

All external pursuits
Of offshoots those hinder subliming attitude
Be axed from Ancient root.

Verse 5

With no pride and no delusion
Evils of attachments who have won
And with Lust who is done
From dualities disengaged
And established in the Self
Undeceived they reach Eternal goal.

1 NO RELATIVE WORLD

Diffusion of relativity
Of contrasts of seeming real, duality
Who kept equal, won.

2

Freedom from false notions
Brings non-attachment to the false
association
Through true devotions.

3 PRIDE

A regent I enthroned
On the inner Kingdom of my own
Unruly to King of kings.

4 DELUSION

Things impermanent so designed
Are desired by man to get
As permanently 'mine'.

निर्मानमोहा जितसङ्गदोषा
अध्यात्मनित्या विनिवृत्तकामाः।
द्वन्द्वैर्विमुक्ताः सुखदुःखसंज्ञै
र्गच्छन्त्यमूढाः पदमव्ययं तत्।।15.5।।

THE MANIFESTATION AS THE SOUL

Verse 6

That abode of Mine,
Beyond sun, moon or fire to make shine
That state having earned
Attain place of no return.

1
Through the unseen course
All luminescence are borrowed
From the Supreme source.

2 COME UP BEYOND EGO
Ego erred to estimate
In the lack-lustre of objects, glazed
Remains shadowed under the Brightest.

3
In the strange dims
Of Sun, moon fire with dying beams
There is Eternal source gleam.

4 SOURCE OF ALL RADIANCE
Beyond relative blurs of light
Transcending duality of all dims
That Brightest source resides.

5 NO DARK-NICHE
That Sun, moon, that fire
Has relative warmth and relative glare
This 's equal in the Source.

6 A SUN BEYOND SUN
This infant Sun
Will die at the day's submission
Eternal sun has no horizon.

Verse 7

All eternal fragments of Myself
In the conditioned world of beings
As a conditioned soul manifests
Onto itself the mind attracts
And six senses are animated
those in Prakriti rest.

1 THE MANIFESTED SOUL
Conditioned to swell
Individual wave forgets at shore
In Eternal ocean it dwells.

2
Once adhered to worldly pull
With God Conscious inherent inner tool
Wise is never befooled.

न तद्भासयते सूर्यो न शशाङ्को न पावकः।
यद्गत्वा न निवर्तन्ते तद्धाम परमं मम।।15.6।।

ममैवांशो जीवलोके जीवभूतः सनातनः।
मनःषष्ठानीन्द्रियाणि प्रकृतिस्थानि कर्षति।।15.7।।

3 THE GENESIS

The Unconditioned and Unmanifest
With little bit of its essence
Puffs in conditioned frame.

4 GYAN

The knowledge commences
Through senses but Perfect Knowledge is attained
Shedding off the senses.

Verse 8

*When the Lord as Jiva**
Acquireth a body or leaves
Mind and senses He taketh
While leaving the Living entity,
He taketh and doth pass
As the wind carries aromas.

1 CREATION OF WORLD-BEINGS

Free Entity of the Lord
Belittles Himself with minute independence
Pigmy dependant on senses.

2

A flower, a visible frame
And into it pollen soul is feelable
Unto Unseen essence aimed.

3

Soul is a breeze
It wafts with it rosy or mephitis,
Depends how its elixired.

4

Senses have aura of Instinct
Mind has aroma of Intention
Soul has charisma of Insight.

Verse 9

Taking up the body gross,
Presiding over mind and senses
Of hearing, sight, touch, smell, taste
In the sensory world the 'Jiva' as God's presence
Is thus engrossed.

*Little living entity Mephitis = stink

शरीरं यदवाप्नोति यच्चाप्युत्क्रामतीश्वरः।
गृहीत्वैतानि संयाति वायुर्गन्धानिवाशयात्।।15.8।।

श्रोत्रं चक्षुः स्पर्शनं च रसनं घ्राणमेव च।
अधिष्ठाय मनश्चायं विषयानुपसेवते।।15.9।।

1
The lesser world Lord made,
For higher delights Jiva be conditioned yet
In lesser he engages.

2 SENSORY WORLD
If bound he pretends
In the iron or even gold chains
Bound he will remain.

3 THE WORLD OF MATTER
Body has senses
Senses have mind which has world
Alas ! in its sub-consciousness.

4
My folly dipped
The mind in bowl of senses
Contaminating 'the inner Deep'.

5
Senses, who have
Those to own mind unruly behave
Are slaves.

Verse 10

The deluded do not behold
Him, who quits body or holds
Under spell of Nature's modes
Him, who enjoys in the mould;
But one with eyes of gnosis
Can alone perceive all this.

1 MIND'S VISION
The Divine Non-thing 'Jiva'
Which the grosser thing has conceived
Refined eye could perceive.

2 IMMORTAL WITHIN MORTAL
A Run crudely peopled
Is blurred by fast changing scene of mortals
The Knower focuses on Immortal.

3
Within grosser 'me'
A subtle individuality which caused me
Précised –eye could see.

4 KNOWLEDGE IN STEPS
Seen by orbs
Perceived by the various levels of mind
Interpreted by Consciousness.

उत्क्रामन्तं स्थितं वापि भुञ्जानं वा गुणान्वितम्।
विमूढा नानुपश्यन्ति पश्यन्ति ज्ञानचक्षुषः।।15.10।।

5 *MEDITATION*

Closed lids open
The eye of mind to realize
'The Closest' to life.

Verse 11

Yogic seekers do endeavour
To behold Him as Inner Dweller
But the Unwise with taints
They do toils in vain.

1
Though workable thoughts
But those of Unrefined and strayed mind
Perceive Him not.

2
Endeavour with Purity
Make more and more opportunity
Then what's due.

3
In the din of senses
The melodious hum of inner songster
Is not perceivable.

4
He sees me sure
Whether I am pure or blurred lore
By taints procured.

Verse 12

The Radiance of the Sun
Whole world, which maketh shine
And moonlight and light in fire
Know ! all splendour to be Mine.

1
Lord equips with fuel
Makes the planets and altars own tool
Thus distributes own aureoles.

2
The Sun is big altar,
Every altar has a Little sun
From One all beaconed.

Aureole = Glory / Aura

यतन्तो योगिनश्चैनं पश्यन्त्यात्मन्यवस्थितम्।
यतन्तोऽप्यकृतात्मानो नैनं पश्यन्त्यचेतसः।।15.11।।

यदादित्यगतं तेजो जगद्भासयतेऽखिलम्।
यच्चन्द्रमसि यच्चाग्नौ तत्तेजो विद्धि
मामकम्।।15.12।।

3
A little sun in cave
Which as glowworm glows; have
The very same astral torch.

4 *'JAGAT GURU'- BHAARAT*
Even closed doors are His
Lord pushes eastern treasure through slits
Make every niche lit.

Verse 13

Into the Earth I diffuse
By My Energy support the fauna
I become the moon's nectarine juice
And nourish all flora.

1 ONE SOURCE
All planets, all planes
All pulses, all puffs all pollens
My plasm alone sustains.

2
The Divine is versatile n' vivid,
Which transmutes even the adamantine livid
Even through the melting moon.

3 *MY CREATION*
I caused microcosm
Which further enlivened gross macrocosm
With My subtlest presence Protoplasm.

4 HIS OWN VITALITY
In every vital touch
Of life in all wides as such
Is His own touch.

Verse 14

I exist as fire that digest
I exist as life's flame-breath
*I 'm to and fro air puffs**
By which I process four fold food-stuffs.

1
In Physically framed energy
There is a fire having its chemistry
Governed by Lord, autonomously.

2 AUTONOMOUS EXECUTION
Living in Physical realm
This Entity is sustained by metabolism
As self-run dynamism.

**Inhaling and exhaling*

गामाविश्य च भूतानि धारयाम्यहमोजसा।
पुष्णामि चौषधीः सर्वाः सोमो भूत्वा रसात्मकः।।15.13।।

अहं वैश्वानरो भूत्वा प्राणिनां देहमाश्रितः।
प्राणापानसमायुक्तः पचाम्यन्नं चतुर्विधम्।।15.14।।

3 LEEWAY AUTONOMY
Puffs of autonomy claim
mechanized fire –Energy that manifests
To work on vital helm.

4 ALL ENERGIZER GOD
Its not known
This unknown vital fire, who owns?
Which makes me a knower.

Verse 15

I'm in all hearts enthroned
And memory and knowledge I own
As well as the forgetfulness,
Through Holy Veds I am all alone
Who is Verily can be known.
Indeed knower of Veds I am,
Indeed Author of Vedanta I am.

1
In Vault He's cerebrum
In words He manifests as Wisdom
Thus He records His Presence.

2
He is divine potential
To transmute man's babbles into sacred Texts
Being Author of All Knowledge.

3 AUTHOR OF HOLY TEXTS
All intellectual concepts
That seem to be exclusively manmade
From Infinite Reality annexed.

4
For experiences Lord is skill
He is forgetfulness, false notions to spill-
He Himself thus fulfills.

5
Whatever inked the page
As evolution of man's sulcii gyrii
Is All Lord's Brain child.

सर्वस्य चाहं हृदि सन्निविष्टो
मत्तः स्मृतिर्ज्ञानमपोहनं च।
वेदैश्च सर्वैरहमेव वेद्यो
वेदान्तकृद्वेदविदेव चाहम्।।15.15।।

THE SUPREME SELF

Verse 16

There, in the cosmos
Two classes of Entities, live
All beings are perishable in gross
Imperishable in subtle world is 'Jiva'

1
All individuality distinct
For unconditioned Unity has inner instinct,
Which is an Unchanging link.

2 JOURNEY
The route of the Born,
Is routine to change sojourns
Then, end unto Changeless Unborn.

3
Changes, which are seen,
Are in regard to which never changes,
All changes are on screen.

4
The change, as culture
Of man by the name of Evolution
The Changeless Lord nurtured.

5 FINAL CHANGE
There is an inner Changeless,
Within changing coil of changing world
Which leads to the Unchangable.

Verse 17

Besides these two entities
Exists Another, called the Supreme Spirit
Unto three worlds permeateth who
Maintainth these worlds too.

1 WORLD OF WORLDLY
In the conditioned environ
Entity is conditioned in fragmented form
Of Unconditioned Lord.

2 LORD PERMEATES IN WORLD
In the man-sized world
Lord compresses Himself from Infinite Spirit
To the Individualized limits.

द्वाविमौ पुरुषौ लोके क्षरश्चाक्षर एव च।
क्षरः सर्वाणि भूतानि कूटस्थोऽक्षर उच्यते।।15.16।।

उत्तमः पुरुषस्त्वन्यः परमात्मेत्युदाहृतः।
यो लोकत्रयमाविश्य बिभर्त्यव्यय ईश्वरः।।15.17।।

3
This individual entity
Beyond the conditioned individuality
Transcends to Supreme Identity.

4
The All-body world
Is sustained by the Consciousness for whom
Bodilessness is Ideal.

Verse 18-20

As I do surpass
The perishable and imperishable both*
In the world and in the Veds,
I am declared 'the Uttermost'.

From delusion whosoever is freed
Know Me as Uttermost spirit,
O Arjun ! all-knowing, he
With his whole being ever worship Me.

Here with Arjun ! O sinless!!
I have taught you most secret
On knowing this, man becomes
Sage and Perfect.

1 OBVIOUS GOD
The Unknowable godliness,
Reveals Himself before the sage--
Knowable as Self-evident

2
Through unlearned perception
Free from delusion, wise becomes omniscient
Innately sees the Omnipresent.

3
His Lordship
Is only worthy thing
For sages to worship.

4 REALIZATION
Where thoughts are innate
Unlearned knowledge perfects to consciousness,
Unto Uttermost awakes.

**The changing and Unchanging*

यस्मात्क्षरमतीतोऽहमक्षरादपि चोत्तमः।
अतोऽस्मि लोके वेदे च प्रथितः पुरुषोत्तमः।।15.18।।

यो मामेवमसम्मूढो जानाति पुरुषोत्तमम्।
स सर्वविद्भजति मां सर्वभावेन भारत।।15.19।।

इति गुह्यतमं शास्त्रमिदमुक्तं मयाऽनघ।
एतद्बुद्ध्वा बुद्धिमान्स्यात्कृतकृत्यश्च भारत।।15.20।।

5

Where perfect knowledge exists
There nothing in hide could coexist
In light of Supreme Spirit.

6

Secret is not in hide
This Infinite Knowledge in fullest size,
To the sinless abides.

7 DIVINE GIFT

Not the pleasure as largess
Its gift of 'Knowledge of the Highest'
Is Highest reward to sages.

CHAPTER SIXTEEN
Divine/Malign Nature

Giant brains
Are all brainless brains
If virtues drained.

Merits author

With radiant ink, its worth

The Heaven on earth.

Chapter Sixteen

ADOPTING THE DIVINE TRAIT

Verse 1-3

The Blessed Lord said –

Aweless-ness, purity of heart
In Yogic wisdom ever steadfast,
Giving of alms and self-restraint
Holy-study, Simplicity and penance,

Harmlessness, Truthfulness, repose
Freedom from wrath, absence of reproach
Compassion for all, absence of avarice
Gentleness, modesty, resolved spirit.

Vigor, forgiveness and fortitude
Absence of hatred, cleanly attitude
And absence of self-conceit
O Bhaarat ! these are Divine merits

1 METTLE
The Courage
Out of womb of fearlessness
Made the first Sage.

2 THE IMPURITY
When mind is set
On hates and baits
Impedingly upsets.

3 DEVOTIONAL CYCLE
Touch of company of Lord
Makes me fearless and this fearlessness
Intensifies company of Lord.

4 THE PURITY
With All-soul's consent
The virtuous purity of mind of Infant
Should grow but remain infant.

अभयं सत्त्वसंशुद्धिः ज्ञानयोगव्यवस्थितिः।
दानं दमश्च यज्ञश्च स्वाध्यायस्तप आर्जवम्।।16.1।।

अहिंसा सत्यमक्रोधस्त्यागः शान्तिरपैशुनम्।
दया भूतेष्वलोलुप्त्वं मार्दवं ह्रीरचापलम्।।16.2।।

तेजः क्षमा धृतिः शौचमद्रोहो नातिमानिता।
भवन्ति सम्पदं दैवीमभिजातस्य भारत।।16.3।।

5 SPIRITUAL JOURNEY
Merits lighten the loads
Merits enlighten the road
In common run to Abode.

6 MERITS
Lord incarnates in routine
In parts, in fragments and as glimpse
As merits in man.

7 MERITS BRING HEAVEN
Merits author
With radiant ink, its worth
The Heaven on earth.

8 DELUDED LIFE
Giant brains
Are all brainless brains
If virtues drained.

9 VIRTUOUS LIVING
This is paradise
On the earth by own choice
Following virtues in life.

INHIBITION OF DIVINE

Verse 4-5

Vanity, arrogance, wrath self-conceit
Roughness, Ignorance the one who is born with
The demonic state meets.
Divine qualities are conducive to Liberate
While demoniacal are for bondage.
But O Pandav! O Arjun be not afraid
Thou art born with Divine traits.

1 HYPOCRISY
Pride is vicious,
With the wrongs, pretending to be righteous
The ugliest face masked.

2 SHAM-ASHAME
The Evil furrows of brain
Use creases of face to pretend
Hypocritically different.

दम्भो दर्पोऽभिमानश्च क्रोधः पारुष्यमेव च।
अज्ञानं चाभिजातस्य पार्थ सम्पदमासुरीम्।।16.4।।

दैवी सम्पद्विमोक्षाय निबन्धायासुरी मता।
मा शुचः सम्पदं दैवीमभिजातोऽसि पाण्डव।।16.5।।

3 UNWISE ASSESSMENT

Arrogance, anger, conceit rise
Who look, keeping back on light
Stretched shadow of pigmy size.

4 'I' VIRTUOUS

I 'm itself the Virtue Incarnate
Shedding off Loads Of evil Traits
Come back to Primal state.

5 NOTHING IS ABSOLUTELY EVIL

As darkness is not Absolute
So the evil too Is Less good
Liberated-one has understood.

6 BETTERMENT

The Good, corrupted by ill
Is evil; and evil if cured of ill
Same evil becomes good.

7 ARROGANT DARKS

Born with no light
Unaware fights not Own Ignorance
Is fueled with extinguishing arrogance.

8 VIRTUOUS JOURNEY

All conditioned savage-moulds
*Gradually sublime From Births' Tight Hold**
Unto unconditioned soul.

9 YOU ARE BORN GOOD / YOU ARE ARJUN

Heaven is all Divine,
And all Divinity Which ever Existed
Now and here I find.

Verse 6

Exist in the world
Two types Of Men
The Divine and demoniacal moulds
O Parth ! from Me of demoniacal listen !
Of the Divine I have earst-while told.

1 TENDENCY

Lord created two designs
But with own gravity, to Demoniac Or
Divine
A man inclines.

2 GOOD MAY TURN BAD

'Bad' be viewed
Within the same mind as- the Good
Is misapplied, miscontrued.

**Inborn traits*

द्वौ भूतसर्गौ लोकेऽस्मिन् दैव आसुर एव च।
दैवो विस्तरशः प्रोक्त आसुरं पार्थ मे श्रृणु।।16.6।।

3 INCLINATION
Where there is glow
There always is a shadow;
Where you go?

4 ETERNAL TRUISM
Where evil is strong
In its sway every one may wrong
But can't wrong the Right.

5 CONDUCT
Behaviour reflects mind
Which the consciousness carves designs
To the traits assigned.

6 IDEAL LISTENER, KRISHNA SPEAKS
Listener Lord but spake
To the one whose life space
Has place for His word.

Verse 7

The Demoniac don't know apart
What be done and what not
And keep themselves Sans
Cleanness, right conduct and Transparence.

1 FOLLOW GEETA
Do's and Don'ts lie
On tested path as Milestone to rely,
Not on short whims-lies.

2 MAN –THE WARRIOR
One Attribute
That works as only war-tool
Is the Truth.

3 'THE INDECISIVE' (ABOUT DO'S N DON'TS)
The confused
Could not pursue
The Truth.

4
Who follow and pursue
The path tried and True
Reach the truth.

5 CLEANLY
Cleanness maintained
Or in and out its refrained
Discriminates Satan and Saint.

प्रवृत्तिं च निवृत्तिं च जना न विदुरासुराः।
न शौचं नापि चाचारो न सत्यं तेषु विद्यते।।16.7।।

Verse 8

Such demoniacs think and express
The Universe has no truth, no base
There is no Master who sways
Brought by no cause that compels
is lust, alone lust nothing else?

1 LOGIC DECLINED

A diabolic asserts
There is no logic that works
Its all magic of lust.

2 NO PLANNER THEORY

A demoniac world
Is all casual not the causal
Its incidental not intentional.

3 THE ETERNAL FOUNDATION

Run of changing streams
Of rivers have its Unchanging basin
Thus changings have a Changeless within.

4

'Ts Diabolic glance
That the world is chanced by chance
Not by causal plans.

5 STICKING TO THE MAYA

Their Mayic view
Relates changes as changeless
Ignorant of Absolute Truth.

Verse 9

By their feeble acumen
By erroneous belief, fallen
Committing many acts inhumane
Bent to ruin world, they come.

1

Only in low
Ferment and grow
a foe.

2 FEEBLE INTELLECT

On shallow furrows stick
The unbeliever's beliefs that slick
On its virtues slip.

असत्यमप्रतिष्ठं ते जगदाहुरनीश्वरम्।
अपरस्परसम्भूतं किमन्यत्कामहैतुकम्।।16.8।।

एतां दृष्टिमवष्टभ्य नष्टात्मानोऽल्पबुद्धयः।
प्रभवन्त्युग्रकर्माणः क्षयाय जगतोऽहिताः।।16.9।।

3 TERRORISM
Where mind is locked
They only toil for key of lock
That can create havoc.

4 INHUMANE HUMAN
The Chill of falsehood
Melts into realistic warmth of sinew
Making stiff, the good.

5 INTERFAITH FRICTION
Mind is better,
Which is empty of any belief, over
False belief that bitters.

Verse 10

Filled with voracious lust
With hypocrisy, hubris; the imposter
With folly possessing delusive impetus
Is sworn to corrupt works.

1 DECEPTIVE MIND
It's desirous whim
Desires to master desires within him
Who actually, is a victim.

2 DELUDED PRETENSE
I know I am
But my folly cannot claim
To know how I am?.

3 VORACIOUS
Lust is Infinite
Its accomplishment has its limits
That makes it further fervid.

4 INCLINED TRAIT
If something has existence
Which can corrupt your pure brain
You are corrupt before hand.

5 BAD IMPETUS
Evil hates
The trait which is not evil
'ts way to deal.

Hubris = arrogance Impetus =Drive fervid = impassioned

काममाश्रित्य दुष्पूरं दम्भमानमदान्विताः।
मोहाद्गृहीत्वासद्ग्राहान्प्रवर्तन्तेऽशुचिव्रताः।।16.10।।

UNNECESSARY CONCERNS

Verse 11-12

Involved in immeasurable concerns,
Only with death those shun,
Engrossed in 'Lust' they claim
Lust as their all and highest aim,

With hundreds of bondages
Of selfish promises
Enslaved by wrath and passion
They, by unlawful fashion,

Do crave to obtain,
And secure the hoards of mammon
For sense gratification.

1 WORLDY AFFAIRS
Among futile concerns,
Only fate of fatal glory, those earn
Man's body-mind-soul burns.

2 INTOXICATED BY WORLD
Mundane lust poisons
In it dipped mind, doped by concerns
Act, to addictive world's terms.

3 SMALL LIFE / VAST LUST
My deadly promises
Till the death, had many misses
For my passion, still less.

4 VAIN ANXIETY
Many vain-worries pervade
Thus the mind get intoxicated till death
But then it's too late.

5 OPEN THE MIND
My concern
Should not be my world
But God's world.

6 DEMONIAC TRAIT
Where lusty urges strive
Transformed into passionate wild drive,
They unlawfully survive.

चिन्तामपरिमेयां च प्रलयान्तामुपाश्रिताः।
कामोपभोगपरमा एतावदिति निश्चिताः।।16.11।।

आशापाशशतैर्बद्धाः कामक्रोधपरायणाः।
ईहन्ते कामभोगार्थमन्यायेनार्थसञ्चयान्।।16.12।।

7
The Wealth is rich
Which masters the senses and greed,
Not enslaved as necessities.

8 TRANSIANT GAIN
Lust and mammon
Are worth to enjoy momentary moments
What abou' rest of life?

DEMONIAC MIND

Verse 13 -16

I obtained this today
I shall obtain now next
This is my treasure
More shall be mine in future.

I have killed this foe
Others will also be laid low
I'm god, enjoyer of riches
I am strong, happy and perfect.

I 'm high and well-bred
Equals me who else?
I will alm
to rejoice is my aim
Muddled thus they say
By ignorance, strayed.

With many such fancies perplexed
Entangled in delusive mesh
By sensual craving enthralled
They fall into foul hell.

इदमद्य मया लब्धमिमं प्राप्स्ये मनोरथम्।
इदमस्तीदमपि मे भविष्यति पुनर्धनम्।।16.13।।

असौ मया हतः शत्रुर्हनिष्ये चापरानपि।
ईश्वरोऽहमहं भोगी सिद्धोऽहं बलवान्सुखी।।16.14।।

आढ्योऽभिजनवानस्मि कोऽन्योऽस्ति सदृशो मया।
यक्ष्ये दास्यामि मोदिष्य इत्यज्ञानविमोहिताः।।16.15।।

अनेकचित्तविभ्रान्ता मोहजालसमावृताः।
प्रसक्ताः कामभोगेषु पतन्ति नरकेऽशुचौ।।16.16।।

1 INVITING HELL

With self-worshipping ego
Equipping in self, making own foe
Turn altar into inferno.

2 INFESTING THOUGHTS

Mind is big belly
Where desires into it's furrows rally
Craving more to fill daily.

3

This strange urge
In desperate anxiety does indulge
Fallen, they never judge.

4 SLEEPING SOUL

Evil Lullaby those crow
At the hypnotic cradle of materialistic ego
Diviner urges into sleep go.

5 FANCY

Ignorance raves
On the commerce of worldly haves,
Further webs it paves.

6 EGO BRINGS MISCONCEPTION

When mind bloats
In the vault it strangulates thoughts
And the vision distorts.

7

Desire full to the shore
With greed, needs its full share,
Which accomplishes never.

8 LOOSING GAME

Game of desire is noose,
Desires toss up whether win or loose
A life diced on gammon.

9

In common run of man,
Rush for more and more mammon
All empty possessions at end.

10 INEQUALITY IN MIND

Where self-conceit is wild
Inflated ego of birth, worth, wealth spoils
And is self-exiled.

11

Alas ! Evil fancies
To get all, including the peace
In din of own conceit.

12 INNER MAKE-UP

A man does prevail
A heaven out of existing hell
Or falls with false.

Verse 17-18

They are fanatic in vain- glory
Drunk with pelf and plume
They perform rituals as Pharisee
Sans the textual holy decree.

Given to egoism and pique
Prone to rage, those lust sick
They berate others and hate Me, who
Am the Omnipresent in them and others too.

1 SATANIC FALL
Thinking of all in all
Heightened pigmies inflated by the false
In reality they fall.

2
With ego's tool hoed
Neglecting the proven, who forged own road
Unto own pit trod.

3
Exclusive quality of man
Is the Ego, yet it disqualifies also
To be a human.

4 ENVY
Even Evils have wisdom
Where diabolic mind deliberately tricks
Through hatred establishes atheism.

5 VAIN GLORY
Accumulating ashes
Of smoldered charcoal with diamond's glaze
Blackens hand, smudges face.

6 HYPOCRISY
The sacred texts
With own fudge whimsically fake
Will be at stake.

7 READINESS-EVERY DAY
The present world
Is the preparation for the next world
With every sun it unfurls.

8
Only in delusion
Its Satanic conclusion
That God is a delusion.

Pelf = Wealth *Plume = Pride* *Hoe = Scrapping in earth with pickaxe*

आत्मसम्भाविताः स्तब्धा धनमानमदान्विताः।
यजन्ते नामयज्ञैस्ते दम्भेनाविधिपूर्वकम्।।16.17।।

अहङ्कारं बलं दर्पं कामं क्रोधं च संश्रिताः।
मामात्मपरदेहेषु प्रद्विषन्तोऽभ्यसूयकाः।।16.18।।

ILL-FATED BIRTH BY BIRTH

Verse 19-20

These envious and cruel
Worst among men I hurl
And repeatedly they are doomed
Into the diabolic wombs.

Entering diabolic species
Deluded birth after birth
O Arjun ! not attaining Me
They fall further into worst.

1 DESTINY

It seems a Supreme ordeal
But It's always how you deal
Makes the Supreme will.

2 KARMIC FATE

Wrong acts
Bring forward the wrong traits
Brought forward in the next.

3 SELF GUIDED

'Ts Incarnate- soul's choice
Among noxious trumpeting Noise
To raise inner voice.

4 DETERMINATION

Fate decides the fate
Until fated by his acts
Those challenge and dictate.

5 TRANSGRESSER

Privileged of free will
When misused by the Evil
Doomed to Supreme will.

6 DARK TRAIT

To the centre of Evolution
The conditioned soul if not attracted, then
Is caught into Centrifugal delusion.

7 MISUSING TRAIT

None is ever condemned
Ladder which dooms the diabolically fallen
To uplift, ladder is same.

तानहं द्विषतः क्रूरान्संसारेषु नराधमान्।
क्षिपाम्यजस्रमशुभानासुरीष्वेव योनिषु।।16.19।।

असुरीं योनिमापन्ना मूढा जन्मनि जन्मनि।
मामप्राप्यैव कौन्तेय ततो यान्त्यधमां गतिम्।।16.20।।

GATEWAY TO ABYSS

Verse 21-22

Lust, ire and greed
For soul ope gates to Hades
One Need to abandon these.

O Arjun ! escaping these three
Conducive to goodness his deeds
To the Supreme, lead.

1 THREE ILLS
Lust tosses mould
Anger possesses the thought and the bias
Greed disposes soul of soul.

2 FALLEN
These three fiends
Have eaten my wings
From free sky I sink.

3 ESCAPING FROM VAIN CONCERNS
Into short-lived concerns
When divine vitality is not burnt
Soul rockets beyond sub-human.

4
Supreme, in every soul dwells
And His promise to redeem every soul
He never fails.

5 DEMONISATION
Dissatisfaction poisoned
And rusted mind through sense gratification
I became my own demon.

6 SOUL'S JOURNEY
Through many moulds
I journeyed from senses to all soul
Achieved the Goal.

7
Same world is the mean
As blooms the bud in sunny wind
In stroke and storms shrinks.

त्रिविधं नरकस्येदं द्वारं नाशनमात्मनः।
कामः क्रोधस्तथा लोभस्तस्मादेतत्त्रयं त्यजेत्।।16.21।।

एतैर्विमुक्तः कौन्तेय तमोद्वारैस्त्रिभिर्नरः।
आचरत्यात्मनः श्रेयस्ततो याति परां गतिम्।।16.22।।

Verse 23-24

He who discardth scriptural provisions
Actth under lustful whim
Attain nor bliss nor perfection
Nor he attains the Supreme.

So, let the scripture be thy guide,
Thy Do's and Don'ts to decide,
Having known what's in Sacred text
Here thou shouldst act.

1 PERCEPTS
Ancient Provisions
Are lead down by ancient saints
After births of experience.

2 WHO ARE TRUE FOLLOWERS
Worlds of the scripture
Are owned by the divine seekers
As if readers are authors.

3 OWN ANOMALLY
Self -made dogmatism
Of untext inferences of whim
Reach no where.

4 GOD AND HOLY TEXT
Befriending the God
Need a scriptural concord
Both being mutual pal.

5 FALL
Precious Scriptural theme
Individually imposed upon by fanatism
Further is degraded by whim.

6 ANCIENT SCRIPTURES
Time honoured is approved
As holy text because its been proved
To be True or become True.

7 COMING OF SCRIPTURES
Timeless texts
Have arisen from intuition of exactitude facts
Making realizable, the Truth.

8 FOLLOW
Boldest scriptures came out
With idea of oneness; so in doubt
Do not stand out.

यः शास्त्रविधिमुत्सृज्य वर्तते कामकारतः।
न स सिद्धिमवाप्नोति न सुखं न परां गतिम्।।16.23।।

तस्माच्छास्त्रं प्रमाणं ते कार्याकार्यव्यवस्थितौ।
ज्ञात्वा शास्त्रविधानोक्तं कर्म कर्तुमिहार्हसि।।16.24।।

CHAPTER SEVENTEEN

Divisions of Reverence

God has created
You, in you keeping all faith
Just reciprocate !

‘Aum’ is shortest hymn

That’s emerged wordless voice from Him*

To merge me in ‘AUM’.

Chapter Seventeen

THREE KINDS OF WORSHIP

Verse 1

Arjun asked –

Aside, those who set
Provisions of scriptural texts
But those performing rites with faith
O Krshna ! What's their state
Is it divine, Terrence or malign trait ?

1
For common run of concern
Arjun asks the uncommon question
To pick standard provisions.

2 MAKING OWN PATH
This faith in mind
With own inclinations different from line
What does that find?

3 ARJUN'S DOUBT
A yogic perception
In the inhibitions and injunctions
What does the inclinations?

4 PATH FINDER / PATH MAKER
Can a seeker
With his own spiritual endeavor
Slowly become a Setter ?

अर्जुन उवाच
ये शास्त्रविधिमुत्सृज्य यजन्ते श्रद्धयाऽन्विताः।
तेषां निष्ठा तु का कृष्ण सत्त्वमाहो रजस्तमः।।17.1।।

Verse 2-3

The Blessed Lord Said –

Inclination of the embodied mould
Has his faith three fold,
Bright-Divine, terrene and malign dark
About all those now you hark !

O Bhaarat ! the accordance of trait
Has it's inclination innate,
The living being is the Incarnate
Of his own trait.

1 MY NATURE

The Soul, which impregnates
The body-mind inclination to set
Trait becomes body itself.

2

Modes of traits assign
The mind, its mould to design
Be divine or else.

3 ATTRIBUTES-INCLINATION

Man has brought
With him inclined chisel of thoughts
Lest straight hammering distorts.

4 ALL TRAITS ARE OBSTACLES

Traits, for mortal cages,
Whether pricking thorns or reposing roses
For transcending, are hedges.

5 ATTRIBUTES MAKE ENTITY

The hue on the brush
In accordance with daubed stuff
The Canvas, colours.

6 INCLINATION

The Present earns
From the Past treasured earnings
Thus shapes the Being.

श्री भगवानुवाच
त्रिविधा भवति श्रद्धा देहिनां सा स्वभावजा।
सात्त्विकी राजसी चैव तामसी चेति तां श्रृणु।।17.2।।

सत्त्वानुरूपा सर्वस्य श्रद्धा भवति भारत।
श्रद्धामयोऽयं पुरुषो यो यच्छ्रद्धः स एव सः।।17.3।।

THREE KINDS OF BHAKTI

Verse 4

The Divine to the Divinities leans
The worldly pay homage to fiends
And the Malign to manes and goblins.

1
My Stature and nature
Decides my offering prayer
To the Pure or Impure.

2 DEVOTED TO WHOM ?
Worship is the road
Which depends on man's mode
Where it prods?

3 INCLINATION
To Seek in human instinct
But what to seek is divine thing
Where one's individuality leans.

4 WHOM I WORSHIP ?
With raised hands
He is further blessed or further accursed
It's on worshippers.

Verse 5-6

Those who go under severe penance
Not enjoined by scriptural ordinance
Given to self-conceit and selfish attempts
Senselessly they torture bodily elements
There by Me, the Indweller also they offend
Know ! these to be demoniacal men.

1 HYPOCRITIC AUSTERITIES
The hypocritic-fuels scorch
The clay-pot, wick, the light, ash, environ
Also singes the Indwelling torch.

2 UNRULY ATTEMPTS
The Unlettered toils
Over the Individualized mortal coils
Is very self to spoil.

यजन्ते सात्त्विका देवान्यक्षरक्षांसि राजसाः।
प्रेतान्भूतगणांश्चान्ये यजन्ते तामसा जनाः।।17.4।।

अशास्त्रविहितं घोरं तप्यन्ते ये तपो जनाः।
दम्भाहङ्कारसंयुक्ताः कामरागबलान्विताः।।17.5।।

कर्षयन्तः शरीरस्थं भूतग्राममचेतसः।
मां चैवान्तःशरीरस्थं तान्विद्ध्यासुरनिश्चयान्।।17.6।।

3 PRETENDER
Whose ego fastens
In vain, unto diabolic world, is lost
At the Indweller's cost.

4 EGO OF WORSHIPPING
Laden by the Ego
The worships, sink and lost in benthos
Sublime not above

5 SPLIT CONSCIOUSNESS
Broken and splitted
Life, keeping mind and Indweller separates*
To the fullest can't manifest.

6 IRONY
Self-conceit efforts
To bring to light own course
Endorses own dark force.

7 UNINTELLIGENT EXHAUSION
He faces fatigue and fag,
By spiritual feed back who is not fed
Being wrongly tracked.

THREE CLASSES OF FOOD

Verse 7

According to the natural traits
Three kinds of food they partake
Their Yagna, Penance and benevolence
Now listen ! these are different.

1
Traits in hide,
Through diet, sight and sacrifice
'The individual stature', decide.

2 MY TRAITS
To whom I raise hands
How I ope palate, how I ope hands
Closely tie with my bent.

3 LIKING ACCORDING TO TRAIT
My liking is a toy
Casts for moments' flavour or life's fervour
Depends on Nature employed.

**Godly soul   Fag=worn out.*

आहारस्त्वपि सर्वस्य त्रिविधो भवति प्रियः।
यज्ञस्तपस्तथा दानं तेषां भेदमिमं श्रृणु।।17.7।।

Verse 8 -10

That promotes purity, strength, livelihood,
Raises appetite, aptitude, attitude
There savory, substantial agreeable food
Is liked by the Divine and good.

Too bitter, sour, salty sizzling, pungent
As burning roasts produce pangs, pains, banes
These foods are liked by worldly men.

Food insipid, putrid worthless to dine
Stale, refuse and unrefined
Are enjoyed by the Malign.

1
It Reflects
Through my palate,
My stature, my state.

2
Pure food has gravity
To attract Purity from far and vicinity
To be annexed to Entity.

3
Valued-devalued food-stuff
Transcendentally diffuse every bit, enough
The conditioned soul to stuff.

4
Tiny food ingredients
Shaped my brain and ingrained my frame
Immortal, mortal or immoral.

5
Not the noise
But the daily noise
Is my voice.

6 FOOD HABITS
Palate is the mean
Unto firm palate-less soul to intervene
Making it tempered to lean.

आयुःसत्त्वबलारोग्यसुखप्रीतिविवर्धनाः।
रस्याः स्निग्धाः स्थिरा हृद्या आहाराः
सात्त्विकप्रियाः।।17.8।।

कट्वम्ललवणात्युष्णतीक्ष्णरूक्षविदाहिनः।
आहारा राजसस्येष्टा दुःखशोकामयप्रदाः।।17.9।।

यातयामं गतरसं पूति पर्युषितं च यत्।
उच्छिष्टमपि चामेध्यं भोजनं तामसप्रियम्।।17.10।।

7
A drop on the taste buds
Transcendent through body-mind into soul
Your universe thus floods.

9 FOOD CONDITIONS SOUL
The stuffs I swallow
Is absorbed, to the Supreme go
With the flavour of soul.

8 Flood Of Food In Life
Be vigilant to victual's role
My favourite greedy food bowl
Lest may swallow my soul.

Verse 11-13

Yagna, as duty who does for no fruit,
And performs following sacred textual route
Is of the nature Divinely good.

But 'Yagna' done in view of benefits
And performed with ostentatious spirit
That Yagna into materialism fit.

That 'Yagna' is condemned as Malign
Which regards not the scriptural lines,
Nor offering grains, nor offering chants
Nor having credos, not giving alms.

1 DUTIFULLY PERFORMED
The ugly or beauteous
Same Yagna is valued cheap or precious
How much it's duteous

2 KARMA
Seed seems tough
But you don't break it for fruits
Seeding is enough

Victuals=food Ostentatious=Pretentious/ show off
Credos = faith, Yagna = Spiritual rite of offering

अफलाकाङ्क्षिभिर्यज्ञो विधिदृष्टो य इज्यते।
यष्टव्यमेवेति मनः समाधाय स सात्त्विकः।।17.11।।

अभिसंधाय तु फलं दम्भार्थमपि चैव यत्।
इज्यते भरतश्रेष्ठ तं यज्ञं विद्धि राजसम्।।17.12।।

विधिहीनमसृष्टान्नं मन्त्रहीनमदक्षिणम्।
श्रद्धाविरहितं यज्ञं तामसं परिचक्षते।।17.13।।

3
All the ritual toils
Even victual morsel feeding mortal coils
Are sown in soul's soil.

4
Yagna is virtual sacrifice
When sacrificed the desire-ridden price
Of the sacrifice.

5 INDEBTED
It's routine I breath
My occasional alms giving, in self-concert
How could pay debts.

6 GOOD PERFORMER / BAD PERFORMER
Oblation in Yagna altar,
Should illumine and ignite a fire
And not incinerate entire.

7 SHOW BIZ
For vanity done,
Those self-centred, self-conceit oblations
The Self, never have own.

Verse 14

Reverence to the Devas, Unborn,
And also to the twice born,
And worship to the Genius and Gurus;
The Purity and ingénue
Continence and non-violence
Are called the bodily Penance.

1 DISCIPLINE
Shaped by discipline man inclines
To the shapeless worshipable divine
Within get enshrined.

2 DWIJ
From imitations womb first born
From world's limitation womb be hatched
Thus be Twice-blessed.

Ingenue=Simplicity

देवद्‌विजगुरुप्राज्ञपूजनं शौचमार्जवम्।
ब्रह्मचर्यमहिंसा च शारीरं तप उच्यते।।17.14।।

3 SIMPLY SINGLE MINDEDNESS
Simply the naivete
Not have his mind-split
Which drains out Spirit.

4 WORLDLY TOILS
Vital Energy conserved and converged,
From vain concerns of body; serve
As penance of body.

Verse 15

The speech which doesn't offend
The speech which is all truthful
Which is non-irritating, beneficial, pleasant
Speech which practices vedic chants
Constitute speech's Penance.

1 BLESSED TONGUE
Supreme Lord hath blessed
Lord's Own disciplined communion to express
With full potential in man.

2 YAGNA OF SPEECH
Every altar of mouth affords
In Yagna of oblating speech, true words
Pleasant words a charity worth.

3 DAILY PENANCE
Invested in Chants
In reflection of truth, beneficence-pleasance
Daily words become penance.

4 SPEECH AS THE WAY TO GOD
Exhaling the truth of tongue
Inhales the truth of word's expression
Transcends to wordless communion.

5 FIRM TONGUE
A virtual speech
In the day to day vocal activities
Is penance of speech.

Verse 16

The calm and content of mind
Mature silence of mind
*Natural continence of mind**
And thought containment of mind
All are Penance of mind.

*Naivete = Simplicity *Purity*

अनुद्वेगकरं वाक्यं सत्यं प्रियहितं च यत्।
स्वाध्यायाभ्यसनं चैव वाङ्मयं तप उच्यते।।17.15।।

मनःप्रसादः सौम्यत्वं मौनमात्मविनिग्रहः।
भावसंशुद्धिरित्येतत्तपो मानसमुच्यते।।17.16।।

1

Thoughtfully becoming
Thoughtless to the worldly entities
Are mental austerities.

2 DAILY AUSTERE

Composed attempts
To sublime posed worldy tempts
Are daily mental penance.

3

Control the self
Before its being controlled
By someone else.

4 SERENTIY

Mature mute of mind
Turns to natural quietude of thought
Gain altitude of soul.

5 MIND-CONTROL

Out of calm, crazy
These worldly teams are won over if
Self-control is referee.

Verse 17

This three fold-Penance
Practiced by persevering men
With the utmost reverence
Who desire no fruit
Sure, tread on Divine route.

1 SACRED LIFE IN COMMON RUN

Work, thought, words
In world are daily means
Of practising penance.

2 FREEDOM

Daily he does metamorphose
And breaks out of body, mind, speech
On wings he goes.

3

No severe penance
But in daily toils, the perseverance
Will do.

श्रद्धया परया तप्तं तपस्तत्त्रिविधं नरैः।
अफलाकाङ्क्षिभिर्युक्तैः सात्त्विकं परिचक्षते।।17.17।।

Verse 18-19

The ostentatious penance
For recognition, respect and reverence
Are said to be materialistic
Those are unstable and impermanent.

Malign Yagna penance
All these based on ignorance
For self torture or other's torments.

1 HYPOCRISY
Yagna and austerity pursued
For cheap respect as rich values
In reality are devalued.

2
Hands raised in worship
With self-centred motives as basest deceits
Are bound to defeats.

3 POTENTIAL TO RISE OR FALL
All terrene deeds
Have potential to slip to the Evil
May! rise in right spirit.

4
Palate and wallet to fill
Whose wanton pride of cherished sin, deal
Fall very low still.

5
Who worship God
And expects for himself worship of world
Is a non -worshipper infidel.

6 SPIRITUALLY NIL
Materialistic austerities
Though better than evil toils
But possess little merits.

7
Misconstrued holy hymns
Distorts and disfigures Truth in him
His whim makes world, victim.

सत्कारमानपूजार्थं तपो दम्भेन चैव यत्।
क्रियते तदिह प्रोक्तं राजसं चलमध्रुवम्।।17.18।।

मूढग्राहेणात्मनो यत्पीडया क्रियते तपः।
परस्योत्सादनार्थं वा तत्तामसमुदाहृतम्।।17.19।।

THREE TYPES OF GIVINGS

Verse 20

A dutiful largess
At fit time and place
To a most deserving person
Expecting nothing in return
As Divine charity termed.

1 BE DUTEOUS IS DIVINE
The charity as conviction,
As a must-'that is to be done'
Is a Divine concern.

2
Kindness of compassion
With no any kind of compensation
Is a Divine donation.

3
Stretched hands, those give
Are extension of mercy of Lord
Those hands receive.

4
The Divine extended elbow
Has no bias when charity is bestowed
Like a laden bough.

5 CHARITY
A good serve
Only observes when and where
And who deserves.

Verse 21

The charity done for the sake
Of receiving a response back
Or looking after resultant fruits
Or done as a grudging act
Are charities of Materialistic trait.

दातव्यमिति यद्दानं दीयतेऽनुपकारिणे।
देशे काले च पात्रे च तद्दानं सात्त्विकं स्मृतम्।।17.20।।

यत्तु प्रत्युपकारार्थं फलमुद्दिश्य वा पुनः।
दीयते च परिक्लिष्टं तद्दानं राजसं स्मृतम्।।17.21।।

1

A selfish giving
Gives no alms but is bartering of things
In commerce of dealings.

2 BARTERING CHARITY

The hands reluctantly ope
But with worldly rewards and godly hopes
To evolve has further scope.

3

His ope hands
Reflects his open heart
Slowly closing to the Lord.

4

As 'Charity' never befits
The gift with its return gift
Has no serving spirit.

5

For others a gift
Is just not for the receiver
But ownself it lifts.

Verse 22

And the charity is malign
At improper place and time
Given to unworthy men
With contempts and no deference.

1

Alms with unworthy aims
Alm asking for earthly claims
Is no alm.

2

Charity without heart,
A gift, though the men described,
The Lord thinks it's bribe.

3

Any good with contempts
Is empty of good, if seeking recompense,
Even if handfully dispensed.

4

All the world treasures
Are the alms-giving by the One
Rest are begging paupers.

5 EVIL-CHARITY

Who invests in charity,
Simply as in Business of bartering trade,
Loses the Divinity.

अदेशकाले यद्दानमपात्रेभ्यश्च दीयते।
असत्कृतमवज्ञातं तत्तामसमुदाहृतम्।।17.22।।

TRIPLE DESIGNATION OF GOD"AUM-TAT-SAT"

Verse 23

Declared the 'Aum- Tat- Sat'
To be Brahmn's triple epithets,
By that were created,
At Genesis, Brahmans, Veds
And Yagyas and secreds.

1 AUM
'Aum' Absolute seed of Genesis
And 'Tat' is the Absolute seat of Genesis,
'Sat' is offspring, the Gnosis.

2 AUM
Among thousands names
This sonic manifestation of Absolutely unframed
'AUM' is the highest name.

3
The knower of Brahmn
Knows that I am not cluster of atoms
But I'm Aum.

4 AUM–TAT–SAT
Aum is the fine cause
Tat-Sat the effect gross
Thus is whole cosmos.

5 'ONE'- ORIGIN
Holy texts, holy deeds
Also chanters and knowers of these
Have one Originator Seed.

6 'THREEFOLD – CREATION'
AUM God's vital drive
'Tat' is God's particle make cosmos survive
Where God conscious 'Sat' hives.

7 AUM – TAT – SAT
'Aum' is energy ancient,
'Tat' is manifested vital element
'Sat' its conscious essence.

8 KNOWER OF BRAHMN
Intellectualizing text
is a little part of knowledge
Of realizing the Veds.

hives = assemble

तत्सदिति निर्देशो ब्रह्मणस्त्रिविधः स्मृतः।
ब्राह्मणास्तेन वेदाश्च यज्ञाश्च विहिताः पुरा।।17.23।।

AUM – IT'S SIGNIFICANCE

Verse 24

Therefore, any performance
Yagna, charity and penance
Of the knower of the Brahmn
Begin with 'Aum' chants.

1 AUM
A perfect prayer begins
With 'Aum' which is manifested
From hush of Unmanifest Origin.

2 ETERNAL VEDS
'AUM' is sound seed
Its offsprings hymns mantras chants
With prefixed 'AUM' turned eonian.

3 MEDITATE ON 'AUM'
'AUM' is Divine
Its vital sap, elixir and wine
Soul Go ! and get drunk.

4
Before the Eternity clocked
And words into texts and chants flocked
There existed the originator Aum.

5
Vibration of Mantra chants
Which fill the universe with its intents
Is one 'AUM' intense.

6 LIBERATING 'AUM'
'Aum' is shortest hymn
That's emerged wordless voice from Him*
To merge me in 'AUM'.

Verse 25

The seeker of Moksha induct
Their rites, charities, Austerities
While knowing these all as HIS
Without the fruit's wish.

** supreme - being*

तस्मादोमित्युदाहृत्य यज्ञदानतपःक्रियाः।
प्रवर्तन्ते विधानोक्ताः सततं ब्रह्मवादिनाम्।।17.24।।

तदित्यनभिसन्धाय फलं यज्ञतपःक्रियाः।
दानक्रियाश्च विविधाः क्रियन्ते मोक्षकाङ्क्षिभिः।।17.25।।

1
Seeker then withdraws
From methods, procedures and those minor laws
Unto 'Tat' once draws.

2 KNOWING 'TAT' REDEEMS
Little boat floats
With wind of 'Tat', in waves that hoaxed*
But boat crossed to Moksha.

3 ALL KNOWLEDGE
Very THAT is 'TAT'
'That' means compressed and expanded Truth
Solves all ifs and buts.

Verse 26-27

And 'SAT' indicates
Goodness and Supreme facts
And in 'SAT' reflects
The sense of a spiritual act.

'SAT' also reflects
In austerity, charity and sacrifices
Performed as the Divine act
In steadfast state.

1 AUM TAT SAT
Very that -'TAT'
Is revealed as highest fact
Through 'AUM' itself.

2 TRUE KNOWLEDGE –'SAT'
Eonian vibration of Aum
When harmonize with consciousness of 'TAT'
Finds 'SAT' of Oneness.

3 REDEMPTION
'AUM' is transcending Medium
'TAT very that is the Mean
To transcendent to Final win.

4
The relative Truths
Of steadfast rites, charity, penance could
Be the Self-same Absolute.

'TAT'=HE, the Lord.

सद्भावे साधुभावे च सदित्येतत्प्रयुज्यते।
प्रशस्ते कर्मणि तथा सच्छब्दः पार्थ युज्यते।।17.26।।

यज्ञे तपसि दाने च स्थितिः सदिति चोच्यते।
कर्म चैव तदर्थीयं सदित्येवाभिधीयते।।17.27।।

5
Steadfastness unveils 'TAT'
Through rites, rituals explores the 'SAT'
Of Oneness of 'TAT'.

6 'REDEMPTION WAY'
Oneness of 'AUM'
As universal Truth –'SAT' invoked in bosom
Finds his one Home.

Verse 28

O Parth ! 'ts no worth
Sacrifices and alms offered
Or austerities without faith
Are called 'NON- SAT' 'not honest'
Are worthless here and in the next.

1
Any spiritual drive
Of practices, its worth derives
Through motives inhived.

2 WORTHLESS TOIL
The beads and deeds
With faithlessness as seed
In the desert reap.

3
On step of faith
What happens very next
Appears the Path itself.

4
An altar is chilled hearth
Half hearted heart has no warm worth
Without fire of Faith.

5
Catching light into fist
A faithless act is a similar miss
Gathers dark amidst all lit.

6
God has created
You, in you keeping all faith
Just reciprocate !

inhive = assemble

अश्रद्धया हुतं दत्तं तपस्तप्तं कृतं च यत्।
असदित्युच्यते पार्थ न च तत्प्रेत्य नो इह।।17.28।।

CHAPTER EIGHTEEN

I promise thee- "The Perfection"

Where Godliness bridles
Man's boasted zeal on wheel
Together win every field.

Among daily war thick

Lord's whispers be loudly proudly picked

Eternal words never contradict.

Chapter Eighteen

RENUNCIATION

Verse 1

Arjun said -

I wish know O Krshna !
Severally, the essence
Of 'Renunciation' and the element
Of Tyaga, the Abnegation

1
Questioning pursues
Not the doubt but more faith
In Master, the Guru.

2 KRSHNA –THE KILLER OF DOUBTS
Doubts are demons
Hover all about the eagerness of wisdom
Certain killing; ascertain !

3
On concerns of quest
What's bound to happen very next
Questions the very faith.

ORDER OF SANNYASA-RENUNCIATION

Verse 2

The Blessed Lord said –

'Sannyasa' defined by adepts
Is renunciation of fruitful acts
Of 'Tyaga' wise have stated
The fruit of action to abnegate.

अर्जुन उवाच
संन्यासस्य महाबाहो तत्त्वमिच्छामि वेदितुम्।
त्यागस्य च हृषीकेश पृथक्केशिनिषूदन।।18.1।।

श्री भगवानुवाच
काम्यानां कर्मणां न्यासं संन्यासं कवयो विदुः।
सर्वकर्मफलत्यागं प्राहुस्त्यागं विचक्षणाः।।18.2।।

1

Where fruitful acts not pursued
Is 'Sannyasa' and 'Tyaga' where fruits
Of acts not accrued.

2 ORDER OF SANNYASA

Duteous hands perform, though
Where beauteous mind to fruits say No
Is worth Holiest Go.

3

He does act
As veritable action, never owns any act
Knowing sole Doer's fact.

ORDER OF SANNYASA

Verse 3-6

Some learned men say
All deeds to forsake
For all these acts have taints,
Yet other declared that Yagna
And charity and the penance
Ought not be abandoned.

Listen ! what I conclude
About 'Tyaga' 'ts final Truth
Yagna of three kinds are said
O Bhaarat ! it's declared in Veds,

Deeds of Yagna, charity, penance
Be performed and not be abandoned,
For charity, penance, sacrifice
Purifies further the wise

O Parth ! here I finally conclude-
Even these acts be pursued
For sure leaving aside the fruits.

Sannyasa=Renounced order of life

त्याज्यं दोषवदित्येके कर्म प्राहुर्मनीषिणः।
यज्ञदानतपःकर्म न त्याज्यमिति चापरे।।18.3।।
यज्ञदानतपःकर्म न त्याज्यं कार्यमेव तत्।
यज्ञो दानं तपश्चैव पावनानि मनीषिणाम्।।18.5।।

निश्चयं श्रृणु मे तत्र त्यागे भरतसत्तम।
त्यागो हि पुरुषव्याघ्र त्रिविधः संप्रकीर्तितः।।18.4।।
एतान्यपि तु कर्माणि सङ्गं त्यक्त्वा फलानि च।
कर्तव्यानीति मे पार्थ निश्िचतं
मतमुत्तमम्।।18.6।।

1 REDEMPTION
On the way to liberation
Domain of action is hurdle to unbroken
State of God-union.

2 DEEDS OF A SANNYASI
Shunning selfish desires
And one who in others, suffers
His actions are pure.

3 INDIFFERENT ATTITUDE
Not only the Action
Also the non-action if attached to fruits
Is baser-the Lord concludes.

4 NON-ATTACHMENT
All things that claim good
Exist because of result of being seed
Of non-attached godly deeds.

5
Non action of liberated one,
Is active performance, lest for redemption
Action be not abandoned.

6 YAGNA
Old order of rites
In ancient course work and purify
All wrongs to right.

7
Creases of hands
Should have ease in the mind
From desires in errand.

8
The Action with thought
Of attachment with anxiety of fruit,
The good action itself rots.

Verse 7-9

Duty of obligatory actions
Should not be resigned
For renouncing these through delusion
Are declared as malign
Escaping from intrinsic difficiles
Of painful actions to deal,
If renunciation has such cause
Is not at all 'Tyaga'

Difficile=trouble

नियतस्य तु संन्यासः कर्मणो नोपपद्यते।
मोहात्तस्य परित्यागस्तामसः परिकीर्तितः।।18.7।।

दुःखमित्येव यत्कर्म कायक्लेशभयात्त्यजेत्।
स कृत्वा राजसं त्यागं नैव त्यागफलं लभेत्।।18.8।।

कार्यमित्येव यत्कर्म नियतं क्रियतेऽर्जुन।
सङ्गं त्यक्त्वा फलं चैव स त्यागः सात्त्विको
मतः।।18.9।।

O Arjun ! when obligatory actions
Are done, for it's ought to be done
With fruits and attachment abandoned
Such renunciation is Divine One.

1
Duties I flunk
From infallible work of Lord I escape
Very 'Tyaga' I bunk.

2 'DELUSIVE TYAGA'
Abnegation self-designed
Where neutrality to God's will is mal-aligned
Is inaction maligned.

3 FOR COMFORT IN TYAGA
Fearing fear of pain,
Whose obligating concerns who refrain
They renounce in vain.

4 TYAGA FOR FRUITS
For the very comfort
Or renouncement for the results
Whole order* he insults.

5 BE DUTIFUL
Not giving up Actions
But leaving delusion of inaction
Is real renunciation.

6
As renunciant who mull
In 'Sanyaas' even daily obligations are null
Their 'Tyaga' is dull.

7 OBLIGATORY ACTS
If men himself subdues
From what God had made due
Entangles more in voodoo**.

8 TYAGA FOR COMFORT
In convenient appeal
Renouncing actions of world is no ordeal
Is more a worldly deal.

9 THE ORDER OF RENOUNCEMENT-SANNYASA
Penance of Saint
Is Tyaga in pain but this pain
Rids suffering of man-kind.

*Flunk=fail. *Order of Sannyasa. **Magic World*

Verse 10

Who abhors not inauspicious deeds,
And adheres not with auspicious deeds
From doubts, ever freed
Being virtuous and being intelligent
He is divine renunciant.

1
With balanced minds
From inequality who resigns
Equals the Divine.

2 RENUNCIANT – THE TYAGI
Who's independent of happenings
Every moment who stays from worldly abundance
Perfects the Abandonment.

3
Man's virtuous virtues
Transcend the world, through and through
Thus a renunciant pursue.

4
Giving up hates and love
Even-mind keeping itself all above
Perfects renunciation.

Verse 11

Truly, its impossible for the Embodied
To abandon completely, deeds
But fruits of action who renounce
Is the one who is truly Renounced.

1 DESIRE
Where body is dominant
The inner dweller soul becomes conditioned
To desire's sub-servience.

2 NO CONTROL ON FRUIT
Inevitable are the actions,
Have conditioned the Action and Inaction
But can't condition fruits.

न द्वेष्ट्यकुशलं कर्म कुशले नानुषज्जते।
त्यागी सत्त्वसमाविष्टो मेधावी छिन्नसंशयः।।18.10।।

न हि देहभृता शक्यं त्यक्तुं कर्माण्यशेषतः।
यस्तु कर्मफलत्यागी स त्यागीत्यभिधीयते।।18.11।।

3
Non-action is improbable
Embodied has only choice to discipline
The dynamic rhythm.

4
It's- 'I who earn'
It's- 'I who learn'
Need be unlearnt.

5 'KARMA'
The Entity conditioned by gross,
In causal body Action is though caused
Desireless actions get applause.

Verse 12

At demise, good, evil and mixed
Triune fruits with actions are affixed
To the Non renounced who does not desist.
But Never triune fate of fruits affix
To the Renunciant, fruits who dismiss.

1 EMPTIED OF DESIRES
Hand-bowl of desires brew
The Elixir, juice and toxins too
On ope hands nothing accrues.

2 REINCARNATION
Future thoughts are caused
By chisel of thoughts hammered in past
Shaped the next cast.

3 ANXIETY OF FRUITS
Results of toil depends
On Anxiety fruit how oil is spent
'Giving up' fruits, fuels at end.

4 DESIRES ARE OBSTACLES
All anxious unease
Is not with action but desire's from it
Which interrupts Release.

अनिष्टमिष्टं मिश्रं च त्रिविधं कर्मणः फलम्।
भवत्यत्यागिनां प्रेत्य न तु संन्यासिनां क्वचित्।।18.12।।

ACTION AND NON-ACTION

Verse 13 -16

Now from Me learn
O Arjun ! O Mighty Armed !!
Five factors of Action
Which fulfill Actions performed
Chronicled in the Samkhya text
Where in all actions terminate.

Body is working platform
Where doer-Ego performs
And organs of senses perceive
The functional organs, those are active
And the Indwelling deity is fifth.

Whatever right or wrong
Endeavours the man performs
By the mind, body and speech
Are caused by five these.

As only doer who think,
Through non clarified knowing
Sees ownself as exclusive doer
Sees not things as they are.

1 SANKHYA, THE WISE APPROACH
*In **spiritual algorithm***
All actions and fruits be renounced to sum
As coefficient of wisdom.

2 CONSUMMATION OF FRUITS
Within root of action
Fruit which seeds, greed root
Needs be weeded out.

Samkhya = Spiritual Algorithm

पञ्चैतानि महाबाहो कारणानि निबोध मे।
सांख्ये कृतान्ते प्रोक्तानि सिद्धये सर्वकर्मणाम्।।18.13।।

अधिष्ठानं तथा कर्ता करणं च पृथग्विधम्।
विविधाश्च पृथक्चेष्टा दैवं चैवात्र पञ्चमम्।।18.14।।

शरीरवाङ्मनोभिर्यत्कर्म प्रारभते नरः।
न्याय्यं वा विपरीतं वा पञ्चैते तस्य हेतवः।।18.15।।

तत्रैवं सति कर्तारमात्मानं केवलं तु यः।
पश्यत्यकृतबुद्धित्वान्न स पश्यति दुर्मतिः।।18.16।।

3 SANKHYA
When Yogic calculus
Divides the five tools of doer status
Remains 'One' primus.

4 FIVE CAUSES OF ACTION
First caused body-element
Then Ego-centred organs of action-reactions
With traits compelling reign.

5 GEETA GYAN
On Working I-ness in murk
Dawned the learning in mind's east
Illumined it as non-doer.

6 EGOCENTRIC CONSCIOUSNESS
Five-fold tools
With all deluding facilities befool
As doer, not the tool.

7 I 'M THE BODY
Only binds
To the body-dominant mind
Is purblind eye.

8 WISE PERFORMER
Wise is aware
himself as just the seeming doer
Real Doer has authored.

9
Through framed work
Vitalized by universal verve of nerve
The One frameless serve.

Verse 17

No I-ness, who feels
With untainted wisdom above good and evil
Though in here battle, he kills
Nor he slays nor he is bound by such deeds.

1 FIGHTING SPIRIT
Lord's hope reposes
Where hope of warrior combatively amuses
Not in tainted excuses.

2 A WARRIOR IN ME
Killing false ego,
Lord as only Doer who know
Are warriors killing, the Killer-foe

यस्य नाहंकृतो भावो बुद्धिर्यस्य न लिप्यते।
हत्वापि स इमाँल्लोकान्न हन्ति न
निबध्यते।।18.17।।

3 KRSHNA URGED TO YOGI

*You are the instrument**
Your brandishing hands with slay them
Whom I have already slain.

4 GOD WITHIN SOLDIER

Seems it's individual will
But Righteous soldier works Godly in field
Kills the Evil.

5 DUTEOUS WARRIOR

Equal mind has Lord's will
Lord's wish only brandish through man's hilt
Thus, the Creator kills.

Verse 18

The knower is subject
Knowable is the object
Is made known through knowledge
Their 'Karmas' triune stimulus act
*The Entity, the instrument** and activity make*
Three fold basis of any Act.

1 IMPULSE OF ACTION

The Knowledge tempts
The knower, further and further to attempt
The Knowable to comprehend.

2 BASIS OF ACTION

*Five factors*** caused the shrine*
By devotee, devotion and statue-these trine
Made the Divinity enshrined.

3 CONTENTS OF ACTION

Lyrics and instruments in quorum
Of song, need a singer's entity stimulus
Make the fullest chorus.

*Also see Ch –11 **Knowledge ***ref to verse 13-14 Ch-18

ज्ञानं ज्ञेयं परिज्ञाता त्रिविधा कर्मचोदना।
करणं कर्म कर्तेति त्रिविधः कर्मसंग्रहः।।18.18।।

THREE GRADES OF KNOWLEDGE, ACTION AND CHARACTER

Verse 19

The Entity, activity and Knowledge
In Sankhya philosophy as texted
Are three kinds matching three traits
Listen ! to Me, apt.

1
Conditioned by the taste
Any work is worked up by traits
Thus basis of work affects.

2
All the traits bind
Good or evil in mind
Only fruitlessness unbinds.

3 MEDITATE ON LORD'S WORDS
Open mind, open texts
But closed eyes listen to Lord
Who whispers in closeness.

4 INCLINATION
Fluid from brain
Elixir or poison heart and hand
Along veins flows work-trend.

5 LISTEN TO 'GEETA'
Among daily war thick
Lord's whispers be loudly proudly picked
Eternal words never contradict.

Verse 20

That Knowledge is Divine in itself
By which Indestructible supreme is beheld
In midst of many divided
it's Undivided 'Oneness'.

1 SCALE
The only gauge,
To evaluate divinity of knowledge
Is valuing Oneness.

2 FINAL KNOWLEDGE FOR ALL
Everything has One sap
In due course, from this undivided
knowledge
The divided can't escape.

ज्ञानं कर्म च कर्ता च त्रिधैव गुणभेदतः।
प्रोच्यते गुणसंख्याने यथावच्छृणु
तान्यपि।।18.19।।

सर्वभूतेषु येनैकं भावमव्ययमीक्षते।
अविभक्तं विभक्तेषु तज्ज्ञानं विद्धि
सात्त्विकम्।।18.20।।

3 REAL KNOWLEDGE

Nor I nor thou
In highest context, individuality is none
All He, all 'One'.

4 DIVINE THOUGHT

The decorum
Of the wisdom
Knows One Kingdom.

5 ONE ROOT/ ONE EARTH

Up in thickets manifest
Many bowers, trees, leaves and florets
Down earth can't discriminate.

Verse 21

But the knowledge is terrene
Which perceives in all beings
Manifold entities, with varieties distinct.

1 EARTHLY ENTITY

The Earth makes difference
When dissolved into heavenly inheritance
Sublimes to Oneness.

2

Before even genesis
What's most Ancient, is
That 'One' with Oneness.

3

My joy in his
And his tears in my crisis
Is above earth, a bliss.

4

Inner Peace of heaven,
Alas ! with the knife of mundane
Pieced to find peace.

5

Scattered plurality compressed
On earth into 'Godly-Unity' expressed
The highest knowledge.

पृथक्त्वेन तु यज्ज्ञानं नानाभावान्पृथग्विधान्।
वेत्ति सर्वेषु भूतेषु तज्ज्ञानं विद्धि राजसम्।।18.21।।

Verse 22

The knowledge which clings
To the singled working effect
Whose thinking mistakes
Fact of 'all in all' who lack
He is narrow constringed
This knowledge is malign.

1 SELF DESTRUCTION
Encircled tightly who discerns
Only his narrow area of concerns
Strangulates what he learns.

2
Narrow and fixed
See nor as they are, turn fanatic,
Having tubular vision's limit.

3
In whim of mirage
One sees own fancy as whole effect
Deserts 'Self' from the Cause.

4 MALIGN WORLD
A worm within
In narrow cocoon of whim
Never metamorphose.

5 MESSAGE OF GEETA
Convert ! to Oneness
From diverts of plural limits of knowledge
From perverts of own craze.

Verse 23

That 'Karma' is duly acted
Done completely non-attached
Without love or hatred
With fruitive results forsweared
As the Divine actions declared.

यत्तु कृत्स्नवदेकस्मिन्कार्ये सक्तमहैतुकम्।
अतत्त्वार्थवदल्पं च तत्तामसमुदाहृतम्।।18.22।।

नियतं सङ्गरहितमरागद्वेषतः कृतम्।
अफलप्रेप्सुना कर्म यत्तत्सात्त्विकमुच्यते।।18.23।।

1 OBLIGATORY
Only work
Done for the sake of doing work
Is worship.

2 WITHOUT TAINTS OF DESIRE
Employed
In unalloyed
Is true joy.

3 NON DESIROUS ACTS
Non-adherent hands
While performing even any adhering acts
Keep soul unaffected.

4
Doing for just 'Doing'
Itself is so fulfilling
Makes it Divine deed.

5
Venomed by the desire
Any action kills itself entire
Making man a Non-performer.

Verse 24

But Karma with colossal efforts
Inspired to satiate Lust
Or performed with egotism
Have only worldly worth.*

1
An aggressive drudge
Guides to the world of the lust
Making more aggressive grudge.

2
Clever desires
Need be changed to wiser pursuit
Of Lustless attitude.

3
'I-act'
Only acts for unsatiable ego
To sate.

4
Freedom from lust
Is no more ego, but
All Soul.

*Terrene trait Drudge=toil

यत्तु कामेप्सुना कर्म साहङ्कारेण वा पुनः।
क्रियते बहुलायासं तद्राजसमुदाहृतम्।।18.24।।

Verse 25

Action that's delusion-bind
Without keeping in mind
Consequences, loss, hurts and aptitude
Which the Ignorance institute
Is 'Malign Karma' they pursuit.

1
Performing will
Without judging own skill
Leads to evil.

2 DELUSIVE AIM
With fanatic head
In folly keeping elbows over-stretched
See consequences ahead.

3 ALERT MOVE
The Act which interacts
With paths and steps
Is backed.

4
To Act first
And reason afterwards
Is worst.

5 EVERY MOMENT IS EVENTFUL
Delusion is blind
Only wisdom sees uneventful events
In daily toil.

Verse 26

Non attached and without ego,
Having firmness and zealous go
Unaffected by success or failure
Are performers divinely pure.

1 DIVINE PERFORMER
Ego once humbled
Perfecting performance attuned as dutiful
Performer becomes Doer's tool

2 SOURCE
Wick and oil
Makes a performing lamp out of soil,
But the Doer lits.

अनुबन्धं क्षयं हिंसामनपेक्ष्य च पौरुषम्।
मोहादारभ्यते कर्म यत्तत्तामसमुच्यते।।18.25।।

मुक्तसङ्गोऽनहंवादी धृत्युत्साहसमन्वितः।
सिद्ध्यसिद्ध्योर्निर्विकारः कर्ता सात्त्विक उच्यते।।18.26।।

3 EGOLESS TOOL OF GOD
Non I-ness is enough,
To be sinew–flesh of Divinity's work
For which embodied and puffed.

4 NOTHING FAILS
Seeming failure is no failure
For performer who works all divine
It's a lesser success.

5 IGNORE FAILURE
For Egoless steps
Seeming failure is halfways
To the Divine success.

Verse 27

Performer, passionate of gains
Greedy, envious and full of taints
Moved by pleasure and pains
In terrene state, he remains.

1
Man's worth
is not measured by work
But by motive of work.

2
Passionate chore
Is no evil, its thirst for more
Is evils' trap door.

3 VAIN EXERTION FOR MUNDANE
Exertive deeds
Not as penance but as greed
Unto more thirst it leads.

4
But even good deeds
Nurtured and watered in environ evil
Become seed with weevil.

Verse 28

In fickle, vulgar, full with conceit
In malicious, indolent and cheat
In procrastinating and dull
A malign performer meets.

रागी कर्मफलप्रेप्सुर्लुब्धो हिंसात्मकोऽशुचिः।
हर्षशोकान्वितः कर्ता राजसः परिकीर्तितः।।18.27।।

अयुक्तः प्राकृतः स्तब्धः शठो नैष्कृतिकोऽलसः।
विषादी दीर्घसूत्री च कर्ता तामस उच्यते।।18.28।।

1

Karma aligned to the mould
In fancies of own low instinct
Remains alien to soul.

2 *PROCRASTINATION*

Tomorrows of the dull
Stretch, as mirage, the unframed time
On canvas all malign.

3

Insight who slight
Though soul lives in mould but such
Mould is soul's parasite.

4 *REBOUNCE*

With self-conceit
Himself dishonestly values a cheat
But cheats himself.

EXPRESSION OF WISDOM, FORTITUDE AND HAPPINESS

Verse 29-30

Dhananjay ! O Winner of mammon !!
What I detail please listen !
There are Understanding three folds,
And fortitude, according to the modes.*

O Parth ! that ken
By which one, understands
What ought to be done, what not
What's to be feared what's not be awed
What's binding what's liberating,
Is pure divine understanding.

1 *DO'S AND DON'T*

No words, no texts
But the understanding of scattered knowledge
Picks the working trait.

2 *NOT CONFUSED*

Where ken is not
Tossed, in consistency of idea engrossed
Decides the ethos.

Ken = wisdom (comprehend) **Nature (Attributes)*

बुद्धेर्भेदं धृतेश्चैव गुणतस्त्रिविधं श्रृणु।
प्रोच्यमानमशेषेण पृथक्त्वेन धनञ्जय।।18.29।।

प्रवृत्तिं च निवृत्तिं च कार्याकार्ये भयाभये।
बन्धं मोक्षं च या वेत्ति बुद्धिः सा पार्थ सात्त्विकी।।18.30।।

3 PERFECT GRASPING
No fickling perhaps*
But execution of text brings firmness,
Lest books are just maps.

4 EXEGESIS
Not the holiness of scripture
But the interpretation is the teacher
That make the understanding pure.

5 KARMA BY YOGIC DISCIPLINE
In the run of world
Yogi takes up all inevitable pursuits
As run by the Lord.

6 NATURAL FIRMNESS
Should n't I long
The throngs of Karma to those
I do never belong.

Verse 31

Ken which can't make out
Between religious and irreligious doubts
Between do's and don'ts of acts
That understanding has a Terrene intellect.

1 BIAS
Where likes and dislikes
Right all wrongs and contrariwise
Is mind of earthly size.

2 SCALE
Veds are the holiest
But my understanding of its text
Defines my worst, my best.

3
Visualizing distorted form
Of clarity of Holiness, perform
In myopic blur.

4 PATH OF 'DHARMA'
Not the marching advance
But the very flow of stance
Make rights and wrongs.

Verse 32

In gloom that perverse
Seeing irreligious as religious
Having pervertedly who see all things
Malign is their understanding.

*Confusions.

यया धर्ममधर्मं च कार्यं चाकार्यमेव च।
अयथावत्प्रजानाति बुद्धिः सा पार्थ राजसी।।18.31।।

अधर्मं धर्ममिति या मन्यते तमसाऽऽवृता।
सर्वार्थान्विपरीतांश्च बुद्धिः सा पार्थ तामसी।।18.32।।

1 THE PERVERTED MIND
The malign
Is preconceived gloomy design
Of the Divine.

2 DARKNESS
The unreasonable gloom blurred
And blinded the life of eternal bloom
Thus deserted reason accursed.

3 RISK TO DISTORT
All is Divine,
But in mind lay on the line
To be malign.

Verse 33

Fortitude, which is fixed
Through all Yogic praxis
Thus controlling the mind
Keeping Praan and senses in confines
This determination is Divine.

1 INTERIORIZED RESOLUTE
The firmness climbs
Through Yogic trails of tiny steps, finds
A mountain within me.

2 RESOLVED NEVER REVOLVE
Fortitude has
Steps, paths and the targets
Its eddy spins, lest.

3 DIVINITY IN FIRMNESS
Untouched to the mundane
Eternal state of firmness remains
In itself the Heaven.

4
Fortitude
As weapon of soul
Conquers the whole.

Verse 34

O Parth ! But the fortitude
Which holds Dharma, pleasure and pelf,
Craving for the fruits
Are Terrene determination in itself.

Lay on the line = to risk harm

धृत्या यया धारयते मनःप्राणेन्द्रियक्रियाः।
योगेनाव्यभिचारिण्या धृतिः सा पार्थ
सात्त्विकी।।18.33।।

यया तु धर्मकामार्थान् धृत्या धारयतेऽर्जुन।
प्रसङ्गेन फलाकाङ्क्षी धृतिः सा पार्थ राजसी।।18.34।।

1 LOWER FORTITUDE
Though firm
But on the lower terms
Is lesser Dharma.

2
A terrene ride though firm
Is surf-ride for pleasure of tides
Make fortitude, a flotsam.

3
The inner patience
Restrained to duties of the mundane
Gains the earthly grains.

4
Earthly fortitude
With desire to enjoy the fruit
Is no Divine pursuit.

Verse 35

That determination which limits
To dreaming, fear, grief and conceit
Is malign fortitude of the stupid.

1
That obstinacy
Which determines through all fancy
Is self willed liability.

2 BAD BARGAIN IN LIFE
In imagery fancies
False firmness inebriates into stuporous fences
At unneeded expenses.

3 WAYWARDNESS
Into such firmness doped
Which intoxicates scope of ordained duties
Keeps, from hope.

4 DELUSION OF THE DULL
Dreaming false zest
Is deemed to get very next
All the regrets.

Inebriate=intoxicate (drunk)

यया स्वप्नं भयं शोकं विषादं मदमेव च।
न विमुञ्चति दुर्मेधा धृतिः सा पार्थ तामसी।।18.35।।

Verse 36-37

Now O Arjun ! from Me listen !
Of the three kinds of contents
By Practices which is obtained*
Brings to end the pain.

Which seem poison at first
But is a nectar afterwards,
Born of purity of mind
Such pleasure is declared Divine.

1
Constituents of instincts
Make up practices very distinct
Variable joys to bring.

2 SPIRITUAL EXPERIENCE
From what we are
To what we should be
Practice makes us.

3 GLIMPSE OF HOPE
Purity be so divine
That ever purity of the Evil
Some pure guidance finds.

4 HOLY PATH / HARD PATH
Pure spirituality composed
Quinined practices seem bitter and over dose
But to nectar come close.

5 SPIRITUAL STRUGGLE
The world evaluates first,
The Divine purity through worldly measures
As poison that depreciates elixir.

6
Seeming toxic experience
Of spiritual struggle elixirs the ingredient
With Eternal content.

7
Bitter soil, bitter root
Pure manure seems poison too
Yet ends in nectar fruit.

**Regular chants, meditation, services.*

सुखं त्विदानीं त्रिविधं शृणु मे भरतर्षभ।
अभ्यासाद्रमते यत्र दुःखान्तं च निगच्छति।।18.36।।

यत्तदग्रे विषमिव परिणामेऽमृतोपमम्।
तत्सुखं सात्त्विकं प्रोक्तमात्मबुद्धिप्रसादजम्।।18.37।।

Verse 38

But the Terrene is such content
Which arise from matter and sense'
Seem' like nectar at first
But is poison in the end.

1 RAVING MUNDANE

The joy which is brief
Is no joy at all but grief
Never eternally relieve.

2 SHORT LIVED JOY

The Joy that wanes
Man tricks to win it, in vain
Even knowing its transience.

3 EARTHLY PLEASURES

Lured by senses and sinew
Debased by chewing the chewed
Sapless life they pursue.

4 WORLDLY JOY

Doped in worldly toxins
Joy of transient slumber need a tocsin
The Eternity to win.

5 A MUNDANE PLEASURE

Sugar coated Joyous sense
Dissolve in mouth of the transience
A bitter pill in the end.

Verse 39

The content which deludes self
At first and in the sequel
Arising from sopor, illusion, torpor
Declared as Malign pleasures.

1 ILLUSION IN WORLDLY TOIL

In desert of illusion,
Pleasure as mirage come to the vision
Wanders in joyless exertion.

2

Bliss is god's will
But joy what arises from evil
Is pleasure's fossil.

Tocsin=Alarm bell

विषयेन्द्रियसंयोगाद्यत्तदग्रेऽमृतोपमम्।
परिणामे विषमिव तत्सुखं राजसं स्मृतम्।।18.38।।

यदग्रे चानुबन्धे च सुखं मोहनमात्मनः।
निद्रालस्यप्रमादोत्थं तत्तामसमुदाहृतम्।।18.39।।

3
Illusive knowledge
In own designed deluded taste
Delights in mirage.

4 PERVERTED MIND
The joy is human
But illusive joy lead by perversion
Is euphoric demon.

Verse 40

There is no existence either
In here or in higher world
Which is free from three traits of Nature.

1 THREE TRAITS
The Earth is heaven, mixed
With more earth or more abyss
Proponent to triple fabrics.

2
Through nature Lord puffed
Some scarce traits and some enough
Thus plurality is stuffed.

3 SUBSTANTIALLY SAME
Mortal and Immortal ens'
Differ in ratio of threefold essence
Have same ingredients.

'KARMA- DOMINANT' SOCIETY

Verse 41

O Arjun ! O Foes' scorcher !!
Of Brahmin the scholar,
Of Kshatriya the warrior, Vaishya the trader
As also of the Shudra, the worker
Duties are imposed according to traits
Springing from their own nature.

Ens= Entity

न तदस्ति पृथिव्यां वा दिवि देवेषु वा पुनः।
सत्त्वं प्रकृतिजैर्मुक्तं यदेभिः स्यात्त्रिभिर्गुणैः।।18.40।।

ब्राह्मणक्षत्रियविशां शूद्राणां च परंतप।
कर्माणि प्रविभक्तानि स्वभावप्रभवैर्गुणैः।।18.41।।

1 NATURE DECIDES ONE'S WORTH

Man's work
What's his worth
Is trait not the birth.

2

From inside every cast
Commissioned one, out of inner four castes
According traits and taste.

3

Birth-right of every birth,
Is to be borne with free choice
Of grading to his worth.

4

Natural caste determined
*By man's response to nature's fruit triune**
Is only genuine.

5 'TRIGUNA'

Any world has social fabric
Grossly graded by traits intermixed
*Into sattvic, Rajasic, Tamasic.***

Verse 42

Poise, Penance, purity, persistence
Probity, Pardon, learnings, Prudence and credence
Are innate Karma of Brahmin
From their own nature, origin.

1

Knowledge brings wisdom
All goodness converts into altruism
Faith bestows freedom.

2 TWICE BORN- DWIJ

Whose birth is florn
Whose work has virtuous sojourn
That reborn is high born.

*Divine, terrene, malign. **Moral, mixed, immoral*
Credence = faith in God Florn = potential of spiritual enlightenment.

शमो दमस्तपः शौचं क्षान्तिरार्जवमेव च।
ज्ञानं विज्ञानमास्तिक्यं ब्रह्मकर्म स्वभावजम्।।18.42।।

3 BRAHMIN ; AS GUIDE
True Brahmin descends
From upper world to lesser planes
Making lesser worlds to transcend.

4 ONE IS BRAHMIN
In every aborn*
He, the Supreme is equally elorn
Who knows, is High born.

5 GOODNESS IS BRAHMIN
All Goodness
For none of the reasons in return
Is Brahmin.

Verse 43

With Valiance, radiance, firmness, finesse,
No lamming from bellum, having generousness and sway
*Are innate Karma of Kshatriya.***

1 WARRIOR'S GOODNESS
True warrior's hilt
Brandish for altruism to meet
The innate inner spirit.

2 TRUE KSHATRIYA
Here mind is a sage,
And beauteous thoughts filled Kshatriy's cage
With the duteous courage.

3 NO LAMMING
True Kshatriya wins first
And battles the enemy afterwards
Never escapes thus.

4 WARRIOR
Life's bellum lethale
Who live and die never to escape
Their Karmas prevail.

5 KSHATRIYA'S INNATE NATURE
Kshatriyas were one
Who had soul as highest weapon
And ultimately won.

*Lamming=escaping, finesse=skill *every birth is equal. **Warrior class*
Elorn = hidden essence

शौर्यं तेजो धृतिर्दाक्ष्यं युद्धे चाप्यपलायनम्।
दानमीश्वरभावश्च क्षात्रं कर्म स्वभावजम्।।18.43।।

Verse 44-45

Tilling earth, ranching heifers
And commerce are Vaishya's work
And to serve others draws
The innate Karma of Shudras,
Committed to own karmic trait
Any man can become perfect.

Now from Me listen !
How can this be done.

1
At commerce and services
Plowing the mind with chaste consciousness
Reap a Divine harvest.

2 NO LESSER DEEDS
Any natural aptitude
By instinct has petty or piety Attitude
To refine from crude.

3 CASTEISM
'Ts All mother's contempt
Whose sons on work distinguishingly attempt
To make womb difference.

4 CASTEISM
God's plan is sacred
For mankind's frame but man has made
It a ungodly hatred.

5 NONE IS LESSER WORK
Even animalistic deeds
Allocated as lesser, may ennoble instead
Virtues make lesser works, The worship.

6 CONDITIONED TO TEMPERAMENT
Temples and Shambles
By birth are installed in every cast,
To manifest as caste.

7 BIRTH ALONE GIVES NAME
That umbilical cord
Strangulates the society; which names in accord
With darks of womb.

8 KRSHNA'S PROMISE
To innate Karma pledged
Worshiping, warring, working of any cage
May perfect to salvage.

Shambles=Slaughter house

कृषिगौरक्ष्यवाणिज्यं वैश्यकर्म स्वभावजम्।
परिचर्यात्मकं कर्म शूद्रस्यापि स्वभावजम्।।18.44।।

स्वे स्वे कर्मण्यभिरतः संसिद्धिं लभते नरः।
स्वकर्मनिरतः सिद्धिं यथा विन्दति तच्छृणु।।18.45।।

9
Self analysis allocates
His own path prod by own traits
And commitment perfects.

10 MOKSHA - PATH
Trader's commerce, bard's words
Pandits' prayers, servers' serve, warriors sword
Redemption equally chanced.

11 'TWICE BORN' IS REAL BRAHMIN
Once born-
For redemption, need be reborn
Alone through his Karma.

Verse 46 -47

From whom the existence originates
By whom all is pervaded
Worshipping Him with one's own trait
Man can become perfect.

Better is own work
Over other's well known work
Who does, No sin incurs
Even if lacking merits
Yet to his own traits befits.

1 DOING ALLOCATED WORK
Self surrendered man
Working in Consciousness of the Creator
Shapes work into worship.

2 EQUALLY CHANCED
Through any trait pattern
Any one on road to perfection
By Innate faith, won.

3 PROPENSITY
With self-created trait
Decreed of Karma's cause and effect
Man inherits in the next.

4
Overpowering destined traits
The work by free-will initiated
Perfects, the conditioned Acts.

यतः प्रवृत्तिर्भूतानां येन सर्वमिदं ततम्।
स्वकर्मणा तमभ्यर्च्य सिद्धिं विन्दति मानवः।।18.46।।

श्रेयान्स्वधर्मो विगुणः परधर्मात्स्वनुष्ठितात्।
स्वभावनियतं कर्म कुर्वन्नाप्नोति किल्बिषम्।।18.47।।

5 WORK WORKS
Man is born to do
Every work of man is worship
If man knew.

6 INNATE TRAIT
As snake's venom
Kills not himself, the innate wisdom
But becomes nostrum.

7 INBORN DUTY
Any pattern of palm-crease
Every born hand has individually better
Path of release.

8
Not my lesser trait
But how sacredly I act
Decides my fate.

9
None be despised
The innate work with its ordained size
Any work is divinely precise.

Verse 48

O Arjun ! one should not abandon
The Karma's trait with which one is born
For all the Undertakings are doomed
As the fire by fumes.

1 FALSE IDENTITY
False status
Enveloping the inborn genius
This incoherence hurts.

2 ALL WORK ARE DIVINE
With whatever propensity
One is born with, seraphic or malefic
Works out for 'Divinity'.

3 TRANSCENDING MUNDANE KARMA
Action with innate trait
Are so spontaneous and self-induced expert
Perfects even in defects.

4
Every work, little or more
Has evil enveloping of core
But like fire its pure.

Despise = condemn.

सहजं कर्म कौन्तेय सदोषमपि न त्यजेत्।
सर्वारम्भा हि दोषेण धूमेनाग्निरिवावृताः।।18.48।।

5
My work worked
For, my natural spark is brighter than
Surrounding fume's murk.

SUMMARY OF ESSENCE OF GEETA

Verse 49

He, whose intellect is ever detached
From worldly desires and ties
Lustless who has won his 'Self'
Gains uttermost state of renounced life,
Actionless state he doth realize.

1
The one ever-satiated
Beyond action and reaction obviously sets
His renounced intellect.

2
Lusty desires of fruits
May rot the lustrous action itself
And spoil renunciation-sap.

3 RENUNCIATION – THE SAVIOR
Mind is the vehicle
Of combustible desire in fiery world
Renunciation defuels.

4
From volatile passion
Immutability transcending farther the action
Is perfect renunciation.

5
Mind is the worst foe
At the same mind 's best pal
Depends, controls or controlled.

Verse 50

Now in nutshell learn !
How he who has attained perfection,
The utmost of wisdom, finds Brahmn.

असक्तबुद्धिः सर्वत्र जितात्मा विगतस्पृहः।
नैष्कर्म्यसिद्धिं परमां संन्यासेनाधिगच्छति।।18.49।।

सिद्धिं प्राप्तो यथा ब्रह्म तथाप्नोति निबोध मे।
समासेनैव कौन्तेय निष्ठा ज्ञानस्य या परा।।18.50।।

1
No stretches of texts
Condensed consummation of all knowledge
Is in inner Oneness.

2
All learnings compress into truth
All the Truths compress into One
All the ones into Brahmn.

3
Truth is the 'Sun'
On the learner's knowledge horizon
Where dawns the Brahmn.

Verse 51-53

Immersed in pure intellect
Whose firmness subjugates 'self'
Forsaking sound and other sense objects
Ever freed from lures and hatreds,

In secluded place who resides
Eating but little and light
Body, speech and mind subdued,
Ever in trance imbued,

Taking the disposition, a refuge
With Ego, power, conceit abandoned,
Lust, anger, greed who has won,
Such serene sublime person
Is fit for God-Union.

बुद्ध्या विशुद्धया युक्तो धृत्याऽऽत्मानं नियम्य च।
शब्दादीन् विषयांस्त्यक्त्वा रागद्वेषौ व्युदस्य च।।18.51।।

विविक्तसेवी लघ्वाशी यतवाक्कायमानसः।
ध्यानयोगपरो नित्यं वैराग्यं समुपाश्रितः।।18.52।।

अहङ्कारं बलं दर्पं कामं क्रोधं परिग्रहम्।
विमुच्य निर्ममः शान्तो ब्रह्मभूयाय कल्पते।।18.53।।

1 PURE BODY/ PURE SOUL
Purity of Inner self
Brings more imperative purity to the surface
Further purifying the depth.

2
Blazing luxuries lure
And unnecessary necessities make impure
In and out seclusion cures.

3 VAIRAGYA
Yogic passion
Is one, that's God-union
Through possession of Dispassion.

4 FOLLOWING GEETA
Little on bread
More on what Lord hath said
Evolves man to Godhead.

5 YOGIC SECLUSION
On this crowded earth
A lonely planet within me
Waits, my heavenly worth.

Verse 54

Becoming one with the Supreme
Soul attaining serene
Yogi not longs nor laments
Equality in all he doth see,
Attains utmost Bhakti towards Me.

1
With weeds of ego
Poise, on unequal soil, cannot furrow
And Bhakti cannot grow.

2
With uneven serenity
All differ in intensity of Bhakti
But have equal opportunity.

3
Falsehood brings turmoil
When pacifies into Truth, brings poise
And divine sky is visualized.

4 EQUALITY
Equal steps
Not the equal road
Needed to cross odd.

Furrow=plough.

ब्रह्मभूतः प्रसन्नात्मा न शोचति न काङ्क्षति।
समः सर्वेषु भूतेषु मद्भक्तिं लभते पराम्।।18.54।।

Verse 55

By the Utmost Devotion
He who knows Me, in My element
'And what I am and Who I am?'
Having known Me in My essence
Forthwith enterth into Me.

1 BHAKTI, THE ONLY MEAN
Alone with Devotion true
The devout, about the Beloved Lord knew
What's what and who's who?

2 GOD-UNION
In surrendered consciousness
Devout's identity can't retain itself
Finds entered into Oneness.

3
No mental presage of non-devotee
But inclined faith with flowing ease
Naturally reach.

4 ENTERS INTO SUPREME
The ego of one spark
Once touches flammable devotion of fueled heart
In Conscious-Flambeau is lost.

Verse 56

Under My refuge, My devotee
Though keep in engaged in world duty,
Obtain by My mercy
The Eternal Unchanging State.

1
Nor just passive surrender
But with dynamism in the obligatory world
Is devotion ideal.

2 'BHAKTI' IS DUTY
A mortal is made,
In image of Immortal love of Godhead
With duty to reciprocate.

3
In the world of duty
The 'Karma' finds a paradise for devotee
In Lord's refuge.

4 SEEKER'S SHELTER
To act is Human
But to act in His refuge
Is Godly too.

भक्त्या मामभिजानाति यावान्यश्चास्मि तत्त्वतः।
ततो मां तत्त्वतो ज्ञात्वा विशते तदनन्तरम्।।18.55।।

सर्वकर्माण्यपि सदा कुर्वाणो मद्व्यपाश्रयः।
मत्प्रसादादवाप्नोति शाश्वतं पदमव्ययम्।।18.56।।

5

By His mercy
All devotees think of their own duties
Are His.

Verse 57

In Me all actions be cerebrated
Me as Highest Goal be intended
Resorting to yoga of gnosis
In Me thy mind be fixed.

1

All the ego
Of doer – sense must go
To reach the Utmost.

2

Ousting bodily ego
Yogic sovereignty of King Soul does know
No lesser gusto.

3 'DEVOTION'-BHAKTI

Let me be engrained,
What I did is all His hand
His wit in my brain.

4 GOD AND WORLD

Work with one hand
Clasping God with other; once job ends
God with both be clenched.

Verse 58

Mind, Upon Me getting fixed
Thou wilt cross all intricacies by My Mercy
If through ego thou dost not heed
The destruction, thou wilt meet.

1

Who is heedlessly closed
To the divine words of Kurukshetra, knows
No Moksha.

2

A heedful Consciousness
Has no deeds unconscionably anxious
Is liberation worth.

Gusto=Bliss, zestfulness

चेतसा सर्वकर्माणि मयि संन्यस्य मत्परः।
बुद्धियोगमुपाश्रित्य मच्चित्तः सततं भव।।18.57।।

मच्चित्तः सर्वदुर्गाणि मत्प्रसादात्तरिष्यसि।
अथ चेत्त्वमहङ्कारान्न श्रोष्यसि विनङ्क्ष्यसि।।18.58।।

3 FOLLOW GEETA

To be freed

From Unsighted darks of blind deeds

Take ! Good heed.

4 EXPLORE HIS WORDS

Heed ! the Lord

To listen to intuitions what He imparts

Kept hidden in heart.

5 HEEDFUL DEVOTEE

In His devotion who falls

Lord raises him as bosom pal

Rights all false.

Verse 59

Under ego's sway
If thou doth state
'I will not combat'
Thy nature will take
And thou wilt have to fight back.

1 UNREASONABLE EGO

Ego identified

Infright dislikes and wrongs the Right

Egoless fights for insight.

2

Ego has a fright

Egoless has a inner might

Of soldier's fight.

3 DUTY TO FIGHT

God puffs a soul

And resolved to put in the mould

Instinct of a soldier.

4 A SOLDIER'S INSTINCT

Not the fronting hates,

But the egoless love backing the soldier

Naturally combats.

Verse 60

Bound to duties inborn,
What through delusion you don't perform
O Arjun ! thou wilt be coerced
Helplessly through thy innate force.

यदहङ्कारमाश्रित्य न योत्स्य इति मन्यसे।
मिथ्यैष व्यवसायस्ते प्रकृतिस्त्वां नियोक्ष्यति।।18.59।।

स्वभावजेन कौन्तेय निबद्धः स्वेन कर्मणा।
कर्तुं नेच्छसि यन्मोहात्करिष्यस्यवशोऽपि तत्।।18.60।।

1
A sense-fighter-wisdom,
Through 'Karma' battles in births to come
For soul kingdom.

2 KARMA
Acquired learning should know
That past earnings have instinctive force
One has to follow.

3
What's earned in past
Once conditioned into performing urges
That 'Karma' is not lost.

Verse 61

In everyone the Lord dwellth
Compelling all into His mayic spell
And revolve, mounted within
O Arjun ! as if to a machine

1
'Ts Lord's resolve
For mechanical body where soul revolves
Finally to evolve.

2 HUMAN
Every piece
The Master made a master piece
Formatting machine of Release.

3 EVOLUTION FOR SOUL
Man consciously grow
To past patterns of to and fro
Lord made no robot.

4 FREE CHOICE OF KARMA
Through Karmic pattern
Within to and fro of chains
To evolve never constrained.

5
This mechanized soul,
Until is shaped to the Supreme Soul
Lord carves and molds.

ईश्वरः सर्वभूतानां हृद्देशेऽर्जुन तिष्ठति।
भ्रामयन्सर्वभूतानि यन्त्रारूढानि मायया।।18.61।।

Verse 62

With all thy efforts
Go to His refuge O Bhaarat !
Thou wilt, get the peace Utmost
By His Grace, get the Moksha

1
'God first'
Is the key word that works
To bless the worst.

2
Dissolving individuality
In refuge of the Eternal Totality
Brings the peace.

3
Being his refugee
Is the only way to get free
From His decree.

4 THE INDWELLER
I never chased
And found, in His refuge so blessed
Within me His address.

Verse 63

Most secretive secret
I have declared to Thou
On this exhaustively deliberated
Do what thou wish to do, Now.

1 KNOWLEDGE
Explore in all wides
Discover, apply knowledge and realize
God keeps no hide.

2
This declared secret
Of words of Lord need be deliberated
To be liberated.

3
Through intuitive grace
Secrets of all secretive knowledge
With its application blessed.

तमेव शरणं गच्छ सर्वभावेन भारत।
तत्प्रसादात्परां शान्तिं स्थानं प्राप्स्यसि शाश्वतम्।।18.62।।

इति ते ज्ञानमाख्यातं गुह्याद्गुह्यतरं मया।
विमृश्यैतदशेषेण यथेच्छसि तथा कुरु।।18.63।।

Verse 64

Listen ! to My Supreme Lore
Because thou art My dear beloved
I tell thou therefore
For thy good what behoveth.

1
Unconditionally Lord guides
But leaves every soul on free-will
For Alas ! a lesser choice.

2 *INTUITION*
May the devotee hear
Over surrounding glamours n bounding clamour,
The Guiding whispers.

3 *REDEMPTION THROUGH GEETA*
Among advents of the Supreme
Incarnation as Words in Geeta's Hymns
In extremes, redeem.

4 *MEDITATION*
With ears of meek
Listen ! in the wordless silence, seek
The Lord speaks.

Verse 65

Thy mind upon Me, fix !
Be My devout and worship !!
Offer homage unto Me ;
For thou art beloved to Me
So My promise is True
Quite unfailing thou
Solely wilt attain Me.

1 *TRUE DEVOTION*
Where life becomes God
There only God breaths and never dies
'Bhakti' eternally survives.

2
God needs no praise
But praises through Karmic-law lays
Man, a raise.

सर्वगुह्यतमं भूयः श्रृणु मे परमं वचः।
इष्टोऽसि मे दृढमिति ततो वक्ष्यामि ते हितम्।।18.64।।

मन्मना भव मद्भक्तो मद्याजी मां नमस्कुरु।
मामेवैष्यसि सत्यं ते प्रतिजाने प्रियोऽसि मे।।18.65।।

3 SURRENDER / BHAKTI
Having endeared ownself
For the Dearest Lord is a motive force
His promises to endorse.

4 DECIDE THE GOAL
Where world is the end
God is means; where God is the End
World is means to attain.

Verse 66

All Karmic bindings abandon!*
Take refuge in Me alone
I will absolve thou of sins
So thou shouldst not moan.

1 WAY ONLY
'With' or 'not with it'
Nor absolve nor solve but confuse
Answers only His refuge.

2
Worldly obstacles
God works as heavenly miracles
Once surrendered.

3 DHARMA OF IDENTITY
Laws of beings
when surrendered to Supreme refuge
Incur no sin.

4
My duties and sins
I surrendered unto His refuge
Remained all virtues.

5 SHARANAGATI
My work
Once surrendered to God
With Eternal hands I work.

**Duties of mind and body*

सर्वधर्मान्परित्यज्य मामेकं शरणं व्रज।
अहं त्वा सर्वपापेभ्यो मोक्षयिष्यामि मा शुचः।।18.66।।

Verse 67

This Lore shouldst never be shared
With who is not austere
Nor with who is infidel, evil
Who serve no devotional
Who does not care to hear Me
Nor to one who at Me, cavils.

1 PRACTISE KNOWLEDGE

Who invest learning wisdom
Into his own living, is the one
Comely bosom.

2 IDEAL STUDENT/ IDEAL TEACHER

The Perfect teachers
Are the seekers who seek
The perfect seekers.

3 SEEKER

He who is mad
For his struggle towards knowledge
He alone is Learned.

4 ELIGIBLE STUDENT OF GEETA

Judge cultivable soil,
As the Immortal Geeta for mortal coil
Lest the seed spoils.

5

Faith is the lens
Through which depth of Lord's comments
One can comprehend.

6 GIFT OF GEETA

Knowledge itself
Of Geeta is the highest largess
Of Geeta's verses.

इदं ते नातपस्काय नाभक्ताय कदाचन।
न चाशुश्रूषवे वाच्यं न च मां योऽभ्यसूयति।।18.67।।

Verse 68-69

He, who will preach
With utmost Bhakti in Me
This Supreme secret to My devotees
Shall come to Me, guaranteed.

This among men who undertakes
Duty towards Me as the dearest
Dearer to Me than him
There wilt be none else.

1 MESSAGE AVATAR
Geeta is Messenger Incarnate
Within Krshna's incarnation; one who imparts
Gets His added grace.

2 HELPING HANDS
Hands those are lowered
In redeeming others are Lord's dearer
Over the raised hands.

3 SHARING DIVINITY
Who have visualized
Become eyes for non-cognizing vision of others
Are apple of Lord's eyes.

4 TEACHER WITH DEVOTION
'Ts not just teaching
It is imparting part of own soul
The seeker to uphold.

5
As Soul of Lord's Soul
Who imparts this Geeta unto Soul -seekers
Redeems and help redeem others.

6 IMPARTING KNOWLEDGE
Elixired with divine bliss
Who nectarize others with Immortal gnosis
Is Krshna's dearest service.

7 PREACHER OF GEETA
Thy Love and Lore
What thou enshrined in my core
Should have ope door.

8
Teacher is a torch
Who illumines others in the darks,
Naturally comes in light of Lord.

य इमं परमं गुह्यं मद्भक्तेष्वभिधास्यति।
भक्तिं मयि परां कृत्वा मामेवैष्यत्यसंशयः।।18.68।।

न च तस्मान्मनुष्येषु कश्चिन्मे प्रियकृत्तमः।
भविता न च मे तस्मादन्यः प्रियतरो भुवि।।18.69।।

Verse 70

And here I state thus,
Who study thus dialogue between Us
Will be worshipping Me by Yagna-Genius.*

1
Soul conversed with Lord
Or Imparted by Lord, as intuitive thoughts
Are Eternal utterance of Geeta.

2 GEETA
These Eternal dialogues
Those echo within, the soul to progue
Make knowledge, the worship.

3
Gnostic Geeta is ship
With wisdom-compass navigates in oceanic dark
To shore to apt worship.

4
Lord declares wisdom,
Accepts devotion opening His bosom
Worship ! Him as bosom friend.

5 GEETA'S MESSAGE
In Eternity's recent past
The Lord talked to Arjun to impart
His heart in every heart.

Verse 71

Who heeds this sacred text
Laden of faith, barren of hates
Even that man, as well
Will be liberated, in virtuous plane to dwell.

1 LORD'S WORDS
Lord spake for all time
Engraved words on Eternal heart of mankind
The blessed path to find.

2 LISTENER IN MUNDANE
Among many shallow reflections
Eyes of faith find deepest perception
To perfect own vision.

*Rituals of wisdom, Gyan Yagna Progue=Goad, direct.

अध्येष्यते च य इमं धर्म्यं संवादमावयोः।
ज्ञानयज्ञेन तेनाहमिष्टः स्यामिति मे मतिः।।18.70।।

श्रद्धावाननसूयश्च शृणुयादपि यो नरः।
सोऽपि मुक्तः शुभाँल्लोकान्प्राप्नुयात्पुण्यकर्मणाम्।।18.71।।

3 LIBERATION IS GEETA'S SCHOLARSHIP
Who reads, even who heeds
Lord's word for them, are word-keys
To proceed and succeed.

4 GEETA IS AVTAAR
Lord's comments
Enshrined into heart, one should comprehend
Shlokas as Lord's Advent.

TALKS CONCLUDE BETWEEN LORD AND DEVOTEE

Verse 72

The Blessed Lord asked –

O Parth ! Attentively havest thou harked
O Dhananjay! O conqueror of wealth !!
Hath thy illusion born darks
Now been dispelled?

1
Before any task
The Lord introspectively asks
To lit the darks.

2 HEARING IS REVERING
Devotees hear
Attentively their Lord's whispers
Thus they revere.

3 ENLIGHTENING MORN
Attentively learn
At delusive marge once dawns Sun
Day is bound to come.

4 BE ATTENTIVE
In worldly din
To intuitive Lord many hear, overhear
But few listen and win.

कच्चिदेतच्छ्रुतं पार्थ त्वयैकाग्रेण चेतसा।
कच्चिदज्ञानसंमोहः प्रनष्टस्ते धनञ्जय।।18.72।।

Verse 73

Arjun said –

O My dear Achyut !
My delusion is removed
'ts all Thy Grace
I regained real knowledge
Now I am firmly established
My dubiousness is vanished
And I am ready to work
According to Thy words.

1 NO CONFUSION STATE

Born of Lord's compassion
From shaking confusion to established equilibrium
This makes thoughts firm.

2 BODY-SOUL COMPLEX BATTLE

What was covered
By God's grace discovered
Conquered.

3 RECOGNIZED AS SOUL

The shrouded mortal design
Once awakened in the Immortality, finds
And perfects into Divine.

4

To serve illusory ill
Or to serve Lord's doubtless will
Two choices in mortal field.

Verse 74

Commentator Sanjay said –

Between Vasudev and High soul Parth
This wondrous discourse
Thus havest I heard
I'm thrilled full to the shores.

अर्जुन उवाच
नष्टो मोहः स्मृतिर्लब्धा त्वत्प्रसादान्मयाच्युत।
स्थितोऽस्मि गतसन्देहः करिष्ये वचनं तव।।18.73।।

सञ्जय उवाच
इत्यहं वासुदेवस्य पार्थस्य च महात्मनः।
संवादमिममश्रौषमद्भुतं रोमहर्षणम्।।18.74।।

1 KRSHNA – ARJUN DIALOGUES
The Mortal revived by word
Of the Immortal, is awakened and his work
Becomes Immortal work.

2
Consciousness of the Supreme
Lit through symbolism, into lesser dims
Every niche to illumine.

3 COGNISION OF GEETA IS RARE.
Shower of Higher wisdom
Perpetually rain on lesser being,
Harvested seldom.

4 SANJAY WATCHED WONDER
Any despondent is endowed
With potential to be dynamic Whole
Which, the wondrous Geeta showed.

Verse 75

Through the grace of Vyasa
This Supreme secret talks
Lame to my conscious vision
And came from Yogeshwar Krsha
What He spake I directly listened.

1
Alone through Spiritual Maser,
May be person, text Granth, blessed words
One masters Supreme Master.

2 THE TEACHER – THE TAUGHT
In disciplic succession
Like Sanjay, one can perceive and listen
Today's words of Krsna.

3 VYASA, UNIVERSAL GURU
The Spiritual Guru
Is non-refractory transparent lens through
Which experience is direct, true.

4 SANJAY'S STATE
In interiorized blissful Union,
Enshrining Guru in introspective perception
Establishes direct communion.

व्यासप्रसादाच्छ्रुतवानेतद्गुह्यमहं परम्।
योगं योगेश्वरात्कृष्णात्साक्षात्कथयतः स्वयम्।।18.75।।

Verse 76

Sanjay, the commentator continues –

O King ! The dialogues wondrous and sacred
O King ! Keshav and Arjun voiced
As I recall and recall those
Again and again I rejoice.

1
*In Sacred Mystics**
Once established; never leaves, ever meets
A transcendental seat.

2 TRANSDENDING EXPERIENCE
Once enslaved mind
Having engraved with Divine Experience
Frames in permanence.

3 SPONTANEOUS REMEMBERANCE
The Experience
Which elixirs and enlivens Consciousness
Becomes the breath.

4 ESTABLISHED STATE
Reaching unending bliss,
Seems ending with some missed beats
Is indelible and fixed.

Verse 77

O King ! as I recall anew
Krshna's That Virat Swaroop
I am further greatly surprised
Again and again I rejoice.

1 CELEBRATE THE LIFE
Man is sent
Introspectively to recall Lord's Advent
To glorify every moment.

2 MEDITATION ON VIRAT
That Vision I recall
That Virat form ; my vermiform extol
And I grow tall.

*Yogic secrets

राजन्संस्मृत्य संस्मृत्य संवादमिममद्भुतम्।
केशवार्जुनयोः पुण्यं हृष्यामि च मुहुर्मुहुः।।18.76।।

तच्च संस्मृत्य संस्मृत्य रूपमत्यद्भुतं हरेः।
विस्मयो मे महान् राजन् हृष्यामि च पुनः पुनः।।18.77।।

3
Virat's Virat zeal
Once elixirs spirit with Divine thrill
Transported soul is fulfilled.

4 MEDITATING ON VIRAT SWAROOP
Visualizing 'The Total form'
My introspection with Lord, arm in arm
Transcends me and transforms.

5 TOTALITY REALIZED
All else dissolves
When resolves 'Total form' for Divine Union
Of the Vision of the visions.*

Verse 78

Wherever is Krshna, the Yogic Incarnate
Wherever is Parth, the archer great,
Such is my firm view,
There will be true
Wealth, victory, verve, virtuous values.

1
With Yogic spirit of Krshna
With archer arrowing on sin
There is ever win.

2
Once the archer surrenders
Before moral guidance of Divine words
Never surrenders.

3
Warrior God was concerned
He took me as His weapon
Thus I won.

4
Where Godliness bridles
Man's boosted zeal on wheel
Together win every field.

5
Right arrows of expertise
Once bow down to Supremacy of Supreme
Never bow in worldly bellum.

6 CONFIDENT ARJUN IN ME
Enemies arrayed tough,
Against Me equipped with desponding bluffs
God is enough.

**Chapter 11/verse 5-47*

यत्र योगेश्वरः कृष्णो यत्र पार्थो धनुर्धरः।
तत्र श्रीर्विजयो भूतिर्ध्रुवा नीतिर्मतिर्मम।।18.78।।